WICKED TIES

THE TETHER TRILOGY
BOOK TWO

SHANORA WILLIAMS

WICKED TIES

NEW YORK TIMES & USA TODAY BESTSELLING AUTHOR

SHANORA WILLIAMS

DEDICATION

*To anyone who has gone through
battles in order to protect their peace.
Don't ever stop fighting for <u>you</u>.*

MAP OF VAKEELI

For a bigger photo of the map, please visit:
www.shanorawilliams.com/blog/map-of-vakeeli

JUST A HEADS UP

Wicked Ties is book 2 of the Tether Trilogy and picks up where book 1, **Vicious Bonds** left off. To better understand this story, I *highly* suggest reading Vicious Bonds first. You can find it on my website or on Amazon.

If you've already read Vicious Bonds, I hope you enjoy this continuation of Willow + Caz's story!

CHAPTER 1
CAZ

WHEN I WAS A BOY, MY MOTHER WOULD TELL ME A tale about a woman living a free and liberating life. She's happy in her own world, getting by as best as she can...then one day, there's a knock at her door.

At the door is a king—a sizable man with eyes as dark as coals and hair as black as raven wings. And it's when that king appears that the story takes a darker turn.

Because in her story, the king doesn't just knock. He eventually kicks her door down, and the beautiful woman panics, having no idea who he is or what he wants.

According to my mother, this free woman had built a cottage between two territories of Vakeeli, an illegal act she wasn't aware of prior to his arrival. Someone had stumbled across her cabin in the forest and reported it to the king of Blackwater for a few rubies, and the king took it upon himself to seek the person who'd disobeyed the law.

The king expected to find someone he wouldn't care about—

1

a person he could shove aside and take the home from just to make a reasonable profit. But when he laid eyes on the free, beautiful woman, he instantly fell for her.

However, the woman did not fall for him. In fact, she was *afraid* of him and wanted nothing more than for him to leave. The king saw her resistance as a challenge and made it his mission to get the woman to love him, so he left that night, but returned many times after, leaving gifts, food, and riches in an attempt to win her over.

The woman wanted none of it. She loved her simple life in the forest and loved growing her own food. And as far as riches, she didn't need them. She either had or could make everything she desired. Plus, the king was not her type. For starters, he was married, and she informed him of this in hopes that he'd stop showing up.

None of the woman's rejects sat well with the arrogant king, and he drowned himself in drinks. When he was full of liquor and frustration, he stumbled to her cabin in the middle of the night.

It is there that the king called to the woman while standing at her door, begging her to come out, begging her to love him. The woman stepped out and told the king to go home—that he was drunk and wasting his time.

Infuriated, the king barged into the woman's cabin, dragged her to *her* bed, and had his way with her. No matter how much she fought, he overpowered her, and eventually she stopped fighting and lay there, waiting for the nightmare to be over.

Realizing his error after he'd sobered up, the king ran back to his kingdom, leaving the woman to cry alone in the night. Two full moons later, she discovered she was pregnant.

Panicked, she sought the Mythics of Whisper Grove, wanting to rid herself of the foreign being inside her.

She begged and pleaded, not caring that getting rid of the baby would send her to The Trench. She didn't want the king's baby and refused to carry it. After the nightmare of that night, she no longer wanted to live. This baby was forced upon her, you see, and she wanted *nothing* to do with it. But all the Mythics denied her—all but one.

This Mythic was a smart man, kind and cheerful. He told the woman he'd help her get rid of the baby without anyone finding out. But it was as he began creating an elixir to rid her of the baby that he told her he could feel the baby's power in her womb. The baby she was carrying was going to be special and would grow up a protector, with a special gift no one else would carry.

The woman didn't care. She didn't believe him. She was set on getting rid of the child and never speaking of it again, so she took the elixir and ran home.

Later that night, as the woman stared at the bottle, ready to abolish the king's mistake, she felt a fluttering in her womb. She felt this beautiful, innocent life inside her moving, and tears crept to her eyes. And when she closed her eyes, she saw a baby boy in her arms, with cerulean eyes and inky hair. The baby looked at her with so much love—more love than she had *ever* encountered in her life—and she thought, "It is not the baby's fault he is in my womb."

Because of what she saw, the woman tossed the elixir into the fireplace, and for the next six months, she carried the baby, giving birth to him in her cabin with the aid of the kind Mythic who promised to help her.

And when she saw the baby was indeed a boy and that her

vision had come to life, she swore to protect this boy with all her might, and to *never* let the king find out about him. For if he did, she knew the wrath the king would take. A bastard son, born out of wedlock. It'd make him appear immoral and he'd kill the boy, or worse—punish him in some way for ever being born.

The woman kept the boy a secret for as long as she could, but as the boy grew, it became harder to keep him in hiding, for he was an adventurous child, stubborn, and she saw many of the king's traits in him. Despite it, she promised she would raise the boy to have a tender heart, so that no matter what he went through, or how much he suffered, he would care for others in the same way he would want to be cared for. Because she knew it was coming…his suffering. She knew she couldn't protect him forever, because there was one enemy who wanted to take her from him. And if he couldn't keep him, neither could she.

This is the story my mother would tell me, and I was happy for the boy, never realizing he was me. And the Mythic who'd helped the woman—that was *Manx*.

For years, my mother said someone would come for us. She'd drive herself mad, pacing the cabin. She used to let me stay with Manx every day until one day, my visits to him came to an abrupt end and she told me to never speak to him again.

I realize now that it was Manx's plan all along to bring me to life. He knew what I would be before I was even born—knew the power I possessed and wanted it to be his—so he convinced my mother to keep me and grew close with both of us until my mother figured out he was Decius. That's what all those late nights in the libraries were for, the pacing of the cabin, the handle of the dagger in her hands as she watched the door, waiting for an unknown enemy to attack.

I see that now as I stare into his eyes, and the cold wraps around me like snakes. Manx is not the compassionate man I thought he was. All this time, he's been *hunting* me, pushing out anyone who cares about me, and waiting for his moment to strike. The realization is such a disappointment.

What good am I if I'm only here to be used by men like him and my father? Perhaps this is the better option, to let him take my body, my mind, and kill me. I'll only be used time and time again…

But there's Willow, and he *cannot* have her. Take my heart and rip it out of me, I don't care, but my mate will *not* be his.

When I get out of this icy mental trap Decius has me in, he's as good as dead.

CHAPTER 2
WILLOW

ALORA'S PALACE

I SUCK IN BREATH AFTER BREATH AS CAZ'S ICE-COLD body is brought back down to the floor. Everyone in the room is in an uproar, shouting with red faces and veins bulging from their necks. They're in delirium.

My chest grows twice as heavy as I focus on Caz's blue body again. He was fine only a minute ago. We were on Alora's balcony after his trip to see The Council. He gave me a protection morsel from Manx to shield us from Decius, but somehow Decius has still gotten to him. This can't be happening. We're supposed to be safe now. The Council gave us a protective bubble and gave Caz their word that Decius wouldn't be able to come after us, so how can this be? Mournwrath can't be taking him.

Tears blind me when I realize I'll lose him too, just as I've lost everyone else. Oh, God, if I lose him on top of everyone else, I don't know what I'll do. I won't want to live anymore. I'll beg Mournwrath to take me and make it quick so I can run off into whatever afterlife Caz awaits me in.

A pair of hands grips my shoulders, and my eyes snap up to find the person their connected to. It's when I look up that I realize I'm hyperventilating. My breaths are sharp as they fill my lungs and work twice as hard to escape.

"Willow, breathe!" Caz's aunt and one of his closest confidants, Maeve, wraps her hands around my upper arms as she gives me a light shake. "Breathe, my dear. Breathe."

I'm trying, but I still can't breathe. In fact, I think trying to calm down is only making it worse. It's as if my body knows something's not right and that my other half is in duress.

Maeve curses beneath her breath, snatches her hands away from my shoulders, and yells, "Get us to Beatrix's house *right now*! Killian, Rowan! Grab Caz's body and let's move!"

I'm not sure how I'm escorted out of the palace and inside the SUV with everyone else. I think Juniper, one of Caz's cousins, helps me. It's all a blur, really, as the tires of the SUV rip over the roads and through the forests. We rush along the tall bridge with glistening waters beneath, Rowan driving faster than he's ever gone, and I know I've lost it because I'm not afraid about the bridge. The first time we went across it, I feared for my life. It was as tall as a giant, with rocky waters beneath that could likely kill you on impact. Now, I don't care if we fly over at this point. We all may as well die without Caz because, whether he realizes it or not, he's the core. He's part of the reason his cousins and even Maeve have purpose and respect in Vakeeli. He's the reason I want to live again. Without him, I'm back to square one.

My eyes drop to Caz as his head rests on my lap. His body is comparable to a slab of ice but having him near and leaving the confines of that room in Alora's palace has calmed my breathing. His skin is pallid, dark circles forming around his eyes. The circles deepen by the second, morphing his face into a hollow version of itself. I stroke wisps of hair off his forehead as Rowan parks the car in front of Beatrix's cabin.

Maeve is out of the vehicle in a flash. Killian snatches my back door open, and I lay Caz's head down gently before climbing out. I stumble a bit when I'm on flat ground, and Juniper rushes my way, holding my elbow and keeping me steady.

Grabbing Caz beneath the armpits, Killian tows Caz's body out of the truck. His feet thunk on the ground as Killian grunts and clutches him beneath his armpits. Rowan lifts Caz's feet and he and Killian carry his body toward the stoop. Caz's cousins and right-hand men know how to handle him.

Maeve is already at Beatrix's door with a gun, and she swiftly kicks the door in.

"Maeve!" Alora, the queen of Vanora, yells behind me.

"BEATRIX!" Rage brews in Maeve's voice—a rage like nothing I've ever heard. I suck in a breath as Alora scurries past me to reach the porch. Juniper curses and chases them, and I follow.

The inside of Beatrix's home is dark and vacant. No candles flickering, no incense burning. The back door of her house is wide open, and a few windows in the kitchen are smashed, the moon gleaming on the sharp, jagged glass. It's not as warm as when I first visited.

As I round the corner of the short hallway, I see Juniper and Alora are standing in a bedroom, shoulders tense and hands in front of them as they stare at Maeve. Maeve has her gun pointed at Beatrix's face, while Beatrix sits on a lumpy bed that looks smaller than a twin with eyes full of fear.

"Please—w-what is going on?" Beatrix exclaims.

"Tell us what the hell is happening to Caspian or I'm shooting you in your bloody face!" Maeve barks at her, shoving the gun forward in warning.

"Yes, I—I can explain! Please!" Beatrix pleads, throwing her hands up.

Maeve's thumb presses down on the gun's hammer spur. "Speak quickly! I'm growing impatient!"

"It—it's Decius!" Beatrix confesses.

"*Decius?*" Alora and Maeve ask at the same time.

"Yes! He's returned!" Beatrix wails. "He made me lure you all here during that attack, but he told me it had to be *after* he saw Caz." She shakes her head, hands trembling as she holds them in front of her. "I knew he was still out there. There were rumors amongst the other Mythics about him taking form as one of us, and when you came to me, I could feel the Cold Tether, and if I could feel it, I'm sure Decius could too. I tried getting Caz and Willow away from each other so it would weaken him—deter him, even—but it didn't work. They fell in love, and now he's much stronger!"

"What does he look like?" Maeve demands. "Do you know? How can we find him and make him end this?"

"He...he...um...he has snowy hair. Blends in with the Whisper Grove community. He's older, but his face is *deceiving*. He appears merry and calm, but he's not. Beneath the exterior, he's *rotten*, and after encountering him, I'm certain he has all of Whisper Grove under some sort of spell."

Beatrix's explanation sends a shock through me. "Wait a minute." I step next to Maeve, who side-eyes me before pointing her focus to Beatrix again. "Does the guy you're talking about go by the name of Manx?"

"Yes!" Beatrix bobs her head. "That's him!"

The confirmation makes my heart sink to my stomach. "Oh, my God." *No.* How could Manx do this? He was our *friend*. He loved Caz!

"Well, he has our boy!" Maeve snaps, and she lowers her gun, but only to grip Beatrix by the upper arm and yank her off the bed. Beatrix cries out in pain as she grips the area where she was stabbed by the men from the attack...the men who I now realize were probably under a spell of his.

"Maeve, we should handle this a different—"

"Alora, I have a great respect for you, but I would encourage you *not* to fuck with me right now," Maeve snarls.

Alora backs away, blinking in shock, and Juniper cuts her a sympathetic look before following her mother out of the bedroom. She drags Beatrix by the arm until they've made it to her tiny living room. When I round the corner, I spot Rowan and Killian beside Caz's body, which is now more blue than white.

"He's dying here, Mum!" Killian shouts.

Maeve releases Beatrix's arm and shoves her forward. "Do something right now. Make this stop."

"I—I can't! I'm nowhere near as powerful as Decius! He's been alive since the beginning of time!"

Maeve presses the gun to the side of Beatrix's head. "Do. Something. Now! I will not ask again!"

Beatrix panics, dropping to her knees next to Caz. She breathes raggedly, wincing as she surveys Caz's body from head to toe. As she does, one of her brows inclines and she shudders a breath. "These veins," she whispers.

"What about them?" I ask.

She traces a hand over his body, hisses, then jerks it away just as quickly. "I—I'm afraid I cannot touch him. It seems Decius has a Mythic repellent in his body. If I touch him, it may alert him and cause him to work faster." She points to a shelf, at a set of vials. "Give me that slim, clear vial with the gold capsules inside it."

Rowan moves quickly, snatching up the bottle and tossing it to Beatrix. She takes it, pulling out a capsule and splitting it apart with thin, shaky fingers. As she does, glowing gold dust sprinkles out of it, and she offers one half to me.

I can't help my frown. "What am I supposed to do with this?"

"You're his mate, and Decius hasn't gotten to you yet. You're still connected. If you take this, there's a possibility it'll temporarily release whatever hold Decius has on him." She glances at Caz again. "Right now, it seems Decius has his mind. He hasn't gotten to his body yet because he's still breathing. *Here.*" She shoves it in my hand, and I cling to it. "Swallow it."

"What will it do?" Juniper demands.

"It will cause her great pain at first, as she absorbs both Tethers. Once you swallow it, Willow, you must touch him. Hold him, so that the veins on his body are shifted to yours. You do this, and the Tether will break...but only for a night."

"How can we trust her?" Killian growls.

"We can't," says Maeve. "But we have no other choice. Willow, swallow it."

I don't hesitate bringing the half capsule to my mouth. This is for Caz. I'll take his pain if it means saving him. The capsule is bitter and acidic going down, but I swallow, then I lie beside Caz, wrapping my arms around him.

Beatrix backs away, as well as everyone else, and I close my eyes, waiting for the pain to steal me away. At first, I don't feel a thing, only the iciness of Caz's body as I cling to him. But then a sharpness pierces my head, like a knife has sliced through my skull and is splitting it in two. I whimper as a dozen visions flood me. Then a million more knife-like slices drag across my body, up my arms, my legs, my chest, and as they do, I let out a bloodcurdling scream.

"Goodness! What is it doing to her?" Juniper wails.

"Leave her! You can't touch her!" Beatrix shouts.

"It's going to kill her!" Rowan barks.

"No, it won't! This only means it's working!"

Everyone goes quiet as my screams engulf the room. I want to open my eyes, beg someone to take this pain away, but I don't. I cling to Caz, who still lies frozen beside me, and scream until my voice is hoarse.

His memories run through my mind at warp speed. I can't grasp any of them quickly enough. They coil around my brain, toying with me, flickering by like old movie films. There's so much sound, so much color, so many voices.

And then it all stops.

CHAPTER 3
WILLOW

I HEAR NOTHING BUT MY SHALLOW BREATHS.

When I open my eyes, I'm in total darkness. I turn my head, noticing a bright blue dot in the distance. I walk toward it, my footsteps echoing on the dark ground, and the light, I realize, is in the form of a tunnel. Chains rattle and the air around me becomes colder the closer I walk through the tunnel. The dot widens with each step I take, the light growing brighter, and that's when I realize it isn't just a dark ground beneath me. Its *ice*, and it's splintering beneath my feet.

I freeze, afraid to move any farther. The ice groans beneath my weight, as if it will crack completely at any given moment and swallow me whole. I don't know if this is real or if it's in my mind, but what I do know is that I *cannot* let the ice break before reaching the end of this tunnel.

I hear the chains rattle again and lift my head. I spot a figure in the distance, bathed in blue light, slumped over and unmoving. It's a person. It's...

"Caz!" I yell. Forget the ice. I need to get to him. I run toward the tunnel end and the ice crackles louder. It splits apart as I run faster, chasing me as I hurry toward the light. I breathe raggedly, arms pumping, before finally diving forward and grunting as I hit frozen land.

When I look back, the ice completely splits apart behind me. A dark tidal wave rises, swallowing the broken ice and dragging it into the darkness, and I can't help feeling a chill whisper down my spine knowing I could be under that water right now.

I press up on my hands, surveilling my surroundings. The chill in the air clings to my skin, sinking deep into my lungs and bones. Tufts of breath surround me as I observe the hills and mountains of snow and ice ahead. The sky is a cloudless, murky blue, the horizon tinged a vicious red. Caz's body was here... but now he's gone. Where did he go?

"You can't find me!" A shrill voice fills the air. To my left, a boy with floppy, dark hair runs past, glowing in iridescent blue light. It takes me a while to realize he may not be real. More of a vision or figment of my imagination. He glows with sparkling blue dust radiating off him and can't be any older than five.

The boy hides behind a shimmering tree, giggling, and I step closer, confusion taking hold of me.

"Oh no!" a woman's voice squeals. "Where could he be? Where has my Caspian gone?"

The boy giggles again, crouching behind the tree as a woman appears, looking all around, pretending not to see him. I remain still as the woman turns in my direction, looking right through me.

"Is he here?" She trots away, popping her head around a wheelbarrow, and the boy's laughter swirls in the air.

"Oh, wait—I think I hear something! Would that be my

raven-haired boy?" The woman tiptoes over, finding him behind the thick tree. She grabs him, tickling his ribs and nuzzling her nose into the crook of his little neck. He laughs hysterically, throwing his arms around her.

"You found me!" he sings.

"My sweet boy," she coos. "I'll *always* find you."

They disappear, fading into blue specks, as if they were never there. The wind blows, whistling past my ears, and I wrap my arms around myself to fight a shiver. Ahead is a trail of more glittering light leading to a place unknown. The sound of rattling chains grows louder, and if I'm not mistaken, the light is leading to that very noise.

A spark appears in my peripheral as I start the trek, then the sound of a horse galloping, its hooves pounding into the land. A loud woosh strikes the air and I gasp, stopping dead in my tracks as an illuminated horse with a bearded man atop it rushes right past me, barely missing my nose.

"Get back here, you worthless piece of *shit!*" the bearded man roars. He's a burly man with angry, coal-like eyes. He has a sword in hand, raised in the air as he chases a teenage boy who throws up his middle finger before jumping a fence.

The horse rides off in the distance, disappearing into the mounds of ice and snow. The rattling becomes louder. I move faster. My feet are practically numb as I climb a hill. Just as I reach the top, I see the person I've been looking for.

"Caz!" I cry.

He's slumped over in a chair, head down, body pale. Frost clings to his dark hair and feathery eyelashes, and if I'm not mistaken, he's not breathing.

With shuddered breaths, I run toward him, my feet feeling like slabs of ice now, but before I can touch him, a dark figure rises from the ground, talons out and sharp teeth bared. The crescent eyes bore into mine, flaming red and devilish.

"Welcome to the prison of Caspian Harlow's mind," Mournwrath croaks.

"Let him go, Decius. *Now.*"

Mournwrath floats higher, smirking. "It's not your turn yet. I'm surprised to find you here so soon, Willow."

I look around him to see Caz again. The chair he's in has now been suspended in the air, his body wrapped in icy black chains. Black veins crawl along his body, snaking up to his temple. My eyes follow the black veins down the length of his body all the way to the ground, and it's a trail that leads to Mournwrath's cloak.

"Why?" I choke out. "I don't understand. Why would you do this, Manx? Show yourself, you traitor!"

Mournwrath is quiet a moment, staring, and then comes the sound of crunching bones shifting beneath flesh. The black monster disappears, transforming into a familiar jolly man with white hair from Whisper Grove.

"Better?" he asks, still floating.

"Oh, fuck you," I snarl.

He releases a petty sigh. "Do you think I wanted it to be this way, Willow?"

I back away as he floats closer to me. He's Manx, but the black still drips off him like whorls of smoke, and they're keeping Caz prisoner.

"How can you do this to him?" I breathe. "He *trusted* you."

"Many people trusted me, I'm afraid."

"You've been hunting him since he was a child," I counter. "You're a predator."

"I do what I need to in order to prosper. It's in my nature. Blame the Regals. They brought this wretched Tether upon us."

"The Regals didn't make you this way," I retort. "You decided to deceive because you couldn't have what you wanted."

Manx's eyes widen.

"Caz told me all about the original Tethered people. Oriah, wasn't it? You couldn't have her, so you killed her mate and then you murdered her. You killed all of them and then tried going for their *children*. You're a sick, twisted monster who doesn't deserve to live. The Regals should've killed you a long time ago."

A darkness sinks into Manx's eyes, and the whites of them turn blood red. I expect a snap back, a lash of anger, but instead he raises his chin and puts on a simple smile.

"Now, now. Don't worry yourself about that, Willow. That is the past, and after I absorb your and Caspian's Tether, I won't need to hunt anymore. As for the Regals, they are simply three bored, miserable beings who don't care about any of their creations. That's why they let me do this, you see? They let me hunt for Tethers, let me feed, let me live on. It is clear they *want* this, and I suppose it's like a game for them now. How long can a couple survive before Decius drains the life from them? Oh, what fun! Better fetch the freshly popped kernels while we're here!"

"I—I don't understand."

"What is there to understand?" His face darkens and that jolliness is gone, his eyes piercing red flames. "This is *my* world, and you're both in it. I'm the one in control of Vakeeli, which means you're as good as mine. As soon as I'm done with him, I'll be coming for *you*."

Something pierces my arm, like a quick poke of a needle, and I look down with a hiss. The veins from Caz's body have attached themselves to me. My skin absorbs them, and I watch as they crawl up the length of my arms and chest. I can feel them on my neck, but they're nothing more than a tingle now.

Manx throws me a bewildered glare. He whips his head to peer at Caz, who groans and shifts in the chair.

"What have you done?" Mournwrath hisses, eyes turning to crescents again as he focuses on me.

I smirk. "I was only buying time. You're not taking us as easily as you think you are."

"Ah. How brave of you, Willow. Let me guess. You got Beatrix to talk. She's helping you...*again*. Love of Vakeeli, you'd think that woman would've learn a thing or two by now." He floats closer to me, the redness disappearing from his eyes. His feet lower to the ground, and he places his hands behind his back. "Here's what I'd like to let you know, though..." A chiming noise rings in the air like a gong, and I spin around to find a black and silver clock floating in the air behind me. "In ten hours, the capsule she's given you *will* wear off. And what they don't tell you is that if you take another to try to prolong this rather pressing matter, it'll likely *kill* you, which will make my work so much easier. I've been waiting one hundred and twenty years to have Caz. What's ten more hours?"

With those words, he transforms completely to Mournwrath again and rushes toward me, shoving me onto the ground. However, I don't fall on my back. I sink into a dark void, arms flailing for seconds that feel endless. Above, I spot the blue light, the snowy hills, and my mate, floating in his chair. And then I land on hard ground.

CHAPTER 4
WILLOW

MY EYES FLUTTER OPEN, AND I FIND MYSELF surrounded by Caz's family again. His body is wrapped in my arms, and the black veins have disappeared from him. When I check my arms, they're spreading like thick threads.

"You all right, Willow?" Rowan asks as he and Killian help me stand.

"Yeah, yeah. I'm fine," I murmur.

"Well? What happened?" Beatrix demands, staring into my eyes.

"I saw Decius," I tell her. "He's aware his time has been set back, and he knows you're helping me."

Beatrix looks all around, worry creasing her forehead. "Okay." She nods, eyes on me again.

"He said something about Vakeeli being *his* world and having the control. No one can stop him here but the Regals. This is going to sound really, *really* crazy, but what if...what if I take Caz back to my portal and to my world, just until we figure out how to get rid of Decius?"

"It'll be impossible getting rid of Decius unless we find the Regal Selah," Beatrix says, head shaking swiftly. Right, Selah. The Regal who created all of Vakeeli and every single person on it. Decius put her in a deep sleep and the only person who can wake her is Caz.

"Well, where can we find her?"

"Only The Council would know," Alora says, "and the person they sent to find her is lying on the ground."

"There has to be a way to get to her that doesn't involve Caz —something we can do," I proclaim. "Can we not talk to The Council? They can't wake Selah without Caz's blood and if he dies, they'll have nothing. Perhaps we can demand them to take all of us to Selah. We can't just let Caz die!"

Everyone looks at each other, then they drop their gazes to Caz as the heaviness of my statement weighs on them.

"I suppose sending him to your world will create a lengthier delay," Beatrix murmurs with a scratching of the head. "Decius is only powerful here because he works through Vakeeli soil. Without it, his powers aren't very useful. He could move through other universes just like any other Mythic, but he'd likely use vessels—you know, animals and people with bad intentions. He'll use whatever works in his favor to get him where he needs to be. And even then, he wouldn't be able to fully use his powers to take the Cold Tether in your world. No vessel would be strong enough so he'd have to find a way to bring Caz back, which could take ages."

"So there *is* a possibility then? An escape for Caz?" I inquire.

"Yes, but *only* if it works. It's never been done before by a

Mythic—sending a Vakeeli-born to another universe. It requires a lot of energy—energy I don't even have right now."

"Beatrix, we have to try," I plead. "Look at him. He's *dying*. I can't just sit here."

Beatrix's misty eyes fall to Caz's body again. She sighs, then gives me a slight nod. "All right. It may weaken me—possibly even *kill* me—but I'll do my best."

"Thank you." I wish I could say I find relief in her words, but I don't, and I won't until I know it's worked, and Caz is safe. It's such a big ask and no, I don't want Beatrix to die, but I'm willing to do anything for him right now.

Beatrix scurries across the room to one of her bookshelves, collecting several thick, leatherbound books into her arms. "Your portal remains in Blackwater, correct?" she asks over her shoulder.

"Yes."

"Then we'll perform the ritual there. Now let's hurry. Time is truly of the essence."

CHAPTER 5
CAZ

BLACKWATER IS NOTORIOUSLY KNOWN FOR ITS COLD winters. I'd like to think I've grown used to the chill, but what holds me now is a different kind of cold.

In my territory, where the wind would howl and the snow would cling to our skin, we'd still have our clothes, hats, and shoes to keep us warm—a barrier to protect us, if you will. But here, I have nothing. Isolated in a cold, dark place, wrapped in chains that feel like bent icicles digging into my flesh.

A weak groan escapes me, and I breathe as evenly as possible through my nose. It's useless. My entire body shudders as the wind whips and the snow clings to me.

A blur of black dashes past, and I look to my left, watching the figure land several feet away. A dark cloak billows behind the figure, dark boots touching the ground. The figure shifts to a person, and he walks closer to me. The black cloak transforms to a stark white, and when I carry my gaze to their eyes, I have the urge kill him.

"You know, Caspian," Manx says, approaching me. "You're much luckier than you think you are."

He snaps his fingers, and a chair appears right across from me. He sits on it, just out of arm's reach. I can't even headbutt the fucker if I wanted to.

"I was enjoying your memories," he goes on. He looks me all over with eyes I used to trust. "Do you have questions?"

I grimace, look him up and down, then spit at his feet.

Manx chuckles, folding one leg over the other. "We have ten hours until I can claim you. Why not enjoy these last few hours we have together, just like old times? Look, I've shifted into someone you trust. That's much better than my true form, which you *do not* want to see, believe me."

Still, I say nothing, and as if that irritates him, he sits forward and says, "Fine. If you don't want to talk, I'll *make* you talk." Shoving out of his chair, he walks away from it and shifts into a person I've never seen before. He becomes a man with short dark hair, like the ink of a squid. His skin turns a grayish white, like dirty dish water, and that cloak of his transitions to black again. His nose isn't round and soft, but hawkish, crooked, and flared. But nothing beats his eyes—dark irises and pupils that have no life or color and seem to go on infinitely. *This* is the real Decius.

He lifts both arms in the air, creating a gray cloud above us. The cloud spreads, creating a moving image, and I wince when the cold chains tighten around me.

In the clouds, I see a woman, and not just any woman. It's my mother. She's out of breath as she bursts into my childhood cabin. I'm just a boy, no older than seven, lying on the floor reading a book.

"Caspian, come quickly!" she shouts, already grabbing my arm and yanking me up.

"Stop this!" I demand, but Decius only looks at me with a smirk, his face as sinister as they said he was in the stories I used to read about him.

He lets out a wicked chuckle. "I knew you'd talk to me eventually."

"Do you get some kind of sick kick out of this?" I snap. "Torturing people about their past?"

"Oh, absolutely. In fact, it gives me much more strength. That's what makes your Tether so sweet. The duress you're under. The pain. The hurt. The resistance of who you *truly* are. Why do you think I led Magnus, your cruel, cruel father, to you and your mother? If he hadn't taken you, you never would've become who you are now. All that pain that festers inside you will only do me wonders."

"Do you remember what I told you about the hidey-hole?" my mother asks, rushing me out the door of the cabin.

"STOP!" I squeeze my eyes shut, refusing to look, but they're immediately pried open again by a needle-like invisible force. I cry out as my eyes are spread open wider, forced to watch what happens next in the glowing clouds.

"Yes, Mum, I think so," I tell her.

"Good boy. I need you to stay in there until I come for you. And no matter what you here, you must stay in there. Do you understand?"

"Why, Mum?"

She ignores my question, trudging through the forest, my small hand clutched in her clammy grasp. She walks around a tree with a large trunk, and a bed of moss and twigs. Releasing my hand, she shoves the twigs and moss aside, revealing a wooden plank. Removing the plank, she uncovers a hole in the ground—one I watched her dig months ago. Back then, I had no clue why she was digging it. "Go on then," she says hurriedly. "In you go."

"But I don't want to go in there! There are spiders, Mum! I'm scared!"

"You must!" she declares, and after she does, the voices of men rise, echoing through the forest. She gasps, dropping to her knees and looking me in the eye. "This is the only way I can protect you right now, Caspian. We have no time. Please get into the hole, and I'll come for you in a few minutes. Okay?" She forces a smile, one that doesn't reach her eyes. If I'd known then what that smile represented, I never would have agreed.

Tears form in my eyes. My vision has blurred, but I nod and allow her to help me into the hole. Once inside, I stifle a sob as she covers it back with the wooden plank, whispering, "It's okay, son. It'll be okay."

She shoves leaves and other things on top of the plank to cover it, darkening the hole by the second, and then I hear her steps scatter away. The voice of the men grow louder, booming as they call for her. "We know you're here, Azira! Give us the boy!"

"Enough!" I shout, glaring at Decius. The sharp grip on my eyes weakens, and the vision in the cloud fades.

"Caspian, this isn't Blackwater. You aren't in charge here," he says, smirking with his hands behind his back.

"I don't care."

"Do you not wish to relive these times? The last moments spent with your mother?"

"Fuck you."

He sighs, moving closer. "I suppose it doesn't make sense to torture you with things you relive daily. I know it's all you ever think about—your mother. Her death. Your *recklessness*. But Willow..." A wide grin spreads across his face, and I jerk forward in my chair. The chains rattle, pressing deeper into my skin, and at this point I don't care if they rip all of it off.

25

"You hurt a hair on her head, and I'll tear you limb from limb, you twisted fuck," I growl. "I swear on all of Vakeeli, I'll find a way to *end* you."

He laughs, his head falling backward. "And there it is. That calm demeanor you carry so well simply vanishes when your mate comes into the equation. You're just like the Tether you descend from. The original, Lehvine. Always throwing threats even when he's unable to do a damn thing. Tell me, how will you do *any* of what you say when you're stuck here?"

"My clan will find a way out for me."

"There's no way to fight it. The only way is through Selah, but that won't happen now because I have you. The Council will have to find another chosen man...and that will never happen. Not when I begin my reign." He taps his chin, looking all around. "How about this? I let you and Willow suffer *together*. That's rather poetic, isn't it? She feels your pain and absorbs your memories, while you get to endure it all over again."

He forms another cloud as I shout at him, but my shouting turns to screams of agony as he continues the memory—the one that ruined my life and changed me forever.

CHAPTER 6
YOUNG CASPIAN

PAST

I CROUCHED IN THE HIDING HOLE WHEN I HEARD THE
thundering voices of men. My heart was beating so hard I could
hear it in my ears.

I wrapped my arms around myself as I looked up, focusing
on the jagged slits of the planks. Through the slits, the sky was
a hazy orange. It would be dark soon, and the thought of that
terrified me because around the cabin at night, it was pitch
black, and there were stories about things that only came out at
night.

As wisps of light gave leeway, I decided to inspect the hole.
There were no spiders or nests, fortunately, only dirt, twigs, and
black worms. One of the worms tried inching away, but I picked
it up and sat on my bottom. I recall my feet being bare and the
cool soil wedging between my toes.

"Mum will be back," I whispered to the worm. I held it close, studying the ridges and lumps on its body.

Then there was a familiar, high-pitched scream. Gasping, I looked up as I heard my mum shout, "No!"

Footsteps followed, swift and chaotic, and I stood promptly as the steps grew nearer. With haste, the plank was removed, and I saw my mother again. She threw her hand at me and when I took it, she yanked me out of the hiding hole.

"Come, son! Now! They know where I've hidden you! We must go!" There was panic in her voice and though I had no idea what was going on, I held her hand tighter. We ran away, but that's when heard the pounding of horse hooves behind us.

"Don't look back, Caspian! Just run!" Mum shouted, but I was only a child. I couldn't help himself. As my feet moved and Mum led the way, I peered over my shoulder again and there were three men riding horses and chasing after us. Two of the men had torches gripped in their large hands and glistening black helmets on their heads, the letter B carved into the sides of them. Back then, to my young mind, they were intimidating, but not as much as the man in the middle, who rode his horse without a helmet and had dark eyes full of fury. A bushy, thick beard swarmed the lower half of his face, and he roared Mum's name repeatedly, demanding her to stop. She didn't.

Instead, she kept running, gunning it through the forest with my hand in hers. Panic set in when I realized this was a chase. These men were trying to get us, possibly even *kill* us. I whimpered and put my attention ahead again, running as quickly as I could alongside her.

The hooves of the horses grew closer. It didn't take long for one of the men to circle us and bring us to screeching halt. The fire of his torch blazed in our faces, the heat of the fire lightly singeing my forehead, as the man shouted, "Give us the boy!"

Mum collected me into her arms with a defensive snarl. Shooting a hand in the air, she aimed it at the man and an invisible force knocked him off his horse and sent him crashing into a tree.

I gasped as Mum dropped her hand. I was in complete shock. I'd never seen her do that before. Ever. But I had no time to ask her what'd happened or how it was possible because she tossed me onto the back of the man's horse before I could fully let it sink in.

"Azira!" the bearded man behind us bellowed, but Mum climbed onto the horse, gripped the reins, and rode off. I was still stunned by what my mother had done. She used to tell me only Mythics and the gilded had powers, yet she'd just killed a man with powers of her own. How was that possible?

The body of the horse was sturdy, and it galloped loudly as Mum shouted for it to go faster. I had the urge to lay my head on the horse, feel it's warmth on my cheek.

"We must reach Vanora," Mum breathed, then shouted at the horse again to pick up speed.

I looked back as the men trailed farther behind, and for a moment, I could taste the safety and the freedom, the feeling wrapping around me like a warm cocoon. We'd reach Vanora as Mum planned and we'd be safe from these random men. Mum would be happy, and all would be well.

But just as quickly as the bliss swam through me, our horse let out a bloodcurdling screech and buckled forward. Its heavy body crashed into the ground, sending us flying across the forest. In flight, Mum sucked in a breath and threw out a hand in my direction. Suddenly, I was wrapped in a bubble of blazing gold light. The bubble felt hot, but not enough to burn. I landed softly on the ground, cushioned by the bubble but Mum...her fall was much worse. Her delicate body slammed into a tree, and I was positive I heard the crunch of bone. The bubble surrounding me faded as his Mum rolled over on the ground with a pained groan.

"Mum!"

Not too far away from her was the horse we'd been riding. Its rear legs were gone and bleeding profusely. They'd been chopped off by something sharp and silver—something that was clearly thrown at it. The weapon, shaped like an oversized axe but without a handle, lay next to the bleeding horse and was cloaked in crimson. My heart wrenched for the horse as it whinnied in agony. It wasn't the horse's fault. How could they hurt a defenseless horse? *How could they?* I snapped out of my thoughts as Mum moaned and rolled onto her back.

"Mum!" I screamed, scrambling toward her. I stumbled over sticks and logs, but before I could make it to her, a large hand grabbed my upper arm and snatched me backwards.

"Get off of me!" I shouted. I thrashed about as the man wrangled me in his arms. "Mummy! MUMMY!"

"Shut up, boy!" the man hissed. The other man with a torch clopped around Mum while on the horse. He hopped off, picking her up by the single thick braid in her hair.

Instantly alert, she swung at the man and missed. The man laughed then kicked her in the back, sending her flying flat on her stomach.

"Caspian! I'm here," she cried, digging her nails into the ground, and attempting a weak crawl in my direction. "Magnus, please!" she wailed, voice cracking. "You can't take him from me! He's, my boy! He's all I have!"

"Shut her up," the man in charge growled. The soldier bent over and grabbed her by the braid to yank her to her knees. She let out a scream as he curled it around his fist and yanked it backward. Blood was dripping from her mouth, and some was on her hand, where she clutched her rib. With his other hand, the man dug into the pocket of his trousers until it was coated in a white powder. He cupped her mouth with the powdered hand, and Mum moaned, trying to shove it away but failing.

"Mummy!" I cried, stretching my arms for her. I'd watched in horror as they hurt her, so young and weak and unable to do anything to help. Completely useless. That's what I was. A useless little boy.

When her body sagged and her eyes closed, I screamed, "LET HER GO!" but it made no difference. The man in charge only held me tighter and squeezed my upper arm so hard, I was certain it would leave a bruise.

"Take her to the dungeons," the man in charge demanded, reeling me back as I sobbed for her. I was crying so hard my stomach hurt. "I'll teach her a thing or two about running away from me."

CHAPTER 7
WILLOW

THE VISION HITS ME LIKE A MURKY TIDAL WAVE. IT drowns me, the suffocating water filling my lungs, and I find it hard to breathe, to see, to do anything.

Even when I try to pull out of it, I can't. I'm trapped in it because I *am* that boy with worry and fear, hiding in the hole, waiting for his mother to return. I *am* him as he screams for her, begging for the big man to stop torturing them. I feel his agony as he reaches for her like his life depends on it, the woman who has clearly sworn her life to protect him.

That boy is Caz, once young and so full of life, now broken and in despair. My heart aches for him.

I sit back in the seat of the car, breathing as evenly as possible as the vision passes. I blink some of my tears away, then look to my right at Juniper who has fallen asleep. The side of her head is pressed to the window. In the back row, Killian stares out the window, and Rowan drives, fully alert. Maeve is rubbing her temples with the pads of her fingers, as if fighting a headache.

I turn my head to peer out the window too. It's still night, thank goodness, and though I was lost in the memory, I didn't react externally. However, I am shaking. The fear and struck my adrenaline.

I turn a fraction, taking a look through the back windshield and spotting Alora's SUV. They have Caz's body occupying the back row. Beatrix believes it's best that I don't touch him now that I'm harboring his half of the Tether. She doesn't want any trace getting back onto him for Mournwrath to work with. Still, I'm worried about him. If I saw that vision, that means he's seeing it too. There's no telling what Decius is doing to him right now.

I face forward again, sucking in a breath and letting it settle in my lungs before releasing it. I have to get Caz out of there. Decius has him trapped in his own mind, and he's tormenting him with these memories. And something tells me what I just saw was only the tip of the iceberg. A sudden chill takes over me, and I clench a fist as pain ripples down my spine. I groan, squeezing my eyes shut as my body tenses in the seat.

"All right there, Willow?" Killian leans forward, eyeing me.

My eyes find his, and I nod. "I...I'm good," I breathe.

He slides his gaze to my arms. I look with him, and a new vein has appeared on the center of my forearm and is crawling its way to my bicep.

"Do they hurt?" Killian asks. "Those marks?"

"Only when a new set forms. Feels like knives slicing my skin."

"Fuck."

"Yeah."

He's quiet a moment. The wheels of the SUV bounce lightly as we drive along a dirt road. "Oi, uh...listen." He scratches his eyebrow. "I'm...uh...well, I didn't mean to take my anger out on you about this whole Tether thing. I've been a bit of an asshole toward you ever since you dropped in Vakeeli. It's just that this is all so new, and we've never faced anything like it." He pauses. "But I see that you're willing to do anything for Caz, so I can appreciate that. *We all* appreciate it," he says, gesturing to his family.

I can't help smiling as I ask, "Is this your way of apologizing for being said asshole?"

The right side of his mouth quirks upward. "It is, so accept it. It won't get any better than that."

I laugh. "Well, then, I accept. And you're right. I'll do anything for Caz. He doesn't deserve to face this alone. It's our Tether. We just have to find a way to survive it."

"What if there is no way?" Killian scratches his eyebrow again. "I mean, what if the whole thing with him going to your world doesn't work?"

I shrug. "We have to try. It's worth a shot."

"He's gonna hate it," he grumbles, sitting against his seat again. "All he's ever known is Blackwater, really. It's his home. His land. Your world will be new territory for him...and I mean that in the literal sense."

"Yeah, well, hopefully he doesn't have to stay in it for long. Just long enough for us to find a way out of this mess."

"Well, we're gonna do all we can from our end," he says.

Silence fills the car again and I sigh. "My brother always used to say I write the script for my own life," I murmur. "Whenever I had a bad day, he would tell me I had the power to spin it into a positive one. And this, I suppose, is our story.

Mournwrath is just a speedbump. We'll get Caz to safety first, then figure out how to get to Selah so she can defeat him. We take it one thing at a time. That's the only way we'll make it through this."

"Your brother was a wise man," Killian murmurs.

I nod, trying not to let the doubt sink its claws into me. Because that's what Decius wants. He wants us to feel doomed, like there's no way out of the situation we're in. But there is *always* a way. He may be old, but he's not invincible.

CHAPTER 8
CAZ

"FINE," I MUTTER AFTER THE VISIONS HAVE STOPPED. If talking helps end them, so be it. "You want me to talk. Let's talk."

Decius cocks his head ever so slightly, his hands behind his back.

"Why go through all this trouble now just to absorb some Tether?" I ask. "Why didn't you just take me while I was young? You had plenty of chances. I used to do some of my studies with you. I spent night after night in your home whenever my mother was away."

Snow falls, and I shiver as more flakes land on my scalp and shoulders. He looks all around, pointing his face upward, letting the snow pelt his skin.

"I do love snow." He sighs, then he turns his head only a fraction to eye me. "If only it were that easy. As I told you, the torment is what I feed on. It fuels me, makes me powerful. Plus, you had to mate, and believe me, I never thought that day would come. Mating is not optional when it comes to the Tether. When you succumb to the desires and have that urge to *fuck* her constantly and to *kill* anyone who dare touches her, *that* is what I need. That is what truly fills me."

"My mother..." I start, but I can't go there—not without getting angry—so I rephrase. "You're the one who told Magnus about me when he needed an heir."

Decius shrugs. "I may have sent him a letter or two."

My hands ball into fists. "She trusted you. You made her carry me, give birth to me, and all for it to come to *this*?"

"What can I say, Caspian?" He cracks a demented smile. "I have so much time on my hands." He folds his arms over his chest. "Listen, for what it's worth, I have always liked you. Much more than any other Tethered male. And considering you're a descendant of Lehvine, oh...you should be grateful I like you because I *hated* that bastard. You and I? We were close, and for a long time, I thought of you like a son, so don't think for a second this doesn't pain me to do. I like you and Willow, and it's nice to finally see you coming out of that depressing shell and being happy with someone...but at the end of the day, I killed my one true love—my *mate*—just to continue living. And I loved Oriah with all my heart, but this hunger inside me is *unstoppable*. Whether I cave to it, or allow the darkness inside me to take over, it will be done. There is no stopping it."

"You're making people suffer," I snap. "Why not just disappear? Kill yourself? You have nothing to live for—no purpose other than sucking away Tethers. That must be a terrible life to live."

He's quiet a moment, lips twisting as he conjures an answer. "You're right, there is nothing for me to live for. I'm an old being. I can't procreate, and I can't die unless Selah kills me herself. I suppose I continue living because my life was going to be robbed from me, and by having life still...well, it's a wonderful slap in the face to those who were so ready to betray me. I never asked to be created. I never asked to fall in love, or to mate, but I did. And because of that, I live in spite. I live because it's a good reminder to feel all those original Tethers again when I've absorbed a new one. It all comes back to me, brings me to life, makes me more powerful. And you know what it's like to have power, Caspian. You're a ruthless monarch, one so many people fear. Having even one sip of power is enough to change you." He moves closer. "And I want to let you in on a little secret. Seeing as you're the son of a hybrid Mythic, a descendent of a Tethered male, *and* you share blood from a line of monarchs...well, my boy, your soul is enough to fill me to the brim. With just yours, I can kill Selah while she's in her eternal slumber and become the primary Regal. Then *no one* will be able to stop me. There won't be any more suffering for the Cold Tethered. They'll have no choice but to come to me if they seek peace, which is much more than Selah ever gave them. I'll be king, and all of Vakeeli will be mine. Hey, maybe Willow's universe will be mine too. I've always wanted to travel to Earth. I suppose I'll do it with a lasting impression."

Every time he says Willow's name, a flame builds in my chest that wants to shoot out like the fire of a dragon. But as angry as I am, I know this anger won't protect Willow.

Raising my chin, I lock on his eyes as he conjures up yet another chair with the snap of his fingers and sits across from me.

"What if I make you deal?" I ask.

38

"A deal?" He tips his chin. "This should be interesting. What sort of deal?"

"You say you only need me to fulfill your plan. What if I let you take me...*willingly?*"

Decius scoffs. "How so?"

"I don't know how—perhaps I can cross thoughts with Willow, tell her this is my choice, and she can tell everyone to stop trying to save me," I state quickly. "But if I do, you *must* leave Willow out of it. Let her live her life. Let her forget about me and the whole world of Vakeeli. Keep her and my family out of all of this Tethered mess."

"Do you really think Willow would want that?" he asks, sneering.

"No," I whisper. "But she'll do it. She loves me, so she'll do it."

"Do you love her?"

His question torments me. A knot forms in my belly, tightening with each cold second.

I carry my gaze to his. "She's my mate. I loved her before I even met her." I lower my head in shame—not for loving Willow. I'd never be ashamed of that. But because I finally found a slice of happiness and someone who completes me, and I must give her up. I must sacrifice my love for her so she can live on.

Smirking, Decius rises and leans down, his face so close that his hawkish nose almost touches mine. "Very well. We can do it your way. It is true that I don't really need Willow's half of the Tether. I just don't like leaving loose ends, but seeing as she's not from here...well, I suppose this is a risk I can take to get this over with sooner rather than later. So long as she goes back to her world and doesn't return to Vakeeli, she should be safe. And if she does come for me, well, that'll be her mistake. I won't be able to control what I do to her if she does." His eyes darken. "Better that you warn her."

"Do I have your word, Manx?" I demand.

"Decius," he corrects, face twisting.

"Do I have your word, *Decius?*"

He grins, revealing slick white teeth. "One thing about me is that I keep my word. Willow will remain untouched, so long as she doesn't come after me when this is all over. Now, hold still." He grips my head, holding on to it tight. I cry out as his talons pierce my skull, and he groans too, yelling, "Send your message to her *now!*"

I let the words form in my mind, despite the pain and the cold. They're likely the last words I'll ever tell her, so I make them worthy.

I love her so much. I only want her safe. It sucks to die this way, but it must be done. I've wanted to die for a very long time, and now the moment has come. So long as my mate is spared, I'll let my fate be.

Decius' talons release my head, and he pants raggedly, staggering backward. I drop my eyes to his hands, and they're no longer the talons of Mournwrath, but mortal hands...just like Manx's. His hands are charred, like they've been burned or forced into a fire. Black smoke whispers off of them, and he hisses in pain, staring down at them.

Decius' eyes flicker to mine, and we stare at each other without a single world. I'm not sure what the hell just happened, but it feels like it was more in my favor than his.

With a grimace, he steps away, and his eyes drag to mine once more, burning with furious curiosity, before he vanishes into thin air.

40

CHAPTER 9
WILLOW

WHEN WE REACH BLACKWATER, THE MOON SHINES boldly in the night sky and the temperature has dropped several degrees. My breaths ripple out, floating past me when I step out of the SUV. It may be chillier here, but it's nowhere near as cold as the prison of Caz's mind.

Speaking of, Killian and Rowan waste no time taking Caz's body out of Alora's SUV. As they do, a voice runs through my head that catches me completely off guard.

Willow, my time is running out. Forget about me. Live your life on Earth and promise to never come back to Vakeeli. And tell my family to let me go. I love you.

"What?" I whisper. *Caz? Caz?*

"What's the matter?" Juniper rushes toward me.

"I just heard Caz's voice telling me to forget about him."

I stare at his motionless body as Rowan and Killian steady him in their hands. Why would he say that? I'm not living without him. What the hell is he talking about?

Caz? Why are you saying that? Can you hear me?

I wait for his response, but it's like I'm speaking into a void again. There's nothing but silence, my voice echoing back to me.

Juniper's brows have dipped with concern. "Are you sure it was his voice?"

"I'm positive. It sounded just like him. I don't know, maybe it was a warning. We need to hurry and get to the portal." I take a sweep of my surroundings. In the dark, it's hard to tell exactly where the portal is, but Killian bobs his head in the proper direction, and I take the lead. We trek through the forest and despite how badly I'm shivering, I walk as quickly as my body will go.

"Make a right at that tree, then a few paces left. I marked the area with a W," Killian says, and sure enough, as Juniper points her flashlight, I spot the W on the ground. "W for Willow," Killian goes on.

"That was very wise of you, Killian," Maeve tells him. "Thank you."

Beatrix rushes past me, carrying a large burlap bag with her. From the bag she takes out vials, bowls, books, and containers filled with various colored liquids, powders, and rocks.

"Lay him on the ground," she orders Killian and Rowan. They place him down and she looks to me. "In order for this to work properly, your bodies must merge."

"*Merge?*" I frown. "What does that mean?"

"The less clothes you have on, the better this will work. Clothes are barriers to Mythic magic, and for something as powerful as sending you both through a portal, I don't want any sort of resistance."

"Oh." My eyes flicker to Rowan and Killian, and then to

Maeve and Juniper. They all stare at each other, then glance back at Alora and her guard, Proll, who stand near the gate a distance away.

"Are you saying she needs to be *naked?*" Maeve demands.

"Not entirely naked, but the less garments she wears, the better." Beatrix pops open a purple vial and sprinkles some of the liquid onto the ground. "Their bodies must touch consistently throughout the process with minimal barriers. He's already shirtless, so I suggest removing your shirt too, Willow."

Maeve and Juniper look at me with sympathetic gazes, while Killian and Rowan glance at each other a fleeting moment before focusing on their mother.

"Is there no other way?" Maeve tries again.

I look down at my cloak and shirt. I'll be freezing my ass off, but...this is for Caz. "It's fine. I'll do it," I tell them.

Killian and Rowan turn away immediately, facing the opposite direction. I don't look to see what anyone else does as I slide out of the cloak and pull the shirt over my head. I unbutton my pants next, sliding them down and stepping out of them. Standing in just a bra and panties, I wince as the cold bites my skin, and a breeze wraps around me. I put my focus on Caz's pale body on the ground. This is for him. *For us.*

"Okay, now I need you to lie on top of him." Beatrix has a book open and is flipping through the pages. As she does, I lie on top of Caz's body. He doesn't make a sound, and I swear it terrifies me. That, and his body being like a block of ice is disheartening, but I cling to him and rest my ear on his chest. His heart still beats, a solid *thu-thunk, thu-thunk.* I find relief in that.

"Now, for everyone else, I need you to leave. If I can manage this, the portal will be powerful. It will suck anyone and anything into it who is in a certain range, and there's no guarantee you'll end up in the same place as the Tethered. There are so many universes—*thousands*. It's a risk I'm sure none of you want to take."

"Right. Fine," Maeve mutters reluctantly.

"Here." Rowan's voice is near, and he walks up to me with a black handgun in hand. His eyes are everywhere and on me all at once. "Take this with you. Caz won't like being in another place without a gun."

I take the gun and place it between us. "Thanks, Rowan."

He nods then turns away just as quickly as he had before, jogging away with Killian.

"We'll do everything we can to find a way for you two to be free from Mournwrath!" Juniper yells as Maeve takes her hand. "We promise!"

I smile, watching as Maeve tugs her away. Juniper looks back once more with a helpless stare as Alora approaches.

"Come to the fields when you're done, Beatrix," Alora commands. "There are still pressing matters to discuss."

"If I make it out alive," Beatrix mutters.

When everyone is gone, Beatrix draws in a breath then exhales. She places the thick book on the ground then picks up a clear vial. Removing the cork lid, she pours a powder out of it to outline our bodies.

"Beatrix?" I call, and her eyes lower to mine. "Thank you for doing this."

She looks at me, perplexed, then asks, "How can you thank me? I betrayed you. Alora will probably have my head if I make it out alive."

"You're making up for your mistake now," I murmur.

Her eyes glisten in the dark. She then clears her throat, blinking the tears away and stepping back.

Putting the lid back on the bottle, she says, "Think of somewhere on Earth that is safe for you, and it will take you there."

"Okay."

After setting the bottle aside, she spreads her hands apart and begins a chant:

When worlds collide, they bring rebirth
Vakeeli tides be carried to Earth
Where tethered bonds shall not arise
And wicked souls will have no worth
Take thine power and give to thee
These hopeless souls who are in need

The first time Beatrix says the chant, an iridescent purple light surrounds my and Caz's body. The second time, our bodies are lifted off the ground. I hold on to him tighter, squeezing my eyes shut, bracing for what's to come. The third time, we spin in the air, slowly at first, then fast—so fast I should be dizzy.

Beatrix screams the chant and I hear pain in her voice, but she doesn't stop, not until purple light beams in the sky like a signal. The air vibrates around us, and when I look down, the ground crumbles. Beatrix is on her knees, purple flames surrounding her. She doesn't stop chanting, despite her expressions of pain. She raises her hands in the air, gesturing to us, and I hear her yell the words, "Regal tether, break thy bond! Send them to a land beyond!"

Her voice fades, and total darkness consumes me. I hear nothing but my ragged breaths. Caz's body is beneath me, cold, motionless.

We float in dark, deafening silence, and I close my eyes, thinking of that safe place—somewhere we will land together. Somewhere Mournwrath won't be able to reach us.

I hold Caz tighter and my stomach drops when we plummet into the dark abyss.

CHAPTER 10

CAZ

THERE WERE MANY THINGS I WAS AFRAID OF WHEN I was young, but nothing was worse than Magnus Harlow of Blackwater. I'd witnessed the relationship between fathers and sons before. The fathers would carry their sons on their shoulders, hold their hands as they ventured through their territories, or play games of mini Chetnee with smiles and laughter. Magnus was not like those men.

Magnus was cold with a temper from hell, and anytime I cried, Magnus would whip me with a steel whip. I learned early on to not cry around Magnus or his wife Lura (who couldn't stand to see me weeping over my mother) but that didn't mean I wouldn't cry for her while locked away in my room.

I'd been robbed of everything—my life, my loving caretaker, even my name. No longer was I Caspian Bizzell, a drifter of all the lands. I was Caz Harlow, heir, and soon-to-be monarch of Blackwater.

I wasn't loved in this new home. I was forced to use a sword and eventually a gun. I was trained to fight, to shoot, to kill. Every Saturday, I was sent out to ride with Magnus and Lura to the village so I could be paraded as the heir of Blackwater. They pretended to be proud, when truly, they hated me.

Every night, I had nightmares of my mother being taken, the horse's blood, and the weapon that'd murdered the horse. I'm imagine her powers and wonder how she could do it. Soon, I learned that she was the daughter of a powerful mythic—that she carried that energy in her blood and had only learned to harness it when I was born. I'd dream of my mother's eyes and how they were filled with helpless tears, her cries, and the way she screamed my name for the last time.

The nightmares were so gut-wrenching that I no longer wanted to sleep, and because I didn't sleep, I'd venture to the castle's dungeons to search for her, to no avail. She wasn't in the castle...and after a few months, I assumed she wasn't alive at all.

Everyone who surrounded me looked at me with expectations in their eyes, eager for the day I'd reign. All did, except Aunt Maeve and my cousins, who lived on the outskirts of the village. They were the highlight of my new life. I was only able to spend one weekend with them every summer, and Magnus made sure to hold back on the abuse and drown me in healing elixir whenever I visited his sister so there was no proof. It wasn't until I was forced to fight in Ripple Hills that Maeve caught on.

Prior to that, there were plenty of times I wanted to tell Aunt Maeve what was being done to me, but Magnus used my mother as a threat. Mythics would reveal her in a mirror in the castle when I stepped out of line, and each time, chains would hang from her wrists and her head was bowed. She would take a breath, and that was when Magnus would threaten that if I said *anything* about it, or how I was brought to Blackwater, he would kill her.

I thought I could hold out. I figured once I was of age, I'd be monarch and would be able to free my mother. But I'd jumped the gun…and it was because of my mistake and impatience that I never saw her again.

CHAPTER II
CAZ

I T ' S   H A R D   T O   I M A G I N E   W H A T   M Y   L I F E   W O U L D   B E   L I K E had I not been a procreation of Magnus. I ask myself often, would I have been happier? Would I have had a better child-hood? A simpler one? One that wasn't so bloody traumatic?

I often wonder why the universe punishes us. Does it feel there are some who deserve it more than others? Is it trying to create a balance on an unknown spectrum, or is it all deter-mined by bloodlines? Perhaps if you're bred into a certain family, there's a possibility your life will be a living hell—a generational curse of sorts.

I don't know the answers to these questions, but they're all I can think right now as I lie in a haze. It feels as if I'm awake. My body hums with warmth and energy, and I feel the breaths expelling from my body. I'm no longer in that frozen wasteland Decius had me trapped in. I'm somewhere else.

"Caz." That voice. It's angelic—beautiful, really. "Caz, wake up. Please."

Willow.

Warm hands press to my chest, and I'm shaken out of a foggy state. My eyes pop open and I draw in a sharp breath, sitting upright. Something heavy slides to my lap. Realizing it's a gun, I pick it up with instinct and point it at whatever is in front of me.

"Caz!" Willow cries. My eyes move from the rows and rows of shelves, books, and boxes, to Willow's as ragged breaths fall through my lips. Her brown eyes light up when I lock on them, and she presses a hand to the top of the gun, lowering it with a smile. "It's okay," she whispers. "You're safe. It's just me."

I stare at her, studying every detail of her face. I never thought I'd see her again, yet here she is in the flesh. Or so I think. This could be another trick of Decius'—another mind game.

I drop the gun, holding her face in my hands. Her brown skin is satiny-smooth beneath my palms, her lips soft and plump as I run the pad of my thumb over them, familiarizing myself with every feature.

"Willow," I breathe, and she nods with tears lining her eyes.

"It's me. Oh my God, I can't believe that worked," she breathes.

I reel her in, holding her close. Her body is warm against mine, and I bury my face into the crook of her neck, wanting to smell her, feel her—wanting *all of her.*

"I thought I lost you." Her voice has an ache to it, one that cuts right through me like a knife through the chest. I still feel her pain, her heartache.

I pull back, holding on to her shoulders. "How did I get out of Decius' trap?"

"Beatrix performed a chant that could send us to my world. I begged her to do it. We're on Earth now."

"Earth?" I can't help my frown as I study the room we're in again. Dust floats about, thick layers of it on the broken-down table surfaces, and there are many boxes around—too many to count. Books varying in thickness are lined neatly against a brick wall, stacked to the ceiling.

"We're on Earth *right now?*"

She nods. "I think so. I'm pretty sure this is the basement of Faye's bookstore."

"Your friend Faye?"

"Yes."

"Why are we here?"

"Well, Beatrix told me to think of someplace safe. It was the first place I could think of. I thought of my apartment also, but…" She lets the sentence fall short, then shakes out of it to stand. It's now when I realize she's only in panties and a bra.

"Willow, where are your clothes?" I demand, standing with her.

"I had to take them off because of the portal stuff." She lifts her arms, studying them carefully. "The black veins are gone. I think that means we've been given more time."

"More time for what?"

"To deal with Decius and to figure out how to get to Selah without him in the way."

"Wait a minute. Can't he just come here, to Earth? If I can, surely, he'll find a way too."

"Beatrix said he can, but he won't be as powerful. Instead, he'll use vessels—bad people or even animals. Whatever fits his motive."

I swallow hard, and the saliva is dry going down. I'm thirsty, and it smells different here—not like Vakeeli. It smells of wet paper and a citrusy scent I can't figure out.

Something thumps above us, and I lift my gaze to the ceiling. "What the hell was that?"

We listen as the thumping grows louder, carrying across the ceiling. Then the sound of a door creaking on its hinges fills the air, and I pick up the gun again, pointing it at the staircase.

I push Willow behind me, aiming my gun at the stairs as they moan beneath someone's weight. I spot one shoe—black and white with colorful strings—and then another. A woman appears halfway down the stairs, a large wooden club in her hand, and her eyes wide.

"Drop it!" I shout, and her first instinct is to scream. Her second is to toss the club and throw her hands in the air.

"Oh my God! You have a gun! *Ay, Dios!*" the woman screams. "Please don't kill me! Please—I just work here! Take whatever you want!"

"Wait—stop!" Willow steps around me, forcing my arm and the gun down.

"You know this woman?" I ask.

"Of course I do!"

"She had a weapon! Is she a threat?"

"No," Willow breathes, moving closer to the woman. "God, no. She's my best friend. This is Faye."

Faye remains frozen on the stairs, looking from me to Willow, who is walking over to meet her.

"W-willow? What the hell is going on?" Faye exclaims. "Are you having *sex* with strangers down here?"

Willow only laughs before drawing Faye in for a hug. "It's him," Willow whispers. "That's Caz."

Faye looks me up and down over Willow's shoulder with

rounded eyes. I stare back, and she finally snaps out of it to grip Willow's shoulders and push her back a notch.

"Okay, two questions: one, *how* is he even here right now? And two, *why* are you both half naked?"

Willow glances back at me. "It's a long story. I'll fill you in, I promise. But before I do that, I have to ask. Do you have a shirt I can borrow?"

CHAPTER 12
WILLOW

Faye makes a run to the closest department store and ends up snagging a jogger suit for me and a black hoodie for Caz.

"How the hell do you put this thing on?" Caz grumbles. I look over, and his arms are tangled in one of the sleeves and opening for the head.

Laughing, I tug my shirt down then make my way over to assist him. "This part goes *over* your head."

"I've never seen anything like this." He watches me pull the hem down to his waist. "Hmm. It's comfortable."

"I'm glad you like it, and that it fits." I turn to Faye, who stands near the stairs with the empty Marshall's bag. "You guys nearly gave me a heart attack. I mean, here I am alone in the shop about to close, and I hear people down here talking. I thought the place was haunted or that someone broke in!"

"So, you come down the stairs with that club of a weapon?"

Caz asks with utter disbelief. "What was that gonna do for you?"

"Well, I didn't expect you to have a *gun*, sir, or for it to be pointed at me," she counters, rolling her eyes.

He quirks a brow, shifting his gaze to me.

"What time is it?" I ask her.

"It's nearing nine."

"Think you can give us a ride home?"

"Sure." She walks up the stairs and I follow after her, Caz hot on my trail. We weave our way through the bookstore, past endless shelves and display tables. The café is closed for the night, but it still smells like coffee and the lingering scent of toasted pastries. Faye collects her keys from the front counter then jogs across the store to set the alarm.

As she does, I look back at Caz who is scanning one of the shelves with his brows stitched together. *"The Subtle Art of Not Giving a Fuck,"* he reads aloud. "Is this an *actual* book?"

"It's a bestseller!" Faye sings, swinging the front door open as the alarm beeps to set.

"That's not a suitable title for literature," he informs us. "It's far too crass."

"Yeah, well, literature is different here," I tell him, following Faye out of the shop. "It's not all about farming, horses, and trading, like the books you own."

Caz makes a *"psh"* noise, watching as Faye stuffs the key into the lock and twists. We follow her around the building to get to the employee parking lot. Her burgundy Honda chirps when she unlocks it, and Caz stops dead in his tracks with a scowl.

"Hold on. We're traveling in *this*?" he asks with wide eyes.

"Yep." I open the passenger door.

"This won't protect us. And look—there are dents and

scratches all over it. How are we supposed to get around in this thing? What if it doesn't work or the engine blows? Are your windows even bullet proof? I literally can see right through them. Why aren't they tinted?"

"*Excuse* me?" Faye's eyes flicker from me, her mouth gaping in pure shock. Then she straightens her back, locking on Caz. "Okay, look, *rich man* from another universe. Don't talk shit about my car, okay?" She sets a hand on her hip. "I worked hard for it. And sure, it has a couple of dings and dents, but it gets me where I need to be and it'll get *you* where you need to be tonight, so get in the car and be grateful for the ride, or you can walk your ass to your destination." She curses beneath her breath as she pulls the door open and climbs into the driver's seat.

Caz continues a frown that's mixed with confusion before focusing on me. I fight a laugh, offering a hand to him.

"It'll be fine," I assure him, trying to be serious. But inside, I'm still laughing because he has no idea what he's in for.

CHAPTER 13
WILLOW

DURING THE RIDE, I EXPLAIN EVERYTHING I CAN TO Faye about Mournwrath/Decius/Manx and how Caz was trapped with him. Faye doesn't say much as I provide my explanation—not that I expect her to. Here she is with a strange man from another world in her backseat, her best friend telling a near-death experience story, and all she's been doing is reading, eating, and sleeping like a normal human being while I was away.

"I just…" Faye works hard to swallow as she parks in the lot of my apartment. She grips the steering wheel, staring ahead at one of the buildings. "And this all happened when you went back? From the *last time* I left you?" she inquires.

"Yeah, shockingly," I breathe.

"That seems like days' worth of events."

"It was about three days."

"But only, like, a day here. That's so strange."

"How long are we going to sit here?" Caz's deep voice rumbles behind us.

I look ahead at my building, anxiety coursing through me. Caz peers out the back window, seemingly confused by his surroundings.

I'm not sure why I'm so nervous having Caz come to my apartment, and that feeling cinches every part of me as we walk up the stairs. I find a key inside the half empty flowerpot next to my doorstep with a dead snake plant still inside it, and stuff it into the lock.

"Love of Vakeeli, Willow. Are you asking to be robbed?" Caz drops his eyes to the key in my hand.

"No one knows that key is there," I counter.

"I do now, as well as your friend Faye here."

"And I trust you two not to tell anyone where I've hidden one of my spare keys."

Through my periphery, I see Caz shake his head as he follows me into the apartment. All the lights are still on, my bed unmade, clothes strewn about. The books Faye brought from Lit and Lattes are still on the bed, my joint papers and baggie of weed still on the nightstand next to it. I hurry inside, picking up loose pieces of clothing, glad there isn't a stench permeating the air like last time.

Faye closes the door behind us, and Caz walks deeper into my apartment, scanning every surface, nook, and corner. I amble toward the bed, placing a pile of dirty clothes on the floor next to it, then pick up my joint papers and weed to stuff into the nightstand drawer.

When I turn, Caz is in the kitchen, picking up a half empty bottle of tequila. He reads the label, blinks with a frown, then puts it back in place.

"So, I'm going to let you two settle in," Faye announces, still standing by the door. "I have to run to the pharmacy for Abuelita, but I'm off work tomorrow, so I can swing by and help out with this Tether thing if you want. Maybe we can find someone else here who has experienced the same thing you two have."

"Doubt it," Caz mumbles, collecting a book from one of my built-in floating shelves and reading the back cover.

I walk up to her. "Thanks, Faye."

"Of course." She swings her eyes to Caz, narrows them as she looks him all over, then puts her eyes on me again. "Text or call me if you need *anything*. And I mean it. *Anything*, Willow."

I huff a laugh. "I will."

Out the door she goes, and when it clicks shut behind her, I turn to Caz who faces me with his arms folded across his chest. "She clearly doesn't trust me."

"Hmm. A situation like this seems familiar, doesn't it?"

He eyes me. "How so?"

"I dropped into Vakeeli, you didn't trust me, and neither did your family at first. Especially Killian."

Caz drops his arms. "He's just protective."

"Yeah, well, so is Faye."

He presses his lips, taking a sweep of the apartment again. "So, this is your apartment in the North Carolina?"

"Yep." I clasp my hands together, fighting a laugh. "As you can see, it's not a castle or anything, but it's only me here, so..."

He bridges the gap between us. "It's fine. Enough for you, I gather." When he's only a step away, he takes my hand and tugs me toward him. I melt in his grasp when he wraps his arms around me. Even here, our Tether is strong. I can feel the power surging between us, as well as his soothing relief. My senses with him are still so high, but…

"Wait. I just realized I can't hear your thoughts," I tell him after a gasp.

He's quiet a moment, then his eyebrows dip as he studies my face. "I can't hear yours either."

"Do you think that means we're not Tethered anymore?"

"I can still feel your emotions, so I doubt it. They run through me—your worry, your anxieties. I felt your relief when Faye found us in that basement, but you're riddled with worry now. What is it that has you so nervous?"

I avoid fidgeting in his arms. "Why do you assume I'm nervous?"

"It's either that, or you're scared."

"I'm not scared." A half-lie. I press my lips, resting my forehead on his chest. "I just thought I lost you, Caz."

He tips my chin with a finger, forcing my eyes to his again. "I'm right here with you, Willow. You made the right call having Beatrix send us here. You're so damn smart."

I can't help smiling at his words, but for some reason, the smiles aren't lasting. As much as I want to be happy, Caz is right. I am worried.

"What if Decius finds a way here?" I ask. "What if he comes and attacks even harder?"

"Then I'll be ready for him this time. He may think he has a hold on me, but the truth is I have the hold on him. Apparently, without me, he can't conquer whatever it is he wishes to conquer. We figure out how to rid ourselves of him, and we can get back to our lives."

"Yeah." I drop my head again. "I guess."

"Oi," he whispers. "Look at me."

I tilt my head so I can find his eyes. They're icy blue and shimmering with emotion. "He won't split us apart, Willow. Not now. Not *ever*. I've got a second chance, and I'll be damned if he captures me again."

I can't help smiling at his words, though I wish I could find comfort in them. I start to say something, but then a growl erupts between us. His stomach is grumbling.

"Oh, wow." I fight a laugh as he smashes his lips together. "Someone's hungry."

He chuckles, and I don't miss the way his face turns a shade of red. He's so easily embarrassed. It's honestly adorable. "You try resisting cold chains and mental warfare and see if it doesn't work up an appetite."

I laugh, going for the purse I left on the sofa the last time I was here. I sling it over my shoulder as I make my way to the door. "Come with me. I know a place we can eat."

CHAPTER 14
WILLOW

I ORDER TWO CHEESEBURGERS AND COKES FROM BAD Daddy's menu.

When the Cokes arrive, Caz eyes his glass suspiciously. "This stuff is poisoned. There are too many bubbles."

I reach for a cheese fry from the appetizer basket, shaking my head. "No. It's just carbonated water, sugar, and some other shit that isn't good for you but tastes amazing."

His frown fades as he brings the rim of the glass to his lips and takes a sip. His nose scrunches as he spits the sip back into the glass and sets it on the table again. "Willow, what the hell is this? Why does it sizzle in my mouth so much? How am I supposed to drink it like that?"

I nearly choke on my fry as he shoves the drink away. "How about a sweet tea instead?" I offer.

"I'll take anything better than *this*."

I flag the waiter down, request a tea, and he brings it back to the table moments later. Caz takes a sip of the sweet tea, his eyes expanding and his pupils dilating.

"This is tea?" he asks after another gulp.

"Yes…with lots of sugar."

"What's *sugar*?"

"A sweetener."

"Oh. Like the grinds of our sweet stalks?" he asks, eyes lighting up.

I look him in the eye and nod, though I have no idea what a sweet stalk is. "Sure, that."

Pleased, Caz takes another big gulp, and the waiter pops over to refill his drink. Moments later, our burgers arrive, and Caz looks down at them, still skeptical.

"It's a burger," I tell him. "Trust me, you'll love it. Try it." I pick mine up and bring it to my mouth, taking a huge bite. Caz watches me, head cocked, before picking up his burger as well and biting a chunk out of it. He chews, and I swear his eyes turn to puddles as they widen.

"Shit," he says, mouth full.

"Good, right?"

"*Very* good. We don't have anything like this in Vakeeli."

"It's pretty easy to make. They also have vegan options. I'm sure I could make some there if I had the proper ingredients." I say all of this, but Caz is biting into his burger repeatedly. He finishes it within four big bites, gulps down more sweet tea, then belches.

"Another," he gasps, and I smile, waving the waiter down again.

CHAPTER 15
CAZ

I'M HARDLY EVER SURPRISED BY ANYTHING, YET WHAT I've encountered on Earth in less than two hours has been rather...*interesting*.

Their way of living is unique. Not a soul walks around with guns or weapons—at least, not that I can see. Everyone has a car, and I've not seen a single horse. There are enormous buildings that touch the sky, taller than any palace or castle I've ever seen. Willow calls them skyscrapers.

It's all so new and fascinating...yet oddly terrifying. Now I see why she was so petrified when she came to Vakeeli. Here, she lives in peace. No one is pointing guns at her constantly or posing a threat with their words. Everyone minds their own or looks the opposite way. That doesn't happen where I'm from. There, we're all in survival mode, trying to stay alive another day.

When we've returned to her apartment, Willow locks the door behind me while I stand in the middle of the main room. There's odd furniture here—a sofa shaped like the letter L with unusual brown material on it and a wooden table in the center. The kitchen is all silver and white, with bubble-ish hanging lights above the island. A wall of windows is ahead, revealing the outdoors. Vehicles are lined up closely, albeit neatly, and face our side of the building. I narrow my eyes to make sure there aren't people inside those vehicles looking in. They all appear vacant.

I shift on my feet and release a slow breath. All of this is strange and foreign, and I've never felt more out of place. As if Willow senses that, she walks to me and says, "How about a shower?"

I nod, and she turns for a closet, taking down a thick white towel then walking across the room to a closed door. She pushes the door open, flips a light switch, and reveals a bathroom. I move closer as she places the towel on the edge of the sink.

"I can wash your clothes so you can wear them tomorrow," she offers as she starts the shower.

"Why would *you* wash them? Where is your house maiden?" I ask.

She breaks out in laughter. "We do our own laundry around here, buddy. Come on, clothes off. I'll see if I can dig through some of my brother's old stuff and find you some shorts or something."

She starts to leave, but I capture her by the wrist before she can go. Her eyes flicker up to mine, soft and burning with curiosity.

"Shower with me," I murmur.

Her eyes expand and her throat bobs as she digests my

request. The truth is I don't want her away from me. I'm afraid to let her out of my sight.

I expect her to find an excuse, but instead, she walks out of the bathroom, collects another towel, then returns, shutting the door behind her.

When she does, the steam from the shower billows inside the bathroom and she drops the towel, pulling her shirt over her head and tossing that too.

"A little hand?" she asks, turning her back to me. She taps at the latch on the back of her bra.

"Right. Those dreadful Vakeeli bras." I unclasp the first hook with a smirk, untie the string that keeps it together, and then undo the second hook. When it's loose, she pulls the bra off, and I can't help looking at her reflection in the mirror. Her breasts sit perfectly on her chest, her brown nipples piqued to perfection. Dropping the bra, she attempts to cover herself up.

"No." I turn her around to face me, my eyes sweeping up and down the length of her. "Don't. Let me look at you."

She breathes evenly, standing before me, a woman in all her glory. I reach for the waistband of her sweatpants and tug them down. Then I help her out of her panties. When she's naked, I scan her body, and my dick spasms at the sight of her. Other universe or not, my body still reacts in an insanely carnal way.

"You're a treasure, Willow."

She fights a smile, biting her bottom lip. "Are we showering or what?"

I step back to undress while she watches every garment come off with awe. When we're both naked, there's a shift in the energy and a buzzing in my blood. We study each other's bodies as if we've never seen each other naked before, and I don't know what it is about this moment, but I find it rather intense. Never have I laid myself bare for anyone, and I feel both powerful and vulnerable.

Here, our thoughts are inhibited, and there's something oddly terrifying about that because now I long to hear her thoughts—to know what she thinks as she looks at me. However, there's an allure to it—us trying to figure one another out. What we want. What we *need*.

I'm not sure what comes over me in this moment, but I want her. I want her more than I want my next breath. I crave her body in my hands, her flesh on my tongue, so much so that I pick her up and place her ass on the edge of the counter.

A small yelp escapes her as I clasp her face in my hands and maneuver my hips between her thighs. Like a flower in bloom, she opens herself to me, thighs spreading farther apart. My dick grazes her pussy and pulses to life as I tangle my fingers in her locs. She cups my face with a delicious moan, and I coax her mouth open, stealing a taste of what's mine.

Dragging my lips from her mouth to the crook of her neck before trailing down to her breasts, I suck each dark nipple into my mouth until they're firm, then drag my lips back up to hers again. There's so much energy running through me, the blood pumping straight to my dick. I'm harder now, throbbing, and I bring her ass to the edge of the counter, angling her hips. I slide one finger inside her, then another, and she moans hotly on my mouth, her fingernails sinking into the flesh of my shoulder blade.

"My mate," I breathe, and she moans. "I need to be inside you."

She nods, kissing the corners of my mouth, my cheeks, my chin—anywhere she can place her lips. "I need that too," she whispers.

I pull my fingers away, gripping the base of my swelling dick, and she spreads her thighs farther apart. The magenta flesh between them glistens, and a wave of heat rushes through me.

I need to taste her. *Right now.*

I lower to one knee as she draws in a breath, brewing with anticipation. My eyes flicker up to hers as I clutch her hips, and when they connect, I bury my tongue in her pussy. Her moans fly to the ceiling, bouncing back, and Love of Vakeeli, she's delicious.

She threads her fingers through my hair, her moans growing louder as I circle my tongue around her swelling clit. I'm dying to be inside her, and I sense that ache as my dick pulses, aching with need, but she tastes too good to stop.

I almost lost moments like this—eating her pussy, devouring her whole. It would've been an unbearable loss, and the thought of it causes me to growl and slip my tongue into the tight hole of her cunt.

"Oh, God, Caz," she whimpers, her back bucking. I look up, and she's tossed her head backward, her hair a waterfall swimming over her shoulders and down her spine. Groaning, I suck her clit until it's swollen then kiss it, nip it, *devour* it, until she detonates. She cries my name with a handful of my hair in her clutches.

The sounds she creates. *Fuck.* I can't hold off any longer. I stand up with my dick hard as Vakeeli steel and thrust halfway inside her. She instantly clenches around me, and I'm surprised I don't come from that action alone.

"Oh, Willow," I groan. I expel a breath, bracing myself for the rest of my dick to be inside her. She feels so good. So tight and wet. She wraps around me like a glove.

I cup her waist, pushing farther in, inch by savory inch. Her mouth parts wider, and when I'm all in, her body tenses and her breath shudders, as if the size of my dick is almost too much to bear. When I thrust, that tension leaves her body, and she melts in my arms.

I lean forward so her back hits the foggy mirror. Her moans grow louder, and she whispers my name as I propel myself deeper, wanting her to feel all of me. Wanting to feel *all of her*.

"Look at you," I breathe, clasping her chin between my fingers. "Taking me so well. So damn wet for me."

Her eyes practically roll to the back of her skull, and I find delight in that—my words being enough to tip her over the edge.

I drop my mouth on hers, crushing her soft lips, swelling inside her, coming closer to climax. She clings to me, her arms wrapped tight around my ribs. The bathroom has doubled with thick steam from the shower, drowning us in a fog, and I don't stop—not until a groan rips out of me and I'm left with no choice but to come.

"Oh, fuck." My forehead drops to her shoulder as I come. There's no way I can pull out right now. Are you kidding me? I'm literally convulsing with this release.

I empty inside her as she holds me close, laying gentle kisses on my cheeks and lips. Then I sigh when I realize *this* is home— here, in her arms. It doesn't matter where we are or what world we're in—as long as I'm wrapped up in her, I'm safe. Sluggishly, I withdraw, and she looks up at me with a sated smile.

"We can shower now," I tell her, and she giggles.

We do shower, but when we're inside, I can't help myself as I cup her waist and reel her in to kiss her again. A heavy moan escapes her, but it's nowhere near as loud as the moan I hear when I press her back against one of the shower walls and drop to my knees.

"Caz," she breathes as the water spills over us.

"Be still," I murmur, then I bring my mouth to her pussy. What can I say? I can't get enough of her taste. She cries out as I feast on what's mine. I circle my tongue around her clit, then lap it up and down, repeating these actions to work her up. I can tell she needs this—to be finished off again, to be *completely* satisfied—and I want to be the one who does that for her. I want to take away all the tension in her body and swallow it down. I want to be the one to rid her of all her worries, if only for now, so I eat my mate's pussy and I don't stop until she hums my name again.

She finishes herself off by thrusting her hips and grinding on my mouth, and when she stills, I lay a kiss on her pelvis. A soft moan fills the shower, and she looks down at me with a warm smile.

Standing again, I cup the back of her head and steal another kiss. I could go on forever, take her in every single way, but this is enough...for now.

A sigh breaks free as she kisses me back, and then we shower (*seriously* this time). I've never showered with a woman before, but it's like we've done it many times together. It comes naturally with the way we wash, rinse, and steal kisses in between.

I like it and I want more moments just like this. And we'll have them as soon as I figure out how to kill Decius.

CHAPTER 16
WILLOW

AFTER THE SHOWER, WE LIE IN MY BED, SMELLING OF Native's coconut and vanilla soap. The apartment is quiet at this hour, several minutes past midnight. There are no cars driving by or noisy neighbors stomping above. The heat pours out of the vents, giving the room a comforting warmth.

I curl into Caz's body, the left side of my face resting on his chest as he lies flat on his back on the bed. One hand is tucked behind his head, the other wrapped around me.

He's been quiet since the shower. I wish I could hear his thoughts right now. It feels weird *not* hearing them for so long while being with him. Now I can understand why some consider the Tether a gift. In moments like this, it would come in handy to read him, figure out what's truly bothering him, because I'm sure if I don't ask, he won't tell me. But I would bet a hundred bucks that most of what has his mind tied up involves Decius.

I reach over Caz for my phone on the nightstand and click

the Safari app, typing in the words *cold tether* and allowing the results to load. I doubt I'll find anything, seeing as I've done this before, but it's worth another shot.

"What the hell is that thing?" Caz asks, focused on my phone.

"Remember that cellphone I kept asking you about in Vakeeli?"

"That's what that is?" He makes a noise of disapproval. "How are there so many words on it? And why is the screen so large?"

"Right now, I'm on the internet."

"The inter-*what*?"

I laugh. "Okay, look." I scroll through the phone, explaining how it all works. He's surprised, even more so when I open Instagram and scroll through images of people he's never seen before.

"And people voluntarily post these videos and images of themselves? For *anyone* in the world to see?"

"Yep."

He shakes his head, blinking several times. "That's absurd. Why put so much of yourselves out there? You're revealing all your weaknesses."

I shrug. "Sometimes in this world, people enjoy seeing others' weaknesses because they can relate to them. It makes us realize we're all human, and that we all make mistakes or have our bad days."

He takes a moment to digest that. "Seems a bit excessive. You can browse for whatever you want on that thing?" He scoffs. "If I were you, I'd get rid of it."

I fight a laugh. "I'm not getting rid of my phone, Caz."

"Well, you won't be seeing me with one of those things." He

straightens in the bed, bringing me back to his chest and burying his nose in my hair. A pleasing warmth swims through me, and I can't fight my smile. I love when he does that—holds me close, nuzzles his nose everywhere.

"I want to ask you something." I shut the screen of my phone off and return it to the nightstand.

"What's that?"

"When we were on the way to the portal, I saw...flashbacks of certain events." I pause, and he tenses beneath me. "They were of you and your mother. And some men on horses, chasing both of you."

He's still tense, and his breathing is now shallow. As badly as I want to look at him, I don't. I want him to process what I'm saying.

"What of it?" he finally asks.

I lift my head, eyeing him. "I didn't know that happened to you."

"Of course, you didn't because I never told you. Or anyone for that matter," he returns rapidly. Then he softens it with, "I just don't like talking about it."

"So you bottle those memories in?" I ask in a low voice.

He's quiet, but I don't miss the way his jaw pulses.

I sit up fully to look at him. He's staring up at the ceiling fan, purposely avoiding my eyes. "Caz, look at me."

He doesn't, so I reach for his face, forcing his eyes on mine. They shine beneath the slits of moonlight. "Tell me what happened with your mom."

"Willow, not right now. *Please.*"

"I want to know."

"Why right now? We've barely even escaped those awful

memories. You saw them? They're fucking devastating, Willow. Why would I want to relive that?"

"I only saw pieces of the man hurting you. I didn't see everything."

Briskly, he sits up and turns his back to me. Propping his elbows on his knees, he drops his head and drags his palms over the length of his face. I watch him a moment as the moonlight highlights his creamy skin, contouring the curves and muscles. I scoot to the edge of the bed next to him, and when he meets my eyes, they sparkle, but not with any sort of happiness. They sparkle with sorrow.

"You can tell me anything, Caz. You know that, don't you? I won't ever judge you," I whisper.

A stretch of silence passes, then he exhales slowly. "You really want the story?" he asks.

"I just want to understand more about you, but if you're truly not comfortable telling me, I understand, and I'll back off."

His head lowers, and his eyes fall to the floor. I take one of his hands, wrapping it in mine and resting my cheek on his sculpted upper arm.

"When I was eight," he starts in a low voice. "My father, Magnus, found out about me. He had no clue that he had a son, and apparently his wife was barren, so he had no heirs." He pauses, looking through one of the windows. "After all this with Manx, or Decius or whatever we're to call him, I realize Magnus found out I existed because of him, and when he did, he sent my mother a message that he was coming for me."

"Why?" I ask, confused. "Why would he just try to take you?"

"He was getting old," Caz informs me. "When you are

monarch and you turn the grand age of one-hundred-fifty, you *must* have an heir. Otherwise, The Council will revoke you of the position and give the role to someone else within the family. Magnus didn't want that. He was a power-hungry piece of shit, and he was willing to do *anything* to keep his place. Sure, he'd slept with women, but he was very careful not to leave any of them pregnant because of his sparkling reputation, according to Maeve. Especially if the women belonged to Blackwater. I'm assuming Manx knew of Magnus' disposition and provided him a solution: me. I'm not quite sure what Manx would have gotten out of that, but it happened. So...Magnus came for me, just to have someone fill the position. He didn't care what my mother wanted, or that he hardly knew a damn thing about me. His goal was to take me and train me to become monarch of Blackwater. But it didn't help that I was a bastard, and what made matters worse was Magnus' wife hated me. She hated me for being born, for existing, and she shoved that hatred down Magnus' throat daily. Here I was, the product of his adultery, and she despised me for it." He sits up taller, drawing in a breath and then exhaling again. "My mum...she tried hiding me when she found out he was coming, but he found out the coordinates of where I was hiding. I assume it was Manx who gave them to him." He clenches a fist, brows stitching together. I rub his hand, and the fist loosens. "She tried getting me away, running to Vanora where we'd be protected, but we had no time. I was taken, and so was she, and after that day I never saw her again. I lived with Magnus in Blackwater up until I was nineteen. Nineteen is when he died, but before that, he wanted to harden me. I was rebellious and didn't want to be a part of the monarch life, so to punish me, he took me all the way to Ripple Hills, where the fighting caves are. He and Rami's father, Buckley, were chummy then."

"Ugh, Rami," I mutter. Rami was the piece of shit who tried to rape me in Ripple Hills. Even though he's dead now, courtesy of Caz blowing his brains out with a gun, I still hate him.

"Yes. That fucker. Anyway, his father and mine casted their bets on me and made me fight. If I lost, they'd beat me, or worse, shoot me with guns and then heal me with a powerful healing elixir from one of their hired Mythics. Sometimes they'd use razors to slice my abdomen or my chest. Sometimes they'd bring other fighters in to team up on me. The punishments were past the point of suffering, but always short of death. But I can tell you, in that moment and many, many years after, all I wanted was for death to steal me away."

I wince at that, remembering the time I saw him point a gun at his own head. I squeeze his hand tighter, and he turns his gaze to me.

"I was just a boy, Willow. I was scared, alone, *afraid*...and Magnus didn't care. He forced me to grow up cold and angry, just so I would become like him—a cold and angry monarch. I'd never felt such relief when I found out the lady monarch had died, and that he would be dying too. I swore when I took over that I'd *never* be like him—that I'd make a change and better the people." He pauses, very briefly. "I realized some people are no better than he was, though, and that there will *always* be others out there who wish me dead or wish harm on the people I care about. I suppose it comes with being a leader. When I took over, Buckley thought he could still control me. He thought that I was afraid of him until I headbutted him and left him with a permanently crooked nose."

"Is that why Blackwater feuds with Ripple Hills?" I ask.

"No. There have been many feuds between us. There are battles and wars that go back centuries. It depended totally on the reigning monarchs. Magnus and Buckley were too arrogant and lazy to feud during their reign, so they were allies for over a century. But when I and Rami took over, we were enemies from the start. I could see Buckley all over Rami, and I despised him. He thought he could come to my territory and tell me what to do, steal my rubies, and make his demands. I shut that down, and if there was one thing spoiled Rami hated, it was being told no."

"Yeah." I roll my eyes. "I remember."

He studies my face, a pained expression filling his eyes.

"What's wrong?" I ask quickly.

He shifts beside me and exhales through parted lips. "When you said in Ripple Hills that I was killing people for no reason..." He trails off, his gaze dropping, and I feel a clench in my chest. "It's never *not* for a reason, Willow. I do it before they can do anything to hurt me."

"Oh, Caz. I'm so sorry I said that. I didn't mean for my words to hurt you. I just didn't understand any of it back then, but I do now. Trust me, I do." I hold his eyes for as long as he'll let me, and he sucks in a sharp breath, as if he finds relief in my understanding.

"As for me mum, well, she died when I was nineteen. I never got to see her again between the time I was taken and when she died...but I could have. At that age, I found out Magnus had been having one of his hired Mythics cast a spell over me. It was a shield of sorts, so that whatever I endured negatively would not be seen by The Council. I only found this out because the Mythic was so bloody drunk one night and angry at Magnus about something, that he told me everything. I was livid when I found out, so I left Blackwater and sought The Council, demanding to be out of his care. I told them all about what he was doing to me, about the fighting caves in Ripple Hills, and even let them see for themselves as they laid hands on me and filled their minds with my memories. And as I've told you before, harm to a child is one of the most punishable crimes. The Council decided to execute him once they found out, and when Magnus was given his sentence, he came to me, full of rage. Then he dragged me to the dungeons my mother had been kept in and had one of his men hang her." Caz's voice has changed. It's thicker with equal parts agony and rage. His hand squeezes tighter around mine, not to the point of pain, but enough for me to feel just how much anguish this confession causes him.

"He killed my mother before he was executed. He did it to spite me. One last punch to the face and stab to the heart before it was his time." He makes a strained noise. "I was so naïve and stupid then. I should've saved her first. I should've found her before going to The Council, but it's because of me that she's dead. I gave him that window of opportunity to kill before The Council came to end him."

"Caz, no. No, you *cannot* blame yourself for that. You were just a kid. You had no idea—"

"I was a *fucking* idiot!" he counters, snatching his hand out of mine. He shoots off the bed and walks across the apartment, raking his fingers through his hair. "I would still have her if I'd just stuck it out, let Magnus die on his own. She didn't deserve it—she didn't deserve *anything* he did to her. He tortured her for years! He *raped* her and got her pregnant, and she didn't have to keep me, but she did. She *did*, and after all that, I'm the one who got her killed."

"It's not your fault." Hot tears creep to the corners of my eyes as I rush across the room to get to him. I clutch his face in my hands, and he tries jerking away, but I hold on to him. "You didn't kill her, Caz. Magnus did. None of what you went through was *ever* your fault. You can't possibly think that. I can't believe you've spent all these years treating his burdens as your own."

"All of it was my fault. *Everything.*" The lump in his throat bobs. "I'm broken beyond repair, Willow. Can't you see that? Everything I touch either gets hurt or dies. Why do you think I rejected our Tether for so long? Why do you think I fought tooth and nail to resist you? Because I couldn't afford *anyone* else I care about getting hurt. That's why I told you to forget about me when Decius had me trapped. You deserve far better than to be with a man as terrible as me."

My head shakes. "I don't believe you're broken beyond repair. Pieces of you may be broken, but they can be mended. I know they can. You have a good heart, Caz, whether you see it or not."

"I've hurt and killed so many people because of my rage—because of this anger *he* poured inside me. He shoved it all down my throat and forced me to digest it, and now I'm this fucked up man who hates everyone and everything, and I can't even enjoy life because I'm so angry and bitter all the time!" His blue eyes glisten as they bore into mine. "How can you still want me after all you've seen? After all I've done? Because you don't even know the half, Willow. I've done so many bad things. Some of it still gives me nightmares."

He's shaking now, and I don't know what to say to that as I look into his teary eyes. I wish I had the words, but I don't, so I pull him in and hug him tight instead. I hug him until his body stops shaking and the tension melts just a little.

"I'm bound to you, Caz. And if that means I have to share

your pain and help you forgive yourself, so be it. I will." I lean back to place a kiss on his cheek. "I'll help you heal. We'll help *each other* heal."

The pain washes over him like a tidal wave. I feel it riding through me, sinking into each organ, nerve, and strand of us. It's astounding that I can still feel his sorrow while on Earth. Makes me think this Tether is so much bigger than anything we've ever imagined.

The grief in his crystal eyes lingers, and I'm not sure what else to say to make him feel better or to bring him out of this darkness that has consumed him, so I lead the way back to the bed.

He spoons me from behind, cradling me in his arms. His warm lips press to the top of my shoulder before skimming up to the bend of my neck, and we remain like this. Quiet thoughts in close proximity.

"I don't know what I've done to deserve you," he whispers on my ear. "You're the greatest thing I've had in a *very* long time, Willow." His arms tighten around me, like he never wants to let go, and I release a satisfied sigh, placing my hand on top of his and closing my eyes.

CHAPTER 17
WILLOW

I FIND IT HARD TO SLEEP AFTER HEARING ABOUT Magnus. It sucks that a name has been attached to that monster. That man wasn't a father. He was an abuser who got what he deserved from The Council. I'm actually thankful that they got Caz out of that situation, and glad they fulfilled some kind of purpose.

After telling that story about his biological father, Caz sleeps soundlessly next to me. I don't think I've ever seen him sleep, but we're on Earth, where there are no red or black tablets to swallow to fight it. It's as if rehashing those awful memories and talking about them lifted some of the weight on his shoulders.

With all this talk about family, I'm left wondering about my own. I feel like I'm further away from figuring out where Warren is. Is he still alive? Has Decius gotten to him? God, I hope not. I miss my brother and I swear after we figure out how to deal with Decius, I'm going to find out where Warren is... dead or alive..

I let the thoughts of my brother drift for now and sit up with my knees to my chest, watching as Caz rests on his back, one hand on his bare chest, the other tucked behind his head. He breathes evenly, and I can't help thinking how beautiful he is. His lips are full and pouty, the sharp angles of his face and nose god-like. His dark lashes caress his upper cheekbone like gentle raven feathers. I see why his mother called him her raven-haired boy.

My eyes fall to his upper body, and I study the scars on his chest. They're all over him, marks from men who tormented and abused him. It's no wonder he's the way that he is. He was taken from his mother and forced into a life he never wanted. I sense he was a carefree child at one point, happy and full of wonder and light, and then it was all snatched away. He was tossed into darkness, left with no option but to drown in it, or in his case, learn to swim the treacherous waters in order to survive. That's my Caz. A survivor.

I drop my legs and trace the pads of my fingers over his scars. I start at the top of his chest, near his collarbone. This scar is jagged and raised, like a knife wound. I rub it gently, as if that'll take away whatever pain he endured, then carry my fingers down to the center of his chest. There's a large wound here, round and slightly raised, probably from a bullet. I don't know why I have the urge to kiss it, but I lean forward, placing my lips on it. Then I move to the next scar, right above his ribcage.

Caz exhales, and one of his hands comes to my head. He buries his fingers in my hair, and I look up to find his hooded eyes on mine.

SHANORA WILLIAMS

I push to my knees and climb between his legs, continuing the kisses, laying them thick on each scar, and he makes a throaty noise. I work my way down until I'm at his pelvis, kissing him there. When I look up again, his eyes are wider, glinting from the moonlight. I pull the hem of his boxers down, freeing his dick.

"Willow," he whispers.

"Is this okay?"

His face softens, and eventually, he nods. "Yes."

I slide the boxers lower down his hips, then take him into my hands. He's already semi-hard, and he tenses as I wrap my fingers around him. He has a beautiful dick, thick at the tip, with a girthy shaft. My mouth aches for him, so I part my lips and take him in, and all the tension melts from his body.

The noise he had trapped in his throat comes out in a guttural groan. I take him deeper, and he sits up on his elbows, watching me with tired fascination and heated lust. I hold his gaze, and his lips part as I swirl my tongue around the head of his dick. He brings a hand down to my head, pushing some of my locs back and caressing my ear with his thumb. One side of my face is cradled in his palm, the tips of his other fingers pressing to the nape of my neck, and I take him deeper, *deeper*, and he moans. Pulling back up, I lap my tongue around his tip, then slide it down to his balls. I suck each one gently, lick them, lap them up, and he throws his head back on the pillow as if it's the best thing he's ever felt in his life.

"Fuck, Willow. That's good. You're *so good*."

Before I can drag my lips back up to wrap around him, he grabs a handful of my hair and tugs it lightly to stop me.

"On top," he commands, and I don't hesitate to climb up his firm body as he rests his head against the headboard. I take off

84

my shorts and panties, then squat above his hard dick as he grips the base of it.

I sink down on him slowly, and with each inch, his mouth parts wider. I hold his attention, pleasure pumping through me as he fills me slowly. When he's all in, a hiss slips between his clenched teeth, and he cups my ass in his hands.

"Ride me." The words come out in a hurry, heated and quick.

I rock my hips forward and backward, and he sinks his perfect teeth into his bottom lip while his hands skim up my waist. He drives his hips upward as I ride him, and I feel *all* of him.

I lean forward to kiss him, coaxing his mouth open so our tongues collide. He buries his fingers into my waist as I rock my hips, and his grip sparks a painful pleasure. I want him to hold me like this every time he's inside me, just so I know he's there. Just so I can feel him.

He sits upward, bringing himself chest to chest with me. His hands slide beneath my ribcage, gripping me as I work my hips in slow loops.

"You're so sexy," he rasps. "I love seeing you like this, on top of me."

I keep riding, keep kissing, and when it becomes too much for me to bear, I gasp and bite my bottom lip, draping my arms around his shoulders.

"Look at me," he whispers, and I do. "I want to watch you come."

His voice. It's always his voice that gets me, so deep and orgasmic. The fact that he's just woken up only enhances it. The sound of it is so raw and primal. I moan, and I swear he feels bigger inside me. He cups my ass again, shifting his hips upward to propel himself deeper, and it's more than enough to make me shatter.

"Oh, Caz!" I moan. "Shit, I'm coming!"

"Mmm. I feel it. Talk to me," he rasps. "Tell me how it feels."

"It feels so good," I pant. "*You* feel so good inside me." I drop my forehead to his, rocking my hips, breathing faster.

"I could spend all night inside you," he murmurs. "I'm so hard right now after watching you suck and fuck me."

My hips don't stop. It's his voice pushing me to the climax again.

"I'll come inside you like this if we don't switch positions," he warns.

I smile. "I'm protected." Fortunately, from the shot.

"Very well." He keeps one hand on my waist, the other wrapping around the back of my neck, and as we look at each other, eyes locked and unwavering, he holds me close and releases a guttural groan.

"Oi, Willow. Do you feel that?" he rasps. "Only *you* can make me come like this."

I rock my hips gently, letting him finish, and he groans as I drop my mouth to his, kissing him once, twice, *three* times.

When the kiss breaks, his blue eyes find mine again, and he cups my face in his hands. He watches my eyes, studies them, then focuses on my lips.

"You're a literal dream come true," he breathes.

"As are you." I smile, and he flips me onto my back, kissing me deeply, still inside me, soft and warm. When he pulls out, he rests his head on my chest, and we breathe in sync.

After several minutes of peaceful silence, he says, "I think I've fallen in love with you."

His words instantly bring tears to my eyes. I blink them away, stroking his hair, his soft cheek, and then his upper back.

"I'm in love with you too," I whisper.

Another silence, only for a few seconds.

"You fought your attraction to me *so* hard." I laugh as he looks up at me.

A smirk claims his lips. "I didn't think I deserved it."

"But you do now, right?"

He plants a kiss on my collarbone. "I do. There's no doubt in my mind that you're mine."

He sits up just enough to claim my lips, hardening again as he rocks himself against me. The ridge of his dick rocks between the lips of my pussy, gently grazing my clit and sending a hot wave of pleasure through me.

When he's fully hard, he thrusts into me, and his mouth descends to the crook of my neck as he levels his breathing. As he thrusts again, he murmurs, "You're everything I need, Willow."

CHAPTER 18

CAZ

WHEN I OPEN MY EYES, THERE IS A FOREIGN FEELING that has washed over me. Calm. I can't remember the last time I've slept so peacefully. It's been ages since I've felt so rested and restored, and despite there being a looming threat out there, I can't deny I've gotten the best sleep I've had in years. No elixirs or pills necessary. Just this quiet little apartment in North Carolina with Willow.

I carry this peace with me as I look around Willow's apartment. A burnt orange sunrise filters through the blinds and I hear birds chirping in the distance. Footsteps thud above me, and I assume it's those neighbors Willow mentioned the first time I heard the steps. I don't know what time it is, but it feels early, and I groan as I roll over, only to find Willow *not* in the bed next to me.

I sit up rapidly, retrieving the Blackwater gun from the nightstand and climbing off the bed. Where the hell is she? Did someone take her? No, that can't be. I'd have heard it. Unless Decius got through somehow…

I march through the apartment, my pulse pounding in my ears as I reach the balcony door and snatch it open. I peer out at the sea of cars in the parking lot, the buildings ahead and skyscrapers in the distance.

Where is she? I should go outside and check. If Decius got to her while I was wasting time sleeping, I'll hate myself. I should've known better. Resting has never gotten me anywhere.

As all these racing thoughts cross my mind, a door creaks on the hinges and I spin around, pointing my gun toward the noise. But it's only Willow. She walks through the front door with a brown paper bag in one hand and a tray of drinks in the other.

Spotting me on the balcony, she starts to smile—that is until she sees the gun pointed at her. "Whoa! Caz? Is everything okay?"

"Love of Vakeeli, Willow. Where were you?" I lower the gun and step inside, allowing my body to sag against the nearest wall as a breath escapes me. "You can't do that to me."

She places all the items on the table while looking at me from head to toe. "Did you think something happened to me?" she asks.

"As a matter of fact, I did."

"I'm sorry, Caz. You have no reason to worry though." She gestures toward the bed. "Did you not see the note I left on the nightstand?"

I swing my gaze toward the nightstand, and there is indeed a square sheet of paper on top of it. I glance at her before walking over to pick it up.

Left to get some breakfast.
Be right back. Love you!
—Willow

"I didn't see it." I swallow, my face and ears growing hot now. This is so fucking embarrassing. Me, about to lose my shit over her absence. Vakeeli's sakes, I need to get it together.

As if sensing my embarrassment, Willow slips out of her jacket and meets up to me. She takes the gun out of my hand, places it on the nearest surface, then drapes her arms over my shoulders.

"I'm sorry," I murmur. "I overreacted."

"It's okay. We're fine for now, Caz," she says, smiling. "We're safe."

"I suppose I'm having a hard time believing that. No one is ever really safe, no matter how much they wish to be."

"For now, we are. And it's funny you say that. It's almost exactly what you said the night before I got sucked into Vakeeli." I meet her eyes, and the brown of her irises shimmer in the rising sunlight. Look at her, so damn beautiful. What would I have done if I did lose her?

"You can't just leave like that," I say. "I don't want to sound like a desperate jackoff, but you just *can't*, okay? I would prefer to have eyes on you at all times."

"Okay, okay. I'm sorry." She pulls away, her forehead wrinkling. "You were just sleeping so peacefully. I didn't want to wake you."

"I don't care about sleep. Take me with you next time if you have to. Please, Willow. I don't beg, but this matters to me. *You* matter to me. I *cannot* lose you."

"Okay, I will." She leans back, avoiding my eyes, but I catch her before she can walk away and collect her face in my hands.

"I'm sorry to get upset," I murmur. "Don't be angry with me. I just...I'm terrified at the idea of losing you."

"I know. That same idea terrifies me too." She presses one side of her cheek deeper into my palm. "I understand, and I won't do it again."

"Do you really? Because I feel like I'm coming off as an overbearing ass and you're getting sick of my shit," I laugh.

She laughs too, pressing her chest to mine. "You are an overbearing ass. Lucky for you, I understand why."

I press a kiss to her lips, then peer over her shoulder at the brown paper bag on the table. "Is that another burger?"

"No." She grins, pulling away. "It's a breakfast bagel from one of my favorite restaurants. You'll like it just as much as the burger."

She unloads everything, setting it up on the table as I sit. When she bites into her so-called bagel, I do the same. The flavors burst in my mouth—spicy, savory, eggy.

"Mmm. What's in this?" I ask.

"Eggs, sausage, and cheese," she answers.

"Mmm." I finish off the bagel, then pick up my drink to sip. "Sweet tea?"

She nods and puts on a coy smile.

"Thank you, Willow. It's delicious."

"Of course." She takes another bite, chews, and assesses me with her eyes. "So, I was thinking you could check in with your family through Cerberus."

My mind has been so preoccupied that I hadn't thought of my wolf Cerberus. "That's a good idea. How do I do that?"

She places her bagel down. "Just think of him. Try to

imagine being him…doing what he does. That's how I got through to Silvera. Maybe you can get a message to your family through him to let them know you're safe for now."

"Okay, sure." I finish off the bagel. "I can give it a try. Would be nice to see how they're holding up."

Just as I pick up my tea to sip, there's a knock at the door. I cut my eyes to the door a fleeting moment before focusing on Willow again.

"Don't worry. It's Faye. She sent me a text thirty minutes ago saying she was on the way." She dusts off her hands. "Apparently she found something so important it couldn't wait."

Willow checks the peephole to confirm, then swings the door open. Faye enters the apartment wearing a tan trench coat and green boots with white polka dots. Never in all my years of living have I seen boots like them—all bright and plastic-looking. How the hell are those things even comfortable?

Faye removes the strap of the leather purse from her shoulder, placing it on the nearest surface before sauntering to the middle of the room with her hands midair.

"You *will not* believe what I discovered," she announces.

I refrain from rolling my eyes. I haven't known her long, but I can tell she loves the dramatics.

"Well tell us. What is it? What'd you find?" Willow asks.

"So last night I was doing some digging about bonds and everything. It got frustrating because there's really not much out there on Tethers, universal bonds, or what have you, so I thought, why not *expand* the search? Instead of looking up information on this rare bond you two have, why not search for things like universal traveling or portal hopping, like you two have done. Well, let me tell you, there were way more results. I went down a rabbit hole about it. *Deep, deep, deep* down," she says, eyes rounding. "Eventually, I found a blog created by this guy who *swears* his fiancée was sucked into a portal and taken to another dimension right in front of him. Apparently, they were hiking, and he says he saw her get sucked into something and disappear."

"Are you serious?" asks Willow, face serious.

"Yes. He claims she legit vanished out of thin air."

"Well, she couldn't have just vanished. People on Earth don't have those abilities, do they?" I ask.

"No, they don't," Willow says. "At least, not that I'm aware of." She turns to Faye. "Who is this guy? Where does he live?"

"Here." Faye whips out her own cellphone thing and carries it to Willow, swiping a finger on the screen a few times before showing it to her. "His name is Phil Patterson and, funny enough, he only lives a few hours away in Virginia. He made a career of gaming on Twitch and was about to get married, but his whole life changed after his fiancée disappeared. He has so many videos talking about it. Here, watch this one."

Willow takes the cellphone from Faye, and I get up to stand behind her and watch it too. On the screen is a video of a brown-skinned man looking right back at us. I'm not sure what kind of sorcery this is, but I'm certain it correlates to all those videos and photos Willow showed me of random people on her phone last night. I still can't wrap my mind around any of that internet stuff, but whatever.

"It's been a whole month and Marney is still missing," Phil Patterson says through a sigh. "I'm sorry, y'all, but this'll prob-ably be my last video for a while. I gotta find out what happened to my fiancée, and with any new findings, I'll keep you posted on my website blog. Everybody blaming me when I had nothing to do with it. I loved her with everything in me, and I know what I saw. Police are try'na call me crazy, think I'm losing my mind, or that I done developed some kind of post traumatic stuff. She disappeared though, and that's fact. She walked right into something and didn't come back, and I'm gonna find out what it was. Peace, fam. I'll be back when I have some answers."

"Was this really his last video?" Willow asks, handing the phone back to Faye.

"Unfortunately. It's the last one he ever uploaded, but he *did* write a blog post about something else he discovered shortly after it," Faye informs her. "His post talks about how he reached out to a woman who knew about universal pulls and portals. He kept calling her a witch, but she didn't like to be referred to as that. Apparently, this woman said she could bring his fiancée back to him—that she knew many things about the multiverse and portals and could even connect with other people from them. But in order for her to do that for him, he had to pay a shit ton of money." Faye pauses, tucking the phone into the back pocket of her pants. "Unfortunately, that's the last blog post he ever wrote. And now...well, here's where my research takes a nosedive."

Willow sighs, as if knowing what Faye will tell her is bad.

"What happened?" I ask, and Faye's bright eyes shift to mine.

"He's in a psychiatric facility in Virginia."

"Of course, he is," Willow mutters, throwing her head back in defeat. "The guy we need to ask questions about portals and other universes is locked in a psych ward. Great."

"I looked up the place," Faye says. "It's Virginia Coast Psychiatric Detention. They do allow visitors every day, from two to five p.m. I know it sounds crazy, Willow, but if we can get to him, ask him who the woman was that was going to help him with the other universes, maybe there's a way this woman can help you through this Tether. Or at least find a way for Caz to return safely and for the threats to be erased."

"That's damn near impossible," I interject. "I'm positive an unknown woman from Earth won't be able to assist us with our Tether. Not with ease. The Tether—Cold Tethers especially—are sacred. They're impossible to manipulate unless one holds the power of the Tether too."

"That may be true, but at this point, it's the only lead." Faye shifts on her feet, looking between us.

"So, we start with this Phil person," Willow murmurs.

I pinch the bridge of my nose. "So let me get this straight. We're putting our faith *and* the fate of our Tether into the hands of a man in a loony bin and an unknown woman who is most likely a con artist?"

Willow and Faye look between each other. "Well, when you put it that way..." Faye huffs a laugh and starts to bite her thumbnail.

"I know it sounds crazy, Caz, but we have to try *something*." Willow steps toward me, her eyes sparkling with hope. "If we don't at least check in about it, how will we know?"

I shake my head, and though I want to look away, I'm having a hard time doing so. Those damn eyes. "Perhaps there's a way to reach the other Regals. Surely, they're much stronger than Decius. And last I heard, they're in hiding as well, blending in, just like Decius was."

"Who are the other Regals?" Willow asks.

"Legend has it that Selah had two sisters who eventually stepped down to become Mythics after Selah created the Tethered. Their names were Hassha and Korah. There are rumors they're still alive and blending in with the commoners. They have great power, and they know many things. It would be easier to signal to them and see if they can help with defeating Decius...if this con artist woman can even give us a link to them."

"We'll try." Willow raises her chin. "We have to. We can't let Decius win."

"You're right. And at this rate, I'll do *anything* to kill him."

"Jesus," Faye whispers. "Is this normal for you? Just saying you're going to *kill* someone?"

"What's wrong with it?" I counter.

"We don't exactly go around saying we're going to kill people around here. At least, not literally," Faye declares.

"Well, I mean it literally. I *will* kill him."

"Okay." Faye blows an exasperated breath then reaches for Willow's hand, squeezing it. "Willow, can we talk? *Alone?*"

She looks from me to Faye, hesitant.

Willow swings her eyes to me as Faye marches to the door. "I'll be right back."

CHAPTER 19
WILLOW

As soon as I shut the door behind me, Faye asks, "He doesn't know that Garrett was here last night, does he?"

"Shh!" I shake my head and grip her by the upper arms, moving away from the door, "No, and I'd prefer it to stay that way, Faye!"

"I know, I know! Sorry! Look, I know it's the last thing you wanted to hear, but I had to tell you. I only met Garrett once the night when he came over for drinks, but last night really freaked me out. You should've seen him, Willow. He was just sitting in his car, looking at your apartment balcony, and he had this look on his face, like he was annoyed or angry or something."

I pull my hands away from her to rub my temples. To say I'm stressed is putting it mildly. Last night, after my phone had charged and come back to life, I saw the text from Faye about Garrett. At that point, it was nearing midnight and I had to delete the text because I was so paranoid Caz would see it and wreak havoc. I tried ignoring it last night and even checked the parking lot this morning, pleased to see there was no sign of Garrett.

"I seriously do not need this shit right now," I mutter. "If he shows up here, Faye, I can't guarantee he won't be *murdered* for it."

A grin splits Faye's face in half, and her eyes bounce around like she's gathering a ton of impractical ideas. "Two guys fighting over you. Gotta say, that's kinda hot."

"*No*, Faye. You don't understand. Garrett wasn't supposed to be in the parking lot. In fact, he shouldn't be anywhere near me because I literally *never* want to see him again."

She straightens her back. "Wait...why not? What did he do?"

"He...put his hands on me."

Her eyes stretch with shock as I rub my upper arm. "What the fuck? Why would he do that?"

"The day after I came back from Caz's world, he...*grabbed* me. Like, really hard. And he called me a bitch because I said I didn't want to be around him anymore. I haven't wanted to be with him for a long time, and I finally called it off. Now, I'm assuming he's pissed about it and is trying to find a way back in, but there is none. I'm done with him."

Faye's eyes are nearly bulging out of her head. "Does Caz know about Garrett? About you not wanting him around?"

"Yes. I told him when we were in Vakeeli."

"Oh." She swallows hard, smashing her lips together. "So, when you say you can't guarantee he won't be murdered for it, you *really* mean that?"

"Yes! It'll be bad if Caz figures out who he is. We just need to figure this Tether thing out, and when it's all said and done, I'll call the cops, let them know...put up a fucking restraining order or something if I have to. I don't know." My eyes are hot and misty. I blink the unshed tears away and shift on my feet.

"Hey, it'll be okay," Faye coos, reeling me in for a hug. "Don't even stress over that worthless *hijo de puta*." She's quiet a beat. "The fact that he put his hands on you..." She lets out an infuriated sigh. "Maybe Caz *should* know Garrett is hovering around. Any man who hits a woman is pathetic and worthless and doesn't deserve to live."

"No, Faye." I pull away and stare at her with serious eyes. "We don't need to be put into anymore chaos. Caz means well, sure, but he doesn't realize our world isn't like his. He could go to *prison*. I need him to keep a low profile if he wants to get back to Vakeeli."

"Right. Right." She blows a breath then tilts her phone, checking the time. "Well, let me know what you decide about Phil Patterson. If you go, I'll go with you guys and just take some time off. I have to run errands with Abuelita today, so keep me posted."

"Sure, but you don't have to go with us if you don't want to, Faye. This is a lot to take in."

"Girl, shut up! I want to!" She puts on a big, dazzling smile. "Believe it or not, I find all of this Tether shit fascinating. I can't believe it's happening. I mean, I think I'm still wrapping my mind around it...and maybe I haven't fully accepted that this world is *so* much bigger than any of us realize, but it's interesting. If I ever get around to writing my memoir one day, or if all the universes decide to collide like some *Spider-Man: Into the Spider-Verse* level shit, I want people to know that I was one of the first to find out about the Tether and all this portal stuff."

"Oh my gosh. You are a mess." I huff a laugh and collect her in my arms again. "I'll see you soon."

She plants a quick kiss on my cheek and walks down the stairs, heading to the parking lot. When she's out of sight, I turn for the door but as soon as I open it, I bump into something—or some*one*, rather.

Caz is on the other side of the door. He pulls it open wider to let me in, and I frown. "Oh my God. Were you eavesdropping?" I ask.

He raises a brow, face hardened. "Where do I find Garrett?"

My heart stutters over the next beat. *"What?"*

"That Garrett fucker. Where do I find him?"

"Caz—"

"You're right. I *was* eavesdropping. Garrett put his hands on you again, and now he has the audacity to stalk you. I want to put an end to it. Now where do I find him?"

I don't even have the words right now. How dare he listen in on our conversation? Where is the trust?

"Caz, this is not Vakeeli! You can't just—"

"Willow, I swear on all of Vakeeli and every fucking universe out there, I *will* find him, whether you tell me or not." I drop my eyes to his fists and their clenching. His knuckles are bone white beneath the thin skin.

I swallow the lump in my throat, staring into his eyes. He can't possibly be serious right now. There are much bigger things to worry about, like Decius, our Tether, his family—even getting him back to his world. So much is at stake! We don't need this.

I fold my arms across my chest. "I don't know where to find him."

"You're lying." He steps around me, grabbing his hoodie from the coat rack.

"Where are you going?" I demand.

"To find him."

I scoff. "How are you gonna do that?"

"Where's your cellphone?"

I feel the weight of it in my back pocket. "You're not getting my phone."

"Fine. I'll find someone else's and demand them to let me use it." He's stuffing his feet into his shoes now.

"Caz, you *can't* be serious. First of all, that's a really stupid plan! No one is just going to give you their phone, especially if you're demanding them to."

He cuts his eyes at me.

"Secondly, you're not here to find Garrett. You're here because you got a second chance at defeating Decius before he can get to us."

"We will do that once I handle Garrett. Why the hell are you even protecting this fucker? He put his hands on you, Willow!"

"Look...okay, listen to me." I grab his hands and squeeze them, forcing his attention on me. "If you get in trouble here, they will send you to *jail*, Caz. They'll arrest you and lock you up, and you'll never get to see your family again. Do you get that?"

"Oh, I get it. I just don't care. They won't catch me." He pulls his grasp out of mine, moving across the room to collect his gun. He checks the chamber for the number of bullets, then closes it before tucking it into the waistband of his pants.

"Well, you should care because if you do something to him —like *kill* him—then they'll come looking for *me*, Caz. They'll ask me questions and interrogate me, and there's a chance they'll assume I did something to him."

He pauses then, side-eyeing me. "Why would they come to you?"

"Because there are people who knew Garrett and I were a thing, and the last time I spoke to him, I was angry. There were people around to witness how angry I was who can prove we were in a heated disagreement. That's just what the police do here, Caz. They dig and investigate until they find out what happened. And if you're with me after he goes missing or they find his dead body, they'll drag us both to jail."

His jaw ticks, then he drops his head, cursing beneath his breath. His grips the gun tight again, swaying it.

"What kind of idiotic shit is that?" he growls. "Why not just take matters into your own hands? What the hell do we need the cops for?"

"I don't know, but that's just how it is. Think of the cops as The Council in Vakeeli. I know the rules are dumb and unfair, but *please*, Caz, I'm begging you. We don't need this right now. It'll only set us back."

I move toward him, reaching for his hand that has the gun. Carefully, I take it away, placing it on the side table. He stands there, body rigid, breathing hard through flared nostrils.

"I want to kill him, Willow. I don't know him, never seen him, but I want to *murder* him. He's tormenting you!"

"I know, I know. But you can't." When I wrap my arms around him, some of the tension melts from his body. Finally, he sighs and encloses me in his arms too.

"Earth and its restricting rules. Bloody ridiculous."

I laugh. "Yeah, some of the rules do suck a little."

There's silence, only for a moment. "If he shows up while I'm here, I can't promise I won't hurt him, Willow. I mean that. If I see him, I'm putting every bullet I have in his head."

I don't know what to say to that, so instead I raise my chin and plant a warm kiss on his lips. "Can you just promise me no violence while you're here?"

His brows pucker. "That's an unreasonable thing to ask of me."

"Caz."

"Fine." He holds me closer. "No violence on Earth. For you."

I smile as he buries the tip of his nose in the crook of my neck. "Good. And we *are* going to see Phil. Sure, he might be crazy, but he could have answers. If we're going to be traveling, we need to get you more clothes, so how about we go shop a bit? Take your mind off of wanting to murder people?"

His lips twitch. "Whatever you want, Willow Woman."

CHAPTER 20
WILLOW

For me, Target runs are better done alone. Every time I go with Faye, she takes it upon herself to stop by *every* department. One time she browsed nearly every shelf and rack to declare what was and was not cute—even down to the bathroom and kitchen cleaners. Then she stopped by the electronics to ask one of the techs about a new device they had on display. So yes, going alone is always better because typically, I'm in and out.

Now, I'm shopping with Caz, and he is ten times worse than Faye. His hyperawareness is making me anxious, and he's hardly paying attention to the clothes I select for him. Every time I ask if he likes something, he simply nods and glances at it before returning his attention to his surroundings. It's come to the point where I'm selecting clothes I think he'll like just so we can get the hell out of here.

I've never seen anyone so paranoid in public the way he is, and I'm sure others are noticing because mothers with children are pushing their red carts with haste to get past him. Every single male is being glared down. Even some of the employees have looked at him strangely. They're probably assuming he's up to no good. Because that's the thing about Caz. He doesn't look away when you lock eyes with him. He stares and stares and *stares* until the other person gives up and puts their attention elsewhere.

To a normal earthling, it's intimidating and unnerving, and he's doing it right now to a poor employee who's placing clothes on a hanger next to one of the racks.

I smack Caz's arm, my phone wedged between my ear and shoulder, and give him a stern eye.

"What?" He frowns, dropping his eyes to me.

"Stop staring at people like you want to rip their heads off," I hiss away from the phone.

"He was staring at me first."

"He doesn't mean you any harm. He just works here. *Jesus.*"

Lou Ann's voice comes through the phone again. "How many days do you plan on taking off?" she asks. I called her when we came to the men's department. If I'm skipping town, I know she'll be contacting me and wanting to meet so we can plan the next event.

"I think just a week," I tell her. "Things are *really* crazy right now."

"Why do you sound out of breath?" she asks around a mouthful of something. "Are you working out?"

"I sound out of breath?" I dump a pack of T-shirts into the red cart. *If I do, it's because I'm trying to focus on our conversation while also keeping an eye on my murderous mate.* "Well, like I said, things are crazy. Will you be okay with me taking a week... maybe even two?"

"*Two?*" she exclaims. "Willow, I like to think that I'm pretty understanding, but this is unusual for you. Should I be worried? Are you in some sort of trouble?"

"No, no! I just…I need some time, Lou Ann. This is more for my mental health than anything, really." I know that'll get her. Lou Ann had a panic attack several months before hiring me. Apparently, she'd agreed to help with an event that was on a tight budget and had given her a short time frame to organize things. She couldn't handle the workload alone and was extremely stressed, hardly sleeping, and completely over-whelmed by it all. When she realized how much she had to tackle, she broke down in the bathroom of the event. Since then, she's hired a therapist to discuss the issue with. She takes mental health *very* seriously, and I feel bad for using that as a cop out…but it's also true. Being with Caz, despite the dangers, has improved my mental health significantly. I don't think about harming myself or wallowing in bed anymore. I have a reason to keep moving—a reason to live—and that's because of him and our Tether.

"Sure, all right." Lou Ann chomps some more from her end. "But when you feel better, we *really* have to get planning. You're my best asset. I can't do this without you. We also have to send the attendees those invites for RSVPs." By *we* she means *me*.

"Right. I'll do that." I watch Caz walk toward a mannequin. He studies it a moment, eyeing it up and down, then grabs the whole mannequin off the stand to set it on the floor. He takes the black trench coat off of it, then slips his arms into the jacket. The same employee who was staring moments ago has his focus on Caz again with a look of pure shock on his face. When he stops what he's doing to walk in Caz's direction, my heart sinks.

Oh God. "Thanks so much, Lou Ann. I'll email you soon." I hang up before she can speak again and rush toward Caz.

"—that you like it, but you can't take the display clothes off the mannequins, dude." The employee is speaking to Caz with a deep frown. His name tag says Jake.

"You're the man who was staring at me," Caz says, bridging the gap between them, and Jake flinches. "Why are you watching me?"

"Caz. No." I press a hand to his chest while putting my attention on Jake. "I'm *really* sorry—he's not from around here. All of this is very new to him."

Jake looks Caz up and down with a continued frown. "Yeah, clearly," he scoffs. "Can you at least put the jacket back on the mannequin? I literally dressed it today."

"Nah, I think I'll keep it." Caz studies the sleeves of the coat. "Nice quality. Fits me well. Black material. It's mine now."

"Dude! It doesn't even have a price tag!" Jake argues, his face reddening. "Just put it back!"

Caz's brows dip. "Jake, I suggest you run along before I shove a bullet up your—"

"All right, let's go. Take the coat off," I insist, already tugging at the sleeve. "We'll find another one. *With* a price tag."

Caz grimaces at Jake while I pull the hem of the sleeve. Jake, to my surprise, doesn't back down, but in his world, he's privileged and safe. He doesn't know that Caz really *will* shove a bullet up his...whatever he was going to say.

I place the jacket on the mannequin's shoulders, smile at Jake, then hook my arm through Caz's so I can lead him away.

"Can you please try to behave?"

"Behave? I didn't do anything wrong, Willow. That man was the one staring at me like I had two heads."

I sigh as I stop in front of a row of coats. "Look—here's a *whole* rack of coats. You don't have to take the one off the mannequin."

Caz studies the coats with an inclined brow. "I don't understand why it's up there if it's not for taking."

"That one is just for display, so that if a person likes it, they can come back *here* to find one on the rack to take home."

"In Vakeeli, if it's on display, we just request it and they give it to us."

"Well, unfortunately for you, this is not Vakeeli."

He still appears confused, but he doesn't argue. He reaches for one of the coats, slides into it, then fixes the lapels and the collar. "I'll take this one."

I release an unsteady breath. "Okay, so I got you a few shirts, and you might have to try these pants on because I don't know your size, but they look like they can fit."

I lead him to the dressing room and have him try all the clothes on, and fortunately, they do fit. The pants are a little loose around the waist, but that's nothing a belt can't fix. When I find a decent belt, we head to checkout, and relief sinks in when I realize we'll be going back home. This man *cannot* be in public for long.

"Can you watch the cart while I use the bathroom?" I ask before we leave.

Caz looks from me to the cart. "Surely, no one will take it while I'm here."

Oh, Lord. I refrain from rolling my eyes and enter the bathroom as Caz stands guard by the cart like his life depends on it. When I walk back out, I catch someone across the way and my heart sinks to my stomach. I freeze, focusing on the man in the navy-blue tracksuit. His curly hair is disheveled beneath a black cap, his lips pinched together tightly. *Garrett.*

My eyes shift to Caz, who has his back to me so he can't see me. However, I believe he senses my panic because his head turns a fraction, and his gaze is over his shoulder to find me.

"Willow?" Caz calls, turning fully to face me.

I look from Caz to Garrett again, who is looking Caz up and down, then he shakes his head and leaves the store. Caz studies me a moment, then turns again to figure out what I've been staring at. When he doesn't see anything, he marches my way.

"Everything all right?" he asks.

"I—I'm fine. Let's go." I grab his hand and rush for the cart. The sooner we pack and get our shit together to see Phil Patterson, the less I'll have to deal with Garrett and his weird ass stalking. I really need to call the police or file a report. If Faye saw him last night, *and* he's here today, he's definitely stalking me. But why? All because I don't want to be with him anymore? He's so damn childish and ridiculous.

I leave the store, surveilling my surroundings. I don't see Garrett or his car anywhere nearby, so I hustle to my car with Caz. I dump the items in the backseat as Caz climbs into the passenger, and when I'm behind the wheel, I start the engine and leave the parking lot.

"I just need to make one more stop," I murmur, checking the rearview mirror. No familiar cars are following me that I can see. That's good.

"You sure you're all right?" I look to my right, and Caz is eyeing me suspiciously.

I force a smile. "I'm fine."

"You look worried. And I feel it too. What did you see in that shop?"

I contemplate telling him the truth. But then I remember what he said at the apartment. If he sees Garrett, he'll kill him. If I tell him Garrett is possibly stalking me, he'll find him and kill him. Oddly enough, I have no doubt Caz will find a way to do it. One thing I will never do is underestimate him. I refuse to let him get into trouble in my world. It's my turn to protect him now, so I say, "All good. You hungry?"

He still stares. "Not really."

"Kay." I turn up the music, and Frank Ocean sings about getting lost. I turn onto a single-laned street, following the directions my GPS provides that lead me to the nearest ATM. Caz watches my phone as it sits on the dashboard on a phone stand, in a perpetual state of awe as the arrow of the GPS guides us.

"I still don't understand that thing," he mumbles. When I'm at a red light, I show him how I made it work. He seems to grasp some of the concept, but not entirely because one of his brows puckers with confusion.

When I park and collect my wallet from my purse, I say, "Wait here."

I don't wait for Caz to speak as I hop out and run to the machine, shoving my card into the slot, and entering my PIN. I peer around at the cars passing by and the vacant lots of nearby buildings. No one around. Just us.

I take out some cash, and as I stuff the money into my wallet, headlights flash in my direction. A navy car pulls into the vacant lot with us, and for a split second it just sits there. Through the window I see the silhouette of a hat and curly hair beneath. Oh my God, that's Garrett's car. The tires of the car screech, and my mouth goes bone dry as the vehicle accelerates toward us.

110

CHAPTER 21
WILLOW

I GASP AS GARRETT DRIVES THE CAR FULL SPEED INTO the passenger side of *my* car, right where Caz is sitting, then reverses just as quickly.

He turns rapidly, veering around the back of my car, but he doesn't get far. In his haste, he ends up crashing into a cement pole. Through the rear window, I watch his head hit the steering wheel from the impact. Still, I can't find it in me to move from where I stand. I'm frozen in a state of pure shock.

Caz stumbles out of the driver's side of my car, eyes wide and full of fury. There's a cut on his cheekbone, and it's dripping blood. That's when the shock wears off and I realize what Garrett was trying to do. He was trying to hurt Caz.

"WHAT THE FUCK WAS THAT?!" Caz shouts.

"I—I don't know!" I shout back.

Garrett's car door pops open, and his body falls out of the car. He hits the ground with a hard *oomph,* and Caz swings his eyes to him, immediately drawing his gun.

"Caz, wait!" I call, but I know it's too late.

"Oi! You fucking asshole!" Caz barks, stomping toward him. "What the fuck are you doing, eh?! You just hit our car!"

Caz snatches Garrett off the ground and slams his back against the side of the car. Garrett cries out in pain. "Oi, did you hear me? You just hit our car," Caz snarls in his face.

"Fuck you," Garrett spits, breathing raggedly. Blood drips from his forehead and the bridge of his nose.

I cup my mouth, unsure what to do. This was not supposed to happen. Why didn't Garrett just stay away?

Caz looks Garrett all over as if finding him familiar. "Willow?" he calls. "Is this Garrett?" His icy eyes never leave him.

Reluctantly, I say, "Yes. That's him."

Within the blink of an eye, Caz has his gun pointed at Garrett's temple. "You're the fucker who put his hands on her."

"Caz," I murmur, stepping forward. "Please. You can't. You *promised* me."

Caz doesn't look at me, but he hears me. I know he does because his jaw is pulsing. He's showing massive restraint right now.

"What are you gonna do?" Garrett taunts, sneering.

"Garrett, I would advise you to shut up, right now," I say.

"That bitch'll just use you and ditch you like she did to me," Garrett hisses at him, completely ignoring me. "You aren't special, you white bastard."

Caz's right eye twitches. Or maybe both eyes do. I can't tell from only seeing his profile, but in millisecond, Caz brings the gun down swiftly to whack Garrett on top of the head with it.

CHAPTER 22

CAZ

GARRETT FUCKER'S BODY CRUMPLES TO THE GROUND, and I feel immediate satisfaction. I swear, I wasn't going to hurt him...not yet. But he called her a *bitch* then topped it off by calling me a *bastard*. Yeah, fuck that and fuck him.

It's almost comical, really. This skinny little shit thinking he's badass. But he isn't. He has no idea who he's dealing with, and I don't give a fuck what world we're in, he'll fucking learn a lesson or two on manners.

"Open your trunk."

"What?" Willow asks, breathless.

"Open it, Willow. Now."

She breathes unevenly, rushing to the trunk and popping it open. I drag his body to the trunk and toss him inside, not caring that his head hits a corner.

"Caz, what are you doing?" she hisses.

I slam the trunk closed. "Let's go."

"Caz, we can't take him! Are you crazy?"

"Do you want me to drive?"

"Caz!"

I ignore her, heading to the driver's side. "Just show me the way back to your apartment. I'll set him free there."

"No, you won't," she says matter-of-factly when she's in the passenger seat, buckling her seatbelt. "His car is still out here. Someone will wonder whose it is since it's crashed. They'll ID it."

I don't say anything to that. Instead, I say, "Which way to your apartment?"

She tells me where to go, but not without ranting about how this is wrong and how we should let him go *before* reaching her apartment.

I've lost my temper, and I know it. All I want to do right now is wake his ass up out of whatever fainting spell he's under just to knock his fucking lights out again.

And I'm not lying to Willow. I *will* let him go...just not so soon.

When we reach her place, she climbs out of the car and says, "Open the trunk. We have to let him go, Caz. We seriously don't have time for this."

She slams her door closed and hurries toward the trunk, but as she reaches to open it, I press on the gas and drive off, taking the fucker with me.

CHAPTER 23
WILLOW

It takes me a moment to remember this is my life now. Yes, I'm back in my world, but that doesn't mean all has returned to normalcy.

The events that are happening right now are *very* real, and no, I'm not in Vakeeli where it's okay to be violent, or where all of it can be swept under the rug. I'm in *my* world, where there are police, the FBI, and even the damn army. There are authorities here, cameras on every block, and he's making this *unbelievably* hard for me right now.

"DAMN IT!" I scream in the middle of the parking lot, just as a man steps out of his car with takeout. He eyes me awkwardly, scurrying toward his building. Under any other circumstance, I would be completely embarrassed, but I'm too angry to be embarrassed right now.

"Okay. Okay. Think," I breathe. I snatch my phone out of my back pocket. I'm glad I grabbed it beforehand. I can't get into my apartment because both keys are now in my purse, and my purse is inside the car. And I can't call him and make him come back because he doesn't have a damn phone. That telepathic bond would *really* come in handy right now.

I walk to the nearest sidewalk and contact the next best person. Approximately thirty minutes after shooting Faye a text, her car appears in my complex. She pulls up to the curb, and when I climb inside the car, I slam the door.

"I can't fucking believe him," I grumble. "I *cannot* fucking believe him."

"Where do you think he went?" she asks.

"I don't know. For all I know he's still driving and coming up with some insane plan."

"Jesus, this is a mess."

I slouch in the seat, pinching the bridge of my nose. I feel a headache coming on, and my fucking mate is out there loose and ready to murder.

"He'll come back," I mutter after a while. "He has to."

"Yeah." Faye grips the steering wheel. "Wanna go to my place until then?"

"Sure."

CHAPTER 24
CAZ

I'VE NEEDED TO SMOKE A BLOOM SINCE I LANDED IN this place. Without them, I get antsy, impatient. *Violent.* And being around Garrett has increased my need for a bloom by ten.

His head rolls, and a strained noise gets trapped in his throat as he tries shifting in his chair. I wait for him to lift his head and figure out why he's been restrained. It takes the mind a few seconds—sometimes minutes—for previous events to register after a mild head trauma, but I have a feeling when he sees me, it'll all come back to him rather quickly. When he spots me standing across the room with my arms folded, his glossy eyes stretch wide, and he rocks harder in the chair I tied him in.

"Glad to see you aren't dead," I say.

He tries screaming beneath the silver tape wrapped around his mouth. It's the only thing I could find in this dreadful place of his. I do have to admit, though, this world of Willow's is quite resourceful. I pulled over about fifteen minutes after taking off from her place and checked his pockets for one of those cellphones. Apparently, many people on Earth have them. I also retrieved his wallet and checked his ID, making sure he *was* Garrett, and what did I find? A location, which I figured was his designated address. With what I remembered from Willow's mini tutorial in the car, I entered the address into the navigational thingy on his cellphone, and it led me here, to his home —a shabby little shithole in the wall that's located in a terrible area, might I add. I saw men outside with their pants hanging below their asses, smoking scented sticks that smelled of chemicals. I hope Willow has never come here. It's revolting and reminds me a lot of Ripple Hills, just with more buildings and streets.

The good thing about Garrett's home, though, is that there's some sort of club next door, and their music is very loud. The bass thumps through the walls, vibrating beneath my feet.

Garrett's eyes swing to the counter behind me, and his eyes grow even wider. I look with him, at the knives neatly lined on the counter, then back at him as he moans behind the tape.

I walk up to him, gripping the top of his head with one hand and snatching the tape off with the other.

"Come on, man!" Garrett wheezes, his eyes damp. "I-It's not like that with Willow anymore, man! I—I didn't do anything to her!"

"You hurt her. And you just tried to kill me with your bloody car," I mutter.

He frowns. "I—okay, yeah, I may have grabbed her a little too roughly a few times, but I can't control myself sometimes, man. It's just a way to keep her attention. I've done it to other women too, not just her. And I wasn't trying to kill you, just scare you."

I step back, assessing him, then turn for the counter. "Should I start with your fingers or your toes?"

"Come on, please!" he begs.

I pick up the thinnest knife. It's nothing like my silver wire in Vakeeli that I use to slice off flesh and fingers, but it'll do.

"The sad thing, Garrett, is that as much as I want to, I can't kill you. You should find relief in that." I glance over my shoulder. "Apparently there are laws here—things I can't do to get rid of you without a whole case coming down on Willow's head. But I *can* hurt you."

"W-why? You just met her, didn't you? Why do you wanna hurt me over *her*? She isn't shit, man! All she does is get high and drunk all day, and her communication is fucking terrible. She hides literally everything about herself, she's a shitty girlfriend, and I won't even lie to you, she sucks bed! All she does is lay there! You'll be bored with her in less than a week."

I withdraw my gun and point it at the center of his forehead. "Say one more word about her and I'll blow your fucking brains out, you ignorant piece of shit. I don't care about the laws. Worst case scenario, I'll take her with me, and no one will ever find her if someone is generous enough to come looking for you. You'll be dead, and she'll be safe."

His bottom lip quivers. So pathetic. Perhaps I shouldn't have taken the tape off. He's just pissing me off at this point. It'll be hard *not* to kill him.

I put the gun back in my waistband. "Right. Let's get this over with, shall we? Where's your nearest hospital?"

"W-what?"

"Never mind. I'm sure I can find it." I grip the handle of the knife and bring the tip of the blade to his left eyelid.

"Please," he whimpers.

"See, where I come from, we don't tolerate men putting their hands on women. In fact, if I hear about it, I kill the bloody bastards who do it."

I drag the blade of the knife across his eyelid, and he rocks in the chair with a loud cry. It takes everything in me not to jam the damn thing into his eye socket. Instead, I take the knife away and grip him by the shoulder, coming face to face with him.

"Oi. Look at me." Tears leak down his face, mixing with blood from the fresh cut. When he doesn't look at me, I slap him once, *twice*, demanding his attention. "LOOK. AT. ME."

He opens his right eye, and when he does, I take the knife and stab it into the meaty flesh of his thigh. His wail pierces the room, and fortunately for me, the club music drowns it out.

"Repeat these words," I command.

"Please...stop," he cries. "Please. I'm sorry, man!"

I press down on the knife, and he sucks his bottom lip into his mouth, holding back another set of tears.

"I will never..."

Garrett drops his head. "I...will...never..." he repeats.

"Put my hands..."

"Put...my h-hands."

"On another woman again."

"On a-another woman...again."

"*Especially* not Willow Austin."

"E-especially not...Willow."

"WILLOW AUSTIN!" I shout in his face. "Say her name!"

120

He flinches. "Especially not Willow Austin!"

"Good on you." I rise, turning for the counter and picking up a bigger knife. It glints in the dim light above as I weigh it in my hands. Not Vakeeli steel, but good enough. "Now be still. This won't take long."

CHAPTER 25
WILLOW

I SIT ON FAYE'S COUCH, A CUP OF HOT CINNAMON apple tea in my hands and my mind running through a million thoughts. She lives with her grandmother, her Abuelita Mariana, the person who has made the tea and has given me a dozen hugs since I walked through her front door.

Abuelita Mariana hasn't seen me in months (she made it clear she wasn't happy about that as she spouted off in her native tongue), but I'd forgotten how much I loved coming here. Have you ever been to a place that you wished was home? A place that's cozy, comfortable, and free of judgement? That's what it's like at Faye's. Her abuelita is so hospitable and is always making sure I'm fed, hydrated, and happy.

In the short hour I've been here, she's made me a turkey, avocado, and provolone quesadilla, provided a grapefruit Jarritos, and then made some tea to ease my stress. Apparently, she can feel my anxiousness, but even so, she hasn't said a word about it—at least not directly to me. And it's not like she can ask me personally—she doesn't speak much English, and what she does ask of me, she directs to Faye, who translates for both of us. Still, there's something about Abuelita Mariana. I've known her since I was a child, and we've always understood each other without saying a single word.

When it's nearing nine p.m., Abuelita Mariana murmurs something to Faye as she slowly pushes out of her recliner.

"Buenas noches, Willow." Mariana plants a kiss on my forehead. She smells like roses. I smile and wish her good night as Faye assists her. Several minutes later, Faye returns to the living room.

"Still nothing?" she asks, plopping down on the sofa beside me.

"Nope."

She huffs. "You know, when you said he was violent, I thought you were being dramatic."

"Why would you think that?" I laugh.

"I don't know. You tend to overreact sometimes."

I place a hand on my chest. "*I* tend to overreact? This coming from the woman who cried because she couldn't get a ticket to the Taylor Swift concert in time?"

"Hey—that was going to be an amazing concert, bitch!" She fights a smile, slouching back. "Anyway, do you think we should go find that crazy guy of yours? He can't be far, right? He doesn't know a damn thing about Charlotte."

"No." I shake my head and sip my tea. "He'll come back."

"What if he kills Garrett, though?" she asks, eyes widening. "Would he really do that?"

"He promised me he wouldn't."

"Is he good at keeping promises?"

"Surprisingly...*yes*."

"Hmm. Well, even if he doesn't hold to that promise, you have an alibi. You've been here all night. And, technically, he's like a John Doe. They'll find prints, but his name won't be in any of their systems. He doesn't exist here."

"Are you trying to justify him killing someone?"

"Well, it's not like Garrett doesn't deserve *something* coming to him." She folds her arms. "Why didn't you tell me he was being aggressive with you before?"

"I don't know." I lift a shoulder, shrugging. "I guess I just felt like it was small in comparison to everything else I've been going through."

"But that doesn't mean you deserve that, Willow."

Silence surrounds us. I look toward the bookshelf, at the collection of Babysitter's Club books lined on the second row. Faye's favorite childhood books. Her comfort reads and the books she turned to when she didn't want to face reality.

"I think I let it go on because it made me feel something, you know? Even if the feeling wasn't good or healthy, I still felt *something*, and it reminded me that I was alive. After Warren disappeared, I swear I thought I was going to be numb for the rest of my life, Faye. So, I guess I clung to that feeling. Wanting it to be *something*, even if it hurt."

She studies me, brown eyes glistening in the light. "I get that." Her head drops, and she tugs the sleeve of her shirt down to conceal the scars on her wrist.

I grab her hand, giving it a squeeze. "We all have our demons, right? We're all just trying to make it."

"Cheesy as fuck hearing that out loud, but yeah. You're absolutely right," she agrees.

I release her hand, laughing and placing my tea on the coffee table.

"I just can't believe out of all the people in the world, it's *me* dealing with all of this with Caz," I go on. "Surely there's *someone* out there who is much more qualified to deal with universal hopping and Cold Tethers."

She shrugs. "Apparently the universe chose you. *Literally.*"

My phone buzzes in the back pocket of my jeans, and I lean forward to pluck it out. At the sight of Garrett's name on the screen, my breath catches.

"Hello?" I answer.

"Willow." Caz's voice is deep and laced with exhaustion.

I spring off the couch, rushing to a corner of the room. "Oh my God, Caz. Where are you? What did you do?"

"Interrogate me later. I'm on my way back to you."

"Do you know where to go?"

"I'll figure it out." The line goes quiet.

In a low voice, I ask, "Did you kill him, Caz?"

He's quiet for so long I think he's hung up. I check the screen, and the seconds are still ticking by. He's still there.

"Caz..."

"No," is all he says, then the phone beeps. He hung up.

I turn to Faye, who is already looking at me with questions swirling in her eyes. "I need a ride back home."

CHAPTER 26
CAZ

SHE'S ANGRY. I KNOW IT. WE MAY NOT BE ABLE TO feel one another as intensely as we could in Vakeeli, but despite the lack of our Tether, I feel her frustrations radiating through me like a searing heat.

When I finally find the lot of her apartment, I spot her sitting on a bench in front of the building with her arms folded and eyes locked on her vehicle.

I push the button for the engine, and the engine dies. Then I step out, shutting the door behind me and meeting up to her.

She stands immediately, focusing on the collar of my shirt smeared in blood (that I'd tried covering with the new jacket she bought), then at my hands, which I washed before coming here.

"You are out of your *fucking* mind, Caspian Harlow!" she snaps through gritted teeth. "I told you to let him go! I told you to just behave—that's it. Behave so we can figure out this damn Tether and Mournwrath and get you back home in peace!"

"I'm sorry," I say.

But she ignores my apology and continues her tangent. "You can't just run off and attack people, Caz! You just can't! That's not how this world works. I know Garrett's a fucked-up person and he had no right putting his hands on me or calling you names, but you *can't* behave that way here. God, I feel like I'm talking to a child or something! If you get caught, I can't help you. I can't pull strings here like you can in Vakeeli. Do you understand that? This is *not your world*! You can't just go around like a damn vigilante trying to set the record straight!"

I reach forward, grabbing one of her hands, and she breathes raggedly, trying to snatch it away, but I don't let her. I hold on to it with desperation, then slowly bring her palm to my chest so she can feel my heart beating. To my surprise, that calms her down just enough to stop resisting me.

"Willow, *I'm sorry*," I say again, and she stares up at me, brown eyes glistening beneath the streetlamps. She's on the verge of tears, and there's a dull ache in my chest that I'm sure is coming from her. I feel awful for it all.

Her bottom lip quivers as her head sways side to side. "If I lose you too...I just...I *can't*, okay? I need you to stick this out with me. I need us to be okay. For once in my life, I want to hold on to someone, not have them disappear on me."

Her words slice through me, like a hot knife through butter, and I realize what I did, though warranted in my opinion, was wrong. This isn't about what I've done to Garrett. I've *scared* her.

"I won't ever do it again," I whisper. I cup the back of her head and bring her forehead to my chest. "Well...not here, at least."

She huffs a laugh.

"Oi, look at that." I can't help my smile. "A laugh."

"Shut up," she mutters, then she pulls away to look me in the eye again. "I'm *really* mad at you right now. You left me standing in the parking lot of my own apartment complex looking like an idiot. Give me my keys." I hand them to her, and she marches to the car, taking out the bags from the shop we went to and then trudging past me to get up the stairs.

I follow along, watching her hike up the stairs angrily. She should stop. Her walk is making her ass look *incredible* right now. I fight the urge to tell her so. She's pissed. I can't get under her skin any more than I already have.

When the door is unlocked, she steps back to let me walk in first. Locking and closing the door, she releases an exasperated breath as she makes her way across the apartment and dumps all the bags on the floor.

"Look, for what it's worth, Willow, I did it for your—"

She crashes into me, her lips colliding with mine. She moans into my mouth, stripping me out of the jacket and forcing me backwards until the backs of my legs hit the edge of the bed.

"You're a lunatic," she breathes, clutching my face in her hands.

"For you, I am," I say.

"You're going to get yourself killed, Caz."

"If it means you get to live in peace, I don't care."

She studies my eyes. "What about *your* peace?"

"My peace is with you. If you're not happy, neither am I." Her head shakes and a pained expression takes over her face, like she wants to resist those words but can't.

The pads of my fingers trace her jaw. "Come here," I murmur, clasping her chin and bringing her lips to mine again. I flip her onto her back, and she yelps from the unexpected action.

Her breath is hot on my lips as she asks, "What did you do to him?"

"Do you really want to know?"

"Yes. Tell me what you did."

I skim my lips over her cheek. "I asked him how many times he'd hurt you physically."

"Okay?"

"He said no more than four times."

"Hmm." Her eyes move past me, as if she's rehashing the number of times.

"And for each time that he did," I rasp, my lips hovering over hers again, "a wound was inflicted."

"Wow." She places her head on the bed and her locs spread around her head.

"I didn't kill him," I remind her. "But it'll take some time for him to heal and recover. He'll think twice before ever hurting a woman again."

"Where is he now?" she asks.

"Dumped him in front of a nearby hospital."

She looks at me, eyes wide with surprise.

"What?" I plant a kiss on the corner of her mouth. "I'm not a complete monster."

To that, she laughs and laces her arms around the back of my neck. When her mouth connects with mine, I melt on top of her. See, this right here—*this* is why I've vowed to protect her. She's a beautiful sight when she feels safe, when she's happy, and if some fucker like Garrett ever tries to strip her down again, I *will* kill him.

I don't prefer loose ends, but there's an advantage here. He won't blame me, or even Willow. He'll wallow in his misery, because I've warned him if he opens his fucking mouth about what happened, I'll come back to snatch all his teeth out with the rusty pliers I found in his bathroom.

"I'll protect you here, in Vakeeli, and any other universe we find ourselves in. You hear me?" I tip her chin, putting her eyes on mine.

"Yeah," she breathes. "I hear you."

With those words lingering in the air, we strip each other out of our clothes.

CHAPTER 27
WILLOW

I CAN'T SLEEP. NOT ONLY BECAUSE OF THE SCARE I had with Caz running off with Garrett, but also because we're going to see Phil Patterson tomorrow, and I don't know what to expect from the trip.

For all I know, Phil is some psychopath who murdered his fiancée and is pretending this whole portal thing happened to rid his mind of the guilt. The only thing keeping me glued to the idea of visiting him is the woman who said she could help him get his fiancée back...the one who Caz believes is a con artist.

If there is a woman who can reach out to other universes, why not try? I used to think supernatural things like that were impossible, but that was before I wound up in Vakeeli. And Caz's statement from earlier still rings true: there could be people on Earth who have powers but hide them for their own safety.

This woman, if she has the power, could find a link to one of the other Regals Caz mentioned, help us get to them, and maybe even help us defeat Decius. It would be simpler if Decius wasn't so powerful. The Regals are at the top of the food chain. They are the creators and the originators, then there were the originating Tether couples, but Decius stole all their energy and killed them, thus leading to him being this multifaceted being that is a cross between a damn wizard and a demon who can manipulate people's mind and cast spells. Then there are the Cold Tether children—people like me and Caz who are descendants of the original Tethered people. However, I'm not sure if we have power. Caz has his power as monarch...but it's more a commoner's thing. The most power we have as a couple is through our love. Hearing each other, feeling, seeing, breathing. We're on the same wavelength and that is a power in itself...but I'm curious if there's more to us that I'm not grasping. This trip may have a small possibility of answers, but a small one is better than none at all.

We've packed and I booked a rental car to pick up by morning. I would take my car, but it's a 2010 model with way too many miles on it, and I don't think it'll make it that far, plus after Garrett rammed into the side of it, I don't think it's worth taking. Faye will be riding with us, and based on the text messages she's sent, she's excited for the adventure. I don't think she realizes how dangerous it could be.

I'm ready for the trip, but I can't help feeling like something is off tonight. I've felt it since the last time I was home, even more so when Garrett would appear. There's an ominous presence lingering over me, weighing me down, reminding me that someone is out there, and he wants me and my mate dead.

The apartment has been eerily quiet. Not even my neighbors have made much noise, no stomping above my head or doors opening and closing outside, which is rare considering they have two kids. The deafening silence could be all in my head, but with where we are now, I'm not sure I can believe that.

I shift my gaze to Caz, who is turned onto his side, resting. After all those nights of not sleeping in Vakeeli, perhaps he needs it right now, so I leave him be and climb off the bed to go to my dresser. I take out a new pair of pajama pants and a camisole, toss my locs into a bun, then go to the bathroom to start the shower.

I crack the door as the water runs and face the mirror, wondering how I've gotten myself into any of this mess.

Multiple universes.

A Tethered soulmate.

A soul-sucking demon wanting to rip us apart.

Something tells me we don't have much time to figure this out. And what if we do all this for nothing? What if Decius takes us anyway and makes us suffer even more because we ran away?

No. I can't think that way. We *will* get out of this, even if it means going through every universe and portal we can find.

I strip out of my clothes and toss them in a pile on the floor, turning for the shower. But it's when I open the glass door that a hiss fills the air.

A cobra, all black with a thick head, glares at me with beady eyes, and I freeze. It opens its mouth, revealing sharp fangs with poison dripping from the ends. Its tongue flickers as it sways left, then right, then rises higher above me, and all the blood drains from my body as I stare at it, stuck in a trance I can't pull myself out of.

I find that I can't scream. There's a snake in my shower, it's clearly about to attack me, and I can't scream. Every sound is trapped, deep, deep, *deep* down.

I slip backwards and my back hits the counter. The snake hisses again, shooting toward me, and I scramble toward the corner, waiting for the bite to pierce me—for its venom to sink into my blood and kill me—but nothing happens.

Instead, the snake remains only inches from my face, and a large hand is wrapped around the throat of it with a white-knuckle grip.

My eyes travel up the arm attached to the hand, and Caz towers above, nostrils flared and lips pinched tight. He wears only a pair of basketball shorts and nothing more. He lifts the snake in the air and raises a knife in the other, and when he brings the blade forward, he slices the head off the snake.

Blood splatters onto the wall, and the body falls onto the floor with a *splat* right next to me. I push up farther against the wall as it wiggles lifelessly.

"Ohmygod. Ohmygod. *Ohmygod.*" The words tumble out of me as I stare at the creature's body. "That's a—that's a fucking *snake*, Caz!"

"I know."

"How did you..."

"Your fear. I felt it." He collects the body from the ground and carries it along with the head of the snake out of the bathroom. I can't bring myself to move as I hear him rustling about. When he returns, his hands are clear, and he reaches down to help me up. My legs are like Jell-O, even as I rise, but he keeps me steady, placing me on the toilet seat.

"Decius is here, Willow," Caz says in a low voice. "He's come to your world."

I swing my eyes up to his, fear dripping into my veins. "Through a vessel," I whisper.

His jaw ticks.

"Beatrix said this would happen. He knows where we are, Caz."

"I fear he's always known."

A paralyzing fear wraps around me. *He knows where we are.* He knows how to get to us. I knew something felt off. It was like a static in the air, and I was waiting with bated breath for something awful to happen, for a shoe to drop.

"We can't stay here. We need to move, find answers. As long as we're moving, he can't get to us," Caz declares.

"But what if—what if he finds another vessel? Another snake? A damn anaconda this time!"

"No." He works to swallow, his eyes bouncing around the bathroom. "Something tells me he'll use something bigger and smarter than a snake next time." He pushes to a stand and turns around to shut off the shower. "Are all your things packed?"

"Yes."

"Good." He grabs my hand. "It would be best if you call Faye now, let her know we're leaving."

CHAPTER 28

HUNTERSVILLE HOSPITAL – 3:45 A.M.

GARRETT'S RIGHT EYE FLUTTERS OPEN AS THE EKG machine beeps a steady rhythm. A whooshing noise drowns out all the other sounds, and his good eye shifts to the white ceiling.

Through the coppery scent of old blood, he smells sterilizing cleansers in the air, hears the soft murmurs of people nearby. He looks around more, his eyeball swiveling to the navy-blue curtain on his right, then the EKG machine and bag of clear fluid.

I'm in a hospital.

He can't remember the last time he's been in a hospital, and as he sits for a moment, digesting his surroundings, he remembers *why* he's there. That white man with the dark hair and wicked blue eyes. He took him, mutilated him, hurt him— nearly *killed* him.

Garrett's body shakes violently on the bed, but he can't bring himself to move the way he wants to. He's too stiff.

"Hey, whoa!" a voice calls. "Take it easy." A nurse appears, dressed in teal scrubs with a medical mask covering the lower half of her face.

"You've suffered a lot of head trauma. I'm surprised you're even awake right now." She gives him a pitiful onceover, and he attempts to speak, but his throat is thick and dry, so the word *"Where"* comes out in an awkward croak.

"Don't worry," the nurse says, scribbling something on the paper of her clipboard. "You're being taken care of. I can't believe you fell off a *building*. You poor thing." She sucks her teeth. "Six broken bones, and you must've landed on something sharp, considering your wounds. That's a miracle, you know."

Fell off a building? He didn't fall off a building. He was knocked out, then taken to his own apartment and tortured by some pale, British-sounding asshole he didn't even know the name of. He was punched so many times he'd lost count. The man had taken a literal meat tenderizer and smashed one of his forearms and shins with it. And the stabbing. *Fuck*, all the stabbing and slicing. That was the worst of it, not because it hurt more, but because it seemed the man truly got a kick out of cutting him. Garrett grimaces and attempts to clench his fist, but his body doesn't react.

"It's a good thing someone found you and dropped you off." She turns to face him. "You thirsty, hun? Probably are. I'll get you some water." She leaves the room, taking the clipboard with her.

As she goes, Garrett breathes unevenly and looks down. His left arm and right thigh are in a cast, and considering how stiff his neck is, he must have a neck brace on. There's a slight pain

137

in his abdomen, a sheer reminder of being stabbed, and another pain...near his groin. He shudders, remember how close that man was to slicing his dick off. He drops his head, sighing. He must be on heavy meds right now, he assumes, because he can hardly feel a thing.

He sits for a heated moment, letting all the events register. He still can't believe that happened to him. Sure, he shouldn't have been following Willow around. Truth be told, it was not in his nature to do such a thing. Lately, there'd been something luring him to Willow. Something he could not resist. His dreams were always about her, and when he woke up, the first thing he wanted was to see her.

It seemed all he could think about was Willow, despite the fact she was pulling away. He knew she no longer wanted him, but there was a voice in his head, constantly telling him to not let her go. Garrett liked to think of it as his own little shoulder demon. The voice would only come out to instruct him on Willow. It told him to hurt her, to scare her. It even told him to *watch* her. The voice led him to search her apartment for more information on her and her brother, find out her weakness. Many people would consider it an obsession, but he was not obsessed. He simply needed her. Anytime he rejected that little demon, it tormented him with nightmares that seemed endless. It was his duty to watch her, look after her. *Be* with her.

No, he shouldn't have gotten angry with her in the parking lot of her apartment complex, or angrier when she told him to leave. And he probably shouldn't have followed her from Target to the ATM, then rammed her car with *that man* inside it, but he couldn't help himself. It felt right to kill him for being with her. He didn't think the man would torture him. Here she was, all chummy and lovey with this other guy—someone she's been seeing for some time now, clearly—and she was trying to leave him for a *white* boy in a trench coat? He knew Willow wasn't shit, but this took the cake.

He stews in his anger as the nurse returns with water and helps him sip it, oblivious to his rage. She places the TV remote in his left hand, where he's only able to use two of his fingers, and when she leaves, he manages to click it on to a boring news channel. His mind constantly goes back to Willow and that man who was with her. He's hurt now, but he'll find her again, and he'll kill that man she's hanging out with.

The hours tick by, and hospital grows quieter. Less people. Less movement. Less things to do, and Garrett, though tired, refuses to sleep. What if that man comes back while he's down? While he's weak? What if he *kills* him this time? No, he won't... will he? He needs to call the cops...but how is he going to explain what he did? Crashing into her car. Attempted murder, really. He'll go to jail. Plus, the man did say if he snitched, he'd come back to really finish him off, and Garrett doesn't doubt it. No, he has to lie low until he recovers. Then he can exact his revenge.

All of it messes with Garrett's head, so much so that he develops a headache. Then the TV flickers off, the lights go out, and his room drowns in darkness.

Garrett cranes his neck just enough to look out the open hospital door. The lights in the hallway are all off, minus one flickering light dead in the center.

His door slams closed, and he sucks in a sharp breath, but he can't move. His heart races, and his fingers curl around the remote. *Fuck, that white boy is probably back. He's going to kill me this time.*

He waits, and waits, but no one comes. Then, in the darkness, he spots a black shadow seeping out of one of the eggshell walls. He watches it take shape, turning into a tall figure—a figure that has no face, just red eyes, the shape of half-moons.

"Hello, Garrett," the creature croaks, and Garrett stares at it, a familiar chill riding through his body. He's seen this creature before, in his nightmares. It's the same creature who chases him and drains him of life if he doesn't do what he's told with Willow. It's that demon who whispers over his shoulder, now coming out to play.

The creature moves closer, glaring down at him with its blood red eyes. Reaching down, the creature presses its taloned hand to Garrett's chest. The talon is cold, penetrating through the fabric of his shirt. It removes its claw, and the casts Garrett wears split open, setting his leg and arm free.

"Find her," the creature growls as Garrett sits upright on the hospital bed. He flexes his fingers. No pain, no more wounds. He's perfectly healed. His eye no longer feels swollen. A dark energy hums through him. He feels strong, powerful. A smirk claims his lips.

"Who are you?" Garrett asks.

The creature says nothing.

Standing, Garrett cuts his eyes at the creature who's been haunting him for years. "What do you want?"

"Kill her," the creature growls. He knows exactly who he's talking about, and with those words, Garrett leaves the room, trudging out of the hospital to find Willow as a twisted vessel of Decius.

CHAPTER 29
WILLOW

WILLOW

After grabbing everything we need, we leave my apartment and drive to Waffle House. It's better than sitting at my place where Decius can return with one of his vessels and try to kill us.

When the waitress asks what we'll have to drink, I request a coffee. Caz asks for sweet tea, which I want to laugh at because he's become a bit obsessed with the drink, but I can't bring myself to find any humor in our situation right now.

He's only here enjoying sweet tea at a twenty-four-hour diner because our lives are on the line. The thought eats away at me so much that I begin biting my thumbnail.

"Hey," Caz calls from the other side of the table, grabbing my wrist. "Relax. We're okay."

"For how long?"

He stares briefly and, unable to answer that question, looks away. Pressing his back to the window next to our table, he lifts his leg, resting his boot on the bench.

"I hate snakes, by the way," I mutter.

He smirks.

"What's funny?" I ask.

"Nothing, I'm just thinking about when I was younger and hung out with Rowan and Killian during the summers. We used to go near Shadow's Peak, where there were nests of snakes— twice the size of that cobra in your shower, might I add." He brings a hand up, rubbing his temples with his fingers. "I could use a bloom right now."

I glance at my tote bag. I don't have bloom, but I do have something else that may help. I dig into my bag to retrieve my wallet, taking out enough cash for the drinks. "Come with me." I'm already leaving the table, the straps of my tote bag in hand. He drops his foot and follows me out of the diner. I round the building, and just behind it is a long strip of grass facing the freeway.

I sit on the slightly damp grass as Caz approaches, and I know he's looking at me with mild confusion as I rustle through my tote. "What about our drinks?" he asks.

"We'll get more later." I tap the spot next to me. "Come on. Sit with me."

He complies, claiming the spot next to me with a light grunt. I take out one of the four joints I had in my nightstand that are already rolled. I'd rolled them what feels like weeks ago, before going back to Vakeeli to reach Caz in his mom's cabin.

I fish around for a lighter, and when I find it, I bring the joint to my lips and spark the end of it, taking a deep inhale. When I lower it and exhale, some of my stress drifts with the smoke—at least, that's how I like to think of it. All that pent-up stress floats away with each puff. I offer the joint to Caz.

He takes it, but not without examining. "Is this the weed stuff you talked about?"

"Yep. Smoke it just like bloom."

He brings it to his lips, inhales until the end turns to embers, and then exhales, releasing a large cloud of smoke. He coughs immediately after, and I burst out laughing, taking it from him when he hands it back.

"'Your weed holds no comparison,'" I say in a voice that's supposed to be like his.

"What?" He coughs again, his eyes watering. "Are you *mocking* me?"

"That's what you said the first day we met. That my weed holds no comparison to your *precious* bloom," I giggle.

He clears his eyes with a prideful smirk. "Well, I clearly take that back. Love of Vakeeli, what kind of concoction is that? Made to knock you flat on your ass, is it?"

I laugh again, and it's the kind of laugh that hurts my stomach but feels good all the same. The kind of laugh I need right now. I take another pull and offer it to him again.

"Not too much," I warn as he inhales. "I don't want you getting high to the point of paranoia."

As he smokes, I stare at the cars driving on the freeway, their headlights slashing through the darkness.

"What was the story about the nests of snakes?" I ask.

"Oh, right." He hands the joint back to me, and I study his profile. The stress has melted away, his eyes soft, body lax beneath his coat. He presses his hands behind him, resting on his palms, and I put out the joint. This is a good place. "So, Rowan was the troublemaker, no surprise there, right? I was hanging out with Kill and Row, we were teenagers around the time."

"Where was Juniper?"

"She wasn't there that day. I believe she'd just started her first bleed." He shudders, and I laugh.

"Her first *bleed*?"

"Yes. You know...when women hit a certain age and begin to...*bleed*. They're, erm, becoming a woman, or what have you, so..." His face has reddened, and I try not to laugh as I watch him nearly tuck his neck into his jacket to hide his embarrassment.

"We call them periods here. A cycle," I tell him.

"Yes, well that. I don't know much about that stuff. Anyway," he continues, clearing his throat. "It was Rowan's idea to steal weapons from Magnus' castle so we could pretend we were warriors. Most summers, Magnus and Lydia were out of Blackwater, so we snuck in there a lot to smoke blooms, drink his whiskey. There was one day when Rowan ended up stumbling across a snake nest, and his whole foot slipped inside. The snakes became extremely hostile and shot out of the nest, immediately trying to bite us. I'm not sure you're aware, but most boys then were trained to kill any and everything in preparation of becoming a Blackwater soldier. I changed that law when I took over, by the way. Never seemed ideal to raise boys to become murderers. Children should be children for as long as they can." He swallows, wisps of hair falling onto his forehead as he lowers his gaze. I reach forward with a smile, pushing some of those loose hairs back. He glances up, returning a half-smile. "So anyway, here we are, three hormonal boys, slicing the heads off of snakes, thinking we're badass." He chuckles, and I can't help grinning while I imagine the three of them fighting snakes.

"Y'all sounded pretty badass," I tease.

He chuckles, and I rest my shoulder against his as the woosh of the cars flying by on the freeway soothes me.

"I know I've only been here for a few hours, but it's put a lot into perspective about my family," Caz goes on. "I used to put up this barrier to block them out when I first met them. They had a life I didn't have. They were free, unlike me, and were never harmed by their caretaker. They had a shit father, but... well, he never hurt them like mine did to me. Just left them to their own devices and also leaving Maeve to be a single mother. I envied their lives so much—still do, really. They're all so close, sometimes I feel like the black sheep." He sniffs.

"That's not true," I argue. "They love you. They see you as one of them."

He presses his lips, and I'm glad he doesn't argue with that. I'm glad he knows it's the truth.

"Well, all this to say, I miss my clan. My *family*," he says quickly, correcting himself. "I know they're worried sick."

"I bet they are. But it's okay. We'll get you back to them, I promise."

He looks at me sideways, the streetlights making his eyes sparkle like cobalt gems. Reaching for my hand, he brings it to his lips and runs them over my knuckles. His lips are warm, soft.

"I don't want any of them getting hurt because of our Tether," he murmurs.

"Right, our Tether. Killian's biggest fear," I return, huffing.

"God, that man. How do you deal with him? What happened to make him so angry all the time?"

"The better question to ask is how does he tolerate *me*?" Caz counters, and I sense that he won't spill much about Killian. If anyone is like a vault, it's Caz. There must be a reason Killian is so hostile and angry, something that goes much deeper than daddy issues. "Besides, he doesn't hate you," Caz says, looking ahead again.

I swing my eyes to his.

"He just doesn't understand you. He's a lot like me. We hate things we don't understand—that we can't wrap our minds around. But sooner or later, he'll be like your guardian. You'll be family, and he won't *ever* let a hair go astray on your head. He's like that with the people he loves. Because that's Killian. The angriest of us all on the outside, but the most tender inside."

There's a warmth to Caz's voice, one that overflows inside me, making me feel comforted and a little emotion. "That's good to hear."

I lower my gaze, my mind going back to the last car ride I took with Caz's family. I could sense some of Killian's tenderness when Caz was out cold. It almost looked like Killian wanted to cry, and Caz and I talk about that as time passes and the sun slowly pours above the horizon, painting the sky in lush lavender and cotton candy pink. It's nice talking to him at this hour, wrapped in a blissful high. If only we could have these moments forever, uninterrupted. Just us.

But we can't. Not right now. And I realize that when my phone rings, and I pull it out to see Faye's name on the screen. I glance at Caz, and he sighs when the reality of our situation sinks back in. He stands and takes my hand, helping me to a stand.

We collect our things, grab a coffee and tea to go from inside the diner, then make our way to the rental car lot where Faye will meet us for our trip to Virginia.

CHAPTER 30
WILLOW

VIRGINIA COAST PSYCHIATRIC DETENTION CENTER sits atop a hill, a wide three-story brick building that overlooks the Atlantic Ocean. The majority of the dark roof is hidden beneath pregnant gray clouds that threaten to break at any given moment, and lawn lights flash onto the building, revealing cracks and chips to prove just how old the building is.

We passed a gate where a security guard stood in a security box and asked for identification. Now, after four hours of being on the road, I'm driving into the parking lot, the wipers on the windshield swinging every few seconds to combat the light drizzle.

It's a gray day, cast with rain and fog, and of course it would rain today, when I'm already paranoid and don't know what to expect. I normally love rain, but not when it comes to visiting a place like this. What the hell was I even thinking by coming here? I should just drive away right now.

I breathe as evenly as possible and find myself parking.

When the car is still, I glance at Caz who has his eyes trained on the building. I look over my shoulder at Faye who is chewing her bottom lip so hard she'll probably make it bleed.

"Stop doing that," I hiss at her.

Her eyes swing to mine, and she stops chewing immediately. "Sorry. Lost in thought."

"Are we ready?" I ask, shutting the engine off.

Caz drops his eyes to his coat, lifting one side of it and revealing the Blackwater gun. "You're sure I can't take my gun?"

"I'm *positive* you can't take it. They're most likely going to check us for weapons and other things."

"Which, by the way, you shouldn't take personally, okay?" Faye adds, as if she's talking to a toddler. "Security checks are protocol in places like this."

Caz removes the gun from the inside pocket of his coat and slides it beneath the passenger seat. "Don't patronize me," he grumbles over his shoulder. "There'd better not be any funny business going on."

"We'll talk to Phil, get the information we need, and then get out," I assure him.

I say the words, but even as I get out of the car and peer up at the building, I feel an uncomfortable buzz ride through me, and my gut forms into a block of lead. I shake it off though and shut the car door behind me as Faye leads the way to the building.

We approach the door, where Faye pushes her thumb on a large button next it. The double doors clink and spread apart, groaning on the hinges, and we walk inside to a sterile white lobby. Ahead are two security guards—a man and woman—dressed in black and standing with metal detector wands in hand, and to our right is the check-in desk, where a woman in all white with red hair sits in a chair behind it, clacking away on a computer.

Her green eyes flicker up to us, and she does a double take as she rises from her chair. Her name badge reads Elana.

"Can I help you?" she asks with a practiced smile.

"Hi, yes. We're here to visit Phil Patterson. I'm his cousin, Faye." Faye trots toward the desk, smiling, just as she practiced. Because that's one thing she didn't find out until we were already on the road—that the only visitors who come here *must* be family or with a family member.

The woman cocks her head. "Hmm. That's interesting. Mr. Patterson has never had visitors before."

Caz stiffens next to me, but Faye continues a smile with a sappy sigh. "I know. Sad right? See, here's the thing," she says, folding her arms on the countertop. Elana almost frowns at the gesture. "I've been so upset with Phil—for years, really. I just...I *hate* that he's in here. We weren't just cousins growing up, we were best friends, and I couldn't bear seeing him in this place. But I've had a life change—you know how that goes, right? And I've realized life is *way* too short to be selfish with my time."

Elana raises her chin, studying Faye a moment before swinging her eyes to Caz and me. "And you brought others with you for a first-time visit?"

"They're friends. We all used to hang out together."

"Only family is allowed, I'm afraid."

"Sure, but can't you allow a mild exception? As you stated, Phil never has visitors. I can't guarantee that I'll make it all the way out here to see him again. I'd hate for him to miss out on seeing all of us."

Elana's eyes twitch as she studies all of us again. "Just a

moment." She sits in her chair, picking up a corded cream phone from the receiver and punching numbers into the base. She cuts her eyes at all three of us again with a suspicious onceover, then says into the phone, "Do you have a list of approved relatives for Phil Patterson?" She pauses. "There is a young woman here named Faye saying she's his cousin, but I don't recall him ever having visitors."

Oh, fuck.

I stare at the back of Faye's head, hoping she'll turn to look at me so we can get the hell out of here. Clearly, this woman knows we aren't family and are wasting her time. But Faye doesn't break. She continues looking at the woman with a confident smile. Caz shifts on his feet, peering around the lobby with unease. I bet he's wishing he had his gun.

The woman's eyes round as she lowers her gaze. "Oh—uh, really? Are you sure? All right. I'll send them back." Elana hangs up the phone then pastes on a smile as she gestures to the sign-in sheet on the counter. "Please sign in and I'll show you the way."

Wait...what?!

When we're signed in and past security, Elana meets us on the other side. It's clear she's not satisfied with Faye seemingly telling the truth by the smile she wears that doesn't reach her eyes.

"How did you just do that?" I whisper to Faye.

"Remember Kaiden?"

"The guy who hacked into your Instagram account?"

"Yeah, well, he owed me a favor—the jackass. I may or may not have asked him to hack into the files here to put my name on Phil's visitor list. He said it was pretty easy, actually."

My eyebrows are nearly touching my forehead. "Shit."

"See?" She smirks. "I'm not completely useless."

"A professional liar though, I see," Caz mumbles next to me.

Faye cuts her eyes at him with stitched brows.

Elana approaches a white door, swiping her badge across a black box to unlock it. She holds the door open for us, and we step into a bright room that smells like bleach and Pine-Sol. The walls are painted a pale shade of green, and ahead is a floor-to-ceiling window revealing the ocean and a miniature black and white lighthouse in the distance. There can't be any more than four or five tables centered throughout the room, each with two or three plastic, blocky seats beneath them. A single green leather sofa is against the far-right wall, shining heavily beneath the lights like it's been wiped cleaned more than once today.

This room is spotless, yet nothing about it is welcoming. There are no portraits on the walls, no TVs (which makes sense), not even any flowers to show a little cheerfulness. It's all so *empty* and lifeless.

"We've let Phil know you're here. Security will be bringing him along. For your safety and Phil's, we lock the door from the outside, but when you're ready to go, just push the buzzer right here—" She taps at a black box on the wall— "and someone will let you out." Elana holds steady for a moment, eyeing each of us again, then she huffs before leaving the room. When she's gone, her heels click-clacking in the distance, I take a look around with a relieved sigh.

"For your information, Caz, I'm not a liar," Faye blurts out when Caz approaches one of the windows. "What I did back there was a white lie, which helped us, by the way."

"If that's what you believe, so be it," Caz says.

"Why do you even care?" she hisses. "I may have lied, but *you're* violent. You kill people for a living."

Caz frowns over his shoulder. "Are those more lies you feed yourself to feel better?

"Jesus Christ." Frustrated, Faye slips out of her pink teddy coat and sits on one of the plastic chairs. I'm glad she stops arguing because I can't stand the bickering. They've been taking verbal jabs at each other since the car ride started. Faye, though she was rooting for Garrett's demise, clearly isn't pleased about Caz's rash decision or leaving me stranded in the parking lot. And Caz is just...well, Caz. He doesn't like anyone outside his clan.

"You put her in danger," Faye had argued during the drive. "Someone could've blamed her for what you did! What if someone saw you stuff him in your trunk?"

"No one saw us," Caz shot back.

Their arguing went on and on for thirty minutes—on and off. They kept talking about what was good for me, what I needed, what worse could have been done, until I told them both to kindly shut the hell up. To my luck, Faye shoved her AirPods into her ears to tune everything out, and Caz huffed and grumbled about how he'd do it again as he stared out the window.

They're at odds, which I find a bit comical because Faye for me is just like Killian for Caz—overprotective and defiant. She's only looking out for her friend, just as Killian was only looking out for his cousin. I can't even imagine Faye and Killian in the same room. They'd have each other in a headlock, I bet.

I take the seat across from Faye, looking her up and down. "Are you two gonna argue the whole time you're around each other?"

"No," she quips. "Only when he messes up. If he's your mate and you're bound to him or whatever, he needs to make sure he doesn't do stupid shit like that ever again. If you die because of that *hijo de puta*, I swear I'll find a way to that Vakeeli place and strangle him myself. I'm not even kidding. You're my best friend, and no one is gonna take that from me." She turns her head, throwing daggers at Caz's back with her eyes. I look at Caz, and when he glances over his shoulder, I'm surprised to see him smirking. Though annoyed, he also finds her protectiveness amusing.

"This coming from the one who says violence isn't the answer," he laughs.

"Whatever. Where is this guy?" Faye sits up in her seat, and as she does, a buzzer goes off and double doors on the opposite side of the room spread apart.

Two men stand there, one in a security uniform and the other dressed in a dingy beige sweatsuit. The man in beige is short with a bald head and wiry glasses on the bridge of his nose. His skin is sable, his lips plump, wrinkles on his forehead from scrunching his face to see us. It's Phil, though he looks nothing like the video anymore. It seems he's aged ten years, and the glasses don't help his case.

He looks at me and Faye, and then at Caz who remains standing by the window.

"Let me know when you're ready to head back," the security guard says to Phil, then he leaves the room, shutting the doors and conjuring another loud buzz.

"Now, wait a minute." The man places his hands on his hips, eyeing all three of us again. "I should've known this was a setup. I ain't ever seen y'all a day in my life." The man's voice is slightly high-pitched, and he has a southern accent, just like the videos.

"You must be Phil." I stand to fully face him.

"That'd be me." He drops his arms. "And who the hell are you?"

I look around the room at the cameras before putting my focus on him again. "Would you like to sit?"

"I will, when you tell me who you are."

"You know me." I laugh, widening my eyes, and he angles his head. Then he glances at the cameras, and his eyes narrow the moment it registers. For a split second, it seems he's going to call for security with the way he shifts on his feet and tosses me a wary look, but then he nods and points a finger at me.

"Right—you're the ol' girl from the theater." He walks closer to me, and as he does, Caz turns fully, watching his every move.

Noticing the motion, Phil looks back at Caz, twists his lips, then makes his way to the table where Faye is. I pull up an extra chair as he sits. Caz remains standing, keeping an observant eye.

"Tell me who the hell y'all really are and what the hell y'all want from me," Phil says in a low voice, his elbows on the table. His elbows are ashy, and I have the urge to take the hand lotion out of my bag and squirt some into his hand so he can use it.

"I'm Willow, and this is my best friend, Faye."

"And that angry man in the corner?" Phil inquires, pointing a thumb back.

"That's Caz...and he's the reason we're here," I inform him. "We, um...we read about you and your fiancée. About the reason you're here, in this place."

Phil straightens in his chair then, his brown eyes turning serious behind his glasses. "If y'all are journalists or these new social media reporters or whatever, you can get the hell out right now. I already told my story, and I ain't repeating it."

"No, no, we believe you," Faye says, raising a hand to calm him.

Phil cocks a brow.

"We drove from North Carolina to come talk to you in person after hearing your story." Faye glances at me for reassurance, and I bob my head. "We're hoping you can tell us what you saw that day."

Phil is quiet as he looks between us. "Why you wanna talk to me about it? Did it happen to you too?"

"Sort of," I answer with a shrug.

"We read your blog posts. We're just trying to put the pieces together about all of this portal stuff." Faye crosses her arms on the table. "Can you tell us what all happened that day?"

Phil narrows his eyes. "What you got on you?"

I look from him to Faye, mildly confused. "Um...what do you mean?"

"Got anything sweet on you? I ain't had nothing sweet in a long time. They never give us treats. Says it messes with our brain chemistry or something like that, but something sweet here and there ain't gone kill us." He scratches the scruff on his chin. "Wish I had a Snicker or something."

Faye's eyes swing to me, and she lifts her hands in the air, the gesture screaming *I've got nothing.*

"Um..." I bring my tote bag onto my lap and dig through it. To my luck, I find a watermelon Jolly Rancher and an Andes mint. Both have probably been in the bottom of my bag for months, but he won't know that. I place them on the center of the table. "That's all I've got."

Phil's eyes drop to the candies, then he glances at me before collecting them swiftly, hiking his shoulders, and peering around the room, like this is a drug-dealing situation. I can't help looking at Faye again. Her eyes are wide and lips are pressed, and she's probably thinking what I'm thinking: this may not have been a good idea.

"All right, so where do I start? Let me see..." He unravels the sticky wrapper of the Jolly Rancher and pops it into his mouth. "Mmm. Damn. I ain't had one of these in years. It's good."

Caz steps closer. "Tell us what happened."

"All right, all right. Hold on, man. Let me savor this shit. I just told you we ain't allowed to have sugar in this place."

Caz refrains from rolling his eyes.

"All right, so yeah, you read the blog posts, so you know the story about Marney. How is my blog doing anyway? Never mind. Look, I ain't lying about it. She really did disappear out of nowhere. We were hiking, right? And it was mad early in the morning. She wanted to go to McAfee Knob to see the stars at four in the damn morning and then watch the sun rise, and I would've done anything for her, so I went. We were walking a trail that leads to the top of a hill and chilled for a second. Then the sun came up and we took pictures, ate a couple of sandwiches and snacks, but when we came back down, that's when we saw it." He leans in, ashy elbows on the table. "It didn't look real at first. It was like blue glitter or something floating in the air. And Marney, man, she was nosy as hell. Always so damn adventurous and wanting to know *everything,* and I told her to leave it alone, 'cause I ain't gone lie to you. I believe in aliens and shit. Like those motherfuckers are out there, probably watching us, and all I could think in that moment was that some alien was about to pop up and abduct our asses. But Marney, she kept going toward it, even though I kept yelling for her to come back." He shakes his head, defeat washing over him. "She tried to touch it, and the next thing I know, she's gone." He spreads his fingers, eyes widening. "Just disappeared out of nowhere. And when she did, all that glitter disappeared too. Wasn't even there no more. I looked all around that forest for her, spent hours calling her name, going back to that spot, trying to see if it would take me too, but nothing happened, and I didn't know what to do, so I called the cops. But they didn't buy my story. They kept interrogating me, asking if we argued, had a fight—crazy shit, you know? Always wanna assume a black man hurt his woman, but I never laid a finger on Marney, or *any* woman for that matter. I'm a good man." He adds the last sentence with more gumption, like he needs us to believe it.

I nod, waiting for him to continue.

"Nobody could help me, and her family—man, she has this brother, Antoine, who always picked on me. He was an asshole, so you know he blamed me, started calling me all kinds of names, said he was gonna kill me because I did something to his sister. And I couldn't sleep after what happened. I kept going back to McAfee, hoping I'd find her, but I never did. So, I started doing some research about what I saw, thinking maybe that would help me get some answers. And when I tell you I fell down a rabbit hole, I did. Did you know there are people out here selling organs they don't need for two hundred dollars, sometimes less? And that some people worship jellyfish? I'm talking, capture the jellyfish, place them in a tank on an altar, and bow down to them. That's crazy, right?"

"Stick to the point," Caz says, irritation lacing his voice.

"Ay, man. What's your problem?" Phil snaps, but it's hard to take him seriously when he's sucking so hard on that Jolly Rancher. "Why you so mad?"

"I'm not mad. We simply don't have time to sit here listening to you talk about organs and jellyfish," Caz tells him.

"All right, all right, Fine. Whatever. So anyway, I did my digging, and I came across this website about a man who got his legs."

"A man who got his legs?" I repeat, confused.

"Yeah. This man said he found a woman who helped him walk. He was a paraplegic, legs didn't work. Wheelchair bound, you know the deal. But he wrote about how he met this woman in New Orleans during a trip. Said the woman saw him and promised she could make him walk. He didn't believe her, but he kept thinking about what she could offer, so he went back to her. She recited a whole bunch of mumbo-jumbo, told him to close his eyes, and he'd see a blue light. When he saw it, she told him to go to the light, and he'd walk. And he did. He said he saw the light and felt like he'd been suctioned into another place. The man walked—only he wasn't walking here, on Earth. He swears he was somewhere else. Somewhere where the world was richer, the trees greener—he was free, and he said he was running. He could feel his legs, his feet on the ground, the grass between his toes, all that. He said it was the best experience of his life, and you know it was because he kept paying this woman just to feel himself walking. He became addicted to the feeling. He swears it was real. The man went into debt because he kept going back to her." He shifts the Jolly Rancher to his right cheek.

"Anyway, it wasn't the fact that she helped him feel like he could walk that got my attention. It was how he mentioned being sucked into a blue light, like a portal or something, and it reminded me of the glitter I saw. I reached out to him, and he kept telling me to trust the portals—that the portals are our friends—that we're capable of all things through them. Some mad shit that I didn't really care about. I asked for the woman's information, and he gave it to me, and I went all the way to New Orleans to see her...and I shit you not, she showed me the portal too." Phil's eyes are nearly bulging through his glasses. "I was so close to it, but she closed it up right when I was about to reach it, said I had to pay her $5,000 if I wanted to see Marney again."

Faye gasps. "Seriously?"

"Yep. And I was willing to do *anything* for Marney, but I ain't have the money then, right? So, I took the money out of Marney's bank account. Her brother caught me and started accusing me of crazy stuff—about how I hired someone to take her, get rid of her, just to have her money. Cause Marney was a big shot—I forgot to tell y'all that. She owned this Tex-Mex restaurant called Bodega's. Big in the V.A. Made good money. And her brother thought I set her up just to take her money."

"Well? Did you?" Caz probes, and Phil frowns, turning in his chair to glare at him.

"Fuck you, man! I'd never do anything like that! Marney was gonna be my wife!"

"Caz," I snap, glaring at him before focusing on Phil again. "Please don't take anything he says personally, Phil. He's...still learning."

Phil's anger radiates off of him, and I turn my head to shoot a glare at Caz again. If he doesn't stop with the snark, we'll never get this woman's information. Caz raises a hand, as if he gets the point.

"Listen, Phil. Caz isn't from here," I say, putting my attention on him again. "He's from another universe. A place called Vakeeli."

Phil's eyes stretch as he observes Caz deeper. "Shit."

"Yeah, and right now he's in a lot of danger. We both are, actually. We're just trying to find someone from here who can help us. This woman who showed you the portal...what was her name?"

Phil tugs on his bottom lip, thinking about it. "She went by Effie, I think."

"And do you know where exactly in New Orleans we can find her?"

"When I went, she had a shop close to the French Quarter. A place called Yakaree, or something like that—smelled like incense and fish in there, and she had these little animal skulls—"

"Did you just say *Yakaree*?" Caz moves in closer, eyes locked on Phil. His face is paler, the blueness seeming to have melted away from his eyes. I frown. What's gotten into him?

"Yeah, that. You say it just like her." Phil chuckles, but Caz is not laughing. His face is grim.

"Caz, what's going on?" I ask.

"Whoever this woman is, we *can't* go to her." His words come out without hesitation. "We'll have to find someone else."

"Why?" I counter. He can't be serious. "We're so close to a possibility. We don't have time to look anywhere else, Caz."

His eyes swing to mine. "*Yakaree* is a Vakeeli term for someone who will soon meet their demise. This woman...her energy can't be good if that's the title she's running around with." He looks at Phil. "What happened to the man who got his legs?"

"Last I heard, he was living with his mother. Lost his job. Drowning in a bunch of debt. Probably gave everything he had to that woman just to keep feeling like he was walking," says Phil.

Caz points his gaze to me. "Willow, I'm not sure about this."

"Do you think she'll hurt us?"

Caz blinks, then lowers his head. "I don't know."

"But who else can we go to?"

A pause. Then another, "I don't know."

I release a frustrated sigh.

"*Yakaree* can mean so many things. Perhaps she means a financial demise, or mental," Caz goes on, pacing a bit. "Phil here was caught taking money so he could give it to her, and the man who found his legs lost all his money by giving it to her." Caz rubs his forehead, trying to wipe away the frown.

"We have to try," I tell him. "She could be from Vakeeli, which could help us. If Beatrix got us here, then maybe this woman tried what Beatrix did on herself and ended up here."

"It's possible, but why the hell would she be hiding here, on Earth?" he asks.

"We can only find out if we meet her." I turn to Phil. "Thank you, Phil. We won't bother you anymore."

"Yeah, and sorry about your fiancée," Faye adds, standing.

"Y'all really going to that Effie woman?" Phil probes.

I look at Caz hesitantly. His brows are puckered, forehead wrinkled as he stares out the window. He doesn't want to do this, but we have no choice. What other option do we have? Someone here has a link to Vakeeli, and we can use it.

"Well," Phil says when we don't respond. "Good luck to you on that one. But if it were me, I wouldn't go anywhere near that money hungry witch again."

CHAPTER 31
CAZ

WHEN WE LEAVE THE DETENTION CENTER, FAYE AND Willow are rambling about this Effie woman and how it makes sense to find her, despite all the dangers that clearly surround her name. All the while, I can't bring myself to say much of anything about it out loud.

My mother told me stories about people who used *yakaree* to hurt others. They'd run to Mythics after being assaulted or bullied, and they'd beg them to put the spell of *yakaree* on their enemies. The next thing anyone knew, the person they'd put the spell on would be dead and had the mark of *yakaree* on their body, the letter Y with a slash through the bottom. I always liked to think it was a coincidence—these people dying and ending up with the mark—but *yakaree* has somehow made its way to Earth, which proves how powerful it is. Though none of them have the mark here, it's clear the stories are true. The demise can happen to anyone, anywhere.

After driving to a rental car lot, Willow sees Faye off. As badly as she wants to come, she can't swing it to New Orleans —something about being there for her grandmother and getting back to work at her bookshop. Frankly, I'm glad she's taking off. She's gotten on my nerves too many times to count.

When they hug goodbye and Faye drives away with her rental car, Willow returns to ours, plopping behind the wheel. The car is quiet for several seconds, droplets of rain splashing on the windshield and blurring our surroundings.

"Do you think we should find another way?" she finally asks, her gaze shifting to me.

I let the question linger. "Depends. Am I allowed to take my gun when we meet this woman?"

She smirks. "I think that would be best."

"Then we'll go. But if she tries to curse us, I'll know it. There's a hidden language in Vakeeli that goes back thousands of years, and if she knows the work of *yakaree*, then she's likely ancient. This woman, whoever she is, is very cunning."

"Well, let's hope she's nice." Willow enters a location on the map app of her cellphone. "Fourteen hours. We'll have to make an overnight stop." She appears nervous as she grips the steering wheel and pulls onto the main road. "I'm worried that if we stop, though, Decius will find us. There's no telling what he'll use this time."

"We don't have to stop if you don't want to. I can drive when you get tired," I offer.

"What if you get pulled over? You don't have any ID."

"I'll drive carefully," I insist.

She considers that. "I guess…"

"You have very little trust in me," I say, laughing.

"It's not that. I just…I get nervous for you. Mostly because you don't handle normal situations the way I would. You're automatically defensive."

"It's just *driving*, Willow. We'll be fine. I can drive and follow the arrow on your navigational thingy while you rest. We'll be okay."

She releases a breath. "You're right. I'm just overthinking."

"That you are." I peer out the window at the passing trees and gray sky. My mind can't help wandering to this Effie woman again. "This woman must've been banished. That, or she's hopping back and forth from here to Vakeeli for fun, and if she can do that, she must be extremely powerful. You said it yourself that Beatrix seemed to be in pain just to send us here, and Beatrix is very old."

"Yes, that's true." She twists her lips a split second. "Can guns stop Mythics?"

"*This* gun can." I sit up in the seat, opening the revolver. "But there are only five bullets in the chamber. Better hope she's not a vanisher."

"A *what?*"

"A vanisher. The kind of Mythic who can vanish into thin air. It's fucking odd, I won't even lie. They disappear and pop up on another side of the room. I had to fight one once during a battle near Ripple Hills. It was *not* fun."

She huffs a laugh. "Sounds freaky."

I reach over to grab the hand resting on her lap. Her eyes flicker in my direction briefly before focusing on the road again.

"We're in this together, you and I," I tell her. "Remember that."

She smiles, bringing my hand up to kiss the back of it. Her

lips are soft, plush, and warm, and the mere grace of them sends a spiral of heat through me.

"Careful," I murmur, grinning. "You'll start something you'll have to finish."

She breaks out in laughter, pulling her hand away to swat at me playfully. "That is the *last* thing we have time for, Caspy."

CHAPTER 32
WILLOW

"I'M RUNNING LOW ON FUNDS." I STARE AT THE number in my bank account. $254.32. With booking this rental, buying clothes for Caz, food, and even the withdrawal for my rent, I shouldn't be surprised, but I am. Ya girl is broke, and I won't be working with Lou Ann for at least another week...and she doesn't pay for time off.

Caz swings his eyes to me as he grips the steering wheel with one hand. "What are you talking about?"

"We don't have rubies here, we have money, and when we run out of money, shit gets rough," I explain.

"I have an unlimited supply of rubies," he says. "Is there not an unlimited supply of currency for you here?"

"No. I work to make my money."

He frowns. "Why? You're above that. You shouldn't have to work for it."

I can't help the laugh that escapes me. We all feel that way on Earth, but society thinks otherwise. I've always hated the ideation of working to live. Why can't we just live to live?

"I'm not a monarch like you, and, unfortunately, I don't belong to a monarch's clan," I inform him. "I have to work and pay for everything myself here."

"Shit. No wonder you're so stressed here."

"It's fine. I'll use my credit card for the hotel room and food."

Caz concentrates on the road with his brows drawn together.

"What? Why are you frowning?" I ask.

"You know, if you ever decided you wanted to make a life in Vakeeli, you'd never have to worry about these *funds* you speak of," he says. "I'd take care of you."

I can't help my smile. "Well, that's very kind of you."

A brief pause. "Would you ever consider that?" he probes. "Staying in Vakeeli, I mean?" When I don't answer right away, he backs it up with, "Never mind. I shouldn't have asked. It's far too soon for you to even consider it."

"No, no, it's not that." I grab his free hand, clutching it. "I just…I guess I'm wondering if *you* would want that. Me staying there…"

"Without a doubt." He replies with a voice drowning in certainty. "Say we do find a way to kill Decius. Say we do make it out of this Cold Tether alive. All that remains is a decision between us. Do we part ways—you in Earth and me in Vakeeli —or do we decide to be together in one universe?"

"Would you stay on Earth with me?" I ask in a joking manner.

He cracks a smile that makes him look younger, more vulnerable. "I could, but I don't think I'd do well fitting in."

"That's how I feel about Vakeeli. I wouldn't fit. I'm not built like you and your clan are. I barely know anything about guns. Hell, I can't even hold one properly."

"Ah, you don't have to worry about that. I'll teach you."

"What about the threats? The people who hate you? The Rippies? If they find out about me, they'll use that against you, and in order for that *not* to happen, our...relationship—if that's what we want to call it—will have to be a secret." I study the profile of his face. "I don't want to be your secret, Caz."

"When we make it through Decius, our relationship won't be a secret. Everyone will know you belong to me, which means no one will come after you unless they're asking to face the barrel of my gun."

I let that sink in. Then I say, "You know, despite how crazy things get in Vakeeli, I can't help feeling like it's my real home. Sure, I was born on Earth, but...my roots are in Vakeeli. Just like yours. And according to the history, it's where I originated."

"That is true. And in Vakeeli, we have power, respect. We can have anything we want."

"It's about control for you, isn't it?" I ask with a smirk.

"How do you mean?"

"I mean, here in my world you don't have that control. You have to follow the rules. But in Vakeeli, you can do whatever you want. And people fear you, which in turn makes them respect you." I can't help smiling as I say, "So, when it all boils down, I believe you *do* enjoy being a monarch. Whether you admit it or not, you enjoy having people under your grueling thumb."

He glances at me briefly before putting his eyes on the road again. "Does that make me an awful person?"

I squeeze his upper thigh. "Not if you use your power wisely."

He huffs a laugh, then shakes his head, grinning. "Are you going to make a changed man out of me, Willow Woman?"

"It's a possibility, Caspy."

He uses his left hand to drive, bringing his right down to grab mine. Our fingers intertwine, and I love the feel of his skin against mine, the heat of his hand.

"Consider it," he murmurs. "I don't want to strip you of the life you have here—I'd never do that. You can always use the chant Beatrix gave you and return to see Faye whenever you want. Or, if you need time away from all the madness of Vakeeli, you're more than welcome to go back to Earth for however long you need to." He pauses, his throat bobbing up and down. "All I ask is that you consider sharing a life with me." He kisses one of my knuckles. "I want to be a better man for you, Willow. I want to live the rest of my life with you, provide for you, protect and take care of you. My heart will only ever beat for you. But if that's not something you want…"

I pull my hand out of his and lean over the middle console to plant a kiss on his cheek. "I'm *yours*, Caz," I murmur in his ear. "No matter where we are."

"Does that mean you'll make a life with me in Vakeeli?"

I sit back in my seat again, and because I like being a teasing bitch, I tell him, "I'll consider it."

He can't help but to smile.

170

CHAPTER 33
WILLOW

I'M NOT SURE WHEN I FELL ASLEEP, BUT WHEN I WAKE up, it's because the speed of the car has decreased and there's an excruciating itch on the back of my neck.

I scratch at it, and Caz peers at me as neon red lights flash on his face. He pulls into the parking lot of the hotel I booked, The Rêvasser, and finds a space to park.

"Everything all right? he asks.

I scratch the back of my neck again until the itch subsides. "Yeah, I'm fine."

I take a look around the dark parking lot. Several cars occupy the lot, bathed in fluorescent red light. The rain has clearly followed us here because droplets cling to the cars, as if a shower has recently passed. Not much surrounds The Rêvasser except a diner across the street and a walking trail behind it.

A group of people bursts out of the front door of the hotel dressed head to toe in flashy attire, most likely on their way to the city.

I collect my tote bag and climb out of the car as Caz goes for our suitcases in the trunk. The lobby of the hotel has a contemporary feel, with abstract walls, down lighting, and a velvety seating area with plush chairs and wooden tables. Many of the chairs are occupied with bodies—men and women with drinks in their hands, chatting and laughing.

Once I collect the room keys from the clerk behind the desk, I lead the way to our room. But as we go, I can't help feeling like someone is watching me, and the itch on the back of my neck intensifies. I scratch the area, and a chill snakes down my spine—a familiar sensation that causes me to stop in my tracks. I peer over my shoulder as a couple leaves the hotel, hand in hand. Caz takes my hand, bringing my attention back to us.

"Are you sure you're okay?" His head is at a slight tilt as he studies my face.

"Yeah. I'm fine." I force a smile up at him, squeezing his hand as we approach the elevator. I press the up arrow, and Caz stares at the brown doors, confused. When the doors spread apart, he takes a leap back, tugging me with him.

"We're going in *that*?" he exclaims.

"Yes, and it'll be fine, I promise." I release his hand and go for the doors, pressing my back to one side to keep them open.

He studies the silver walls and mirrors inside the elevator then enters with tense shoulders. I walk in and stand next to him as a woman boards with us. Caz presses his body to the back corner of the elevator, glaring a hole into the back of the woman's head. I notice him reach for the inside of his coat, but before he can, I grip his hand.

"What should we have for dinner?" I ask, and he drops his eyes to mine, frowning. When he sees the warning in my eyes, his shoulders relax a bit, but that doesn't stop him from staring at the woman.

I fight a smile as he says, "Not sure."

"You should dry Mandina's!" the woman insists, turning halfway to eye me. I smell wine on her breath as she leans in a little closer. "Me and my husband went last night—incredible! The shrimp linguini and garlic bread are the *perfect* combination."

"Thank you." I smile at her. "I'll have to check it out."

When the elevator stops on floor three, she waves at us and trots off. As the doors come together again, closing us in, Caz expels a long-winded breath.

"I will never understand why you're so eager to talk to strangers," he mumbles.

"It's common courtesy. And don't be so nervous," I tell him as the elevator rises again.

"Why couldn't she wait her turn to get on?"

"There are no turns for the elevator unless it's already packed," I say, laughing. "Anyone can get on if there's enough space."

"Such strange customs."

The elevator stops, and the doors groan a bit as they open. "Come on. This is our floor." I step out, marching down the green carpeted hall to room 412.

Relief sinks in as we enter the room. We're safe, if only for now. I flip a switch, and the darkness is replaced with dim, gold lights. A king-sized bed is pressed against one of the walls, the headboard black and upholstered. The curtains are black as well, a sheer ivory one behind it. This particular hotel has been around for one-hundred-twenty years, and I gather that by the smell of old carpet and the undertone of cigarettes, though this is now a non-smoking hotel.

I set my suitcase aside, and Caz dumps his on the floor, walking through the room to survey it.

"How long do we stay here?" he inquires.

"Just one night. I googled the Yakaree place, and it's not far from here."

"You *what?*" he asks, confused.

"I searched for information on my phone. Anyway, her shop is only a mile from this hotel."

Caz maneuvers to the window, pushing one of the thick curtains aside with a finger. As he peers out, studying his surroundings, he asks, "What are we to do if she's not willing to help us?"

I sit on the edge of the bed, huffing. "I…really don't have an answer for that." Then I chew on my thumbnail because the question taunts me. What *are* we going to do if this woman doesn't help us? Where do we go from here? Do we just keep running and hiding, hoping Decius can't get to us? Because that won't work. We can only run for so long. There is a chance we can return to Vakeeli together, but there's also a possibility that we'll be killed as soon as we land with Decius drifting around.

"Oi."

I look up, and Caz is watching me, his brows slightly pinched together. He walks my way, slipping out of his coat and dropping to one knee before me. "Let's take our minds off the negative. This would be a good time for me to tap in with Cerberus, see what he and my clan are up to. Will you show me how you did it with Silvera?"

I smile up at him as he offers his hands for me to take.

"Are you trying to distract me?" I ask, rising with him as he tugs on my fingers.

"I am. Is it working?"

"It is."

He walks around the bed, one of my hands clasped in his, and sits in a large, cushioned chair in the corner. He clutches my waist, hauling me down on his lap, and I yelp then laugh as he wraps his arms around my middle.

"So, what did you do first?" he asks after laying a kiss on my jawline.

"Well, the first time it happened, I was thinking about you."

He grins. "About me, eh?"

I playfully roll my eyes. "Don't get a big head. I was just worried about you."

"Couldn't get me off your mind, could you?" I hear the humor in his voice. "Don't worry. I couldn't get you off my mind either." He holds me tighter, stroking his thumb over the flesh on the back of my hand.

"Anyway, when I tapped in with Silvera, I felt this cool draft. And then my surroundings changed. I was back in Vakeeli, mentally but not physically."

"Okay…"

"But the second time I did it, I went some place quieter, and I could control it. I just closed my eyes and thought of Silvera. Let's just try it."

"Okay." He sits against the back of the seat, and I turn my head, watching him inhale and exhale with his eyes closed. His eyeballs move behind his eyelids, and then he's cracking a smile.

"Hey, boy," he murmurs. "It's just me. You behaving yourself?"

"Can you see through him?" I whisper.

Caz nods, eyes still closed, then he grabs my hand. When he does, a coolness rushes through me, from my head to my toes. I close my eyes, and the first thing I feel is the cool air of Blackwater along with a light mist. I hear the sounds of the ocean, the rustling of the tree leaves, and the swishing of tall blades of grass. And through someone else's eyes, I spot Blackwater Manor. The dark, pointed roof is hidden behind thick, gray clouds. Mist dampens the ivy that trails across the front and wraps around the corners. Normally, there are sconces burning outside the castle, but not today. The house simply sits there, muted and empty.

When I look down, there's something bloody on the ground —a white rabbit with beady silver eyes. Two puncture wounds are on its bleeding neck, one of its hind legs mangled and broken. I look to my left, and Cerberus is right next to me, his snout in the air as he sniffs.

"I'm not there, boy, but I'm with ya." Cerberus whines and sits on his hind. "Oi, don't start your whining. You and Silvera been hunting? You better be sharing with her. I know how selfish you can be."

I have the urge to open my eyes and look at Caz, but I don't. I'm afraid I'll lose this moment, but I admit it is cute hearing him speak to Cerberus like he's his child. Perhaps he is. His little fur baby.

"That's a good boy. Do me a favor, eh? Take me to the family."

At that, Cerberus growls and rises to all fours again. He huffs and backs away, then he's howling at the sky. Caz stiffens beneath me, as if he's been struck by a bolt of lightning. Still, I keep my eyes closed.

"Go to them, boy. Show me where they are," Caz commands.

Cerberus runs off, and Silvera is hot on his trail. They dash toward the castle, but as they approach, I notice the door is wide open and it's completely dark inside. Cerberus stops, refusing to go in.

"Something's not right," Caz whispers. "What's...what's happened? Where is everyone?"

Another whine from Cerberus.

"Cerberus, I need you to take me in there, boy. Show me where everyone is."

Cerberus grunts, backing away, and Silvera watches him turn his back to the door before focusing on it herself.

"Go, girl," I tell her, and she does, but not without caution. She enters the mansion with her head tucked, taking slow steps through the foyer. She passes Caz's office and it's drowning in darkness, not a single candle burning. He's right. Something isn't right.

As Silvera goes deeper into the castle, I realize none of the lights are on, and it's so cold I can see her breath. A noise sounds behind me, and Silvera looks back at Cerberus who has gathered some courage and is following her lead. Silvera keeps going until she's rounded a corner and entered a large room. It's the main area—where sofas, tables, and extra chairs are for seating. Juniper explained to me that it was where family was supposed to hang out, but they never spent much time in there because they were all so busy. There's a fireplace ahead, smoke tendrils wafting out of it, like the fire died not too long ago.

Then, there's a crackling noise. Silvera whips her gaze to the right, and what I see next causes my stomach to drop and my heart to pound so hard and fast it hurts.

CHAPTER 34
CAZ

It takes a few seconds for me to digest the scene before me. For just a moment, I imagine that I'm dreaming, or that Cerberus is making this all up in his head...but he's not.

My clan floats in the air, wrapped in thick black vines with sharp points similar to barbed wire. Their eyes are closed, their skin gray, and their lips blue. Dark veins crawl up their skin, just like the veins I had, and my breath falters. All of them are here—Maeve, Juniper, Killian, Rowan. Even Della, my housemaiden.

A blue sheen of light blocks one half of the room in front of them, and when Cerberus lunges at it, trying to break through it, he yelps. I wince, feeling the sting of it on my skin. It's a barrier, keeping them contained.

A deep laugh erupts in the room, and my clan goes flying toward one of the walls. Their bodies merge to it, and ice trickles from their heads to their feet, wrapping them up in glacial cocoons. Cerberus barks, and I try speaking to him, but I can't wrap my mind around this. My clan should have been safe. I thought Decius couldn't hurt them. Shouldn't The Council be able to stop this? The Regals? *Someone?*

A silhouette appears from a corner, and when he steps into the minimal light from the windows, he sneers down at Cerberus. His black cloak drifts behind him, dragging across the ice shards on the floor. His skin is white like snow, lips a deep purple, and his eyes are just as black as his clothing, not a pupil in sight. He snaps his fingers and my clan—*my family*—is completely buried beneath the ice.

"No!" I yell.

Cerberus growls at him as he steps forward, and I don't need to say his name in order to know who he is.

Decius.

"You send your wolves to do the dirty work?" Decius stops in the middle of the room, studying Cerberus and then Silvera. "Rather smart, actually—these wolves. Your mother was always three steps ahead. Not for long though."

I clench my fist on my lap, squeezing my eyes shut tighter.

"She knew the Gilded, Mythic, and Tethered cannot harm Tethered animals."

He walks closer, and Cerberus' growl deepens. Silvera snaps at him, daring him to come closer and baring her teeth to prove her point. I wish they'd both attack this fucker, eat his damn face off and be done with him, but something's stopping them. I can sense Cerberus' anger. I can feel him wanting to rip this man to shreds, but not being able to do it. What's stopping him?

"But what your mother forgot is that I'm no ordinary Tether," Decius goes on, pacing the space in front of the wolves. "I was an original and one of the most powerful, might I add. And these wolves? They're *useless* without their owners in the same universe."

He raises a hand in the air, and a tightness builds in my chest. Cerberus stumbles on his feet, choking for breath. He wheezes painfully, small whimpers slipping through as he collapses on the floor. *No.* He's stopped his lungs. I feel his invisible hands wrapping around them from the inside and clutching tight. My wolf can't breathe, and Decius' unseeable grip is growing tighter around his lungs.

"Stop!" I shout, but I'm breathless, feeling all the pain Cerberus endures. And I'm aware Decius can't hear me, but he knows I'm here. He knows.

Silvera tries lunging at Decius, but she can't break through whatever barrier he's created, which only makes her angrier. Her barks boom through the room, but Decius keeps his focus on Cerberus, glaring right into his eyes as he lowers to a squat. "Do you feel this?" he rasps, a sneer toying at the edges of his lips. "If you don't return and fulfill your end of the bargain, I will end your wolf, your entire family, and then I will come for Willow."

Just when I think Cerberus won't be able to take another breath, Decius rises to a stand and backs away. Cerberus whimpers as he staggers to all fours again. When he realizes that he was attacked, he barks viciously at Decius. Because that's my wolf. He never backs down. But I need him to right now. I never thought I'd see the day. He has to go. I can't lose him.

"Go into hiding, Cerberus. *Now*," I demand.

Cerberus prowls the room, snarling at the gloating Decius, eyes locked on him.

"I said *now*, Cerberus!"

My words bellow inside me, reverberating, and Cerberus finally does as he's told, rushing out of the castle and toward the fields. Silvera rushes out right behind him, and they sprint toward the forest.

When I can't take it, I open my eyes and suck in a sharp breath. My hand presses to my chest as the oxygen sinks back into my lungs.

"Hey, hey." Willow clasps my face in her hands. "Look at me, Caz. Breathe. *Breathe*, you're fine." She holds my face tighter, looking deep into my eyes.

"He—he has my family, Willow! You saw it! He fucking has them!" She climbs off my lap, and I shoot out of the chair to pace the room.

"I know, but we're going to get them out of it!"

"He's going to kill them if I don't fulfill the bargain. We need to get back! I—I have to. I can't let them die. Not for me."

She watches me rush to the window to snatch the curtain open, and after a few silent seconds she asks, "What bargain did you make with him?"

I turn toward her slowly when the desolation in her voice rings clear. *That's right.* I didn't tell her what we'd agreed on. I hadn't planned on telling her because I didn't think I'd have to commit to it after landing on Earth. I didn't think it would matter, but I was wrong. So, so wrong.

"Is this about that telepathic message you tried to send before Beatrix sent us to Earth? Something about me living my life and forgetting about you?"

I drop my gaze, working hard to swallow. "Yes." I can't lie to her. She already knows. I see it on her face.

She takes a step closer, squaring her shoulders. "What was the bargain, Caz?"

"Willow, I didn't think…I didn't think I had a choice. I was willing to do *anything* to save you."

"Tell me," she pleads, eyes glistening.

I focus on her brown eyes, and even while knowing I'm going to break her heart, I say it. "I told him that I'd let him take my Tether if he promised to leave you out of it."

Her brows furrow, and the sharpness in her shoulders dulls. "You were going to give up, is what you mean."

"No, I wasn't giving up! I felt like it was the only thing I could do so that you and everyone else remained safe!"

"Okay," she breathes, holding her hands out to level the tension. "I can understand why you did that. You felt there was no choice. I understand…but you don't want that anymore, right? You aren't trying to go back to Vakeeli just to give yourself to him, are you?"

"I wasn't before because I thought we were safe and had a fighting chance, but I have to do something now, Willow. He has my family! I can't just stay here while he torments them."

"You promised me you'd *fight*," she counters, voice cracking. "Giving yourself to him is *not* fighting, Caz! We can still make this work without you running to him and handing over your life! He's only trying to scare you!"

"Do you think I wanted this?" I snap, stepping closer. "I *never* wanted *anyone* I care about to suffer, yet you all are and it's because of me!"

"It's not because of you, Caz! It's because of the stupid Regals for creating the Cold Tether!"

"Look, we need to get back at once, Willow. If I don't, he'll kill them. I can't let that happen. He was waiting for me to show up. He knew I would find a way to check in on them, or that I'd return somehow. He's probably tracking us right now."

She grimaces. "You are out of your fucking mind if you think I've done all of this just for you to die anyway! If that's the case, I may as well go back home and leave you here!"

"Willow, you see where we are," I plead. "There is no winning this."

"We haven't even gone to see the Effie woman yet! She could have answers, Caz! She could help us, or at least find someone who can!"

"And if she doesn't?" I demand, and her eyes grow wide, watering again. "We must face the reality here, Willow. I hate it as much as you do, but if this woman can't get us back, if she can't help us, I have to take Decius' bargain. I will *not* let him have you, my family, my wolf, or *anyone* in my clan. He wants me. He can't gain full control of Vakeeli without *my* energy and *my* blood. If that means sacrificing myself so you all live, then I'm going to do it. Do you understand?"

Her bottom lip quivers, and as badly as she wants to cry, she doesn't. Instead, she steps away and turns for her tote bag on the bed. She snatches it up and stomps to the door.

"Where are you going?" I ask as she swings the door open.

"I just...I need a moment to myself right now."

She starts to walk out but stops dead in her tracks, swinging around to face me again. "I don't know this side of you, Caspian," she says with a tight frown. "I get that you're afraid for your family and for me—and trust me, I am too—but you're letting him win. And I know I haven't known you long, but from all that I've seen firsthand, you don't just let others beat you down and use your weaknesses against you. You'd take the power back and find a way to put an end to all of this so that it *never* happens again." Her eyes search my face while hers crumples with anguish. An ache builds in my chest, so raw and intense that I want to drop to my knees and cry. I feel her. I hurt right along with her. "You think I don't know that you want to kill yourself?" she asks in a near whisper. "I saw it the day I walked into the office when you had that gun pointed at your head. Decius is handing you that loaded gun right now, and you're just going to take it. I won't stand for it."

She holds my eyes until a tear skids down her cheek. Angrily, she swipes it away with the back of her arm, gives me her back, and walks out of the room. I close my eyes and sink into the chair after the door slams.

CHAPTER 35
WILLOW

THE HOTEL LOBBY HAS DOUBLED IN BODIES AND noise since we arrived. I've only been to New Orleans once before, and that was for a bachelorette party for one of Lou Ann's clients. I hardly knew the bride-to-be, and I remember only going because all I could think about was drinking. I admit, since having Caz around, I haven't felt the urge to drown myself in liquor. He's been my new addiction—the feel of his arms wrapped around me, hot kisses on my skin, and his presence completing me.

But I suppose that's what happens when you become addicted to something...eventually you'll have to kick the habit to the curb...or perhaps you develop a new addiction.

When Caz and I first arrived, there were only a few squatters lingering around the bar. Now, there are dozens of people in groups, clinking glasses after making toasts, or men cursing at the sports game on TV.

I scan the bar, complete with a dozen wooden stools, and

spot an empty one toward the end. I push through the rowdy crowd until I finally reach the empty seat. When I sit, I let out a loud sigh and focus on the lineup of liquor on the glass shelves. One of the two bartenders comes in my direction, a woman with pink hair. She's petite, wearing a black camisole and leather jeans. Sleeves of tattoos embellish both her arms and even crawl up to her neck, and the neon red sign above glints off her septum piercing.

"You alone tonight, hun?" she asks, eyeing me as she dumps an empty glass of ice into the sink.

"Yes."

"How much you plan on drinking?" She sets the glass upside down while I hesitate with my response. I can't tell if she's serious or not. When a slow smile spreads across her lips, I relax. "I'm kidding," she laughs. "I don't give a damn how much you drink. Just make sure you have a ride beforehand, 'kay? I've seen too many chicks come in here, get drunk, and not have a ride. Then I have to shoo the drunk guys off and make sure she gets home safely. Call it the angel in me."

"Ah. Well, I should be okay," I tell her. "I'm staying in this hotel. As long as I don't fall and bust a knee or something, I'm good."

"Say no more. What can I get you?"

I request a gin and tonic, and she nods, turning away to get to work. "Want a tab?" she asks once she's concocted the drink.

"Please." Because I'll definitely need it tonight. I pick up the drink and take a long swig. The alcohol burns going down, bringing on that delicious heat I crave when I'm stressed. I release a slow sigh. Yeah, I'll need about four more of these before going back to the room to face Caz.

I can't believe Caz is so willing to give up—to give it all to

Decius. I get he wants to protect his family, protect *me*, but what's the use in us doing all this (running to Virginia to talk to Phil, coming to NOLA to find some mysterious woman, getting nearly attacked by a cobra and God knows what other vessels are on the way) if he's just going to go back to Vakeeli and turn himself in to Decius? It makes no sense, and the thought of it makes me take a bigger swallow.

The bartender slides me another glass, and I look into her eyes. "Seems like you need it. Name's Noni. Call for me if you need me, babe."

I smile at her as she turns to assist someone else. The doors of the hotel swing open and more people file into the bar, meeting with friends, laughing, living their lives. It's all so simple for them. Simple human beings doing simple, simple things. Eating hot wings and guzzling beer. Sipping colorful, blended drinks with silly smiles on their faces. I face forward again, sipping the remainder of my first drink.

I can't help wondering why I'm so upset. It can't just be about Caz and his willingness to turn himself over. No, it's something deeper, and I stew in it, sipping several times until it dawns on me.

After Warren went missing and before meeting Caz, my life had no purpose. Sure, I worked with Lou Ann, and I hung out with Faye, but what was my purpose, really? All my life, I've felt like I don't belong here, and after meeting Caz, I understand why.

Now that I've met him, my life has meaning again. There's someone to share my time with, someone I'm unconditionally, irrevocably *in love* with, no matter how hard I try *not* to be. In my hands is someone who I'm willing to go to the ends of the earth—or any universe—for, and if I lose him, what will be left of me? There's a possibility my brother is in Vakeeli, yes. But if Caz dies, how will I ever find Warren? Would I even want to, after all this? Or will I end up like Phil, trapped in a psychiatric detention center, thinking of all the what ifs?

That's why I'm angry. Because the one man I've fallen madly in love with may not be mine forever, and to be frank, it fucking sucks. Everyone I love either leaves or is forced to go. I didn't ask for this life, but I'm putting up a fight for it, damn it, and so should he.

I finish off my first drink and dive right into the second. After a large gulp, I take my phone out of my bag and send Faye a text.

> Made it to NOLA. Mad at Caz.

Faye responds almost immediately with:

> Why? Did he try to kill someone AGAIN?

> No, but he's contemplating getting himself killed just to stop Decius.

> Ugh. Seriously, he is super dramatic and complicated

I chew on my bottom lip, my thumb hovering over the keyboard.

> If that's what he wants fine. Whatever. If I didn't love him it would make letting go so much easier.

Faye isn't so quick to respond this time, and I keep reading my message, slowly regretting sending it, until her conversation bubble appears to show she's typing. Her message pops up:

> He's yours, Willow, and he needs you.

> But if you don't want that life, don't be in it. Find a way for him to go back and be done with it. You don't have to subject yourself to that kind of life if you don't want it. It'll be hard, I'm sure, but it's possible.

I read her message several times, blinking my tears away. God. I have never felt so much aching in my chest. My heart yearns for this man, to rush up to our hotel room and collapse in his arms. But a part of me also wants to run away because Faye is right. I didn't ask for *any* of this. Why should we be Tethered? Why does our love have to be so damn complicated?

I feel warmth on my back as someone hovers behind me. Arms wrap around me from behind and draw me back so that my back is touching his chest. The arms mold around me, as they've done many times before, and when I smell him, a sigh escapes me. He somehow still smells like Vakeeli, like it lingers in his skin and hair—ocean air, salt, and a little bloom.

He drops his chin to my shoulder, and I shut the screen of my phone off, melting in his arms. *Ugh.* Who am I kidding? I can't run away. This is what I crave, what I want most. Even now, I'm supposed to be mad at him, but how can I be? His arms are where I belong. I'm centered within them and don't want to be anywhere else.

"I'm sorry, Willow." His deep voice falls into my ear, sending goosebumps crawling up my arm. He plants a kiss on my cheek. "I'm very sorry."

I remain quiet, staring at the ice in my glass tumbler. "Should I just go back home and forget about all this?"

"Absolutely not." He steps to my side, his body still close to mine. He tips my chin with his forefinger, and I carry my eyes up to his. "I'm fighting," he assures me. "I panicked about my family, but it was only for a moment. They mean a lot to me. My wolf. Blackwater. All of it matters to me much more than I realized." He strokes my chin. "But *you* also matter."

"I get why you want to sacrifice yourself, but I don't want Decius to take you, Caz."

"What if it comes down to it? What if it's the only way to save you all?"

"If we have to run to Selah ourselves, we will. I don't care how we do it, but it *can* be done. Decius isn't unstoppable. As long as we're together and fighting, we're safe."

"You're right." He drops his head, dark lashes touching his cheekbones. "If I can get back to Vakeeli and send a contact to The Council, perhaps they'll give me another spell of protection."

"Yes, like they did last time," I return, hopeful. I'm glad this is where the conversation is going. Filled with hope and tenacity.

"But something tells me that as soon as Decius senses I'm back in Vakeeli, *and* if the Council doesn't get to me in time, I'm out of luck again."

"Maybe Beatrix can give us something."

"Maybe." He takes my hand, wrapping both of his around it and bringing my knuckles to his lips. He kisses them as he looks into my eyes. "I won't give up."

"Promise?"

"With my whole heart, I promise."

Satisfied, I pull my hand away and lace my arms around the back of his neck. He plants a kiss on top of my head just as someone yells, "Get a room!"

I laugh as Caz finds the culprit and grimaces at him. "They're just joking," I laugh. "Just people being drunk and stupid."

"We have a room," Caz says. "What he said doesn't even make any sense."

"Oh, boy. Here we go."

"What? It doesn't, not if he's speaking literally."

I fight a laugh as I pull my arms away and pick up my drink, downing the rest of it. As I fish into my purse for some cash, someone walking past roughly bumps into Caz. Caz grunts as he catches himself before stumbling into me, and the person stomps away.

"Oi! Jackass! You just bumped into me!" he shouts at the man's back.

I look past Caz at the man who is rushing through the bar in a brown hoodie. He doesn't look back as he leaves the hotel, and I frown, watching him go, and then there's that itch on the back of my neck again. I give it a scratch before placing cash on the counter.

"I hate this world," Caz grumbles. "Can we get back to the room now? Prepare for tomorrow?"

"Yes. Let's go." He helps me off the stool, leading the way out of the bar and toward the elevators.

"I didn't take the elevator down, by the way," he says. "Couldn't figure it out, so I took the stairs."

"Did you really?" I feel that annoying itch on the back of my neck again, and when I press the button for the elevator, Caz rubs the area.

"Why do you keep scratching there?" He pushes some of my locs out of the way. "Leave it be. You're causing a rash."

I rub the irritated patch of skin as the elevator doors spring open and we walk inside. As we ride up to our floor, a pounding builds in my head, and then the elevator comes to an abrupt stop. Ice splinters up the walls, cracking the mirrors and freezing the buttons. Caz grips my hand, pulling me into him and holding me close.

"What's happening?" I gasp.

Caz says nothing as the elevator darkens, minus a flickering light above. The elevator begins to rattle, then it lurches and causes us to buckle, going at a speed that's much too fast. Caz pulls me even closer as a voice croaks, "You will be mine, Caspian Harlow."

Decius.

The elevator continues to rattle a few seconds longer and then it just...*stops.* The ice fades, and the elevator illuminates with the original LED lighting. The cracks in the mirror are gone, and the buttons are as they were.

When the doors separate, dumping us onto our floor, we hurry to the room and lock the door behind us, though I'm not quite sure that'll save us.

"He's found another vessel," Caz pants, peering out the window again.

"How do you know?"

"He's getting stronger. He's using something. Or *someone.* He has to be close."

I scratch my neck again then hiss when my nails break the skin. Caz rushes to me, pushing my locs out of the way again. He stiffens at my side. "Willow," he breathes.

"What? What is it?" I ask as he stares at the back of my neck.

"How do you take pictures on you cellphone thing?"

I dig into my tote, fishing it out, showing him how, then dropping it in his palm. He snaps a picture of the back of my neck. When he brings it down and I see the picture on the screen, my breath stalls because it's no longer a rash on the back of my neck. They've turned into veins.

"Does this mean he can get into our heads again?"

Caz works his jaw, head shaking. "Do you think we should go to the Effie woman tonight?" he asks. "If all these people are partying, surely, she's up too."

"We can try, but the hours for her shop said one to five p.m."

"Sure, but that doesn't mean she isn't there. Look, if he's found a bigger vessel, there's no way of me knowing it. A snake is easy, but if it's a person, it could be *anyone,* and if they capture me, that'll give him way more energy. He'll take us right back to Vakeeli, back in his grasp, I'm sure of it."

I slide the straps of my tote onto my shoulder. "Let's go by her shop and see what we can find."

Caz has his gun in hand before I even turn for the door.

CHAPTER 36
WILLOW

YAKAREE IS ON THE CUSP OF CENTRAL CITY AND THE Central Business District. Being only a five-minute drive (and fifteen-minute walk) from the French Quarter, I can understand how this Effie woman remains in business. She's not entirely on the bad side of the city, but she's close, and the location gives any tourist an excuse to be adventurous without crossing too far into crime-ridden territory.

Night has fallen, the autumn air cool, spilling through the slit windows of the vehicle. I park along the curb in front of her shop and tighten my grip on the steering wheel.

Effie's shop is a tiny place with a brown exterior. Large bold letters spelling out Yakaree are painted at the top of the shop, and pillar candles flicker on the sill from the inside. Iron bars line both windows, as if imprisoning anyone who dares enter, and a three-step stoop leads to a dingy black door that appears to have been knocked down and replaced too many times to count.

Caz stares at it, shaking his head furiously. "I gather nothing but bad energy from his place."

A silhouette moves past the window just as he says that, the shape of a woman with big, poofy hair who I *swear* has claws as she reaches for something in front of her.

I level my breathing, though I get the same bad vibe he does.

"You have your gun," I remind him, keeping my voice steady.

"My gun'll be useless if she's a vanisher," he reminds me.

Right. The vanishing Mythics. "Well let's hope she isn't one." I unclip my seatbelt as Caz pushes his door open. When I meet up to him, he keeps an eye of our surroundings. I take the three broken steps up, stopping at the door. "Ready?" I breathe.

Caz raises his gun to his chest, providing a simple nod.

There's a doorbell next to the door, and I jam my thumb down on it. The tiny house rings to life, chiming like church bells.

We wait for the door to be answered, but after a few seconds, nothing. I try the doorbell again, and this time I hear rapid footsteps moving throughout the shop.

Immediately, the door is snatched open, and a woman appears, her hair a voluminous snowy afro trailing all the way down to her waist. Her piercing ice-blue eyes narrow as she glares at me, her skin complexion similar to damp coffee grounds. Her eyes are blue and electrifying, quite similar to Caz's. Alluring and intimidating. She shifts her gaze to Caz, and before I can say a word, she lifts a flat palm in the air, blows dust into our faces, and everything fades to black.

CHAPTER 37
WILLOW

I OPEN MY EYES WITH A GROAN AND TRY TO SWALLOW, but my mouth and throat are so dry, it feels like the saliva is riding on sandpaper. I shift in the chair I'm on and jerk forward, realizing I've been restrained.

When I look down, I don't see anything wrapped around me —no rope or cords or chains. I try again, but my arms don't budge. There's something there though. I feel it constricting around my arms, pressing into my skin.

"What the hell?" I breathe, trying to move again and failing.

A deep groan rumbles next to me, and I look to my right at Caz. His head lifts, wisps of hair clinging to his damp forehead.

"Caz? You okay?" I whisper. Talking makes my mouth feel dryer.

He blinks a few times before finally focusing on me. He also tries moving out of his chair but is forced back into the seat.

"What the hell is going on?" he demands.

When he turns his head to look around, I do the same.

We're in a dark room with vintage floral wallpaper, minus one wall that has a mid-size mirror on it. The mirror's frame is intricately designed with a gold border. Candles flicker before it, plants surrounding it, alive and dead. I carry my gaze up, and instead of a ceiling, dead flower stems dangle from above.

Ahead of us is a two-top table, a round glass bowl in the center filled with Mardi Gras beads, and a container of strawberries. More candles are on the table, the wax from them dripping onto the aged wood. Just like Phil said, it smells of incense and a whisper of fish. The incense give off a sage and dragon's blood aroma, and I see them burning next to the mirror on a stand, small embers falling off and turning to ash on the floor. The fishy smell has me confused. I'm not sure where that's coming from, and I don't have much time to figure it out because a person appears at the opening behind the table. The woman who answered the door steps around the corner with her hands at her sides and her chin raised high.

I hold back a gasp as she makes her way toward the middle of the room, looking us over with piercing blue eyes. She wears dark colors like blacks and deep greens, and she's dressed in so many layers that I can't decipher what part of the outfit is what. A kimono, a corset, a camisole, waist beads, leggings beneath a billowy brown skirt. And her nails—I see why they looked like claws from her silhouette outside the window. They're long, stiletto-shaped, and painted a striking silver.

She's quiet as she strides around our chairs, her head cocked, studying nearly every detail of us. Then, finally, she speaks.

"You're Cold Tethered." Her voice is soft but husky, and she has an accent similar to Alora's.

I look to Caz, who is glaring at the woman with a rapidly

ticking jaw. His eyes move to the right at a shelf, and I look with him. His gun is there, not too far out of reach. If only we could move, he could grab it and use it.

"Let us go," he demands.

The woman clasps her hands in front of her. "You angry little boy," she murmurs, more to herself than to him. "How did you find me?" She swings her eyes to mine, awaiting my answer.

"Research," I reply softly.

"Hmm." A smirk curls at the edges of her lips. "Research," she repeats, then she moves across the room, taking down a wide brown chest from the shelf.

"So, you've found Yakaree. Well done." She opens the chest, taking out a silver dagger with a tip painted blood red. "But you shouldn't have come here. I'm not quite sure how a Cold Tethered couple has made it to Earth *together*, but whatever issues you carry with you, I want *nothing* to do with them." Then, in the blink of an eye, she's standing behind Caz, pressing the blade of the dagger to his throat. No, she did not walk, or skip, or hop to him. She moved from one side of the room to the other, faster than I could blink.

"No!" I scream.

"Fuck," Caz croaks as she presses the blade deeper into his throat. "I knew she'd be a vanisher."

"So. You're the Vakeeli born," she says breathily. "Good to know. It'll do me good killing you first."

"Wait!" I call just as she presses the blade deeper, drawing blood on his throat. "*Please*—look, we're not here to cause trouble. We just have questions. Yes, it is true, a Cold Tethered couple isn't supposed to be on Earth, right? It's likely *never* happened before, and you're probably confused and don't want to deal with it, but I can explain, okay? A Mythic sent us here. She helped us escape Decius before he could steal our Tether."

The woman's icy eyes slide to mine, but she doesn't remove the blade. "Decius," she hisses.

"Yes—him. He's after us, and we need a way back so we can get to The Council. We were just hoping you could open a portal, take us to them. They provided a way to protect us from Decius before, and if we can just get to them—"

The woman raises a hand, and relief sets in when she snatches the knife away from Caz's throat. Blood drips to his collarbone, and he grimaces as she walks around him.

"Decius is after you?" she asks.

"Yes."

"And who is the Mythic that sent you here?"

"A woman named Beatrix."

"So why did you pop up here with a weapon? Clearly to hurt me, no?" The woman's eyes slide to Caz. "Speak, boy," she demands.

"We're not here to harm you. However, the name of your shop is the reason I brought a gun with me," Caz states. "My mother told me about the term *yakaree*. It's a word used to cause someone's demise. You lure people here and create their downfall. I was only preparing for any tricks you had."

At that, she smirks. "Tethered descendant of Lehvine. Such a bullheaded man."

She looks at me. "Daughter and one of the twins of Jesha and Valkee."

"So, you've studied the history of the Tether. You know all the original Tethered and their children, I reckon?" Caz asks. "That means you can help us, correct?"

The woman waves a dismissive hand. "No, it does not."

"Then how do you know so much about Vakeeli?" Caz counters.

The woman raises her chin at him and then she snaps her fingers, and the invisible restraints on us fall away.

"Because I am Korah, Regal of land, air, and all living things of Vakeeli *except* the Tethered."

CHAPTER 38

CAZ

"I quite favored Jesha and Valkee. They kept to themselves. Stayed out of trouble. Took care of their territories, which I appreciated because I worked hard on those lands. A shame Decius got to them." Korah the Regal speaks, but I can't wrap my mind around what's going on. How is this possible? All this time, the rumors said she was hiding in Vakeeli. Many said she'd created her own island that was not made for man and was living on it, but she's here.

It makes sense, the power she uses to send people to Vakeeli, if only for a moment, and it explains how she can travel through universes without pain or weakness. No Mythic can do that. It'd require far too much energy, but a Regal can do anything. Their energy is strong enough to split mountains and wipe away the existence of men with a single snap of their fingers.

She hands Willow an odd-shaped berry and tells her, "Looks like a regular Earth strawberry, but I only disguise it as one. Eat it. It'll quench some of the thirst." Then she offers one to me, but I turn it down, though I am thirsty.

Instead, I get up from my chair and walk across the room, collecting my gun from the shelf.

"Do you plan on shooting me with that *thing*? A Vakeeli weapon?" Korah asks. I turn, and her eyes are trained on me.

"Straight from Blackwater," I answer, tucking it into the inside pocket of my coat. "And no, I don't plan on shooting you, though I'm sure you could dodge a bullet if you needed to."

"Sure, I could. But do you really think an item like *that* will kill Decius?"

"No. But it'll protect us for now from whatever vessel he uses on Earth."

"Ah yes, vessels." Korah runs a finger over the wooden table next to her. "Have you encountered any yet?"

"One. A snake," Willow answers, then visibly shivers.

"When was this?" Korah asks, tapping the table with one of her claw-like nails.

"Last night," Willow responds.

"There will be another soon. If there's one thing I remember about Decius, he becomes very impatient when he's close to his targets."

Korah sighs and faces the table, and I wait for her to speak— to address this colossal elephant in the room about Decius—but when she picks up the container, opening it and plucking out a berry for herself, I can't help the question that slips out of me. "Why are *you* here?"

She looks me up and down. "In my own house?"

"On *Earth*."

She bites into the berry, and juices trickle from the corners of her mouth. "I'm certain you heard the rumors while you were in Vakeeli. What are you, around one hundred and twenty years old? Yes, about right. Anyway, if you've heard them, then you know about Decius overthrowing Selah."

"So, you just left her there? Didn't even try to set her free?" I ask.

Korah stands tall. "I warned Selah not to create the Tethered. Hassha and I both did, but she didn't listen to us. Now she's paying for that mistake."

"Why didn't you want her to make them?" asks Willow.

"Because we knew it would disrupt so many things. Creating land, animals, and other creatures was simple. They can't overthrow us because they have no mind of their own. But creating beings who can think for themselves, and who also carried more energy from Regals, well...it was bound to go horribly wrong. Selah gave the original Tethered too much freedom—too much *power*. She thought they'd all worship her and stay in their place. She was wrong, and now they're all dead, and they continue to die because of it. All but one, anyway."

"Isn't there a way to wake her up? We heard that she's the only way to defeat Decius," Willow goes on. She cuts her eyes at me, and I'm glad she doesn't mention that it will require *me* to wake her. If this woman really is Korah the Regal, she either knows for a fact who I am, or she has another solution to waking her sister that she hasn't tried yet.

"I don't know anything about that, so I can't help you." Korah moves across the room, plucking items from the shelves and placing them on the center of her table. Feathers, jewels, rocks. Pointless things. "I will be having after-hours customers soon, so you need to leave and never come back."

"So that's it?" I step closer to her. "You're just going to send us off to die like the rest of them? Why are you so afraid of him?"

She whirls around to face me, and her eyes glow an electrifying purple. Ah. There she is. Korah the Regal with her energy brimming to the surface. She narrows her eyes as she points a stern finger in my face. "I am *not* afraid of him. I no longer wanted to tolerate him, or the disgusting place Vakeeli has become. You've seen it. Look at you. I can feel it all over you—the agony that place has put upon you. You reek of it, you sad little boy. Why would *anyone* ever want to go back to that retched world, especially someone like me? Someone they'd hunt down just to harness my power?"

I clench my jaw, refusing to look away, even though I feel prickles in my brain, like she's prodding it with her sharp nails, going through the crevices and searching for all my truths.

"I have family there. I'm monarch of Blackwater," I inform her.

She scoffs, turning away again. "Look, you may cherish your precious Blackwater and all its...well, *black* water, but I don't care. I can't help you, end of story. I suggest you stay on Earth and keep killing whatever vessels come after you. That would be much easier than going back. Decius will likely tire of it eventually...at least until you both die and a new Cold Tether couple is reborn."

"And if he doesn't?" I counter. "If he finds a way here?"

"He won't." She peers at me over her shoulder. "He has no way here unless it's through corrupt vessels, I and Hassha made sure of it. And with the corrupt, I cannot control that because I don't use my energy for wicked things. Only for good. Now *leave*."

"Please." Willow's voice is faint, but we both hear it. I know

Korah hears it because she lowers her head, hiding her eyes as she arranges the items neatly on the table. "I get why you don't like what Vakeeli has become. Trust me, I understand it more than anyone. There's violence everywhere, darkness, and hardly any regard for women. I can't imagine what people would do if they got a hold of you. They'd have no respect for all you've done, all you've created, and that's not fair seeing as you gave them so much to live with. But…I sense there is a reason you left instead of destroying it all. You still have faith in Vakeeli, just like me and Caz do."

Korah's shoulders tense.

"Caz has a family there, and in the short amount of time I've been there, his family has become mine too. Plus, my twin brother…he may still be alive somewhere in Vakeeli, and I would hate to not find out if he's still alive all because Decius decided to kill us. And Caz…he's trying to make Vakeeli a better place. He and the queen of Vanora are. There are people who want to make it a good world again, but we can't do that if we don't put an end to Decius and all this fear. So, I'm *begging* you, Korah. Will you please help us?"

The room falls into a fizzled silence. One of the candles crackles behind me as I focus on Willow. Tears have lined her eyes, but she blinks them away, awaiting Korah's response. I have no idea how she can still remain so hopeful after being flat-out rejected.

With an exasperated sigh, Korah turns her head and faces Willow. "It is your empathy that will help this sad boy," she proclaims.

Love of Vakeeli. If she calls me *sad* or *boy* one more time…

Willow smiles at her with shimmering eyes.

"Look, I can't promise that I can help you defeat Decius. I

haven't been in Vakeeli in over four centuries, so my energy is not what it once was."

"Well tell us how to kill him," I insist. "There has to be a way. He may be powerful, but he's not immortal. The other Tethers died because of him. That means he can die too; it may just require more of something."

Korah walks past me to get to a shelf, taking down a thick green tome. It's bound in leather and engraved with her name on the front cover. She carries it to the table and opens it, spreading the yellowing pages and revealing paragraphs of cursive script. None of it is written in modern word. It's all in ancient Vakeeli symbols and letters. I only know some of it, but not all, and I wish I'd paid attention more with those tutors Magnus hired instead of picking fights with them.

"Hassha and I found out the wood of a Trench tree doused in Regal blood can weaken him. It's why the Trench has practically become a wasteland. He tried burning all the trees, but after so many years, I believe there are still some that can be found. Shape the wood into a spear or any weapon with a pointed tip, have Hassha add a little blood, stab him with it, and he will weaken—possibly even die. We tried it once and it kept him down for centuries, but somehow, he returned. By the time we realized it, our lives had changed, and we didn't want to deal with Selah's creatures anymore, so we went into hiding. Wood from a Trench tree could work because it's his origins— he was born there and was overseer of The Trench. It's where his roots are, you see, so anything from there has a possibility of defeating him if mixed with *our* blood. We are the creators of Vakeeli, and what we create, we can also destroy."

"Sure, all right. I just can't believe you haven't gone back for your sister. She's your family," I mutter.

"My sister and I didn't want to die for Selah's mistakes," she snaps, fixing her gaze on me. "We told her to test it out with one of the Tethered, not run off and make *seven* of those abominations. She'd drained all of her energy creating the Tethered, and we knew it was going to take years for her to gather that much energy back." She looks between us. "No offense. You two seem decent enough."

"Do you think Selah is still alive?" Willow asks.

Korah gives her a funny look—one I can't discern. "I *know* she's still alive."

I consider telling her that I know where Selah is with what The Council told me with Inferno Isle, but I'm not sure it would matter. I'm the only one who can awaken her—whether Decius is alive or not. If she senses there's another way of getting to Selah *without* having to interfere with Decius, she may not be so willing to help us end him, and I can't risk that, so I step away, studying the mirror on the wall instead.

"Is this where you create portals?" I ask.

"It is. If you must go back, there is a possibility I can send you to Hassha. Like I said, my energy is weaker now that I'm on Earth. I'm not sure my blood will help you defeat him, but Hassha has never left Vakeeli, so her blood is potent. She can find a way to protect you from Decius while you're in Vakeeli, and even find a way to get the wood from a Trench tree. Only thing about her now is she has a family now, and she does *not* like intrusions. She and her warriors will kill you first then ask questions later. I don't know if that's a risk you're willing to take."

"Is it possible for you to give us some blood and send us to The Council?" I ask. "That way we won't have to bother Hassha."

"I can't get you all the way to Luxor. The Council have energy blockers around their borders. If they sense mine, they'll put up a guard, prevent visitors. That'll only delay you. I've never liked The Council, and they most certainly don't like me." Korah blows a breath. "I'll get you to Hassha, or as close to her as I can, and you tell her everything you told me. And take this." She turns for the brown chest again, withdrawing something. She places the object in Willow's palm, and Willow looks down at it before closing her hand around it. I get a glimpse of it, something small and gold.

"Show her this, and she won't deny you," Korah says, clutching Willow's wrist. "She'll know I sent you personally."

CHAPTER 39
WILLOW

THERE'S A HUM IN THE AIR AS KORAH STANDS IN front of the grand mirror. Her hands are raised, eyes closed, and Caz and I stand behind her hand in hand.

He grabs my hand when Korah begins chanting in a language I don't understand, and the mere action, though simple, makes me feel safe.

The atmosphere becomes charged, the hairs at the nape of my neck rising, a dallop of unease swimming through me. A neon purple light appears on the center of the mirror. Korah breathes deeply, tips her chin, and the purple dot grows in size. It stretches along the wall, bright and blinding, and Korah steps backward, closing her hands to fists.

"Move toward the portal," she instructs us. "You must go through one at a time."

With Caz's hand in mine, we move forward. A wind rips around the room, whipping at my hair and Caz's. Caz looks to me, the purple glow bathing half his face.

We can do this.

I gasp when I hear his voice in my head. Oh, that precious voice. I haven't heard it within me in days, and I've missed it. My lips part as I focus on him.

I can hear you.

He smiles. *Must mean it's working, eh? You ready?*

I think so.

Good. His faces the portal again. *I'll go first.*

He releases my hand, but my heart sinks when I feel that itch on the back of my neck again. When he takes a step closer to the portal, something thuds behind us, and the portal immediately closes.

I spin around to find Korah still there, but she's not alone. Someone familiar stands behind her with a knife to her throat.

And that someone is *Garrett*.

CHAPTER 40
WILLOW

"I can't let you go through that portal," Garrett snarls.

"Garrett? What the hell are you doing?" I shout. "Let her go!"

Caz steps in front of me with his gun drawn. When I glance at him, his eyes are narrowed as he looks Garrett over from head to toe.

"Not a scratch on you," Caz mumbles. "Impossible, considering I broke several of your limbs."

"Fuck you," Garrett spits at him.

"He's been touched by Decius," Korah says raggedly. "I feel it!" Her eyes flash purple, and she vanishes from his arms. She appears on the opposite side of the room, near the mirror again, and when she does, Caz raises his gun at Garrett and shoots him in the head.

I cup my mouth after the ring of the gunshot and the thud of

Garrett's body on the floor. It's so eerily quiet afterward that all I hear is the beating of my heart, my pulse pounding in my ears.

I expect him to be dead, for that gunshot to have ended it all, but then Garrett's hand twitches. He sits upright, and when he staggers to a stand, the bullet in his head pops right out and clinks to the ground. Not a wound is in sight.

What the hell? How is he not dead? The snaked died with one slice!

"Fuck," Caz curses, and with a smirk, Garrett charges toward Caz, slamming him down on Korah's table. The table smashes to bits on the floor, and Caz grunts as he manages to shove Garrett onto his back and wrap his hands around his throat and squeeze.

Garrett sneers, like the choking doesn't bother him—like he's breathing despite the hands locked around his throat—and Caz blinks down at him, just as shocked as I am.

Someone mumbles behind me, and I swing around to spot Korah facing the mirror again. This time, the portal opens immediately, and she grabs me by the wrist to drag me toward it. "You must go first. Get to Hassha and show her that piece of broken crown I gave to you. Tell her who you are and what's happening. She will help you. *Go.*" She drags me closer to the portal, but I resist.

"What about Caz?" I cry.

"He will meet you there!"

"No—I don't like this! I can't go back without him!"

"You must!" she shouts.

I look over Korah's shoulder, and Garrett flings Caz across the room, throwing him into one of the shelves. A loud grunt falls out of Caz when he hits the shelf and lands face down on the floor. His gun scatters across the room, and when he rises to his knees and attempts to reach for it, Garrett kicks it away.

"Korah!" I scream. "You have to help him! Please!"

Korah's purple eyes are wide with panic as she peers back at Caz. Picking the gun up, Garrett points it down at Caz, and Caz's eyes swing to mine.

I'm not able to run to him after that, despite how badly I want to, because Korah shoves me into the portal.

I'm sucked into blinding purple light, arms flailing, but I can still see a glimpse of Korah's shop. Korah has her back to the portal, her hands raised at Garrett, who has dropped the gun to clutch his head. Blood drips from his eyes and nose, and he roars loudly from whatever pain she's inflicting.

Garrett staggers toward the portal as Caz lumbers to a stand. But whatever Korah is doing doesn't last long because Garrett snatches his hands down and glares at her. He grimaces at Korah, and as she rushes across the room for one of her daggers on the floor, Garrett chases her.

Caz looks into the portal, his eyes landing on mine. I shake my head because I know what he's thinking. I hear his voice in my head, telling me it's his only option right now. *He must.*

Before Garrett can reach Korah, Caz tackles him with all his strength and brings him into the portal with us.

CHAPTER 41
CAZ

I EXPECT THE DROP FROM THE PORTAL TO BE GENTLE. It is anything but. Being dragged through the electrifying purple tunnel, thrashed around, holding my breath—it takes all the breath from me and causes my heart to race and my belly to drop.

I see the opening when I'm flipped over, revealing treetops and lush green lands. Willow goes down first, crashing through the treetops aimlessly. I look back, and the Garrett fucker is scrambling, trying to reach for something to hang onto and failing.

I have no time to consider him as the portal spits me out, then come the trees, its branches whacking me in the face and leaves slapping me in the eyes.

I tip to the right and land on a hard branch that cracks with ferocity, holding back a yell and clenching my jaw instead as I wait for the fall to be over. But what I hope for most is that Willow isn't being hurt this badly with the fall.

214

Then, after that hellish drop, I land.

I drop flat on my belly, and all the wind gushes out of my lungs. My head throbs with unspeakable pain, and my mouth tastes of copper. I spit, and a glob of blood lands on the bright patch of green grass beneath me. I try looking around, but the world is spinning, and the urge to vomit is imminent.

Flipping onto my back, I stare up at the sapphire sky. The last thing I see before closing my eyes is a body landing right beside mine. It thuds on the ground too.

It takes me a while to come to. When I do, it's to the sound of Willow's voice.

"Caz," she calls, lightly tapping my cheek. She looks down at me with bright brown eyes, blood dripping from her forehead. "We made it. Wake up!" She taps my right cheek again, and I groan. A sharp gasp escapes her as she whips her head to the right.

"No!" she screams. "Stop!"

In that moment, her fear awakens everything inside me. I feel her like I once did before, the way her heart drops and her belly clenches with fear. I hear her thoughts screaming, *Why is he coming after me? No!*

"Stop, Garrett! Please, just stop!" she screams.

My eyes pop open, and I sit up just as Willow dashes away from me. Someone hustles past, their feet pounding into the ground, and I realize it's Garrett chasing after her.

I push off the ground, whipping my gun out and chasing him. They don't get far. He tackles her, and I taste nothing but bitter rage as he pins my mate to the ground.

In the air, he raises a dagger—the same one Korah had to my throat.

"NO! Let her go!" I shout, running faster. He looks back at me with a menacing glare, and with a bloody sneer, he brings the dagger down and stabs Willow in the chest.

CHAPTER 42
WILLOW

THE PAIN SURMOUNTS THE FEAR.

Garrett looks down at me with empty, wicked eyes, and I'm left wondering how he went from the man who brought me pastries and coffees in the morning, to the man now trying to kill me.

A flash of black appears and tackles him to the ground, knocking him off of me. Garrett was still holding the dagger and it rips out of my chest, making me scream.

I clutch my chest where the wound is, hardly able to breathe. Blood builds up to my throat, and I try coughing, but that only makes the pain worse. From the cough, blood splatters on my face. My hand grips tighter around the gold object in my hand, hoping the sharp edges of it will steal the pain away, but it doesn't. When I turn my head, I spot Caz on top of Garrett.

He's taken the dagger from him and is stabbing him repeatedly in the chest, neck, and stomach. The blood flings off the dagger with each stab, Caz roaring with anger, his face crimson with rage. Then he plunges the knife into his throat, and Garrett bleeds but he doesn't die.

With a loud grunt, Garrett manages to shove Caz off of him while he's in his state of fury and escapes, fleeing toward a line of trees with a limp. Blood drips off his body, leaving a trail, and Caz shoots up, about to chase after him, until his fury wanes and he remembers.

Willow. I hear his voice, loud and clear. I want to savor it as darkness dims my line of sight.

He rushes back to me as I touch the would in my chest.

"No, Willow. Please, no." He assesses the would, even starts to touch it, but snatches his hands away just as quickly, as if touching it will cause me to die faster.

I hiccup more blood. I guess I'm going to die. *We got here for nothing. All of this was for nothing.*

"It wasn't for nothing. Don't say that. I won't let you die." Caz scoops me into his arms and crosses the grassy field with blood stains on his face. As he goes, I hear hooves pounding into the ground, and for a second I think it's his heartbeat. And then I see the horses galloping in the distance.

Caz stops in his tracks, holding me tighter as the horses near us. On the horses are women dressed in tribal gear with white paint on their faces. Their clothes are ivory, their sashes and weapons laced with brown. All of them are strong with tight grimaces on their faces and weapons in their hands. The weapons range from swords and curved spears to bows and arrows. A line of the women already has their bows drawn at us, arms angled, ready to release their arrows. A set next to them carries gilded shields with a large K engraved on the center.

Caz shifts on his feet, and the wound in my chest aches even more. I clutch a handful of his shirt, wheezing.

"Which one of you is Hassha?" he asks as I drop my head. I clutch the gold piece of crown Korah gave me tighter in my other hand.

Through my periphery, I notice one of the women hop off her horse and march toward us. She shoves Caz on the chest, and Caz stumbles backward.

"What the hell is wrong with you?" he snaps. "We need help, don't you see that?"

"Who are you to be asking for Hassha?" the woman demands. I cut my eyes at her. She's a large, brown-skinned woman with thick, muscular arms and white paint covering half of her face. Her dark hair is braided into thick cornrows with miniature gold chains threaded throughout.

"I'm Caz Harlow, monarch of Blackwater. I need your help. *Please*." The last word comes out hard, forced, but desperate. He hates asking for help. "My mate, she's hurt. She was stabbed by a man who is now running free."

"Who sent you here?" the woman demands. "How did you cross our borders?"

"Korah did. She told us to ask for Hassha."

Just then, another woman walks through and murmurs something in the dark-skinned woman's ear. She raises a hand, gesturing to the other women, and they lower their bows.

Taller than Caz, with bronze skin and white paint on her face, is the person who I assume is Hassha. The paint that stands out most is the large crescent moon on her forehead, as well as the tiny stars peppered across her cheekbones. A single white line runs from the bridge of her petite nose to the tip. Her eyes are two different colors—the left one a sapphire blue, the other hazel, and her hair is the whitest I've ever seen, like snow and textured like silk. Atop her head is a crown, nestled in the braids of her hair. She's not dressed like the other women. She wears a white chiffon dress with gold armor bands around her wrists and ankles, though she does carry a sword on her back. The gold crown on her head appears broken on one side. *Ah. I see now.*

She stops a foot away from Caz, looking him up and down. I wheeze a bit harder as she assesses me. Then, with a heavy accent, she says, "Kill them."

The women don't waste any time bringing their weapons forward as Hassha backs away.

"Wait!" Caz calls. "You can't be serious! Your sister sent us! We're Tethered—a Cold Tether, created by Selah! She said you would help us!"

"You, a man, come to my land spouting lies about my sister," Hassha hisses, and just before she turns away, I find the strength to raise my hand with the gold crown piece in the air.

The piece falls out of my hand, landing on the grass, next to Hassha's foot. She bends down to pick it up, and the gold piece transforms to what looks like a hair clip with prongs on the end. Immediately, Hassha's eyes expand, and she looks from the piece to us again with curiosity swirling in her eyes.

She removes her crown, and the other women murmur amongst themselves as they watch Hassha press the piece to the broken side of it. It bonds to the crown with a gentle lavender spark that crackles.

"Korah," Hassha whispers, her face crumpling with emotion.

"Please," Caz pleads, and this time it's sincere, not demanding, or angry. "You have to help her. She'll die if you don't."

Hassha cuts her misty eyes to Caz. "Place her on the ground. Quickly," she demands.

Caz does as he's told and settles me on the grass. I cry out as the pain worsens while Hassha drops to her knees and heavily presses her hands to my chest. Never in my entire life have I felt this much pain, but it rips right through me, shocking every nerve in my body. I can't help but scream.

An iridescent blue light emits from Hassha's hands. Heat circulates through me, the pain fading by the second and my nerves calming. When Hassha pulls her glowing blue hands away, she looks to one of the women.

"Take her to Wellness Bay right away," she commands, and the woman moves toward me, along with another. One of the women comes around with a wagon attached to her horse, and they place me on top of it. The wagon jolts, rocking and bumping, and I look up at the sky as white birds soar overhead, and not a single cloud is in sight.

I don't feel like I'm dying anymore...but I am sleepy. Caz appears at my side, eyes chockful of worry.

"You'll be okay," he whispers, grabbing my hand and kissing it. "I'll be here. I love you."

I try to smile but find that I can't. He releases my hand as the wagon continues rolling, and I close my eyes, falling into a comatose sleep.

CHAPTER 43
CAZ

"WHERE ARE YOU TAKING HER?" I TURN TO HASSHA AS she grips the reins of a white horse.

She looks at me through the corner of her eye. "To Wellness Bay. We can heal her better there." She gives me a onceover. "She has a dark energy in her that I haven't felt in a very long time. We have things that can draw it out of her, but it will take time."

"Do you believe us then? About Korah sending us to you?"

She exhales, reaching for the crown on her head. She removes it and studies the section that she'd previously attached. A splotch of Willow's blood is on it, and she wipes it away with her thumb as if it's a random smudge. Then she narrows her eyes at me, replacing it. "You say she's your mate, but she doesn't feel Vakeeli born."

"That's because she's from Earth."

"Ah. Explains how you got to Korah then."

"My queen!" someone shouts, and Hassha's head turns to find the voice. A woman in white rushes our way with two younger girls trailing behind. These girls can't be any older than nine or ten. One has skin as dark as Korah's with hair as snow-white as Hassha's. Her striking blue eyes are set on Hassha, an excited expression on her face. The other girl has skin that's just as pale as mine, her hair dark, eyes silver. Both wear dark tribal clothing and are barefoot. They continue making their way toward us while dragging something behind them in a black net.

"The girls found a man!" the woman announces.

"Mum!" the young dark-skinned girl shouts. "We took him down! See? We did good!"

"You shouldn't have taken *anyone* down because I told you two to stay in hiding!" Hassha scolds her with a frown.

The pale girl looks at the other, eyes widening.

"We know, Mum," the blue-eyed one continues, oblivious (or careless) to her mother's anger. "But we saw this man running toward the village and you *always* tell us to protect the village no matter what, so we came out of the hiding tree to stop him!" The girls stop dragging the net, and Hassha walks toward them, dropping to one knee.

"I know I say that, but this time was not safe," she murmurs. "I do not know this man. He could have hurt you."

"Sorry, Mumma," the pale one apologizes.

"No, he wouldn't have!" the blue-eyed one retorts, then she backs away from Hassha and whips a sword out of a leather sheath attached to her hip. It's not large like the other women's, but its blade is flat, wide, and the tip gleams in the sun. "If he'd tried to hurt me or Maia, I would've gutted him like a fish and cut off his head," she declares triumphantly.

"Minka," Hassha sighs, and I notice she's fighting a smile. "What will I ever do with you?"

"Who is this man?" Minka asks, pointing the tip of her sword in my direction.

Hassha forces the girl's sword down, then side-eyes me as I step closer. She then rises to a stand again, putting her focus on the net the girls dragged over.

I look with her, and it's Garrett, bloody and mangled. He's still alive, panting raggedly.

"Let me out!" he shouts.

Love of Vakeeli. His voice infuriates me. I don't know how he's still alive, and I don't care to stop my reaction. I deliver a swift kick to the side of his head, and to my surprise, that knocks him out. Really? A kick? After all the stabbing and punching I did beforehand?

"Ooohhh!" Minka squeals, waving her sword in the air. "I like this man! Mum, can we keep him?"

"We will not be keeping anyone, now you two get back to village with Carra," Hassha commands.

Hassha watches the slim woman in white who approached with the girls steer them away, and when they're distant enough, she asks, "Do you know this man?"

"Willow does," I answer. "Apparently she was seeing this piece of shit while on Earth."

"Willow. That is your mate's name, correct?"

"Yes."

"Her name runs through your mind a lot." I start to ask her what she means, but she continues with, "How did this man wind up in Vakeeli?"

"He was going to attack Korah, so I knocked him into the portal she'd opened for me and Willow in order to stop him."

With that, Hassha tips her gaze to mine. "You saved my sister's life." She steps away from Garrett, scanning him. "There is a dark energy feeding off of him—the same energy I felt on your mate. This man, he's angry about something, and he's being controlled by it."

"I believe he's a vessel of Decius, and I'm looking for a way to kill Decius so something like *this* never happens again." I gesture to Garrett.

Hassha looks at me, stunned. "Decius is hunting you?"

"Me and my mate, yes. And he has my family right now. He's threatening to kill them if I don't return to him. I can't let this go on any longer. I need him dead, and I'm certain you Regals know exactly what needs to be done in order to stop him."

She squares her shoulders, looking off in the distance. I can tell she doesn't want to deal with any of this, even more so when she clutches the end of the net Garrett is in and attaches it to one of her horse's armored legs. "Come with me to the village. There, we can discuss more about Decius."

CHAPTER 44
CAZ

I'D HEARD MANY RUMORS ABOUT THE ISLAND OF Kessel in my lifetime, but none of them live up to what I'm facing right now.

No one has ever really known what the island is like other than its inhabitants. Many men and women have tried venturing to the island only for their boats to explode or to simply fall apart. It could never be explained why no one could venture to Kessel, yet the people of Kessel could come and go as they pleased.

There have been stories about how it is the most beautiful, vibrant place in all of Vakeeli, even better than Vanora, and how there is freedom in living, no concerns over currency, and that all the water found on the land keeps you healthy and youthful. In Vanora, there was only the Lake of Youth, and that's where we collected our barrels. But on Kessel, the source of water is everywhere and available to everyone.

The fruit is better, the animals healthier, lives are much

longer. And there is one rumor that I never believed but turns out to be true: there are no men. Only women live on the island of Kessel, and that would be any other man's dream, but not mine because they all stare at me with questions in their eyes.

It's been said time and time again that any man who entered Kessel was an immediate threat. Apparently, Kessel had been created by a colony of women who had been given the gift of procreation without man from one of the Regals. I now see that that particular Regal is Hassha. This meant that they could become pregnant when ready through a water ritual and conceive their own babies.

I always thought it was bullshit, but I see it now, as I sit in front of a large bonfire. There is nothing but women and children around, all chatting, laughing, and eating. I've been offered vegetable kabobs and wine, but I can't stomach a damn thing because Willow is still in the Wellness Bay. She hasn't woken up, though I've been informed that they've ridden her of Decius' energy. And Garrett is currently wrapped in chains Hassha has touched that will soon rid him of Decius' control. She still has no plans for what she'll do when he's clear, and that alone irritates me.

I feel eyes on me and look to my right, spotting the twin girls and Carra sitting between them. Minka shoots up and rushes toward me. Carra reaches to stop her, but she isn't quick enough. The other girl pops up too, and Carra gives up, shaking her head and leaning against the log behind her.

"Milandra says we shouldn't trust you," Minka tells me matter-of-factly. "She says you're a man, and all men only want one thing."

"And let me guess. Milandra is that large woman standing beside your mother, still wearing her armor, and holding her sword?" My eyes flicker to Milandra, who already has her eyes pinned on me. She's the woman who shoved me when I had Willow in my arms. I won't lie, she's not a woman I'd pick a fight with. She's enormous, probably bigger than Killian. And there's a menacing look in her eyes, like she'd strip me of all my skin and use my bones for a stew.

"Yep. She's our godmother," Minka goes on. "She told us not to talk to you."

I smirk. "You're being quite rebellious then."

Minka shrugs and smiles, then points a thumb at Maia. "This is Maia. She pretends to be shy, but she told me she thinks you're *very* handsome."

"Minka!" Maia wails, shoving Minka on the arm. Minka hardly stumbles and instead laughs, finding her embarrassment humorous. Maia's face turns as red as a ruby as she backs away, avoiding my eyes.

"Well, I'm glad someone around here likes me in some way," I say, pointing my gaze to Maia. She smiles, her face still red. "No sense in bothering with a man like me, though. You're better off looking for someone the opposite of me as you get older." If only she knew. Too bad her tiny mind can't comprehend it.

Her silver eyes drop to the gun on my lap, and I pick it up. As I do, Milandra takes a giant step away from Hassha's throne, raising her sword. I ignore her, showing the gun to Maia anyway. If she wanted my head, she'd have it already.

"Ever seen a Blackwater gun?" I ask.

"No," Maia quips.

"They're quite dangerous. Probably not as dangerous as your Kessel weapons though."

"That's right," Minka says, arms folding. "My mum always

says real weapons are those made from scratch and graced with Regal energy. Not man-made things like yours."

"Is that what your weapons are then? Graced with Regal energy?"

"Yes, all of them are." Minka whips out her sword for the second time today, and I'll be damned. She's good with it, swinging it all sorts of ways and throwing jabs at invisible enemies. She draws back, her hand stuck out to show me the blade. "One cut of our blades and you'll easily die."

"What if you cut yourself?" I ask.

"It won't kill us. Only our enemies. Our weapons are bonded to us as we age."

"I see."

I shift my gaze to Milandra who has lowered her guard, only a bit, and only because Hassha has pressed a hand to her shoulder.

"So, is that woman in Wellness Bay your wife?" Minka asks. "Maia wanted me to ask."

Maia goes rosy again, and this time she punches Minka in the arm. I can't help the chuckle that escapes me. These girls, they're adorable...and so innocent. I haven't encountered anyone like them in ages. So young and carefree, living their lives and doing what siblings do best: pick fights with each other. How nice it must be to not have to worry about things you can't control, like abuse from a father, or your mother being tortured and murdered.

"She not my wife, no, but she is my mate. I'm Tethered to her," I inform them.

"Isn't a Tether a bad thing?" Maia asks in a soft voice.

I start to answer, but someone approaches them from behind. Hassha places a gentle hand on their shoulders, bowing her head to drop kisses on the tops of their heads. "It's time for bed."

"What?" Minka whines. "No! Can we stay up a little longer? *Pleeeasseeee*, Mum!"

"Pleaseeeee?" Maia clasps her hands together, begging too.

"I'm afraid not, my loves. Come on, run to Carra. Get to bed."

"Yes, Mum," the girls say in unison. They walk around their mother to meet with Carra who is already standing near a trail. Carra takes their hands and guides them along the trail leading to overwater bungalows.

When they're out of sight, Hassha sits next to me, facing the fire. The flames crackle, even more so when one of the women tosses more logs into it.

"My colony believes you've seen too much," she states, eyes still forward. "We normally end the lives of men who see what Kessel provides."

"Why?" I ask.

Hassha glances at me before focusing on the fire again. The flames dance in her multi-colored eyes. "Do you know that ever since Selah created the Tethered, men have tried dominating everything?"

I drop my gaze to the dirt. "Have they?"

"Yes. There are the gilded, who were an army of men at first before they slept with or raped women and had offspring with the same abilities. There is The Council, who were all men at first, as well as the appointed monarchs." She presses her lips, as if agitated by the facts she's presenting. "It's fortunate a woman has finally taken over Vanora and still runs it now. But the man who ran it before that, he was just as bad as you and your father."

"What makes you think *I'm* bad?"

"I read energies and thoughts. I normally avoid it, but I've had to tap into your mind to make sure you aren't a threat."

"And am I? A threat?" I ask.

She cuts her eyes at me. "I know you've done bad things. I know you've tortured many people, just to have your way, but no...I do not see you as a threat. But let me inform you that if you lay a finger on my daughters, or *any* of the women on my island, I will take your head myself. Decius be damned."

I huff a laugh, nodding. Fair enough. "I don't hurt women or children."

"Yet?"

"Ever."

She draws in a breath. "But you *have* hurt many people previously." It's a statement, not a question.

"Only when necessary."

"Oh, please," she scoffs. "Some of it was not necessary."

I drop my gaze again. I'm not sure what she's seeing or how deep she's gone into my memories, but whatever she's seen, I'm sure it's what Korah saw too. Their fault for prodding around in my brain and digging between the cracks. My mind is no place to linger.

"When can I see Willow?" I ask, shifting the subject.

She stares at the fire again. "When she's awake."

"And when will that be?"

"Whenever she wakes."

I release a slow breath. "We're in a bit of a hurry."

"Are you always so impatient?"

"She's my mate, and Decius is trying to kill us. Right now, my patience is very slim."

"If you think Decius will ever come here to Kessel, he won't.

231

His energy is useless here, and if he ever manages to set foot on my island, he's aware that I will kill him on sight."

"Why don't you just kill him now? Why wait for him to possibly attack one day?"

"There is no need. He is not a threat to me or my people. He cannot penetrate my energy."

"So you've been okay with him robbing Tethered mates of their souls?" I demand.

"I suggest you remove the bass from your voice," she warns, and I straighten my back, softening my shoulders. She is right. I'm in her territory. Hell, I'm in her world.

"I apologize. I just can't wrap my mind around this Decius thing, or the fact that the Regals are letting him do as he pleases. What if one of your daughters grows to have a Tether? Then what? Because you know he's not just after Cold Tethers anymore, right? He's after any Tether he can find, even the commoners, so long as it gives him some sort of energy."

"It's impossible," she counters while shaking her head. "I gave birth to them and rid them of all Regal origins. They live a normal life with none of the chains of my past. They will never have to worry about being Tethered or an attack from Decius because they are protected with my energy. And even if I die, the land of Kessel will shield them."

"I see." After a few seconds of silence, I say, "They're beautiful girls."

"I know."

"Were you the first to grow life without man?" I ask.

She cuts her eyes at me, nostrils flaring. "If you're asking about their father, that is none of your concern," she snaps.

I lift an innocent hand in the air. "I was only curious. I heard stories about how women in Kessel can conceive on their own. Wasn't sure if that included you."

Hassha swings her eyes to the trail her daughters took, where the tips of the bungalows are faint in the night. Standing, she says, "Walk with me, Caspian."

I push to a stand, following her around the fire. Milandra appears before we can reach another footpath.

"Your majesty?" she calls.

"We will be fine, Milandra," Hassha murmurs. "Stand down."

I look back as we continue along the path, and Milandra scowls at me, then huffs before turning away.

"I'm certain she wants to kill me," I say.

"She wants to kill *every* man, not just you." Hassha chuckles, leading the way between a grove of trees. "Caspian, women have always been seen as lesser than. Men in Vakeeli think we are their objects. They assume women know nothing, that we have no power, that we don't belong unless we're in their beds, on our knees, or in their kitchens. In Kessel, we don't have that. Here, the women can thrive. They can be themselves. They can laugh and nurture and still be strong and fierce. And any man who dares come here and disturb that peace will have his bloody head chopped off."

"I completely understand."

"I can tell you're not like those men though, despite your horrid past. You carry something that keeps you from being like them." She pauses. "Or should I say from being like the man who raised you."

My jaw clenches, and I fight the urge to stop in my tracks. "Get out of my head."

"Oh, I'm not in your head. These are surface thoughts. I hear them very clearly."

The path shifts from grass to sand, and we're facing the ocean. The water shimmers beneath the moon like indigo jewels, and Hassha turns her face up at the moon, drawing in a deep breath. When she exhales, a large wave rises and drifts toward us, bringing a boat with it. The boat's exterior is made of Vanorian Steel with ivory sails flapping in the breeze.

"We will get you and your mate to safety," she assures me. "I've created this boat for a fleet of my women to take to The Trench. They'll gather wood from a Trench tree, bring it back, and we'll create weapons. But be aware, Caspian. I will *not* send my women to war for you. They have peace here, and they shall continue to have it. The same goes for me. I must remain here for my daughters."

"Just get me the weapons. I'll handle the rest," I tell her.

"What about your mind?" she probes, tapping her temple. "He can get in there and stop you. He starts there first."

"Can you protect my and Willow's mind?"

"I can, but only for a few hours. If I am not with you, it cannot last for long. If you were my creation, that would be different." She shakes her head, focusing on the boat. "I always told Selah she made the original Tether too strong. She gave them too much at once."

"Yeah, Korah said the same." I look past Hassha at the bungalows perched above water. The warm gold lights glowing in the dark bring peace, comfort. This place is an oasis. I see why they protect it so fiercely.

"You and Korah must be stronger than Decius when you're together, right?" I ask. "Surely, you could've killed him before now. He's only causing torment and pain. It's not fair, especially not to me and Willow."

Hassha sighs. "Back then, I never signed up for protecting anyone but my sisters. Not the Tethered. Not the babies, nor those who came after the Tethered. It was never my job to do any of that because I didn't ask for it."

"But you protect people now."

"Yes, *now*. I protect people who are understanding and *not* looking to overthrow a Regal. Believe it or not, it took me a while to trust commoners. There was only one I trusted, many eras ago." She smiles, but just as quickly as that smile appears, it vanishes. "I gave him a bit of my energy, and he became a Mythic. He shared his energy with others and since then, there have been Mythics running wild with part of what makes the Regals powerful. Believe it or not, after my encounter with that man, I tried not to be too upset about Selah creating the Tethered because I see how easy it is to create something, only for it to backfire in many ways. Plus, the Tethered aren't all so bad. The original Tethered were loyal and dutiful—all but Decius. As for the Cold Tethered, well you and your mate are the first I've ever met, and I wouldn't say I'm fond of you, but I do think I will like her. She's strong, and I sense that she's kind. Then again, I think women are better than men in general, so I digress. Why do you think there are only women and girls here? I made it so that all we birth are girls."

"Still, wouldn't it be easier for Decius to just be *dead*? He took down Selah. What makes you think he won't take you down too?" I ask.

"If he comes for me, I'll be prepared, just as I've always been. But it has been centuries, and I've heard not a peep from Decius. I have my warriors. They have my energy in their weapons. He knows this. He doesn't bother me, so I don't bother him. As for Selah, we told her this would happen. There is nothing we can do for her now."

"Hmm."

"Besides, it isn't like he can take over the world. He's not *that* powerful."

"Oh, but don't you see? That's his goal. When he had me, only for a split second, he told me my half of the Cold Tether alone would be enough for him to take over *all* of Vakeeli. With me, he says he can do it, and that you and Korah don't stand a chance. And if he does, well good luck to you and your warrior women. I'm sure his first mission will be to take you down, then The Council."

She stares at me, unblinking. "Do you mean to tell me that you have all three binding bloods in you? Monarch, hybrid Mythic, and a Cold Tether?"

"According to The Council, yes."

"But I...how can that be possible? This wasn't supposed to happen, ever. How can I not *feel* it?" She looks me from head to toe. "I should be able to feel it."

She points her gaze another way, the moon causing her silver eye to glisten. "It's no wonder you made it to Earth, that you are not dead yet. He's waited a long time for someone like you. You are right. We *must* take him down."

"That's what I've been telling you all along."

"But once he's gone..." She taps her chin, eyes distant. I don't even think she's talking to me anymore, just thinking out loud. "Once he is out of the way, it is what comes after that will..." She trails off, and a fiery blue light emits from her hands and builds into flames. She gasps and shakes her hands, ridding herself of them.

"What do you mean what comes after?" I take a step toward her. "Hassha, is there something I should know?"

She turns her gaze to me, blinks a few times, then walks past me, the blue fading from her fingers. "It's nothing we can't handle. Come on. I'll take you to your mate."

She walks away from the bungalows and rounds the island, but I still sense some unease within her. She's not telling me something, I know it. She and Korah are hiding something, and it doesn't sit well with me, but who am I to demand answers? One stroke of Hassha's finger, and I'm as good as ash.

We approach a white shelter on thick wooden stilts nestled between towering trees. The leaves brush the walls of the shelter as it overlooks the ocean, and I notice a large wrap-around porch with chairs upfront. Lights illuminate from the inside, pouring onto the porch, and a marble staircase leads to the front door.

"You'll find your mate in there," Hassha says, pointing upward. "Give her a few hours, and she'll be awake and better than ever."

"Thank you, Hassha. I appreciate your hospitality."

She nods and starts to turn away, but before she goes, she says, "Oh, by the way, I took your Blackwater gun." She raises it in the air, and I drop my hands to my coat, feeling around for it with no luck. "I assure you it's not to punish you, but my daughter Minka tends to develop these wild ideas in her head. I already heard her thinking about stealing your gun to try to use it, and to keep us all safe from random bullets, it's best that I hold on to it." Hassha flashes a smile. "I'll give it back when you leave Kessel. Goodnight, Caspian."

CHAPTER 45
WILLOW

I OPEN MY EYES TO FIND MYSELF IN A DIMLY LIT room. My body is weak, my mouth dry, and one of my legs is numb. I try moving one of my feet, but it doesn't budge.

My eyes shift to the right when I hear rustling, and I spot Caz adjusting himself on a two-seater sofa in the corner. He's shirtless, his pants low on his hips. I try calling his name, but it comes out in a croak. He rapidly swings his gaze to me and rushes my way.

"Willow?" He sits on the edge of the bed, stroking his thumb across my forehead. "Nice to see those beautiful brown eyes." He smiles, and I can't help smiling with him. "How do you feel?"

I shake my head. It's the most I can manage at the moment.

"Tell me through here." He taps two fingers against his right temple.

It feels like something's been lodged down my throat, my mouth is dry, and my whole body is sore.

238

I'm sorry to hear that. Want some water? Caz starts to stand, but I tap his hand, rapidly shaking my head.

I don't think I can drink right now even if I wanted to.

Yeah," he murmurs. "The nurse said you might wake and that your body will still be going through the effects of the purging elixir. Give it another couple of hours and you'll be all better." He cradles one side of my face, and the comforting silence lingers. I hear the sounds of the ocean, the waves crashing to shore, and everything rushes back. The fall through the portal, the women on horses, the bronze, goddess-like woman with multi-colored eyes.

Where are we? I wonder.

"Kessel," he responds in a low voice. I peer up at the skylight in the ceiling. The sky is like a velvety indigo blanket with bold stars threaded throughout. Light from the full moon pours onto the gold and white quilt on top of me.

"I'm going to kill Garrett," Caz says after a while.

I look up, eyes stretching. *Is he not already dead?*

"No. They have him in a prisoner's cell. They're trying to rid his body of Decius' energy, which is why it was nearly impossible to kill him, but they say it'll be a while. I told them it'll be better if I just end it all by slitting his damn throat."

I sigh. *He didn't ask to be Decius' vessel.*

"He still smashed into your car on Earth. And I don't even know how many times this makes that he's hurt you. Plus, he's in Vakeeli now. No one will *ever* find the body, so they'll never be able to trace it back to you."

I roll my eyes even though it hurts and brings on a headache.

"He *stabbed* you, Willow. All I keep thinking is I should've left him back there with Korah. She could've handled herself,

I'm sure. If I hadn't pushed him into the portal with us, it never would've have happened, and you wouldn't even be in this situation." He grabs my hand, clinging to it with desperation. "Imagine if Hassha and her tribe hadn't found us in time. I don't think I'd have been able to save you. I had *nothing*." With a long pause and eyes filled to the brim with torment, he says, "He almost took you from me."

I grip his hand, bringing it to my chest. *But he didn't.*

"I don't care," he grumbles. "He still needs to die. He's had too many chances."

Caz.

"No. I'm sick of being the better person when it comes to him, Willow. He *has* to die." He looks away, avoiding my eyes, jaw ticking. I hear him thinking about all the ways he can kill Garrett. He'll take his gun back from Hassha, and if he can't do that, he'll find a spear and lodge it through Garrett's eye socket. He'll wrap his hands around his throat and choke him so hard his eyes turn red. His mind is venturing into dark places, and I don't like it.

"Caz," I say out loud this time. My voice is raspier than usual, and he drops his eyes to mine again. The anger melts off of him when our gazes connect.

Sometimes vengeance isn't the answer. Not for people like Garrett. Send him back to Earth. Let him suffer. Who cares? We'll never have to deal with him again anyway, so long as we're in Vakeeli.

His eyes light up. "Does that mean…"

I smile, listening to his thoughts now reveling in the idea of us making a life together in Vakeeli.

"Does that mean you'll stay?" he asks, still smiling.

Only if you promise to behave.

A smirk rides his lips and he leans forward, planting a kiss on my forehead. "Sure. I suppose we can discuss that later. For now, get some more rest, Willow Woman."

I sink deeper into the plush pillows as Caz brings the quilt up to my chin. He stays at my side, stroking my cheek as he looks out the window facing the ocean. It's peaceful like this, with him at my side, his gentle caresses, the warmth of his breath on my skin, and the sound of gently crashing ocean waves.

I'm not sure if it's all in my head, or perhaps the elixir is causing me to conjure up ideas just for the hell of it, but after another forehead kiss from Caz and before I've completely fallen asleep, I swear I hear him whisper, "I love you more than anything."

CHAPTER 46
WILLOW

WHEN I WAKE UP THE SECOND TIME, I HAVE WAY MORE energy buzzing through me. I press a hand to my chest, searching for the aftereffects of Garrett's stabbing, but nothing is there. The wound is gone, and my skin is clear.

I sniff the air when something divine slips up my nostrils and turn over in bed. On the bedside table is a wooden tray topped with a beautiful parfait filled with a yellow cream and fruit, nuts in a dish, a hefty chunk of brown bread, and a green juice in a slim, crystal glass. There's a piece of brown paper on the tray with words written on it in jagged script.

I pick it up to read it.

If you wake to this, I'm near Moon Village where the huts are. Find me after you eat.

Your one true love,
Caspian

My one true love? *Really?* I grin at the letter, placing it down and picking up the tray. I devour the food, gulp down the green juice, then set the empty tray back on the table. When I climb out of bed, something yellow catches in my peripheral. A chiffon yellow dress hangs on a wardrobe with a note pinned to it.

I asked Hassha for something you could wear. She gave me this dress. What the hell was she thinking! You'll be the sexiest woman on the island!

I can't help the laugh that bubbles out of me as I take it down by the hanger and run my fingers along the material. There's an outdoor shower just outside the glass door on the balcony, and I undress quickly, sliding the door open and stepping out. I stand beneath the warm stream, allowing the water to pour over my bare body. I don't care that my locs will likely be frizzy in a few hours when it air dries because this shower feels *incredible* right now.

I face the ocean, which appears to be endless. The sky is a beautiful turquoise, the sun bold and bright, beaming between the fronds of the palm trees above the shower. The palm fronds, I realize, create a barrier of privacy, and attached to the trunks of the trees are gold flowers, similar to the Vanorian Bloom Caz picked for me near his mother's cabin. I pluck one off the leaf, sniff it, and it smells like honey and rain. Wow. Kessel is so beautiful.

After the shower, I wrap a towel around myself and find a bathroom tucked away inside. The bathroom contains only a toilet and sink with a mirror above, but the windows occupying the walls make it appear a lot more spacious.

There are more folded towels on a built-in shelf, bars of soap wrapped in kraft-like paper, and brand-new toothbrushes made of wood with dark bristles placed neatly in a wooden container on the counter. I can't tell if all this stuff has always been here or if it was placed recently. Caz mentioned a nurse being around last night, before I fell asleep again, so I suppose she put things in place for me.

Thankful, I brush my teeth, pull my hair up into a loose ponytail, slip into the dress, then walk out of the bathroom to reach the front door.

I carry myself down the marble stairs, burying my feet into the powdery sand as soon as I touch it. The ocean breeze soothes every part of me, and I throw my head back, allowing the sun to bathe my skin. This place is absolute paradise.

Looking to my right, I notice overwater bungalows that come in different sizes, the exteriors made of wooden planks with steel roofs. I make my way in that direction and spot mothers playing in the water with their children. I notice all the children are girls. Laughter rings, and it's a joyous noise that is much needed after so many hard days. Some women are styling younger girls' hair, while others help build sandcastles and domes. A few other women sit crossed legged beneath a shady tree, stripping some type of material that looks like cotton off of sticks and stuffing them into braided leaf baskets. One of the women with honey-brown skin and a copper afro notices me and stops what she's doing to smile.

"Hey-ah! Do you need help?" she asks, approaching me.

"Uh, hi. Yes, actually. I'm looking for Moon Village. Is it around here?" I ask.

"It is. Just make a right around the bungalow there and follow the moonstones in the ground. They'll lead you straight to the village. You can't miss it."

I thank her and leave the beach to round the bungalow she pointed at and reach the path. When I find it, the moonstones are the first thing I notice. I wasn't sure I'd know what they were when she said it, but it's very clear when I bend down and rub one of the silvery stones protruding from the ground. It's shaped like a crescent and shimmers in the sunlight. They appear to have grown from the soil, almost like someone planted them underground to allow them to bloom. I follow the stones the rest of the way, and I know I'm close when I hear the laughter of children.

A clearing appears and, sure enough, there's the village that can't be missed. This is no ordinary community, though. The shops are built *into* trees with thick branches that ascend upward as if trying to touch the sky. The miscellaneous shops and huts between have roofs made of gold. The shops sell baskets, clothes, weapons, food, while the huts seem occupied by families.

As I walk through, one of the women—elderly with peppery hair—stops me by offering me a square-shaped fruit. The skin is orange, and it has been cut in half to reveal yellow seeds reminiscent to a pomegranate. I take it from her with a smile, and she returns to the table in front of her shop, cutting more fruit.

It's as I cross an overwater bridge that I spot a collection of picnic tables on a flat stretch of grass. Each table is spread out around a large firepit, and not too far from the pit is a throne. The throne is made of gold, with shapes of the sun, moon, and stars carved into it. Another round of children's laughter echoes through the field, and I look to my right to find Caz seated at one of the tables with two girls who can't be any older than eight or nine. They have flowers in their hands, and as I approach, I hear Caz grumbling, "I can't tie the stem of this thing."

You have to do it like this," one of the girls says, a dark-skinned one with beautiful white hair. She shows Caz how to tie the flower stem with her own set.

The other girl, dark-haired with milky skin, sits right beside him. "Finished," the dark-haired one says, then she climbs onto her knees on the bench and places a flower necklace around Caz's neck that matches the blue and white flower crown on her head.

"You made this for me? Really?" he asks, and the girl nods, blushing. "Thank you, Maia. It's beautiful. Now, if I can figure out how to tie this thing, I'll have a gift for you too."

Oh. My. Word. This is the *cutest* interaction I've ever seen in my life. Look at him with these girls! I've never seen him so...*soft*.

As if he hears my thoughts, Caz's head turns, and his eyes find mine. I wave from where I'm standing, several feet away from his table. He hops off the bench almost immediately, excusing himself from the girls, but they trail right behind him as he ventures my way, like two little shadows.

"Am I interrupting?" I ask, partly teasing.

"Just the masterpieces of flower necklaces and crowns. You know how that goes." The edges of his lips quirk up. "I'm glad you're up and about."

"Yeah, me too. I feel much better."

"You have a weird accent," the dark-skinned girl says. "Why don't you sound like us?"

"Oh, right. Well, I'm not exactly from Vakeeli. I'm what Earth would call an American."

"Ah-mah-ri-cuhn?" The girl frowns as she sounds it out.

I shift my eyes to Caz again, smiling. "I see you have your own little fan club now. Super adorable."

"Oh. Right." He turns a shade of red, looking between the girls as they step closer to me. "They've been lots of fun. Very welcoming too." The dark-skinned girl folds her arms across her chest, while the paler one brings her hands behind her back with a coy smile.

"My name's Minka." Minka, the dark-skinned one, still has her arms crossed. "This is my sister, Maia."

I drop to one knee. "It's nice to meet you, Minka and Maia."

Minka's face changes, like she's pleased that I've lowered to their level. "I'm only upset right now because Maia will probably be upset too," Minka announces.

"Upset about what?" I ask, tilting my head.

"About you being awake, of course," Minka says. "She was hoping you'd stay asleep another day, so we can hang out with Mr. Harlow a little longer. She knew when you woke up, he'd have to leave."

Maia drops her head, a flush creeping up her neck.

"Well, Maia, if it helps, I only need to talk to him for a few seconds. Hey, maybe we can all hang out. Would you like that?"

Maia bobs her head eagerly. "Yes, please!"

"Great! Why don't you find me some flowers too? I'd love to make a crown."

"Oh, I can make you one!" Minka shouts.

"No, she told me to do it!" Maia retorts, and they both run off toward a line of trees, trying to outrace each other.

When they're out of earshot, I slide my gaze to Caz who is already looking at me.

"Why are you staring?" I laugh.

"Look at you," he breathes. "How can anyone not?"

I tuck a loose loc behind my ear, fighting a blush. "How long was I out for?"

"About twelve hours. You woke up around the fifth hour for a bit."

"Yeah. I remember." When he said he loved me more than anything.

Caz takes my hand, walking across the field with me. As we go, I can't help feeling like everyone is watching us. I look over my shoulder at the woman who shoved Caz. She stands next to the bridge, the wooden handle of a spear clutched tightly in her hand, the bottom nestled in the ground. Her eyes are slightly narrowed as she watches our every step.

"They still aren't trusting us about Korah?" I ask as we sit.

"Hassha believes it," Caz says. "Milandra...well, she's a different story. She wants to rip my head off, that one."

"And I can assume Milandra is the woman standing by the bridge with the spear in her hand?"

Caz's gaze flickers to Milandra. "That's her. At this point, she's just waiting for me to breathe wrong."

"Hmm. And where is Hassha?"

"I'm not sure. I haven't seen her since this morning, but she's already sent a boat with some of her strongest women to look for some wood in The Trench. They'll bring it back here, and we can make weapons. Hopefully they can find something."

"That's great news!"

"Yes, it is. Oh, while you were out, I tapped in with Cerberus again." A look of concern washes over him. "He's too afraid to go back to the castle. I feel his fear. He wants far away from Decius."

"Poor wolf. It's probably best that he stays away. Was Silvera with him?" I ask as we sit.

"She was. I believe they've been side by side since we left them." He looks toward the throne. "I need to get to my family soon," he says in a lower voice. "Once Hassha's people return and those weapons are made, I'll have to go to him."

My brows dip. "Don't you mean *we*?"

"No, Willow. *Me*. I'll have protection from Hassha for an hour, at the least. I'll kill him and free my family."

I drag my thumbnail over the back of my hand. "And where will I be during all this?"

"You can stay here, in Kessel. I've already spoken to Hassha about it. It's the only place Decius can't get to you. Here, he can't get into your mind, and if there is any danger, they'll handle it. These women are warriors. They know how to fight."

"But I want to be with *you*, Caz. I came back to help you."

His lips press together, and he grips my hands, squeezing them on top of the table. "I can't have another scare like yesterday, Willow. *I can't*. I'm not losing you. I'd rather you stay here where you'll be safe and taken care of."

"But what if he hurts you—or your family? If I'm not there, how can I know you're okay, Caz? I don't like this plan."

Caz's head drops just an inch. "I'm going to do everything I can to get them out of his clutches. He wants me, not my family."

That is true, but who is to say Decius won't kill them—or hasn't already—just to prove a point? I shake my head, looking toward one of the shops where they sell weapons.

"I don't like this," I mutter, lowering my eyes to the table.

"I knew you wouldn't."

"You shouldn't have even told me," I mutter again.

"I wanted to be honest. I could have left without telling you, then you'd have been angrier with me."

I cut my eyes to his. "Who says I'm angry now?"

"I can feel it. Maybe not anger, but you're upset."

"Because it's unfair, and you know it. I know I'm not the best fighter, but I'm sure I can help." I lean in closer to him as a group of women pass. "If I lose you, Caz—if you never come back—I don't know what I'll do."

"I'm putting up my fight," he reminds me, bringing my hand to his lips. Right. I did tell him to at least try...but I don't want it to be like this. "Relax. Don't worry about me," he goes on. "I'll have protection from Hassha when I leave the island, and it should last me long enough to take down Decius and free my family. Once I do that, I'm all yours, and we'll never be threatened again."

I want to put up an argument, but I won't right now. Not in front of everyone, because though they all seem to be minding their business (everyone except Milandra), I know they're still watching. And even if I wanted to, I can't because Minka and Maia come running back to us with arms full of freshly picked flowers.

They dump them onto the table, and Minka says, "Here! Now what's your favorite color?"

I laugh and tell her pink, and she and Maia get straight to work. I sit and collect a few flowers for myself. As I do, a woman approaches with a glazed, handmade mug in hand.

"I'm Carra," she says, and she takes the spot next to me, sliding the mug in my direction. "I'm sorry you were stabbed, but I'm glad you're all better. Have this tea. It's star berry, a favorite in Kessel."

"Wow. Thank you." I take the mug, cupping it in my hands.

"Are you the nanny for the girls, Carra?" Caz asks as I sip my tea. It's delicious. Tastes like berries and mint.

"I'm their caretaker, yes. It is my assigned role in Kessel." She moves in closer to me, pressing her bosom against my arm while studying my hair. "Your hair is so beautiful. May I?"

Normally, I don't like people touching my hair, but she brought me tea, so I play nice. "Sure, yeah. Go ahead."

Carra rises, moving behind me and pulling the hair tie out of my hair. My locs swim down to my back, and she murmurs, "Such beautiful hair," again before picking up a few pieces and braiding them into sections.

"After this," Carra says, twirling one loc around her finger. "Maybe I can show you to my bungalow. I have lots of hair accessories. Or we can simply relax and have more tea. What-ever you want."

I look to Caz with inclined brows. *Am I tripping, or is she hitting on me?*

Caz remains passive but doesn't take his eyes off Carra.

"Do you like mine, Caz?" Maia asks, stealing his attention away.

"I do, Maia. It's lovely." He pushes to a stand, clearing his throat. "If you'll excuse me, ladies. I'm going to find Hassha. See if she has an update for me."

"Do you want me to come with you?" I ask as he takes a minor step back.

"No, no. Stay here with the girls...and Carra." His eyes flicker to her again, but she's in her own world, toying with my hair. "I'll be right back." He plants a kiss on my forehead before walking away.

I watch him go but can't help sensing something else is going on with him. Whatever is on his mind, he has his wall up, so I can't hear him.

"There. Pink, blue, and gold." Minka captures my attention, walking around the table to place the necklace around my neck, but not without bumping Carra out of the way.

"Mind your manners, Minka. Love of Vakeeli," Carra mutters.

Maia ambles around too, handing her pink, yellow, and white necklace to me.

I put it on then smile at the girls. "Thank you, ladies. They're gorgeous."

CHAPTER 47
CAZ

TRUTH IS, I'M NOT LOOKING FOR HASSHA.

I don't need a status update. It's simply the women here. They're *extremely* hands on, and I'm starting to feel the pain from touch again. I was hoping that wouldn't return, but it has, and I felt it with Minka and Maia. Those girls, as kind as they are, are very handsy. I'd love to spend more time with them, truly, but I can only handle so much before the touch begins to burn and I become irritable. The last thing I want is for them to witness my irritation.

I leave the village, taking a winding footpath that leads to an overwater bridge. Vines hang from the bridge, wrapped around the thick rope and between the gaps of the planks.

Beyond the bridge is a russet mountain with a wide mouth that leads into a dark cave. A woman stands in front of the cave, a spear in hand, white paint on her olive face, and a single braid resting on her shoulder. She's much taller than I am, with thick, muscular arms and legs. It's her job to watch the cave, make sure the prisoner doesn't escape and that no one enters. I only know because I found this cave last night, shortly after Willow had fallen asleep. I know she doesn't want me killing Garrett, but everything inside me tells me to do it. That man doesn't deserve her mercy, and he definitely doesn't deserve mine.

"Is he awake yet?" I ask, approaching the guard. Her name is Lilith.

"He is, but our grace has ordered that I not let you in," Lilith replies.

I narrow my eyes at her. "Why not?"

"Because she knows your intentions. You want to kill him, but our queen has not given you the order. She has told me to not let you in."

"What?" I snap. "Why would she do that?"

"Caspian." I look over my shoulder. Hassha walks toward us in a linen brown dress and her hair braided into a halo with the gold crown on top of her head.

"Hassha, please give me an explanation," I demand. "I have every right to end that man's life. You know what he did to Willow."

She gestures to Lilith, who nods her head and enters the cave. When she emerges, she's clutching Garrett by the arm and dragging him with her. He looks nothing like he did before, full of arrogance and anger. Instead, he appears afraid and weak, and like he might cry. The bloody wimp.

"Follow me, Caspian." Hassha turns away before I can protest.

Annoyed, I follow her across the bridge. Lilith trails behind with Garrett until Hassha stops in the center of the forest. Birds caw, and strips of sunlight filter through the leaves, highlighting her skin.

Lilith walks around me, dumping Garrett onto the ground between us. He lands with an *oomph* and slowly sits up.

"What is it you're most afraid of, Caspian?" Hassha asks.

"I'm not afraid of anything," I counter.

"Losing your mate," she retorts, and I press my lips. "And spiders," she adds.

I avoid a sigh. I *really* wish she'd stay out of my head.

"I know how angry you are at this man, and I know how badly you want to murder him. But while you are on my island, I will *not* allow reckless bloodshed. This is not Blackwater. Do you understand?"

I swallow to rid my throat of dryness. "Yes."

"Now, I sense that Willow would rather us return this man to Earth so that he can go on about his life, but I refuse to do that. He's seen parts of Kessel that no man should ever see, and if he was a vessel of Decius before, he could become one again. I've asked him if he has family on Earth, and he has informed me that he doesn't. I've searched his mind inside and out, and the sad truth is that, other than Willow, no one will care that he's missing."

"What are you getting at?" I grumble, resisting the urge to punch the hell out of Garrett right here, right now.

Hassha gestures to Garrett as he draws his knees to his chest. "What I'm saying is you have a choice right now to turn him into *whatever* you want."

"What do you mean?"

"What I mean is if you want him to become a spider, I can turn him into one."

"*What?* How would that even help me, Hassha?"

"If you feel the urge to step on this spider and crush it

255

beneath your boot, I will not stop you," she continues. "And perhaps it will help you overcome your fear of them."

I stare into her eyes as they flicker to silver.

"No—seriously! No!" Garrett tries standing, but Lilith shoves him back to the ground then points her spear in his face. "I don't know what's going on, but this is fucked up! You can't kill me! I don't deserve to die!"

"Is it true that you were laying your hands on Willow? Abusing her?" Hassha asks, lowering her flaming silver gaze to him.

"I—I didn't do anything! She—she made me do those things!"

His response makes my blood boil. Fuck turning him into a spider. I'd take way more pleasure in ripping him limb from limb as the piece of shit he is right now.

Hassha points her gaze to me. "Well, Caspian?" When I say nothing, she sighs. "It's this, or he rots in that cave forever, because I won't let him go. I'll let him decay, and during his final breaths, he'll know he's dying because he laid hands on a woman."

My breaths come out ragged. I'm so full of rage as I stare down at him. All I need is one minute to destroy him. But it's not an option, and I realize that when I finally step away and shake my head. Willow would be angry with me, disappointed even. She'd be hurt if I did anything to him without consulting her first.

"It shouldn't be my choice," I finally say.

Hassha tilts her head. "No?"

"It should be Willow's."

Her lips curl to a smile. "I like that answer."

Hassha nods at Lilith, and Lilith snatches Garrett up. "Let's go." She drags him away, heading toward the bridge again and disappearing beneath the curve. I let out a frustrated sigh, clenching my jaw so hard I swear my teeth will crack.

Hassha places a hand on my shoulder, and to my surprise, her touch doesn't burn. It hardly feels like it's there at all. When I meet her eyes, they've softened, as well as the anger brewing inside me.

"Vengeance should never be hasty. You of all people should know this," she says, voice low. "I saw your memories about your mother, and what your father did to her."

I clench a fist at the sheer reminder of my mother and the mistake I made that got her killed.

"Her death was not your fault."

I close my eyes, breathing harder, faster.

"Caspian, look at me."

I wait for my breathing to slow before finding her eyes.

"Your mother's death was not your fault. Do not let the hurt from your past and your blind rage rush you into doing something you'll regret later. You were wise to think about Willow first."

"He deserves to *die*, Hassha!"

"Sure, but the pain he inflicted was never yours. It was hers. Don't go behind her back making decisions *for* her. Let her choose what should be done so that she's at peace with it." She removes her hand, and I'm not sure why a sadness falls over me. Hassha is tampering with my emotions. She's putting logical reasoning into my brain, regardless of how badly I want to soak in my anger.

I'm saddened, not because I don't get the chance to kill Garrett, but because my love for Willow is so much stronger than I realized, and she means so damn much to me.

Hassha is right. I can't kill him. It's not what Willow wants, no matter how badly he treated her, and that tears me in two because her heart is good. It's *so* good, and I don't deserve the love she pours from it. She could have ordered me to end that man the same night I captured him and stuffed him in the trunk of her car, but she didn't. Even in fear, she displayed nothing but compassion for that worthless fucker. I truly don't deserve someone like her.

"Come now, Caspian." Hassha's voice snaps me out of my thoughts. "Your mate is awake, thriving, and her heart yearns for you. Let's get back to her."

CHAPTER 48

CAZ

WHEN WE ARRIVE IN MOON VILLAGE, MY EYES MOVE to Willow who is now being offered a fruit basket from Carra. When Willow takes it, Carra drops to her knees and begins massaging her feet. Willow looks around, clearly uncomfortable, but too kind to tell her to stop.

I soften a bit, my guard wavering as I watch her. She's so stunning in that dress, the yellow making her brown skin more luxurious. I want to take her somewhere and lay kisses all over her body, but it'd be rude of us to just disappear while Kessel has taken us in. Still, just five minutes with her, and we'd both be satisfied.

Carra smiles up at Willow, stroking her heels. Seriously. What the hell is up with that woman?

"Do you all massage other people's feet as a custom thing here? Like Carra is doing?" I ask because I've never seen or heard about this in my studies.

"Hmm." Hassha ponders it. "Depends on the person, and if they can benefit us. Don't worry. It's a gesture of great respect."

I look to Willow again as she eats some of the fruit. She places a hand on Carra's, politely thanking her while pulling her feet away.

"Why don't you do something fun with Willow?" Hassha offers. "Take her for a stroll. Perhaps that'll ease your mind and you can discuss the situation to her about our prisoner."

"A *stroll?*"

"Yes, women love that, don't you know?" Hassha asks, her eyes lighting up. "Walk near the ocean, play in the water. Take a swim. It's romantic."

"Hmm. Well, there you have it." I shift on my feet. "Romance isn't really my thing."

"Romance requires vulnerability. You care about her, don't you?"

"Of course, I do."

"And you want to see her happy?"

"Always."

"So be vulnerable with her. Don't hide it. Let it all show. As a matter of fact, after tonight's feast, you can take her to the Cave of Stars. It's quite beautiful. I should know. I made the cave myself—a place for my women to escape when they need to have a swim, unwind, and breathe. I've not tried being romantic there, but some of my colony has."

"Wait. You mean…" I can't even finish the sentence.

As if Hassha reads my mind, she says, "Some of the girls kiss and lick each other here. My women, they love to serve one another in many, many ways."

Holy shit. My eyes grow wider, and I slide my gaze to Willow. Carra is now massaging Willow's shoulders. Now I have the urge to walk over and tell her to get away from my mate. No wonder she's been all over her, giving her tea and fruit, doing her hair, and even inviting her to her damn bungalow. She's *attracted* to her—I see it now. It's in her eyes, the hungry way she looks at her. That woman wants to *kiss and lick* my mate. I could tell her to back the fuck off, but who am I to do that? A man jealous over a woman? Any man would die for that, I'm sure, but man or woman, Willow is *mine,* and I don't *ever* want to share her.

As if she senses the unease coursing through me, Willow finds my eyes and tilts her head. **What's wrong?**

I throw up my mind's wall, and Hassha laughs beside me. "Aren't you the jealous creature?"

"Don't even," I mutter before Hassha can say another word. If anyone is going to be doing any *licking* or *fucking* Willow, it's me, so I ask, "Where can I find this Cave of Stars?"

"It's a short journey from the bungalows. Take the path toward the hill where the moon lilies grow. When the sun sets, you'll see them. In fact, you can't miss them. They turn a soft lavender, very beautiful in the night. Follow the trail of lilies, and it'll lead you to the cave. But fair warning—Cave of Stars is a magical place. *Anything* is possible there. Any desire you or your mate have, it's theirs while in the cave."

"Anything?"

"Absolutely *anything,*" she says, then she moves closer, whispering something into my ear that causes my jaw to go slack.

CHAPTER 49
WILLOW

A DINNER COMMENCES, AND A BONFIRE ROARS TO life in the middle of the clearing. The women eat, drink, and dance while a group of five tap away at conga-like drums or play melodies through flutes.

Maia and Minka run in the clearing with other girls, playing tag, or using sticks as pretend swords. The shops are now closed, and everyone has gathered here to cap the night.

Women young and old flit around with chatter and laughter, and it's like one big family reunion—only Caz and I are the outsiders. We don't belong, but the women of Kessel don't make us feel that way. They give us food and plenty of wine.

Carra tries getting me to dance with her, but I shake my head with a smile, and she shrugs, finding another woman to dance with.

"She wants to lick your pussy, you know?" Caz says with his eyes ahead.

I nearly choke on the swig of wine in my mouth. "Excuse me. *What?*"

"Hassha says the women here serve each other, and that the whole rubbing of the feet thing…well, it's done when someone develops a great respect and admiration for another in Kessel. So yeah…Carra there, wants to *fuck* you." The flames reflect off his blue eyes as he sits forward with his elbows on his thighs.

I'm not even sure what to say to that. First of all, it's the bluntness of his statement that caught me by surprise. He said it so casually, like he told me his favorite color was blue or something.

"Well…" I clear my throat. "That's…interesting to know."

He glances at me. "You wouldn't let her, would you?"

"What? Caz, no!"

"Good. Because I can't fight off a woman. But if that's something you want, well…who am I to stop it?"

I laugh as he drops his arms to pick his wine glass up and bring it to his lips. "Wow. You are seriously so jealous."

"Hey, what's mine is mine. Besides…" He sighs, leaning back on the log we're on and spreading his legs farther. "It's the Tether that makes me so territorial of you. I think of anyone having their hands on you other than me, and I want to rip them to shreds."

Caz places his wine glass down while I polish mine off and shoot to a stand. "Come dance with me," I insist.

His eyes slide up my body before shifting to the women around the fire. "Don't you think Carra will be offended that you turned her down if she sees us dancing?"

"Don't change the subject! Come on." I grab his hand, tugging on the tips of his fingers.

"Willow," he laughs. "I can't dance."

"You can't, or you *won't?*"

He eyes me, head going into a tilt. "I'll make a fool of myself. None of these women want to see a man dancing."

"Who cares? The point of dancing is to have fun, let go. Be careless."

He looks toward the fire, then lets out a long breath as he swings his eyes to mine again. "Very well."

"Yes!" I cling to his hand and lead the way toward the fire with a wide smile. The music is lively and fast, and I have no clue what I'm doing or how to dance to it, but I move anyway, twirling my hips and throwing my arms in the air. Caz watches me, hardly moving.

"Dance!" I shout, grabbing both his hands and reeling him toward me.

"This is ridiculous," he mumbles.

"I don't wanna hear it. Come on." I force him to move his feet with mine while lacing my fingers with his. He finally moves, shifting left to right. "Good. Now loosen those hips. I know you know how to do that."

He smirks at that, those blue irises connecting with mine, and finally livens up. For the first time in my life, I watch Caspian Harlow dance. His hips shift and thrust, his feet stepping in rhythm. He takes my hand, raising it in the air and rocking with me. I can't help the laughs bubbling out of me as he tugs me in by the hand and steals a kiss.

When the music slows in tempo, I drape my arms around the back of his neck, and we sway on the field. The moon is full, beaming on us as the stars twinkle in the background. I hear whispers from the women, and I bet they're all watching us, but I don't care.

We move in sync, the heat of the fire caressing my skin. I

toss my head back, closing my eyes and taking a deep breath. His hands skim down my waist, slowly moving down to cup my ass. He gives it a squeeze, and a deep groan fills the base of his throat.

"Why can't it always be like this?" I sigh.

He says nothing to that, so I look up. He pulls his hand from my ass, but only to grab one of mine and lead me away from the fire.

"Wait—Caz! What are you doing? Where are we going?" I ask, peering over my shoulder. The music has picked up again, and the women have resumed dancing.

Caz makes his way toward a path, shoving branches out of the way, my hand fastened in his. Ahead, I notice glowing purple flowers shaped like lilies and gently swaying with the breeze. Caz finally slows down, and I work to catch some of my breath as I stand at his side. I touch one of the flowers, and it's silky to the touch. Up close, it's not fully purple. Only the tips of the petals are. The rest of its body is white, the thick stems a deep green.

"Wow. These are so pretty," I breathe.

"They are," he says. "But wait until you see what this path leads to."

He walks by my side on the path, past more groves of the glowing lilies, until we're met with a large body of water. The water shimmers in the night, glowing a wondrous, luminescent blue. It's a lake surrounded by trees, bushes, and more flowers, and at the end of the body of water is the mouth of a cave.

"Care for a swim?" Caz is already taking his shirt off, the blue lagoon glowing on his skin. His muscles ripple as he tosses the shirt, and when his pants are off, he lobs them aside too.

"Meet you in." I'm not allowed a word as he runs ahead completely naked and cannonballs into the water.

There's a loud *splash*, and when he resurfaces, he sucks in a breath, then smiles. "Come on, Willow Woman! It's warm!"

"Are you sure? How do you know there aren't any sharks or anything?"

"Willow, you'd see the bloody sharks. The water is as clear as glass," he shoots back.

I bite into my bottom lip, studying the body of water. Caz tips backwards, floating on his back, and my goodness, his dick looks amazing in this light.

"Okay, fine!" I call.

Once my dress is off, tossed into a puddle on the side, I do the same as Caz and run naked toward the water.

When I cannonball, he is indeed correct. The water *is* warm and feels amazing right now, like a lukewarm bath. When I resurface, Caz chuckles, then swims in the opposite direction.

"Follow along."

"You're going *toward* the cave?" I shout. Now he's really out of his damn mind. Going into a cave? At *night*? In another world with all kinds of crazy shit around?

"Don't worry!" he calls. "There's nothing inside. I made sure."

I swallow hard, and with a bit of reluctance, swim after him. When he disappears into the darkness of the cave, my heart is pounding. Everything inside me tells me to turn back and not to make this a Black and White thing, but Black people don't just willingly wander into caves at night.

But I remember I'm with Caz, and he'd never let anything hurt me. As I swim past the rocky mouth, I realize the cave isn't so dark inside. The water still glows, and on the ceiling of the cave, wedged between various sized stalactites (funny, I remember the term from when Warren used to read all those National Geographic books), are specks of light scattered across. They appear to be stars, running from the top to the rocky edges and trailing into the water.

There's a soothing glow inside, and suddenly the cave doesn't feel so daunting. In fact, it's *so* mesmerizing I figure I must be dreaming.

I point my gaze ahead to find Caz climbing out of the water to sit on a built-in bench near one of the cave walls. The bench is made of gold, with stars reflecting off of it. It has a wide seat that can fit up to at least four people, with a base built beneath that keeps it a level above the water.

I study Caz in all his naked glory, taking deep breaths as I float. His chest rises and sinks, his dark hair clinging to his forehead like wisps of ink. His body is like a god's, chiseled in all the right places. His abs are pronounced, beautiful pecs I want to lay kisses on, and his chest is firm as he flexes. Even with the scars and bruises, he's gorgeous. His eyes flicker up to mine, and he looks at me beneath dark, damp lashes.

Come here.

I swim in his direction until I'm floating between his legs. I can't help looking at his dick, the way it sits on his lap, thick and glistening from droplets of water. I have the sudden urge to take him into my mouth, but I refrain, and as if Caz senses it, he laughs.

"You know it's yours, right? You can do whatever you want with it."

I fight a smile. "I know."

I swim backward, and he eases into the water, collecting me into his arms when he's close. His lips meet mine once, twice.

The third time, his tongue slips between my lips, and he tastes like wine and fruit.

"I have a question for you." His voice is husky.

"Okay?"

"What's something you desire most?"

His question catches me completely off guard, and my mouth falls open. "What makes you ask that?"

"I'm just curious. You're my mate. It'd be nice to know what you *really* want. Sure, I can read some of your thoughts, but I haven't heard you thinking about anything of that nature."

I let that marinate a moment, while also aiming not to let other thoughts slip. I don't want him to hear it before I tell him.

"Okay, well if you must know..." I can't help the giggle that bursts out of me. That damn wine. It's got me good. "This is going to sound so silly out loud."

"Go on," he encourages, a tiny smile claiming his lips.

"Okay, well, in my world, women have what we call...vibrators. When I feel lonely and horny, I use it."

"Ah. Yes, we have vibrators in Vakeeli as well."

"You do?" I ask, eyes widening.

"Yes. They're quite expensive actually."

"Oh. Well...it's good you have them." I clear my throat. "Anyway, I've always wanted someone to use it on me while doing...*other* things."

"Other things like what?" he asks, voice husky.

"You know, making out, sucking...licking."

"You mean having someone use it on you to make you come over and over again?" His question is more of a statement.

I shudder a breath as his mouth nears mine. "Sure, that."

"That I can do." His lips crash down on mine, and I moan,

stroking his dick beneath the water. He groans, growing harder by the second.

"*Fuck*. Those hands of yours always get me."

When he's hard in my palm, I pull my hand away, and a guttural noise erupts in his throat. I smirk as I swim to the other side of the cave.

"So, a vibrator, eh?" he asks, coming close again.

I shrug, dipping lower into the water. "Yeah, but it's not like it can happen right now. I highly doubt they have vibrators in Kessel."

He moves closer, the water rippling between us. "What if it *can* happen?"

I narrow my eyes. "How?"

Caz tilts his chin so that he's looking at the stars above. "Hassha says this cave is magical—that if you ask for what you truly desire, you will have. But only in here."

I take a moment to look around at the glittery stars, then whisper, "Seriously?"

He nods with a smirk.

"Wow, that's…" I huff a laugh. "That's very interesting."

"So, what do you say? Shall we give it a go?"

"We can…but only if you're sure."

"This isn't about me. I want *you* to be sure."

I look around the cave again. We are completely alone in here, and there's something alluring about that…but there's no way a cave can create a vibrator. How would that even be possible? Then again, this is Vakeeli. Many unexplainable things have happened that I have *not* been prepared to witness.

Sensing my hesitation, Caz looks me all over before settling on my eyes and says, "Let me put it to you this way. I want to satisfy you in *every* way, Willow. I want to take care of you, protect you, *please* you." He brings his lips closer to mine, so close I can feel his breath spilling down my chest. It makes me shiver in the most delectable way. "I want you to get *everything* you desire and more, especially if I'm allowed to be involved."

"Okay," I breathe as his lips press to my cheek. "Fine. Let's do it."

CHAPTER 50
CAZ

"ALL RIGHT, LET'S SEE IF THIS ACTUALLY WORKS." Willow swims toward the bench, towing herself out to sit on it. I'm right in front of her as she draws in a deep breath. "So *how* does it work, exactly?"

"Just ask for what you want," I tell her. "But call it by its name, the Cave of Stars."

"Okay." She pauses, her eyes bouncing around the cave. "Cave of Stars? What I desire most requires a...vibrator." She's practically blushing as she avoids my eyes. "Can you bring one to us? A big, powerful one!"

The cave is quiet a moment, the soft sounds of water lapping and trickling. When several seconds have passed and not much changes within the cave, Willow releases a breath and says, "Maybe I'm not asking for it the right way."

We wait quietly, peering around the cave again. Then, stars plummet from the ceiling of the cave, forming into an iridescent line that dips into the water. Beneath the surface, the stars merge into a sphere, and it grows in size, forming into an object and floating above the water.

It glows, settling in its form, and Willow sucks in a breath when the object turns into a starry, transparent, and rather large midnight blue vibrator.

Willow gasps, shooting her eyes to me. "Caz...that thing is *huge*."

"Well, you did use the words big and powerful in the same sentence." I swim toward it, retrieving it from the air. "Shall we see how powerful it really is?"

Willow presses her lips together, eyeing the vibrator and then locking on my eyes. "Would you like me to lead?" I ask.

She nods, her teeth sinking into her bottom lip. I want so badly to unleash that caged lip just to trap it between my teeth.

"Right. Lie back on the bench."

"Okay," she breathes. She leans back, planting her elbows down.

"Now, just a fair warning, I'm going to make you come several times," I tell her, and she nods eagerly, her tongue running over her lips. "And when you've had enough of this thing, I'll be buried *inside* you, just to make you come again. Then when we're finished, there'll be a pretty little mess of my cum and yours between your legs. Are you okay with that?"

"Yes," she breathes again, and I watch her hips buck just a little. When they do, I feel an ache in my balls, a yearning just as extreme as hers.

I smirk and press a button on the vibrator that brings it to life. The vibration echoes throughout the cave, and Willow's eyes expand as she watches me bring it toward her. When she spreads her legs, I press the tip of the vibrator on her clit. She moans and shakes instantly, and I clasp her hip with my free hand, lowering the vibrator and thrusting the length of it into her. It goes in easily because she's already so wet.

Her mouth forms into a wide O, and I take that opportunity to push it deeper as my mouth closes around her nipple.

"Oh, Caz. Yes," she sighs. She presses a hand to the back of my head, and I steal a glance up at her. She's already looking at me, eyes oozing with lust and heat.

When her head tips back, she breathes raggedly, clutching a handful of my hair as I move to the other nipple and bring it to a peak.

"Oh, I'm gonna…"

"Gonna what?" I rumble, laying a kiss on her chest.

"I'm gonna come if you leave it like that."

"So come," I tell her, and she sucks in a sharp breath before her body bucks forward. Her cry of pleasure fills the cave, and I hold on to her waist while slowly moving the vibrator in and out.

"Oh, fuck," she gasps when I pull it away completely.

"Look at that," I murmur. "All your cum." I bring the vibrator to my mouth, licking some of her cum away, and her eyes light up. Her heart is racing, and I hear the same words running through her head: *He's so sexy. I need him to fuck me right now. What's he waiting for?*

I climb onto the mildly gravelly bench and sit next to her. She looks sideways at me with hooded eyes before lowering her vision to my dick.

"Sit on it," I order.

She doesn't waste time climbing onto my lap, but instead of facing me, she faces the opposite way. I watch as she squats above me, my dick as hard as a rock and already throbbing from watching her orgasm, and as she slowly sinks down on me, a groan builds in my throat. When I'm all in, that groan slips through my parted lips.

"Fuck, Willow," I rasp. "I feel you. You're so wet."

"Yeah?" she breathes.

"Hell, yes."

When she starts to ride me, I question whether I'll be able to sustain myself. It's never been so simple for me—*sex*, that is. It used to require a great deal for me to finish, but one ride of Willow, and I'm like a teenage boy.

I rest my back against the bench and instruct her to bring her legs up so her back is resting against my frontside. She shifts, and I groan again, pulsing inside her as she settles that warm, wet pussy on top of me.

"Right...now I'm going to bring this vibrator around and rest it on your clit," I tell her. "And when you come, I'll come."

"Okay." She nods, resting the back of her head on my shoulder. I start up the vibrator again and bring it down to her pussy, and as I kiss her neck, she sighs, then moans when the vibration takes over.

How does it feel? I wonder, allowing her to hear me. As if my voice is both a shock and a delicious factor, she lets out a noise that's a mixture of a gasp and a moan.

Then I hear her voice in my head saying, **It feels amazing.**

Better than you imagined?

Ten times better.

Your pussy feels so good wrapped around me like this. Oh, are you clenching? I chuckle as she giggles. *Keep doing that, and I'll come soon. Is that what you want? For me to come inside you yet again?*

Yes.

You love having my cum in your pussy, don't you?

She moans in response, thrusting her hips to move against

the vibrator. My dick spasms inside her. I groan as her hips roll and dip. Yeah, surely it won't be long now.

I increase the power of the vibrator, and that sends Willow over the edge. One of her hands comes to my thigh, clutching it tight. Her nails pierce the skin, and a wave of pain and pleasure strikes me.

"Right there?" I ask aloud.

"Yes. Right there."

"Mmm." I keep the vibrator still as she rolls her hips. Kissing the crook of her neck again, I bring my free hand around to cup one of her breasts, and she breathes harder, faster, and my dick is so hard and swollen that she's leaving me no choice but to let go. All the blood in my body has shot down to my dick. I'll come, I know it.

And when she cries her bliss, I unleash my own. She jerks on top of me, savoring the feel of my dick and the vibration, and I can't help sinking my teeth into her back, not too much to hurt, but enough for her to feel me here too.

As she moves her hips slowly, I feel the warmth of my cum spilling down my shaft and to my balls. Or perhaps it's both of ours. Whatever the case may be, it feels too good to dare pull out.

Willow whimpers as her body relaxes, and I turn the vibrator off and toss it aside. She then climbs off of me, but only to turn around and face me with a lazy smile. Cupping my face, she presses those soft, plump lips to mine and coaxes my mouth open so our tongues collide. My dick comes to life all over again, throbbing with need, knowing her warmth is only mere inches away.

This moment is bliss. The way she smells like flowers and fresh rain. Her calming sighs behind each kiss, so full of love that it makes me weak in the knees. I'm so in love with this woman that it's *maddening*. When the kiss breaks, she closes her arms around the back of my neck, and our lips graze each other, that electric feeling floating between us that I adore.

"I love you more than you'll ever know," she whispers.

I feel my eyes stretch. My word. So, she *did* hear me last night? Well, good. At least she knows.

I can't help myself when I hear those words fall from her lips. I grin, kissing her until our mouths are tired, and when my dick has hardened all over again, I take her one more time in the Cave of Stars.

CHAPTER 51
WILLOW

I DON'T EVEN KNOW WHAT TO THINK AFTER GOING TO the Cave of Stars. That experience—which truly doesn't feel like the proper word—was something beautiful and otherworldly, and it *never* would've happened on Earth...at least not with a vibrator like *that*. A toy made from stars. How...interesting. I wonder what else those stars can do.

I can't lie, my entire stay in Kessel has me thinking about a life in Vakeeli. Perhaps if I stay, it wouldn't be so bad. After we take out Decius and free Caz's family, we could consider it a possibility. But...what happens when more threats arise? When the love we have transforms to something much deeper? When thoughts of marriage and happily-ever-after's are seared into my brain? It's all I can think about, and I have my mind's wall up because I don't want him to hear any of it.

Though we left the cave together, Caz's arm draped over my shoulder, still smelling of salt, stars, and sex, I sense his unease.

Even more so now that we're in a free bungalow Hassha offered us and have changed into comfortable clothing. Through the wide skylight above, the moon burns bright in the clear, indigo sky, the stars acting as backup dancers as they glimmer.

Caz lies with me on the bed, and my head is on his chest. I listen to the steady rhythm of his heartbeat, feel his soft breaths falling on my skin. He has his wall up too. He's been quiet since we showered and lay down.

"What are you thinking about?" I ask after a while.

He continues staring up at the open ceiling, rubbing circles on my shoulder blade with the pad of one of his fingers.

"My family," he says after some time.

"Oh."

A stretch of silence falls on us.

"I'm getting this odd feeling about them. Like something isn't right. We've been in Kessel for nearly two days, and I'm sure Decius has sensed it, regardless of Hassha's protection."

"How would he?"

"We're all linked through this Tether Selah created." I look up, and his face has warped with a mixture of aggravation and sadness. "I just hope nothing has happened, is all. If something does, I'll blame myself."

"We can't blame ourselves for what Decius does, or for any of this Tether nonsense." I sit up on one elbow, catching his eyes. "But when it's time, I'm going with you to Blackwater."

He frowns. "No, you're not."

"Yes, I am."

"We can argue about this until your pretty face is blue, Willow. You're not going."

I roll my eyes. "How will you stop me?"

"I'll find a way."

"And what if I find a way out of your way?"

"Then...I'll circle around to another solution. You must forget I'm a monarch. I'm constantly thinking ahead." He sits up fully and places a hand on the scar on the center of my chest. "This is why you should stay." His finger grazes the vertical scar. "I don't need you getting any more of these."

I grab his hand, squeezing it. "I'll carry all the scars if it means we're together."

His lips twitch and his eyes incline, landing on mine. "What's something you really want in life, Willow?"

I hesitate a bit. "What do you mean?"

"I mean, when you picture your life and think of what fulfills you, what does that picture entail?"

I twist my lips, allowing his words marinate. Was my wall up? Did he hear me thinking about a life in Vakeeli before? No, I'm positive it was up. "Well, now that I've met you, I want you in the picture."

His lips quirk to smile.

"But I guess that picture includes a group of people I love too. People I can be with, who I trust, and who I know will never leave my side, no matter what. I want to nurture and protect the ones I love. I want to live a healthier life too, not drown myself in liquor and weed all the time because I'm so sad." I huff a sarcastic laugh as he continues a smile. "And believe it or not, I've never really been great at anything. Some people are born to be athletes, artists, or writers. Some become models, or dancers, or inherit big corporations. Some even become monarchs, or kings and queens," I add, and that makes him smile wider. "But for me, I didn't get any of that. I just *exist,* you know? But I'm okay with that, so long as I can exist in a place where I belong and where I matter. As long as I can take care of the people I love, talk to them, cook for them, dance with them...that is what will fulfill me. I'm okay being me and being the kind of person who's ready to put a smile on another person's face. And maybe that's my purpose, you know? Being myself. I don't believe all of us are born and destined to do greater things. I think some of us are just here to exist, and to make the world a better place than we left it when it's time for us to go."

A soothing silence wraps around us, floating through the bungalow, and Caz is so quiet I think I've said something wrong. Perhaps I went too deep for him—or maybe all that I've said is dumb and doesn't make any sense.

"Anyway, I know it sounds stupid, but—"

"No." He cups my cheek, eyes glistening. He's revealing that beautiful smile I love, his teeth bright in the moonlight. So boyish. So handsome and vulnerable. "It's not stupid. Not at all. It's the most honest thing I've ever heard anyone say. You don't want to be anyone but yourself, and I love that about you. I love it more than you realize." He kisses the tip of my nose. "You're a treasure, Willow. Truly."

I can't help my smile as he brings our foreheads together. I want to bask in this moment, let it continue forever. Us beneath the moon and stars, surrounded by a beautiful ocean, on the center of a large, comfortable bed that has already conformed to the shape of our bodies. I want this so much...but of course what I want never lasts.

And in a matter of seconds, a foghorn sounds and Caz's smile collapses. A sinking feeling drops into our stomachs like a block of lead, and he jerks away, rushing toward the window to peer out of it.

I climb off the bed with him and gasp when I spot women running out of their bungalows with weapons and zooming past in a blur. I look in the direction they're running and spot a boat floating toward the shore.

My chest tightens when I realize the boat is on fire.

CHAPTER 52
CAZ

WILLOW AND I DRESS RAPIDLY BEFORE BOLTING TO the shoreline with the other women. Their shouting is boisterous as they watch the flaming boat rock toward us.

Hassha appears, pushing between a thick line of women. The flames reflect off her silver eye, and her lips part as if this is the last thing she expected. The flames ignite from the sails to the massive wooden body, rippling through each crevice and corner.

Hassha swims in the water, climbing up a flameless half of the boat and returning in a matter of seconds with a woman in her arms. She lays her on the sand then springs onto the boat again like a force of nature, going back and forth until she's rescued three other women. All of them cough and splutter as the others gather around, lowering to their knees to assist them.

"What's happened?" I ask when Hassha returns. Her white

hair clings to her forehead and cheeks. Soot is on her arms and legs.

"It's Decius," she says. Her voice is so low I almost can't hear her. Then, in a flash, she's on the boat again, this time coming off with a charred barrel. She places the barrel in the sand, then faces the enflamed boat again. One mighty kick from her foot sends the boat flying toward the middle of the ocean to collapse in ruins.

"Open the barrel," Hassha orders, pointing her gaze to Milandra. Milandra rips it open, revealing thick chunks of black wood with silver linings. The silver of the wood emits a menacing glimmer—one that doesn't appear to be from this world at all.

Hassha turns to me, shoulders squared. "We'll make your weapons, and then you must go. I'm afraid the longer you're here, the more danger my tribe is in."

"What did Decius do?" Willow asks.

Hassha stifles a sigh, holding it in and swallowing it down. "He must've known they were coming here with the wood and tried setting fire to it before they reached Kessel borders."

"How would he have known?"

"It was always a possibility," Hassha releases that pent up sigh, focusing on Willow. "He was ruler of The Trench, so he still has a connection to it, whether he's there or not. Though I covered my warriors with my energy so that he could not harm or feel them, there are eyes all over The Trench. Someone must've informed him." She gestures to the women. "My protection is why they are still alive and not roasting on that boat."

Everyone stands a moment, allowing her words to digest. My eyes shift from her to the burning, sinking boat, and then down at the silvery chunks of wood. We're fortunate the wood inside didn't completely burn.

A rapid splashing noise sounds in the distance, like someone is chopping water. The warrior women turn quickly, raising their shields and pointing their spears toward the ocean.

Willow clings to my arm, and I squint my eyes, trying to find the source of the noise. At first, I don't see a thing but the boat collapsing in the distance, flames reflecting on the waters. The warriors take a step toward the shore in unison, eyes alert, the moon causing the silver points to gleam.

Something is coming.

It's out there.

I *feel* it.

The chopping stops. The water settles. Breath bated, we all watch the ocean, searching the expanse of the waters. Then, something shoots into the air, bringing a surge of spray with it.

"Kessala!" Milandra hollers, and the warriors raise their shields as the drenched figure plummets from the air full speed.

The creature collapses on top of Milandra's shield, and with a grunt, she shoves the creature onto the ground, sending it flying several feet, but it only rises again, its bones cracking, neck bent at an alarming angle. It raises its arms like a spider about to attack its prey. Its flesh is saggy, it's teeth sharp like brown razors as they gnash at the women.

"What the hell is that?" Willow's voice is laced with fear as she stands behind me.

I glare at the creature as it takes a step forward, despite the warriors pointing their spears at it. If I'm not mistaken, that thing was a person before. It appears to have risen from the dead, its skin pallid and dense.

"Kassala, heel!" Hassha roars, and she rushes around her

warriors, her hands ignited and a blue beam firing toward the creature. It dodges the beam, its body bending and cracking as it lands on all fours. It's head jerks right, neck cracking to look directly at me and Willow. I push Willow into Milandra, who catches her and tows her away, just as the creature leaps in the air then tackles me to the ground.

CHAPTER 53

CAZ

THE CREATURE CLIMBS ON TOP OF ME, RIPPING AT MY shirt as it gnashes its slimy teeth. I grip it by the throat, trying to shove it off, but it holds on tight. It grips me by the head, squealing, and as it does, my breath is sucked from my lungs. The sunken eyes of the creature transform into red crescents, and he stares into mine until the world around me goes black. Willow's screams grow distant, and the creature disappears.

No longer am I in Kessel. What appears before me is the main room of my castle. It's dark inside, and I can hardly see a thing. I push to a stand, my breath coming out in cloudy tufts as I peer around. The room has become a frozen wasteland, a thick layer of ice on the walls and furniture.

But that's not what captures my attention. On the east wall ahead, just as they were before, is my family. They're still wrapped in black vines, trapped in those icy cocoons. I take a step toward them as something rustles to my left.

Decius stands on the opposite side of the room with a sneer, but he's not alone. Wrapped in his arms, a knife to her throat, is Della. Her eyes are full of dread as she looks directly at me.

"Della," I call. I run across the room in an attempt to help her, but I don't make it far. I come to a halt as the floor opens up before me, revealing a bottomless pit. The pit is too wide to jump. Decius' cackle rattles the room, and he presses the blade deeper against Della's throat.

"You've wasted too much of my time, Caspian. I've never had to wait this long for something owed to me. You avoided my vessels. Now you've run off to the Regals. Don't you understand it by now? The Regals don't give a damn about you or me because this is *our* fight, not theirs."

The edge of the blade sinks deeper into Della's flesh. Blood drips down her throat.

"Stop!" I shout. "Let her go right now! She has no part in this!"

"It's okay, Mr. Harlow," Della whispers, tears skidding down her cheeks. "You've done for me what no one else would have. You gave me purpose after so many losses. Perhaps my purpose has been fulfilled now. Protect your family. Protect your *mate*." She attempts a smile, but it does nothing to conceal the sorrow.

"Decius," I growl, my throat burning from unshed tears. "Let her go. She's done nothing wrong."

"No." It's a simple word. A mutter, really. I can hardly hear it, but I feel the venom of the word sinking into me like a weight. With one swift motion, he slices the center of Della's throat.

"NO! DELLA!"

I watch in helpless horror as she drops to her knees, clutching her neck. She hits the floor sideways, blood trickling down her chest and spilling on the floor. Her blood crawls toward the pit, dribbling into infinite darkness.

Fists clenched, I carry my blurry gaze up to Decius who has his eyes pinned on me. "You have one hour to get to me," he says, then he's moving across the room toward my family. "Or next time, it won't be the housemaiden. It'll be someone even closer to you." He stops in front of Maeve, and I have every urge to rush him, tackle him to the ground, but I'm useless here. I'm not really with him. He's in my head, showing me what he's doing through that disgusting creature.

"Perhaps Aunt Maeve will be next. She guides you, keeps a straight head on your shoulders. If I kill her, imagine how your cousins will feel. They'll blame you forever, Caspian. For as long as they live and breathe. They'll *never* forgive you for what you put them through." His eyes flash blood red. "One hour, or I kill them all," he snarls, and just like that, I'm back in Kessel.

I suck in a breath, coming face to face with Hassha who has her hands on my upper arms. The creature is gone, and her hands are a blazing blue. She must've killed it.

"What did you see?" Hassha demands, those bright eyes swirling with confusion.

Willow grabs my hand, helping me to a stand.

"How fast can you make the weapons?" I ask.

"Within twenty or thirty minutes if I have all my sword-smiths working," she answers.

"Good. Because I only have one hour to save my family."

CHAPTER 54
CAZ

"I'M AFRAID THAT I CAN'T LEND YOU ANY OF MY warriors, Caspian." Hassha has brought me and Willow to her bungalow, where her girls are still sleeping. She talks in a hushed tone, seeing as their bedroom is just around the corner. "It was risk enough sending them to The Trench. I'm afraid I can't go to Blackwater to help you either. If the commoners hear word that I've been around, it becomes a risk for Kessel. My duty is to protect my daughters and my tribe, no matter the circumstance."

"Understood." I rake my fingers through my hair and find that I'm still shaking. I don't shake...not anymore. But he...he killed Della. She's gone, and I couldn't do a damn thing about it.

"Why would he kill Della?" Willow asks quietly, seated in a chair in the corner. She still can't wrap her mind around it. I told her along the way, wanting what'd happened to be an awful nightmare, but I know it isn't. He really killed her. That wasn't

289

a figment of my imagination. I feel that ache deep in my chest, knowing she's gone.

Della was a good woman. She didn't deserve what he did to her. It's *my* fault she's dead. I waited too long. I should've gone back to Blackwater as soon as I landed in Kessel.

"No, you shouldn't have." Willow rises from her chair, fixing her gaze on me.

"Get out of my head, Willow. Right now is *not* the time," I mutter.

Hassha looks between us. "I can get you to Blackwater without a boat. It'll require a lot of my energy, so we'll have to do it in an open field."

I cut my eyes at her. "Fine."

It feels like an eternity for the weapons to be made. Hassha and Willow talk amongst themselves about that creature Decius sent, which I've come to learn is a Trenchmite. Hassha informs us that they're creatures Decius creates from the bodies of wicked commoners who've died in The Trench. He brings them back to life and fills them with his dark energy, using them to venture to places that he can't. According to Hassha, he'd sent several of them after her and Korah when Selah disappeared. Whatever that thing was, I hope to never see one again. Fortunately, she turned the one that attacked me to ash. She's certain it snuck onto the boat on Decius' orders and waited for its chance to find me.

"So, it was a zombie," Willow says, brows dipped. "On Earth, they're made-up things that rise from the dead and eat people's flesh or brains."

Hassha stares at Willow a moment. "Trenchmites do not feed on flesh or brains, but they can steal the life of someone good and use their body as their own."

Willow shudders. "So what did Kessala mean?" she asks.

"It's a Kessel warrior call," Hassha explains. "Means to stand guard, prepare for an attack."

"Oh."

Finally, a knock sounds at the door, and Hassha opens it. Three women are on the other side with rattan baskets in hand. They enter the bungalow, dropping the baskets on the wooden table in the middle of the room.

In the baskets are weapons made from the wood of the Trench tree. After Hassha slices the center of her palm and drips blood into the basket, it emits a rapid blue light before going back to normal.

"Doused with Regal blood," Hassha murmurs.

I draw out a knife and a sizable machete while Hassha turns for a shelf, taking down a white container. Lugging out my gun, she offers it to me, and I accept it immediately. Sure, they have their blessed weapons, but nothing beats a Blackwater gun. I've been trained most with guns. They're a part of me and will be with me so long as I live and breathe.

Hassha faces one of the women standing next to the door, and the woman approaches, dropping something into her bloodied palm.

"I had wooden bullets made as well, compatible with your gun." She takes my hand, and I open it so she can place twelve bloodstained bullets in my palm. "I want you to be aware that these weapons won't kill him, but they will weaken him, especially if you aim for the heart. Once you have him down, you must keep a piece of the wood in his heart so he remains weak."

"So he won't die?"

"I'm afraid not.

I would prefer he's dead," I mumble.

"Yes, but without Selah, we simply will not be able to kill him. We can hurt him as much as we can, weaken him, take his energy, but he will still breathe. Selah is the only way and she…" Hassha's words turn to a whisper. I know there isn't more she's telling me, but I don't have time to wait around for an explanation. Take Decius down first, then figure out how to wake Selah up so she can kill him. That's the goal and I have to be quick.

I accept the bullets and shove them into my pocket. I tuck the gun into my waistband, collect two daggers, then tell Hassha, "I'm ready to go."

"I'm coming with you," Willow says, snatching out her own dagger from the basket.

"No." I leave the cabin before she can protest, following Hassha.

"I'm not staying here, Caz! I'm going!"

I shake my head, ignoring her. Hassha side-eyes me as she continues walking, pushing through a thicket that guides us to an open field. The grass is dark in the night, the blades swaying with the breeze.

"Caz!" Willow shouts when we stop.

I whirl around. "Willow! For once, would you *please* just listen to me?" I grip her by the shoulders, forcing her to look into my eyes. "I am not sending you into that fucking trap, okay? Your best bet is to stay here or go back to Earth! He can't harm you in either of those places."

Her eyes glisten, and her mouth turns downward. "And what happens when *you* walk into that trap and he kills you?" she demands. "You die, and I'll be dead too. Or have you forgotten that?"

"Not if I stick to my bargain."

"You and I both know it's too late for that, Caz! He killed Della! He'll kill everyone, just because he can!"

"Just stay here where it's safe, Willow. I'll try to tap in with you mentally when I've done what I need to do."

Her head shakes defiantly. "No. I don't care how you feel about it, I'm not letting you go into this fight alone, Caz. If you die, I die, remember? And if I'm going to die, I'd rather go out *with* you. Now shut up and get over it because I'm coming with you, and you can't stop me."

I snatch away from her, shifting my gaze to Hassha. "Is there any way you can keep her here?" I demand.

Hassha delivers a slow headshake. "I won't deny her what she wants."

I groan. "Love of fucking Vakeeli! You women and your stubbornness!"

Willow folds her arms, smirking. Hassha smiles at her and tosses a wink, as if proud.

"Fine," I snap. "But if she dies, Hassha, her blood is on your hands." I face Willow again. "If you go, you have to promise you'll listen to me. Whatever I say, goes. Do you understand?"

Willow nods, a bit too eager for my liking, but I won't win this fight, and I'm wasting time. If Hassha won't stop her, how can I? She's so much safer here. Why won't she just stay?

"Hey." Willow's hand falls to my arm. "It's you and me 'til the end, Caz. You won't fight your battles alone. Not while I'm here."

I hold her eyes, wanting to be angry and proud of her all at once. I think of the woman who landed in my forest not too long ago, how she'd have run the other way if faced with a situation like this, but now she's willing to do the opposite. Now, she's here, and I'm not normally one to thank the Regals like all the other crazed commoners, but I do. I thank them for giving me a mate and a partner riddled with compassion and determination. Someone who truly will go to the ends of the world for me, just as I would her.

I take Willow's hand in mine, facing Hassha again.

"Very well. Send us to Blackwater."

CHAPTER 55
WILLOW

I'M NOT SURE HOW SHE DOES IT, OR HOW IT HAPPENS so quickly, but one minute we're standing in the field beneath a dark blue sky, and the next, we're in a forest, surrounded by an infinite number of trees.

The sky is gray with thick clouds. I can smell rain in the air. I look behind me, and there's the gate I've seen many times before, the one that cuts off the forest from the castle.

"This way." Caz turns toward the gate, pushing it open when he's near it. It creaks on its hinges, then he stops, looking at the dark castle ahead of us. But not only is the castle there. A group of people are too. And not ordinary people. The freaking Trenchmites again.

"Oh, God," I whisper.

They stand in a straight line, side-by-side, their arms raised. There are at least six of them. Their eyes glow red like Decius', and they snarl and gnash their teeth, ready to attack.

When one of them takes a step forward, Caz immediately

whips out his gun, swapping out the metal bullets for wooden Trench bullets. He does it swiftly, the revolver slinging shut with a satisfied snap. I can't wrap my mind around how this man is so good with his guns. If it were me, I'd have shot my own hand off by now.

Storing the bullets in his coat pocket, Caz says, "He's created an army." He watches the Trenchmites carefully, how they don't move any closer, just stare, waiting for us to act first.

"Listen to me closely, Willow. The stables across the field," he says, cocking his head to my left. "Go now."

"But Caz—"

"*Now*," he demands, and I clamp my mouth shut, stepping backwards. I promised to listen.

I look toward the downward hill where I assume the stables are and turn that direction, glancing at the line of Trenchmites before looking back at Caz. He tips his chin just as fat droplets of rain fall from the sky.

When he raises his gun, pointing it ahead, the Trenchmites snarl and run toward him with powerful stride. I gasp, running downhill. I spot one of the black stables ahead and rush to the door. I struggle to slide it open due to the mud, but I manage. I close it as far as I can, then spot Onyx, Caz's horse, standing in one of the stalls, neighing loudly and rising on his hind legs.

"Whoa—easy, Onyx! Easy! It's just me," I whisper. He continues his whinnying, throwing his hooves up and huffing.

Something thumps outside and I gasp, pressing my finger to my lips as I look at Onyx, before moving to one of the empty stalls. I spot a tall stack of hay and hide behind it just as another thump sounds at the door of the stable. I hear sniffing, huffing. *Oh, God.* It's one of the Trenchmite. It followed me.

I withdraw my knife, gripping the handle and bracing myself

for the creature. If I jump out, I'll have the advantage. It won't see me, and it can't take me. The urge to do it is high, but before I can, a blur of white enters my stall and pounces on me.

"Oh, my God! *Silvera?*"

She pants raggedly, wagging her tail and nuzzling her nose on my cheek. "What are you doing here?" I whisper. "I almost stabbed your crazy ass! It's not safe out there!"

Then again...maybe it is. If Silvera is here, that must mean none of the Trenchmite have run toward the stable after me.

I hear gunshots ricocheting and leave the stall, going toward the window. I can still see the roof of the castle here, but I can't see Caz, nor can I hear him.

"We have to do something," I whisper. Caz won't be able to get through all those things alone, and even if he does, Decius will know, and he'll be waiting. Like Caz said, it's a trap, and he'll be walking right into it. And my mate may be a lot of things, but he's no fool. He'd never walk into a trap without a plan.

My eyes slide to Onyx just as one of his large beady eyes focuses on me. I open the door of his stall and drag a palm along his sturdy back. "Hey, boy. Wanna go for a ride?"

CHAPTER 56
CAZ

I'VE TAKEN DOWN THREE OF THE TRENCHMITE WITH bullets to their heads. I reload my gun as one of them scrambles toward me, then raise it, shooting it in the head. They could probably die with regular bullets but I'm not taking any chances. The last two spring in the air, and I point my gun up to them, sending a bullet flying through the hearts of both.

They drop to the ground, squealing and turning to ash.

When all their bodies have disintegrated, scattering with the wind, I face Blackwater Manor.

"Where are you, Decius?" I shout. "You had your fun! Now face me!"

The wind howls, whipping at my coat. Thunder rumbles and the sky opens up, bringing the rain down harder. The door of the castle creaks open, and a black silhouette slips out the door. It dashes across the damp field, slinking low in the grass, and I raise my gun just as it appears several steps away from me.

Crescent red eyes flash in my direction, a wicked smile clinging to his lips. I pull the trigger of my gun, and Decius disappears.

Something sharp stabs me in the back, and I expel a sharp breath. A chill descends over my shoulder as Decius says, "Look at that. It only took you forty-two minutes to get to me."

He snatches the knife out of my back then shoves me onto the ground. I land on my stomach with a hard grunt, turning onto my back and raising my gun at him.

With a sneer, he lifts the bloody dagger in his hand—the same one he used to kill Della—and wipes my blood on the sleeve of his jacket.

"Just take me," I mutter, breathing raggedly. "Let my family go."

"Are you still on about that silly bargain we made? That option is long gone, Caspian. You betrayed me by going behind my back to the Regals. Where are they now, anyway?" he asks, peering around. "Not here to save you, I gather. You were a fool to rely on them."

"I don't need them to save me," I grumble.

"You poor boy. Everyone requires saving, especially when *I'm* involved. You truly believed you could face me all on your own?" His mouth curls into a wicked smile.

"Of course not," I pant, my eyes shifting over his shoulder. "I have *her*."

Just as the words leave my mouth, Willow nears us on the back of Onyx. Decius turns but isn't quick enough to move as she dashes by, plunging a Trench sword into the center of his chest. The sword penetrates his body, and he cries out a piercing noise that drowns out all others.

I push off the ground, dusting myself off. There is no pain. I was never hurt and only pretended to be when he stabbed me. How could I be when Hassha sent me off with her energy?

This was our plan before landing in Blackwater. I was to deal with whatever trap Decius laid while Willow ran to the stables for my horse. I had a feeling Decius would know Hassha put some kind of protection over me, but with it being such a rush to get to him, I figured he'd assume I was vulnerable. It was a major risk, seeing as Decius reads energy, but Hassha is smart. She protected me without leaving a trace for Decius to find. And with his focus solely on me, his blood broiling with hunger, I was willing to take whatever risk was necessary to weaken him.

"Now that," Decius laughs dryly, blood smearing his teeth. "That was low. But you missed my heart." Hopping up, he snatches the sword out of his chest. He doesn't do so without pain, but even so, he manages to point a hand toward Willow, shooting an invisible force her way and knocking her off the horse. Onyx squeals as she hits the ground.

"Willow!" I scream as Decius tosses the sword aside with a stagger. A blur of black and white sprints toward him, and he lets out a howl as Cerberus and Silvera sink their teeth into his arm and ankle. He flings them about, but their jaws are locked.

I rush to Willow as the wolves' growls sharpen. "Willow, are you okay?" I ask, bringing her to a stand.

"Yeah. I'm fine." She grunts a bit as I wipe dirt from her forehead. Her eyes expand as she peers over my shoulder. I look with her, and Decius has managed to fling Cerberus and Silvera off him to run. "He's getting away!" she yells.

"No, he's not." I pull out my gun, watching as he ambles toward the opposite side of the field while clinging to his chest. "Stay here. I'm going after him."

"Wait—Caz." She grips the lapels of my jacket, tugging me in and kissing me hard on the lips. "I love you," she breathes. "Now go kill him."

I smile, kissing her one more time before hopping onto Onyx's back and riding after Decius. It's no surprise he's running toward the Dark Cliffs. It's a place that brews with dark energy—a land no man ever ventures to—and he'll likely try to use it to his advantage. But I'm still protected by Regal energy for now, and no matter what tricks he tries throwing my way, they won't stop me from ending him once and for all.

CHAPTER 57
WILLOW

I watch Caz ride off on Onyx with Cerberus right on his tail, and I pray to God and to the Regals that he'll be able to catch Decius and take him down.

Something flashes in my peripheral, and I tilt my gaze toward the castle. The lights flicker on, inside and out. The sconces outside the large front door burn brightly, as well as the torches attached to the terraces. All that darkness has now transformed to light, which must mean Decius' energy is fading. Good.

Silvera meets me as I take a step toward the castle. I have no idea what I'll find inside, but with Decius weakened and away from the castle, it can't be too bad.

I snatch the Trench knife I was carrying out of my waistband and push the door open. Despite the lights being on and the heat kicking in, the place is still freezing, and ice remains all over the walls, running in jagged, ominous lines. I round the corner where the main room is, and to my surprise, the ice is melting away into dark pools on the floor. Caz's family is still pinned to the wall, no longer in their icy cocoons; however, the dark vines still cling to them. Their bodies shift, along with a wave of moans and groans.

Killian's eyes open first, and an instant grimace takes over his face as he looks down at his feet dangling in the air. "What's happened?" he snaps. "Who did this?"

"Wow." I rush toward him with a relieved sigh. "I never thought I'd be so happy to hear your voice, Killian."

"Feel the same way about you, Willow," he returns, and I huff a laugh. "How did you get here? Where's Caz?" he grouses.

Juniper moans next to him, her head rolling sideways. "Love of Vakeeli, my head," she groans, squeezing her eyes tighter. "Feels like I have a bloody hangover."

A rush of relief sinks into me, even more when Rowan's eyes pop open. A frown takes over him as he studies the vines wrapped around his body. "What the hell is going on here?" Rowan demands. "It's that demon fucker, innit?"

Maeve groans, blinking several times. "Willow?" she breathes. "You're here. Tell me he's been defeated," she pleads.

"I don't know," I whisper, then I carry my knife toward Killian.

"There's no way you're killing someone with *that* thing," Rowan laughs. "Looks like a baby's dick!"

"These vines, I assume, are still connected to Decius." I saw at one of the vines wrapped around Killian's chest, surprised when the knife cuts right through it. I slice at the rest, and he falls to the ground, landing on his knees. "It worked," I breathed.

"Where's Caz?" Killian asks again.

"Yeah, where's our brother?" Rowan demands.

"He went after Decius," I inform them. "I weakened him by stabbing him with a sword made from wood from a Trench tree. He ran off, and Caz went after him."

"To where?" Killian asks.

"Wait…you stabbed Decius?" Juniper exclaims.

"I can't really say. Decius ran to the left of the castle," I offer to Killian, though Juniper's question makes me want to shout "Hell yeah I did!"

Killian looks from me to everyone else, his face growing solemn. "He's leading him to the Dark Cliffs."

They stare at one another with wide, worried eyes.

"Get me out of these things!" Rowan grunts, shifting beneath the vines. "We need to help him."

"What are the Dark Cliffs?" I ask as Killian takes the knife from me and slices at Rowan's vines. Once Rowan is freed, he marches out of the room, only to return with a massive gun when Juniper and Maeve have been freed too.

"It's a forbidden part of Blackwater," Maeve explains. "People only go there to commit suicide or to cause someone else's death and make sure a body is never found. To reach it, you have to venture through Rukane Forest, and there are rumors about that place. There's a tale that goes way back—long before even *I* was born—about how a general named Rukane lost his mind during a war with Ripple Hills and led his fleet to a forest, killed them all and then himself, but not before asking a Mythic to bind his and their souls to the forest. They say now that there are shadows that come out to rob your soul just to find their way back to the mainland, but we'd never known because we've never dared going there."

"I don't understand." My head shakes, boggled by this tale.

"Why does a place like that even *exist* near here? And why is Blackwater Manor so close to it?"

"Caz placed Blackwater Manor next to it to prevent others from venturing to it," Maeve responds, swiping a palm over her dress. "Many people have gone missing, and none of the monarchs could ever find the answers, so they built a steel barricade around it to keep visitors away. There's only one point of entry...and only the Blackwater clan know where it is."

Killian bristles by. "If Decius is leading him into that haunted place, not only will he mess with Caz's mind, he'll get him where he's weakest just to take him down."

"And Caz knew this and *still* went after him?" I ask.

"This is *Caspian* we're talking about. He swears he's invincible," Maeve scoffs. "Let's go. We have to find him." Maeve starts to turn but gasps immediately when she passes the desk. I rush around to look with her, and my breath catches in my throat when I see what she does. I didn't see her when I first walked in.

On the floor is Della's crumpled body with sticky, dark blood surrounding her. She lies sideways, eyes wide open, and my stomach twists into a painful, unrelenting knot.

"He killed her?" Juniper gasps. "That monster! How could he?"

"It was bound to happen to one of us," Maeve murmurs, and despite how strong her words are, I don't miss the way her eyes well with tears. She lowers to a squat and reaches forward, running two fingers over Della's eyes to close them. She saunters across the room, grabbing a quilted black blanket from the leather sofa. "We will give her a proper sendoff when we return." Maeve stands again, facing us all. "Let's go save our Caspian and make sure that monster *never* hurts us again."

CHAPTER 58
WILLOW

OF COURSE, WE DON'T LEAVE THE CASTLE WITHOUT stopping by the armory first. Killian and Rowan dress in bullet-proof vests and retrieve three guns each, while Juniper and Maeve do the same. I'm pretty sure the vests are useless, considering we're going up against a soul sucking Tethered Mythic, but I dress in one anyway.

Maeve marches across the room and slams a fist on a lone black door. The door falls open, revealing gray cases lined neatly in black foam. She unzips one, and inside are golden bullets with stark white tips.

"If we're to go into the Rukane Forest, we cannot do so without ash from Luxor Mountains," she declares. "They're the only thing that can stop those wretched shadows, and these weapons are filled with them."

Killian walks up to her, opening one of the other cases to reveal daggers. He takes two for himself, and Rowan and

Juniper follow his lead before venturing to the bullets and loading their guns.

"Here." Maeve places one of the daggers in my hand.

"These weapons won't kill Decius," I tell her as they all grab last minute things like grenades and round silver discs with blades on the end. I'm not sure what the discs are, but when Rowan switches one of them on and a red light flashes in the center, I figure they must be equally as lethal as the grenades.

"Hassha said only wood from a Trench tree can kill him," I go on. "She gave Caz wooden bullets."

"Hassha?" Maeve's eyes widen as she stops everything she's doing to pin her focus on me. Her green eyes are bold beneath the blinding light of the armory. "Where did you see her?"

"I was with her on an island called Kessel. Me and Caz were."

Maeve continues staring at me as if I've lost my mind. "She still lives," she murmurs. "And she's allowing this bloody Mournwrath creature to go around killing people? How could she? We believed in her. I believed in her."

Her voice cracks, and I'm not sure what to say to her. I know that Hassha hasn't gone after Decius because it wasn't her creation, and because Decius could never harm her or the people she loves. Kessel is a quiet place that goes undisturbed, and I'm certain Hassha has worked hard to keep it that way, but ever since my and Caz's visit, I believe all of that has changed.

Regardless, if I tell Maeve that Hassha has been in hiding for hundreds of thousands of years and that she has, in fact, been avoiding Decius and the commoners to protect her peace, it might further upset her. I can't say I blame Hassha, really. She has a family, and the women of Kessel rely on her to thrive.

I try coming up with a viable answer for Maeve because it

SHANORA WILLIAMS

seems she genuinely wants an answer, but I have none, and I'm relieved when Killian speaks up.

"We can talk about Hassha and all that bloody Regal stuff later. If we don't get after Caz, we'll never get the answers we need."

I press my lips as Maeve shifts her gaze to Killian, then she shakes her head furiously, picking up a thick handgun with a silver handle and tucking it into the sheath attached to her hip. "Our bullets aren't for Decius. They're for the creatures who'll come before we reach Decius."

When we step outside, Silvera is already sitting by the door, waiting. She stands at my side as everyone else walks past, going toward an inclining hill. I can see the forest they're heading toward from here, the tips of the pointed trees buried beneath thick clouds. The trees seem to run infinitely, and I shudder at the thought. Still, I follow along, hiking up the hill. The ground shifts from grass to gravel the closer we get, and Killian cocks one of his guns as we approach the steel barricade Maeve mentioned. It's a silver wall that goes higher than I can see. There are no doors to be found; however, Killian takes a step ahead and jabs at a spot on the barricade. Red lights emit in the shape of symbols, and he taps in the code, then the lights blink white followed by a clunking noise. A rectangular gap appears, spreading just enough for a single person to walk through. The other side is so very dark, as if the leaves are bunched together, refusing to allow any light. My heart beats faster, but I swallow some courage because I have to go with them. I have to do this for Caz.

"Mum, you don't think it'd be best if the ladies stay outside the wall?" Killian asks after peering in. "Me and Row can find Caz, kill that Decius character, and bring him back."

308

Maeve sucks her teeth and walks past him. "Not on your life. You forget that before I ever had you, I was a leader of The Watchwomen. The *only* reason I stopped taking part is because I met your father, got pregnant, and ended up with you three." She slips through the entryway, disappearing into the darkness. Killian works his jaw but goes right after her, as well as Rowan.

"The Watchwomen?" I ask, glancing at Juniper.

"Yeah. They were a group of women back in the day who sought their own peace and justice," Juniper explains. "They mostly went after men who assaulted or raped women and children. If they heard about it, or someone came to them for help, they killed the man. It was a whole thing before I was ever born, but my mother told me all about her missions."

"Oh." A thought crosses my mind. "But what about…Tom? That teacher who…" The teacher who molested Juniper.

Juniper raises her chin, nearing the entryway. "I made her promise not to go after him."

"Why?" I ask as I follow her.

"Because karma is a beautiful bitch and she's twice as powerful."

This, I suppose, is true. Caz took care of it and blew Tom to smithereens.

"Come on. You ready?" Juniper is already stepping through, so I nod, following after her. As soon as we're on the other side of the barricade, we're immediately swallowed in darkness. Silvera brushes against my side, fully aware something isn't right about this place. Ahead, there is nothing but dense fog and curving tree branches hovering over a slim footpath ahead. Maeve, Killian, and Rowan are already on the path, venturing deeper into darkness with flashlights and guns aimed ahead. Everything inside me goes against moving forward, but I stay by Juniper's side, my feet moving while my mind revolts.

The deeper we go, the less light there is. I look back, and the light from our entry point is turning into a speck.

"Did Caz tell you what he did to Tom?" I ask, aiming for a distraction.

"No. But Rowan did. I rather admire the idea of that wretched man being blown to bits instead of shot in the head."

"Wait." Killian stops abruptly, raising his gun, and I freeze in my tracks.

Rowan's gun has a red laser on the end, and he swings it left when a tree branch snaps. Maeve and Juniper stand behind the men, shoulders hunched, eyes wide, fingers wrapped around the triggers. I reach for my Trench tree dagger, though I'm not sure it'll stop whatever's in this forest.

"Up ahead," Killian says in a low voice.

I peer over his shoulder, and ahead are dark figures hanging from sloping trees. At first glance, the figures look like people hanging from rope by the throat, and I'm instantly reminded of the story Maeve told. The general lost his mind, sought a Mythic to murder his fleet. There is Mythic energy in this place —dark energy that hums in the soil beneath my feet. I can feel it.

When Killian raises a flashlight, pointing it at one of the silhouettes, I see that it's not a person, but a thick bundle of branches wrapped in pale moss. Some of the moss drips onto the floor of the forest, and the branches they hang from creak and moan, almost in warning.

"They look like people," Juniper whispers.

"Probably were," Rowan mumbles, visibly shuddering.

Killian lowers the flashlight, moving ahead again as Maeve says, "Try not to touch them."

We carefully move through the path, weapons in hand, avoiding the hanging moss. A twig snaps again, followed by a heavy *crunch*, and Killian and Rowan swing their guns, pointing the barrels to the right this time. "That's the second time. Something's out here," Rowan breathes, and my heart drops.

When several seconds tick by and nothing appears, they face forward again, picking up the pace this time. I stay close to the group, gripping the handle of my knife tighter, relieved when I spot the light of an opening ahead.

"Not far to the cliffs," Killian murmurs.

I can taste the salty ocean, hear the waves crashing. There's water on the other side of this forest and light. My heart beats faster the closer we get, but then Juniper lets out a bloodcurdling scream and her gun goes off, the fired shots echoing through the forest.

Killian grunts, and his gun is knocked out of his hand. He's shoved to the ground, and a pair of dark hands grip him by the ankles, dragging him away. Maeve gasps when something wraps its arms around her from behind and yanks her back, just as dark as the hands that grabbed Killian's ankles. Then it takes Juniper too.

My heart beats so hard and fast, I can hardly hear a thing. But I see it all. Something has taken them.

Rowan points the gun in the direction his family were taken, but it's too late. The dark figure behind her shoots into the air with her locked in its arms, and her scream carries through the forest.

"Shit!" Rowan hisses, pointing up with his gun, the laser bouncing off the thick, dark trunks. "Willow, stand behind me," he orders, and I rush his way, taking out my other dagger with the Luxor ash.

"What are those things?" I ask.

Rowan remains quiet, slowly swinging the gun ahead of him. His ear twitches, and with rapidness, he spins around and says, "Duck."

I drop, and he points his gun behind me, sending a bullet flying. Silvera stands over me, growling as something screeches. When I look up, one of those shadowy figures is there. It has no face, no true form. It's like a black ghost, however not transparent. The bullet is lodged into the heart of its chest, glowing now like fire embers. The creature continues screeching until finally, it explodes. Black ashes scatter around us, drifting with the stiff breeze.

Rowan grabs me by the arm, helping me to a stand again. "You all right, Willow?"

"What the hell was that?"

"One of those dead soldiers, I presume. I need all the eyes I can get. Press your back to mine, keep a lookout." He turns away, and I press my back to his, my breaths pouring out raggedly. "What have they done with my family?" he mutters.

Just as he says that, more gunshots go off. They're close by, but I can't see where they're coming from because of the fog.

"Keep that eye out, Willow," Rowan orders. "More are coming, I'm sure."

My breathing becomes shallow as Silvera growls, baring her teeth while looking at the other end of the path.

Another dark figure appears, and I can't bring myself to call Rowan's name because this one is massive compared to the first one, and I swear to God it has *two* heads.

It moves at rapid speed toward me, and I finally find it in me

312

to scream Rowan's name. He spins around me, shooting at it, but the figure dodges the bullet and zigzags behind the trees. In seconds, Rowans' gun is knocked out of his hand, flying away, and the shadow shoves him backwards.

Rowan hits the nearest tree trunk with a grunt, and I back away until my back is pressed against a trunk too. The shadow's head turns, and though it has no eyes, I know it's coming for me next. I grip the handle of the dagger tighter, ready to slash at it.

Silvera continues a growl, a fair warning to make the thing stop, but it doesn't. It inches closer, drifting across the forest floor, and Silvera pounces forward, biting into it. As she bites, black liquid spills, dripping onto her chest and paws. The shadow makes no noise as it shakes Silvera off, flinging her several feet away.

"No!" I scream, and I raise my dagger, aiming for its heart, but the figure grips my arm and slams me into a curved tree trunk. The dagger flies out of my hand and slams on the ground as the shadow's grip on my arm grows tighter. It's other hand wraps around my throat, ice-cold and menacing, and it's because of the cold grip that I realize I've felt it before. It's the type of cold that sinks into your bones and tries robbing your soul. Sure, the shadows may want to claim us, but Decius also has control of them right now, and he's trying to stop us from reaching Caz.

"I'll kill his family first," the creature croaks. "Then I'll drain every drop of blood and energy from his body."

I grit my teeth as the figure tightens its claws around my throat. My eyes shift to Rowan who shakes his head, sluggishly pulling out another gun that's tucked into a strap around his ankle. Something knocks the gun out of his hand, then grips him by the throat too, pinning him to a tree. It's another shadow.

More shadows appear, carrying the Blackwater clan in our direction and slamming their backs to tree trunks. Each of us is pinned and struggling for breath while Silvera barks at them all, unsure where to attack.

My vision grows blurry as I watch them all fight, and it hits me that they're suffering because of a Tether Caz and I share. I think to myself, *there's no way this is it*. There's no way we've gotten this far just for a handful of shadows to end it all. Decius deserves to die. He *can't* win.

As quickly as the thought forms, a bold lavender light appears in the forest—so bright that it's damn near blinding. The shadow with its grip on me hisses as it jerks away. I fall to the ground, sucking in breaths and looking up. The shadow attempts to flee, but a beam of the lavender light hurtles right after it, blasting the shadow to ash.

The rest of the shadows drop their captives and attempt an escape, but more beams race through the forest, slamming into each of them. The shadows screech all at once, their wails ringing through the forest like screams from lost souls.

I rub my throat as Juniper and Maeve suck in breaths and Killian and Rowan pant raggedly. The lavender beams circle back to where we are, hovering above us. I study the one in front of me shaped like a spear with tiny bolts of lightning crackling through it.

Someone approaches, their feet crunching over sticks and gravel. The spheres surrounding us race back to the person and settle into their palms, and when I can finally see this familiar individual, I gasp.

CHAPTER 59
WILLOW

I can't believe my eyes.

Korah stands several feet away, her white hair braided into two single braids that carry down to her waist. Her hands are lit in lavender flames that create enough light to shine down on us and highlight this section of the forest. My eyes find hers, fiery rings around her pupils that shimmer purple, and a smirk claims her lips.

"Korah," I breathe. How is she here? I thought she was never coming back to Vakeeli.

"*The* Korah? The Regal?" Maeve gapes, climbing to her feet. Juniper, Rowan, and Killian do the same, staring at the Regal with a mixture of shock and fascination.

"In the flesh," Korah says, and the flames fade from her hands. Her eyes remain lit as she takes her time studying each of us.

"You saved our lives." Maeve drops to her knees, bowing her head to the Regal, and her children follow suit.

"Please don't bow to me," Korah says, and Maeve tips her chin.

"It's an honor to be spared by a Regal," Maeve insists.

"I understand, but no need for formalities. Please rise," Korah demands.

They all stand again, dusting off their clothes, and I move closer. "What made you come back to Vakeeli?" I ask.

"I didn't have enough power to kill that vessel of a man *and* keep the portal open when I sent you and Caspian back," she states. "Your mate seemed to know this, and he saved my life by taking Decius's vessel into the portal with him. I suppose I couldn't let him have one up on me."

I crack a smile at that, shaking my head. I know that's not the truth, and that it goes so much deeper than that, but if that's what she wants to stick with, I'll take it.

"I flew past the Dark Cliffs," Korah states, more serious now. "I saw Caspian. He's tracking Decius by his blood. He's lost a lot, Decius. This is a good thing."

"Can he still hurt Caz?" I ask.

"That depends. Did Hassha offer him protection?"

"She gave it to both of us...which doesn't make sense if those shadows attacked me. But I think Decius sent them after us. I could feel it, and I heard his voice."

"He's using what's left of his energy to prevent you from reaching Caspian. He knows the presence of your Tether along with the Trench weapons is more than enough to defeat him." Korah's eyes travel up and down the length of me. "I do not detect Hassha's energy on you. That means her protection is wearing off, and if yours is, so is Caspian's."

Korah strides toward me, placing her hands on my shoulders. Her touch sears through my shirt, but I don't budge

316

despite the heat. The warmth of her hands travels through me, touching every organ, until she finally pulls away.

She moves to Maeve next, placing her hands on her shoulders as she did mine. She does this to everyone, and when she's done, she finally says, "I don't have much in me, but this should protect you for at least another hour."

"How do you get your energy?" Maeve inquires. "Perhaps we can help you restore it."

"My energy comes from many things combined. I swim, I fly, I lie on a large field full of flowers and plants and absorb it all. All the land, water, and vegetation of Vakeeli fill me. However, it requires *a lot* of rest, a lot of eating, and many chants. I haven't been able to do that in ages." Korah blinks then steps away, her hands conjuring purple flames again. "Caspian is this way. Follow me."

CHAPTER 60
CAZ

ONYX HUFFS AS HE CLOMPS OUT OF THE FOREST, then stomps his front hooves repeatedly when he hears the ocean. Poor boy. He's never liked large bodies of water, so as soon as he sees the dark ocean beyond the cliffs, he panics.

"Hey. Easy." I climb off his back, stepping in front of him and dragging a palm along the side of his face. "You're safe, and you've done enough." I pat his jaw, and his body sways. He stares at me with beady eyes crowded with lengthy lashes—eyes I can see my reflection in. Sometimes I think he understands me more than anyone else by the way he looks at me. It's the deepest stare that often steals my breath away.

"Stay here."

I cut my eyes to Cerberus. "You too, Cerberus. Stay here. Don't follow me." Cerberus whimpers, trying to give me puppy eyes, but it won't work. Not this time. I have to walk up that cliff *alone*. I know Decius is up there, and judging by the fresh trail of blood on the ground, he's weak, and right now is my time to end him. No distractions.

There's a possibility this could be a trap, but I have several Trench bullets remaining as well as the machete. And as far as I'm aware, Hassha's protection still lingers inside me, otherwise he'd have gotten into my head by now.

"Stay," I whisper again to Cerberus before turning away. I move ahead, taking the steep rocks upward that lead deeper to an opaque fog. The thick moisture clings to my lashes and skin, and I rub the tip of my nose before raising my gun. Something crackles to my right, and I swing my gaze to find the source of the noise. Rocks crumble from the edge of the dark cliff, drifting to sea. Gravel crunches ahead, and I grip the gun tighter.

"*But if I'm a raven, what does that make you?*" a voice asks. It's a soft voice, young. A boy. I frown as it whispers by.

"*I'd like to think I'm a swan. But not just any swan. A black swan. Still beautiful. Still graceful. But she stands out, and she doesn't care because she knows her power.*" A woman's voice, warm and familiar. Mum.

"No." I shake my head, squeezing my eyes shut. That's Decius. He's in my head again. Hassha's protection must be wearing off now.

"*But aren't ravens bad?*" the boy asks again.

"*I don't think they are,*" Mum says. "*I believe everything the universe offers has beauty to it. Ravens only seem bad because they're carnivores. But if you look at them, really look at them, you'll see they're smart as whips, and they're not afraid of danger. I believe that's why people think they're bad. Because they're smart and they know how to survive. That's you, my raven-haired boy. You know how to survive. You'll always know how.*"

"Just not right now," a louder, deeper voice bellows in my

head. I open my eyes again, walking deeper into the fog. I need to find Decius before Hassha's protection has fully worn off.

The cliff has leveled out and is much flatter beneath my boots. To my left and right are black, jagged rocks protruding from the ocean. The water laps at the rocks, waves splashing over them, a futile attempt to drown them.

"I love you, Caspian," Mum whispers. But it's not her voice. It *can't* be. She's not here.

A silhouette appears at the end of the cliff as the fog drifts. I aim my gun at it, moving toward it slowly, just until I can make out what or who it is.

The silhouette stands at the edge of the cliff, overlooking the dark ocean. They wear an ivory dress, a bleak contrast to the black cliffs and rolling gray sky. Her dark hair is braided into one braid that swims down to the center of her back, loose tendrils flying with the damp breeze.

I freeze where I stand, looking at the familiar woman who has her back to me. She turns a fraction, and when I see her face, I stumble backwards, my heart hammering in my chest.

My mother turns to face me, looking like she never left this world. Her green eyes sparkle despite there being no sun, and her smile causes gleeful wrinkles to sink into the brown skin around her mouth and eyes.

"My raven boy," she coos, and I lower my gun, staring at her in disbelief.

"Caz!" someone screams behind me.

I look over my shoulder, and Willow is stumbling up the cliff, her brown eyes wide with terror. "Caz! Stop!"

"Willow?" As she appears, so does another person. This person is familiar, her white hair catching in the fog. "Korah?"

320

"Don't step any closer to her, Caspian," Korah warns, her hands lit in purple flames.

I swallow hard when my clan appears behind them. Their guns are raised, lasers coming off them, ready to shoot.

My family. They're awake now? I thought they wouldn't be until I killed Decius. I stare at them with glistening eyes—that is, until I hear that familiar voice again.

"Caspian," she calls. I turn my head, and my mother now stands next to me.

"You've grown so much," she whispers, grabbing my hand. I lower my gaze to our hands, how they merge as two different tones. I always liked that her skin was different than mine. I was always in awe that I'd been conceived by her—that someone with such beauty and grace created me. Her hands are much smaller than mine now. "Come with me," she says, her voice a melody to my ears. I've missed it so much. I want to cling to the sound of it, allow the notes of her voice to wrap around me and squeeze tight. "We can finally be together. We can get away from this awful place and all it has done to you."

There's an ache in my chest as a coldness sinks into my body. I stare at my mother a moment longer, then peer over my shoulder at Willow, whose head is shaking repeatedly. Korah has a fiery hand clasped around Willow's wrist, and I can tell it's taking everything in Willow not to run to me.

That's not her. Willow's voice whispers through my mind, and I feel that pain in her chest, her yearning for me to come to her. *Please, Caz. It's not her.*

"They'll never love you the way I do," my mother continues. One of her hands grips my face as she forces me to look at her. Her blue eyes swim with certainty. "You're *my* sweet Caspian.

My beautiful, mighty Caspian. Come away with me. Come now."

My throat thickens as she grips my hand and tugs on it, and Willow cries my name again. I allow my mother to lead me toward the edge of the cliff where the ocean and all its jagged rocks are only a fall away. I carry my eyes to hers again, and a vision hits me.

I remember when she took me to Vanora for my seventh birthday. We went to the beach and played in the ocean, and then she spread out a towel, opened the picnic basket she'd brought along, and took out jam sandwiches and black potato crisps. Afterward, we went to the market, and she bought me a miniature chocolate cake with gold truffles. It was the best birthday of my life, and I want so many of those moments to come back. I want *her* back in my life, and if I could have her, I would take her...

But that's an unrealistic thought.

She cups my face in her hands again as Willow's faint calls drown with the wind. "Ready?" she asks, and a chill emanates from her body as she wraps her arms around me. I bring her closer and bury my face into her hair, my throat burning from unshed tears. One jump off this cliff and we're done—gone together, away from this world. I've always wanted that...

My mother lets out a loud gasp. I bring her body closer to mine, so close we're practically one, shoving the blade of my dagger deeper into her heart. She leans back, and I stare at her as she withers away, the edges of her face becoming sharp and shifting into man.

Sure, I've always wanted to run off with my mother and leave this world...but that moment was stolen from me because of Decius. I can't say I didn't expect this—Decius using the image of my mother and all my fond memories to take advantage of me. I hate him with every fiber of my being, so despite the tears that slide down my cheeks, I yank the dagger out, push him off of me, and stab him in the heart again. He drops to his knees, blood sputtering out of his mouth, and the façade completely breaks. The ivory dress turns to black, the long black hair falling away, the blue eyes now pits of darkness. He morphs from my mother to his original self—an old, ugly man who's lived too long and has done so much wrong. He stares up at me with those soulless eyes, and I'm reminded of Manx and everything he taught me. I'm reminded of the man who pretended to care about me, who sometimes took me into his home when I needed an escape from Magnus. Where is that man now? How has he become *this*?

He lied to me. Used me. *Ruined* my fucking life.

"It's a good thing I turned out a bit like Magnus, eh?" My upper lip twitches as I raise a foot, stepping on his chest and forcing his body off the blade. "Just like him, the death of the people I hate satisfies the hell out of me. Especially when it's by my hand."

He lies there, curled over, coughing up blood, and I'm so tempted to kick him over the edge, but I need to make sure he's dead—that this fucking Trench knife worked.

Korah appears at my side, lowering to a squat and looking him over. "After all this time, I finally get to see you go down."

Decius croaks, clutching his chest.

"Why can't he just die?" I grumble.

"The Trench tree weapons were never meant to kill him, just drain him of his energy. Without that energy, he's nothing. Do you have a smaller Trench knife?" she asks, surveilling the blade of my dagger cloaked in blood.

I withdraw a smaller dagger from my coat, and she accepts it. She flips Decius onto his back, breaks off a piece of the wooden blade, and shoves the splinter into the wound on his chest.

Decius wails in nothing but pure agony, a sound that's music to my ears, as Korah works the wood as deeply as she can into the wound. When she's done, she raises a bloodied hand over him, and fierce purple light wraps around his entire body.

"I'll see to it that he's locked in a bloody coffin made of Trench wood too. It's all I can do for now. Without Selah, I can't kill him, but I *can* keep him contained. She's his creation, so she has to be the one to officially end him." Korah blinks, then her throat shifts up and down. I feel there's more she wants to say, but she doesn't say it. Korah and Hassha...they're lying. Something isn't adding up about Decius and Selah and I honestly don't have the energy to demand the truth.

"Caz!" Willow runs my way, her body crashing into mine as she throws her arms around my neck. "Oh my God, are you okay?" She clutches my face, looking me all over. "You scared me!"

"I'm okay." I smile, cupping the back of her head and bringing her face to my chest. She nestles her face into the center, sighing.

When I look up again, my family appears, still clinging to their weapons. Willow steps out of my arms, and the first person to run to me and replace her hold is Juniper. She throws her arms around me, holding on tight and smashing her cheek against mine. Her touch burns like hell, but I allow it and hug her back. When she pulls away, Rowan and Killian move forward, clapping me on my shoulders and smiling.

"We almost died in that forest because of you," Killian grumbles.

"Ah, wouldn't be the first time you almost died because of me, would it?" I smirk.

"Nah. About the thousandth, more like," Rowan responds, and it feels good to have them here, to know they're alive and healthy.

But nothing tops Maeve who approaches me with a tearstained face. Everyone steps out of the way as she rushes toward me and instantly wraps me in her arms. "I love you, Caspian. I love you to the ends of Vakeeli," she whispers.

I nod, holding on to her as long as my body will allow.

Decius was wrong, you see.

I may miss my mother, but these are *my* people too. They're my family, Willow too, and they mean more to me than anything in this world.

"To the ends?" Killian rumbles, gripping my and Rowan's heads and pressing his forehead to ours.

I smile and nod. "To the ends, brother."

CHAPTER 61
WILLOW

To our favor, Korah doesn't have us go through Rukane Forest again. Using her energy, she transports us to the front of Blackwater Manor—all of us, including our wolves and Onyx. Before doing so, she kept Decius wrapped in her light and told us we'd likely never see her or him again.

Now, the first thing Caz and his family do is run to find Della's body. Caz snatches the quilt away, as if she'll be awake now that Decius' reign has been annulled, but no. She's still dead, her skin ashen, old blood caked in her gray hair.

Rowan sniffs, Killian shakes his head, and Juniper presses her knuckles to her mouth, fighting tears. Maeve presses a hand to Caz's back as he stares down at Della.

"Before you go blaming yourself, just know that it's not your fault, and that Della loved you," Maeve says in a hushed tone.

Caz continues staring at the body a few seconds longer, his jaw clenching. *She's gone because of me,* I hear him think. *I'm no good. No fucking good. Couldn't even keep her safe.*

"Caz?" I grab his hand, and he finally pulls his gaze away from Della to slide those glistening blue eyes to mine. "What do you want to do?"

His chin inclines as he puts his focus out the window. "A proper send off," he says after some time. "We change her clothes, wrap her in black silk, and send her off with the ocean. It's what she would have wanted."

"On it," Killian says, then he taps Rowan's shoulder. They bend down to pick up Della's body after wrapping it in the quilt and carry her out of room.

"We'll find some clothes for her," Juniper murmurs, turning away with Maeve.

When they're gone, Caz stomps out of the room too.

I follow him into his office and find him yanking a drawer open and snatching out a silver case. He cracks the case open, plucks out a bloom, then scrambles around another drawer for something else. When he doesn't find whatever he's looking for (I assume a lighter), he opens another drawer and shuffles around it chaotically until finally he slams it closed and yells, "FUCK!"

He launches the silver case across the room, and it crashes into a wall, thudding on the floor. Several of the blooms escape, rolling toward a floor vent. Slumping down in the desk chair, Caz drops his head, and his face falls into his palms.

"Oh, Caz," I whisper. His chair faces the window, and I drop to one knee in front of him. His face is red behind his hands, veins visible and throbbing on his neck. The room goes absolutely still until he unleashes a gut-deep sob. The sob wracks through his body, and he removes his hands to place his head on my shoulder. My throat closes in on itself, but I fight my tears, rubbing circles on his upper back.

"It's okay," I whisper.

"It's not okay. I failed her," he says, voice thick. He picks his head up, and his eyes are red and glistening. "I told her I'd always look after her, and I failed her."

There's a burn in my chest, and at the sight of his bloodshot eyes, my vision becomes blurrier. What do I say to him when it comes to this? Loss. First his mother, and now Della. What do I say to a man who continually blames himself for these losses?

There isn't much I can say because I feel all that pain balled into a tight knot in the center of his chest. This knot won't go away, won't fade. It only lingers, taking up unwanted space. And the truth is, no words will *ever* erase that sort of pain. No matter how many words people say or how much they try to encourage you, *nothing* will resolve the agony until you heal. Trying to ignore the grief is like putting a tiny Band-Aid over a gash. It's useless.

So, I don't speak—not because I don't have anything to say, but because after all we've been through, with the sight of his dead mother being wickedly impersonated, and now the slap back to reality about Della, it's a lot to take in, and he needs to pour it out. My Caz is in so much pain, but I'm here. I'll *always* be here.

I push higher onto my knees and lace my arms around his neck. I bring his face to my chest, and his quiet sobs continue, tears dampening my shirt, body shuddering as he sucks in breaths. I stroke his hair, rub his back, rest my cheek on top of his damp head. I allow him to dwell in his sadness, his vulnerability, his hurt.

After several minutes, the tears stop, but he stays glued to my chest, breathing evenly, the knot in his chest slowly loosening. I pull away, placing a kiss on the apple of his cheek as I stand. "I'll let you have a moment to yourself."

Before I can move away, he catches my hand, keeping me close. Raising his chin, his damp blue eyes find mine. **Don't leave.**

I blink my tears away and nod. *'Kay.*

CHAPTER 62
WILLOW

DELLA'S SENDOFF IS NOTHING SHORT OF HEART wrenching. I'd felt Caz's pain in his office, and it still lingers. The ache within him is intense as he stands in front of the shore, watching Rowan and Killian carry torches toward a black plank. The sky was a hazy gray but has now shifted to a muted dark blue. Thunder rumbles above, the clouds rolling by quickly, as if they sense the heartache and would rather be any place but here.

On the plank is a body wrapped head to toe in silk. Rowan and Killian lower the flames of their torches, placing them on the loose edges of silk to spark it.

Slowly, the body is lit in bright flames, sending a wave of fiery heat rippling toward the head. Juniper takes the torch from Killian so that he can push the plank deeper into the ocean. The wave carries the plank away, and we watch it rock gently, drifting toward the endless sky. There's nothing beyond these black waters that I can see, so there's no telling where Della's body will end up. Perhaps she'll float forever, rocking in peace, almost like a baby being soothed. The idea of that is comforting, actually. Much more comforting than being buried six feet under.

Caz lowers his head as if he can't watch a moment longer then turns away, marching up the stairs that lead to the castle grounds.

I watch him go, aiming to hear his thoughts, but nothing comes. He's blocked me out. This time, he wants to be alone.

When we return to the castle, Maeve and Juniper pull out a simple dinner they'd cooked while preparing for Della's sendoff, and I'm glad to see it's things that are familiar. Chicken, green vegetables that remind me of green beans but skinnier, and wild rice. We eat quietly at the twelve-top table, our eyes wandering to Caz's empty chair. I can't find it in me to eat anything because I'm worried about him. I checked his room, and he wasn't there. He's not in his office either.

"Just give him time." Maeve steals my attention by patting my hand. "He'll come around. He always does."

"He's one of those people who needs an ample amount of time alone in order to recharge. But when he needs us or wants to be with us, he pops up like a wart," Juniper teases, but her wittiness isn't as sharp as usual.

"Yeah. It's best I give him space right now," I murmur, running the prongs of my fork over the bed rice.

"Sure. Don't leave him be for too long, though." Juniper's eyes bounce around the table, at her brothers and then her mother. "Too long, and his mind ventures to dangerous territory."

"He tries to hurt himself," Rowan states before shoveling rice into his mouth. "Kill himself, even. It's fucked up."

"Language," Maeve sighs, but there's hardly any effort to her tone. I can tell she, too, wants this day to be over with. Or to at least get some sleep.

I notice Killian stiffen and clutch his fork tighter. "He would never do that," he grumbles.

"I dunno," Rowan says. "A man can only handle so many losses, brother."

"He wouldn't do that *to us*," Killian snaps this time, slamming his fork down and pushing away from the table. He stomps out of the kitchen without looking back, and the dining room is wrapped in a suffocating layer of silence.

Juniper sips some of her wine and Maeve leans back, pulling out a bloom and sparking it. Rowan twiddles his fork around in his fingers with his eyes on his plate.

"What if that's the one thing I can't save him from?" I ask, looking at all of them. "Himself?"

Maeve pulls from her bloom, and when she exhales, the smoke tendrils fall to her lap. "I believe you are exactly where you need to be. He knows you're here. He knows the pain it would cause you if he ever…" Her voice trails, and she shakes her head. "He loves you. He'll hang on." She pushes my plate toward me. "Now eat up. I know it's not as great as Della's cooking, but you need your energy."

CHAPTER 63

CAZ

BY THE TIME WILLOW FINDS ME, THE SKY IS BLACK and the branches of the trees outside my balcony cave inward like an umbrella. The rain came down hard about an hour ago, pelting on the leaves and weighing them down. I'd been tempted to go inside, but the drops that did land on me felt nice on my skin and cooled the burn inside me.

The rain has stopped, and now the moon is a round chip in the sky, beaming down on me. There's a chill in the air, I'm shirtless, and my hands and feet are cold, but I have no desire to go back into the room and light a fire.

After the last couple of days, I'd rather stay out here and freeze—feel something just so I can remember life's precious moments. If I sink too deep without feeling, I may never come back up for air, so this is where I need to be. On the ice-cold balcony, staring at the ocean and moon.

"I can feel you," I say after taking a pull from my bloom.

Willow steps out, her bare heels landing on the damp

marble. She's changed clothes. A fresh ivory gown. Her hair swims down her back. She immediately wraps her arms around herself when she realizes how cold it is.

"How long have you been out here?" she asks.

"Since I came back in."

"Oh. I came in here to look for you but didn't see you. Guess you were out here the whole time."

"You guessed right." I heard her come in. heard her call my name. As badly as I wanted her, I didn't want her to see my anger. Because that's what I was after Della's send off. Angry.

I put out my bloom, and her eyes drop to the ashtray on the side table next to me. It's full of stunted blooms, and I'm ashamed to say many of them are from today.

Willow remains standing, shivering while eyeing me. Sighing, I get out of my chair and wrap an arm around her, leading her inside.

I shut the balcony door and draw the curtains closed while she walks to the bed, sitting on the edge of it. The lamp on the nightstand illuminates one half of her face.

I move to the fireplace, tossing in a few logs and finding the matchbook on the stand next to it. I light the match, toss it inside, and the fire crackles to life.

I stand again, looking at her as she looks at me. I want to sit next to her, but I can't. I've thought about it all on the balcony —how I want her to stay with me, how I want a life with her... but how can I have *any* of that when she'd constantly be at risk? Her life is quite literally in my hands, and I want to protect her, I do, but I can't be with her at all times—it's impossible as a monarch—and I saw it with Della. A few days away from her, and now she's gone. If I'd been here, she never would've died, and if the same happens to Willow...*fuck*. I don't know what I'd do to myself.

So, I don't sit with her. Instead, I walk to the closet, taking out a shirt and pulling it over my head.

"I'm not going to leave you alone," she says when I step out of the closet.

I look her over, lowering my mind's wall just a bit to hear what she's thinking.

No one trusts him alone. He'll hurt himself. I have to stay with him.

"I will not hurt myself," I snap, and her brows dip. "Besides, it's better to leave me alone than to sit there staring at me with pity in your eyes."

"I don't pity you," she counters.

"Please. Everyone pities me. It's why they all tolerate me. I'll always be that sad boy who was ripped away from his mother and tormented by his father. Didn't you get the memo?"

"They tolerate you because they *love* you. And I don't know why you're taking this anger about your mother and your father out on me all of a sudden."

I turn my back to her, facing the balcony doors. "I'll be fine, Willow. I don't need you checking on me like I'm a child. I just need a moment to think."

"Think about what, exactly?"

I drop my head. "Please, Willow. I don't want to play your game of questions right now."

"Well, I have to ask you, Caz, because you're blocking me out. I don't get why you're doing it, but I want to understand."

"Understand what?" I snap, whirling around to face her. Her eyes stretch, alarmed by my anger, but she blinks it away. "There is nothing to understand. A woman is dead because of me. That's it. And Decius may be wrapped up and put away for now, but we don't know how long that'll last. We don't know if Korah will go back to Earth, abandon all of this, and leave Decius out there. She's done it before. Why wouldn't she do it again? We don't know a damn thing of what's to come or what will happen."

"I get that," Willow replies, much calmer than I anticipated. "But being angry with me and avoiding me won't help you, and you know it."

"I never said I was angry with you," I mutter.

"You don't have to say it for me to see it." She climbs off the bed and moves across the room to me. "If me being here and our Cold Tether is causing you to resent me, then I can leave. The portal is right there. I still remember the chant. I can say it and I can go."

"Love of Vakeeli, I never said that."

"I know you didn't, but I can sense it, Caz. All of what you've been through is because of our Cold Tether, and I know the bottom end of it sucks because sometimes it sucks to me too. But you and I can both agree I was safer on Earth, and you were safer here without me. When we were apart, no one died. Everyone was fine."

I grasp her face between my fingers before she can step away, forcing her eyes on mine. "Willow, how do you not get it by now? I want you more than the air I breathe. I want you in this life, and the next, and whatever life comes after this, but all of these Cold Tether issues is new territory for me, and if I lose you in this lifetime, I'll kill myself. I know I will. And I'm struggling with that—coping with the idea of your loss, but also wanting you in my life every single day and night. You don't think I want to wake up to those beautiful brown eyes of yours every morning? To kiss your lips until they're raw every night? I want all of that and more, but it's fucking *terrifying* to have that here, Willow. I know I said I want you here with me, that I would love for you to make a life in Vakeeli, but losing Della made me realize this isn't a game and that I need to get my ego in check. I won't always win, and I can't fathom another loss."

Her eyes are glassy, and my vision has blurred, but I continue holding her gaze. When she blinks, tears slide down her cheeks. I stroke them away with the pads of my thumbs.

"No one has ever spoken to me that way," she whispers.

I tip my head back a bit. "Did I say something wrong?"

"No." Her head shakes, and she brings her arms up to lace them around the back of my neck. "You said everything right." Her lips press to mine, warm and sweet with wine, and I sigh, drowning in her touch, her kiss...*all of her*. I stumble toward the bed and collapse when the backs of her knees hit the edge.

"I'm terrified," I confess on her lips. "I'm scared to lose you."

"I know. But you won't."

"You don't know that. This world is fucked up."

Her lips find my cheek, and she places a tender kiss on the apple of it. "We're all a little fucked up. I can deal."

She shifts beneath me, adjusting herself enough for me to wedge between her legs. I thrust against her, and all that anger, fear, and pain morphs into something else entirely. It is true when they say love is the most powerful thing—more powerful than any emotion your body can conjure.

She is my safe haven. She is love.

I pull off my shirt and lower my joggers, mounting the bed as she takes off her panties. I cage her head between my arms and lower my chest to hers, and as I thrust inside her, I expel a trapped breath. She's so warm and wet. I don't want to be anywhere else but here.

"I can leave if you want me to," she breathes.

"No." I draw my hips back and propel them forward again. Her lips part, and I lower my hands, entangling our fingers.

"Should I stay?" she whispers.

"Yes," I groan into the crook of her neck. "I want you forever and ever. You make me whole. You center me. I'm scared, but I can't let this go. I love you."

She wraps her legs around my waist, guiding me deeper, and I kiss the crook of her neck, working my way up until my lips are on hers. All that anger I felt before tapers off. The pain still lingers, but here she is, taking some of it away. My mate. My beautiful, perfect mate.

I clutch her hands and unfurl a groan, my dick throbbing inside her as I come. She sighs when my head falls on her chest, then buries her fingers in my hair, stroking my scalp.

We lie here for some time, the moon beaming through a slit in the curtains and shining down on us. I pull out and look down at my glistening dick now coated with both of us and blow out a satisfied breath as I lie beside her. I bring her closer, nuzzling my nose on one of her breasts and inhaling her feminine scent.

She's mine. All mine.

CHAPTER 64
WILLOW

"Perhaps it's karma. Isn't that a universal thing?" Caz wonders.

I lie on his chest, staring through the small gap of the balcony doors that reveals a sliver of the ocean.

It's been well over twenty minutes (I think) since we made love. For the most part, we laid in the dark and crossed thoughts here and there. Only a few times. Caz mostly kept his wall up when he wanted to keep some things to himself.

"Yeah. We believe in karma on Earth too," I tell him, attempting to push away the feral thoughts. Even his voice is doing it for me right now. The rumble of it sneaks through me and stays between my legs. Good Lord, what's wrong with me. *Focus, Willow. Focus.* I'm glad Caz either disregards my thoughts or is too lost in his to react to them.

"Perhaps that's what all this is then," he says. "Losing Della. Decius trying to hunt us. Losing my mother. It's all karma, and I'm playing in its wicked game."

"Karma can be good and bad," I offer.

"I think I only end up with the bad." He's quiet a moment, and I listen to his steady heartbeat. "I told you before that I've done a lot of bad things. Do you remember?"

"Yes, I remember."

"Well, it's true. I have. It was only a matter of time before karma came back to deliver a dose of herself. She took Della from me, and that woman…" I hear him swallow, his body tensing. "She was like an aunt to me, just like Maeve. She may not have raised me from childhood, but the moment I met her, I knew I could trust her. And when she came to me and asked me to help find the people responsible for murdering her son, I didn't hesitate. There was something about her eyes, you know? She had this way of looking at you. This innate ability to look at people like they *belong* to her. She looked at me like I was hers—like she'd do anything for me. She made anyone feel like family…made them feel special."

"Yeah," I agree. "In the short time I knew her, I did like her. She was very nice to me. And honest. Plus, her cooking was great."

"Ah, yes. The cooking. She was a great chef. Believe it or not, she owned a popular restaurant when Magnus was monarch. It was a hot spot, everyone loved it. She'd serve the best seared duck, and her desserts were literally sin. I had some of her blackfruit cake once, and it was the greatest thing I'd ever tasted."

"That sounds good," I laugh.

"It was." He pauses. "She stopped as soon as she found out her son was missing. Sold the restaurant to someone else so she could pay bounties to track him down. This was shocking to many because Della had been poor once, she and her husband.

340

They didn't have the rubies to afford youthwater, so when her husband fell sick, he couldn't properly heal from it, and the only reason she had the restaurant in the first place is because the previous owner committed suicide and handed it over to her. He just gave it to her. I suppose he was fond of her too. Anyway, after she'd come to me with the knowledge that the Rippies had killed her son, I couldn't stand to know she was alone, so I had Juniper bring her to Blackwater Manor. I showed Della the wing she would use and let her know it was hers now—that she could have it and do whatever she wanted with it. She thought I was fooling her," he laughs. "She had no idea why the monarch would want *her* living in his castle. And I couldn't quite explain why I wanted it either, I just did. But with Della being Della, she didn't take it at first. She liked to work for what she had. So, a day later, she comes to me while I'm at the tavern and says, 'Fine. I'll take the position.' And I go, 'What position?' She says, 'The position to be your house maiden. I'll cook, clean, stitch up your clothes, wash them. I'll do whatever needs to be done for Blackwater Manor.'"

He lets the memory steep, and I look up to find a small smile on his lips and his eyes distant. "I told her there would be no pay, really. That I wasn't exactly looking for another house maiden, and that I just wanted to let her know she was safe and protected. She said pay wasn't necessary. She said..." He clears his throat. "She said to me that day that working for me would be the greatest honor of her life."

"Wow," I whisper. "That's so beautiful."

"Yes. And we had another house maiden around, but she paled in comparison to Della, so I let her go. Kept just the one. Never regretted it."

I laugh. "She really loved you. And she took pride in her

work here. I can tell." I hug him tighter, pressing my ear to his chest again.

"Loving me may as well be a death wish."

"Stop doing that," I groan. "Please. You are not a burden to me, or your family, or to *anyone* else in your life. You're not to blame for bad things happening. Bad things happen regardless. Look at me. A woman from Earth, with an estranged father, a dead mother, and a missing brother."

At the thought of Warren, I sit up rapidly. "Oh my gosh, Warren! We are still going to find him aren't—"

"Yes," Caz laughs, pulling me back down to his chest. "We will look for your brother. But not at this moment." With a sigh, he wraps his arms around me and holds me close to his chest. "Right now, I only want to be with you. Everything else can wait a while."

CHAPTER 65
CAZ

As the sun splits through the clouds, shining through the window of the balcony doors, I watch Willow sleep. The warm rays spill onto her bare back as she rests on her stomach, breathing softly. Her warm brown skin is smooth to the touch as I run a finger down her spine. She sighs in her sleep, and I smile before focusing on that glint of sunlight.

It's interesting because the sun hardly reveals itself in Blackwater, yet it shines today after all that chaos like a symbol of victory. It's a brilliant reminder that life goes on, and that I still have much to be thankful for.

Hell, perhaps the rising of the sun is the work of Hassha. She knows what we've gone through, and she controls the way the sun, moon, and stars work. Regals supposedly feel and know nearly everything about the people they encounter, and I'm sure they can sense the dread that has filled me that is bordering on depression. The only reason I'm *not* losing my mind is because of Willow. She's been with me all night, not daring to leave my side. I'm grateful for that—to have someone who cares. Someone who can be right here with me without it hurting.

She held me the majority of the night until she drifted to sleep, her head on my chest, her soft palm on my stomach. It felt nice, and I savored every second of it.

With the comfort I have here in my bedroom, I can't bring myself to go downstairs with my family right away. I hear them as they march through the corridors. Killian and Rowan are usually early risers, but no one beats Maeve. Despite the large-ness of the house, I hear her in the kitchen making a ruckus. I bet she's wishing Della were here.

Della...

I keep asking myself if it hadn't been Della—Regals rest her soul—then it could've been one of my other clan members. How do I face them knowing one of them could've died? Knowing they could've been taken from me within the blink of an eye?

The question torments me and I sigh, picking up my case of blooms from the nightstand and walking to the balcony. I step out, sparking it and inhaling, allowing the smoke tendrils to wash away with the breeze as I exhale. The sun rays bathe me in their warmth, and I draw in a cleansing breath, slowly releasing it before taking another pull of the bloom.

I have so many regrets. Though the sun shines and it's a new day, my family won't be safe forever, and neither will Willow. But I have *power*. And when I think of that power, I pull from my bloom again and stare out at the sea. There's work to return to, and nothing about my role has changed.

The Council still remains, and I'm certain I'll hear from them soon about the trip to Inferno Isle, that wretched island made of lava, flames, and creatures that can kill a man with one swipe of its claw. I'm positive they're aware of the events that have occurred with me being sent to Earth and dealing with the Regals but it's highly unlikely for them to cut me a break. They'll be chasing me down soon. Then there's Rami's son, the boy I'm supposed to mentor and train to become a monarch. I must get to him before people fill his head with ruthless thoughts and lies about me. There are the rubies we must mine for, for the Rippies. I'll have to chat with the Blackwater citizens, lay it out on the table and let them know the truth about the mining, but in doing that, I'll have to reveal who my mate is and why I acted against Rami in the first place, and that doesn't come without jeopardy.

Still, it must be done. Monarchs don't get days off to mope around and grieve. I'd love to be locked away in this room another day with my mate, forgetting about the world and all the anarchy and destruction it brings, but I can't.

I take one last pull from the bloom, stab it out on the ashtray, then step into the bedroom again, shutting the balcony door behind me.

Willow remains asleep, her dark locs strewn over the pillow, half of her face buried into it. She sleeps soundlessly, peacefully. It's good she can now that Decius is gone. No longer will he haunt her dreams.

I don't bother to wake her. I did last night, interrupting her sleep to bury myself inside her another time. I wanted to stop my mind from racing, and she was so tired, but she sleepily opened herself up to me. As soon as I was inside her, all the questions and tension melted away. The way she makes me feel is worth more than words. I crave her even now, but I bet she's feeling raw now, and it's best I let her rest.

I make way to my closet, taking down a fresh set of clothes and a hat. I take a quick shower, rake some pomade through my hair, and dress for the day.

Before I go, I scribble a note on a notepad, fold it, and place it on Willow's side of the bed. I stifle a laugh. *Willow's side of the bed.* That's got a ring to it. I like it. I'll share everything with her, so long as I get to keep her.

I give her one last look over my shoulder before leaving the room and shutting the door quietly. As I walk out, I spot Rowan leaving his chambers from the other side of the castle. He's tucking a gun into one of the holsters at his waist as he rounds the curve of the banister.

"Caz, brother!" He raises his hands in the air and starts to hug me but stops just as quickly. "Good to see you're up and at it."

I clap him on the shoulder. I don't care about the burn. "It's gotta be done. Listen, Willow told me about what happened in Rukane Forest. She said you saved her several times from those shadows, risked your life for her, even. Thank you for that, Rowan. I know you didn't have to."

Rowan dons a proud smile, raising his chin. "Oh, it was nothing. You should've seen me though, Caz! I had my gun and was blasting those fuckers to smithereens with the Luxor bullets! They didn't even see it coming!"

I laugh. "Yeah, I bet. Which gun did you take? I noticed a laser on one of them."

"Oi, that's my GX-36. You know I love it."

I continue a smile as we near the bottom of the staircase. I spot Killian walking around one of the corners with a bowl of cold oats.

"It's about time you two came down." He slurps a large chunk of wet oats into his mouth. "Simpson says you have some things to sign off on, and I was thinking, Caz, about the mining for rubies thing. There might be a way we can mine for them for the Rippie debt *without* putting anyone's life on the line."

"Well go on then. Let's hear it." I stop at the bottom of the staircase as Killian places his half-empty bowl on a nearby table.

"I wanted you to hear from me first that Whisper Grove is waking up from some sort of spell. Pretty sure it has something to do with Decius. Last night, one of them stopped by Blackwater Tavern looking for you. He said his name was Conan and that he's been in Whisper Grove for nearly four hundred years. Apparently, he couldn't remember what happened before Decius arrived until last night. This Conan person was Whisper Grove's tribe leader up until Decius took over and altered their memories to make them believe *he* was their rightful leader. Turns out he's been controlling them for centuries, Caz."

"Four hundred years?" My eyes round. "That's way before our time."

Killian nods. "Right."

"That would explain the attack against Beatrix and why that barman Alexi was there," I add. "Decius must've been controlling them."

"Exactly. Anyway, This Conan man is desperate right now. Their fields are dying at rapid speed, they have no electricity, their horses are suddenly sick, and it turns out they have no rubies or gold. All of what they've had the last four-hundred years was some sort of illusion. The truth is they weren't living. They were just existing while Decius hid in plain sight. It was a cover up of sorts."

"Shit." I lower my gaze a bit, letting all of this new information sink in. "How couldn't The Council see this?" Or perhaps they did but decided to ignore it. Ignorant fucks.

"This is a great opportunity to have Whisper Grove help us in the mines," Killian goes on, running a hand over the top of his head. "Sure, we'd have to mine for more to cover their asses down the line, seeing as they need rubies, but maybe Alora can help us with getting them some gold, and even give them horses and food and whatever else they need in exchange for their assistance in the mines. This way our men can work their regular hours and the Whisper Grove people can take shifts."

I blink at Killian. "And you came up with this solution today?"

He nods, shifting on his feet. "I did."

"Well, damn, Kill. Who would have thought you had brains behind that beefy head of yours?" Rowan teases.

"Shut up." Killian jabs Rowan in the chest, but not without smirking.

"That's very smart, Kill. *Really* smart. I'm proud of you for thinking this all up while I took time to myself," I say.

His smile grows a bit wider, his head higher. He's proud of himself too, as he should be. "Just wanted to lift some of your burdens."

"I appreciate that. It helps a lot."

Something clatters in the kitchen, along with shattering glass, and Maeve hisses a curse word that travels down the foyer. "That's it!" Maeve stomps around the corner, her face red and her dark hair strewn all over her head. "I can have children and raise them, make a pot of tea, and make a simple dinner, but what I *can't* do is be a house maiden. That's not my place. We need to hire another one, Caz. I know it's soon, and I apologize if the timing seems inappropriate, but this place will turn to shambles if we don't get help."

"Don't stress yourself, Maeve. Everything will be fine," I tell her. "See if you can find someone who's willing to help. Run background checks, be thorough. You know how it goes."

"Yes. Of course. Thank you." She softens a bit, moving closer and placing a hand on the arm of my jacket. "How are you feeling?"

"Better today."

"Good. Blackwater won't survive without you, you know?"

I smile at her as she pats my arm then rises on her toes, kissing my cheek. Her kiss, of course, stings, and when she pulls way, my cheek feels like it's on fire, but I endure it.

"Will you do me a favor?" I ask her.

"Anything."

"Willow needs clothes. Can you see to it that she has something to wear for today, then take her to the village so she can pick out more clothes she'll be comfortable in during her stay. Normally Della would—" I clamp my mouth shut, the mere mention of Della making my chest twist.

Maeve gives me a warm smile. "I'll take care of it. Don't you worry."

She then kisses Rowan and Killian on the cheek and coos with a smile, "My boys. I remember when you stopped at my shoulders and would sneak all the chocolates from my purse. Whatever you do today, be safe, do you hear? Caz, I'll be using your office to put together a list of house maidens. Contact my transmitter if you need me. Killian, take that bloody bowl to the kitchen sink and wash it while you're at it. Rowan, you still have crust in your eyes. Why didn't you wash your face? And where the hell is Juniper? She was supposed to be helping me this morning. *Juniper!*" Maeve marches up the stairs on a mission to find her daughter.

Killian takes his bowl and ambles toward the kitchen as Rowan stands by the door, digging into the corners of his eyes. I fight a laugh as I make way to my office and retrieve my transmitter. When we've all met again, I let them know we're going to the tavern first before heading out the front door. I stop immediately when I spot a barrel at my doorstep. It's charred at the bottom, soot clinging to it. I make my way down the steps, taking off the lid of the barrel and finding Trench tree weapons inside.

"What is that?" Killian asks, stepping to my side.

"A gift from Hassha," I tell him, replacing the lid. "Right, let's get these in the car, bring them with us."

"What do you need us to do today?" Rowan asks as Killian hauls the barrel up and tucks it beneath his armpit as best as he can.

"First thing we need to do is get to Blackwater Tavern so I can sign off on papers. Second, we'll contact Alora, see if she's willing to help with this Whisper Grove situation if it holds true. She's never had any animosity with Whisper Grove, so I'm sure she won't mind. Third, we make a trip to Whisper Grove with a small fleet so I can speak to this Conan person face to face. Make sure his confessions are true and that his story holds up. After what went down with Decius, I don't want any more surprises, so contact Veno and tell him to round up a few men from the Barix. Tell them to bring guns and to meet us at Blackwater Tavern, and to be subtle about it."

"I'll make the contact," Killian says as we near the garage where Rowan parks his car.

"And I'll drive," adds Rowan.

Killian dumps the barrel in the trunk of the vehicle, and when we're nestled inside, Rowan starts the car but gives pause as he clutches the wheel.

"So...with that Decius creature gone, does that mean Willow will be staying in Vakeeli now?" he asks.

I keep my eyes ahead. "She's still thinking about it."

Rowan grips the wheel, reversing with a slow spin of the steering wheel until we're on the concrete path. "Well, I hope she does," he says, driving forward now. "She makes you give us compliments."

I huff a laugh. "What?"

"It's true. I don't remember you *ever* telling me that I'm smart for anything," Killian interjects with a chuckle.

"I've called you smart before," I counter.

"Sure, you have," he boasts. *"Sarcastically."*

Rowan breaks out in laughter, driving onto the main road that takes us away from Blackwater Manor and toward the village. As he goes, my eyes fly past the dark trunks of trees that stretch to evergreen treetops.

"She's putting a change in you already." Rowan turns on the air conditioning. "Keeps you looking ahead. Makes you smile. You needed someone like her in your life. I swear you were a desolate bore before."

"She saves you from yourself," Killian adds.

I angle my head just enough to see Killian in the backseat. "I thought you didn't trust her."

"Long and gone, brother," he declares. "After all this Cold Tether shit, it's clear she has your best interest in mind."

I stare through the windshield, my heart thumping. Love of Vakeeli, my heart is jumping around in my chest like a wild rabbit thinking about her.

"She's my better half," I say, and though it's out loud, I say it more to myself. "I'll do anything for that woman."

CHAPTER 66
WILLOW

I WAKE TO THE MUTED ROAR OF THE OCEAN. IT'S A soothing sound, one that makes me want to stay in bed all day and never leave it.

My eyelids flutter open, lazily sliding to the thick tinted glass of Caz's bedroom balcony. The dark waters ripple beneath the sunlight like black jewels.

I'm still lying in his bed, naked beneath the black sheets. The delicate space between my thighs aches as I remember what we did last night, and even during the early hours of the morning before the sun was anywhere in sight.

Yawning, I look to my right and notice Caz's side is vacant. I rub a hand along his side of the bed, and it's cool to the touch. I sit up against the headboard, and my eyes fall to the nightstand. There's a folded sheet of ivory paper on it with my name scrawled in black ink. Caz's handwriting.

I smile at the thought of him writing a note before running off to wherever he's gone.

I pick it up and read it.

You were sleeping so peacefully that I didn't want to wake you. I have some things to do today but make yourself at home. Will return within a few hours.

I love you,

Caspian

His name is signed skillfully, like he's had to sign it so many times before that it falls from his fingers naturally. A smile sticks to my lips as I hold the letter to my chest. A door slams from a distance, heavy like it could be the front door of the manor.

A burst of red catches my eye, and I look to my left. There's a red outfit hanging from a steel room divider, and on the chair next to it is a black shopping bag. I wrap myself in the sheets and rush over to pick up the bag. Inside are panties, jewelry, toothbrushes, and feminine products like tampons and pads, which I'm glad are similar to what we have on Earth. I'm pretty sure I'm due for a period soon.

There's a note attached to the bag, and I pluck it off.

Self-care first, then we have fun.
- Maeve

I tuck the letter into the bag with a smile then take down the outfit, running my fingers through the soft, cottony fabric. Of course, it's red, a color that seems to be a favorite of Maeve's.

I carry all the items to the bathroom and hop in the shower, taking a moment to breathe and let the warm water wash over my skin. I relish in the calmness, feeling a sense of peace when I realize things can go back to normal...whatever that normal may be for us.

No more running away from danger. No more worrying about sleeping in case Mournwrath tries to attack me in my dreams. I wonder where Korah took him, actually, and if we'll ever see her again. At least one more time. I actually really like her, despite how hardened she is. Has she gone back to Earth? Is she still here? Has she paid her sister a visit? Maybe she and Hassha can go find Selah now that Decius has been put down. I'm certain they'd survive and can wake her without Caz.

There are so many possibilities, and I'm feeling optimistic for the first time in a long time, so I finish washing, then step out to clean my face, brush my teeth, then style my hair as best as I can with water. There are gels in Caz's cabinets, but no oils or sprays. That's one thing I'll have to look into while I'm here because I *cannot* walk around with dry locs.

When I'm done and dressed, I place two ruby earrings from the bag into my earlobes and stare at my reflection.

I look brighter, cheerful.

Wait.

Oh, my goodness. I'm *glowing*. Is that what this is? Wow. I have to admit, the glow looks good on me. I've never properly glowed before.

I leave the bathroom, and for some odd reason I start thinking about Garrett. Is he still in that tomb? Will they send him back to Earth? He's a loose end that I want to talk to Caz about. Hassha can't just leave him in a cave. I won't feel too good about him until I know he's back on Earth and far away from here.

I brush the thought aside, and the sound of clinking glasses fills my head. I smell bloom and liquor as well as toast and something sweet, like chocolate.

I gather you're finally awake. Caz's voice fills the hollows of my mind. The clinking continues, and I also hear a scratchy noise, like pen scribbling on paper. He must be at the tavern.

I smile, shaking my head as I make the bed. *Are you gonna listen to everything I do now?*

Might as well make use of it. Now tell me why you're worried about that Garrett fucker.

Oh my gosh, Caz. Seriously? I huff a laugh, making the bed.

I'm just curious. Why not be satisfied with the idea of him rotting?

"I don't know," I say out loud with a sigh. "I know he was wrong but...he didn't ask to be Decius' vessel. And if he goes back to Earth, he can't prove any of what happened in Vakeeli. Isn't there a way they can erase his memory or something? And send him back as less of a piece of shit?"

Hassha would never risk it, but there are alternatives to keeping him quiet.

"Like what?"

Before we left Kessel, Hassha told me to leave his fate up to you. She gave me two options: let him rot in the cave or turn him into a spider and let me crush the shit out of him with my boot.

"What?" I ask aloud. "Turn him into a spider? That's...so Vakeeli-ish."

"Well, she was doing the spider thing more so in my favor, so

that I'd feel satisfied about it. But she quickly made me realize that it's not up to me what happens to him. He's your pain from your past so, ultimately, it's up to you."

I sit on the edge of the bed, peering out the window. "Well...I don't want him dead." I air the statement because it's true. As much as I don't like Garrett anymore and don't want him having any part of my life, I don't think he should die. I'm not God. I don't get to decide who does and doesn't live.

Of course, you don't. I don't think he intends for his words to come out bitter, but they do. Mildly.

"I'm serious, Caz. I know he's a piece of shit, but killing him won't sit well with me. I'll feel guilty about it." I run a thumbnail over one of my cuticles. "I guess if Hassha doesn't want him going back to Earth, then...he should rot and die on his own."

Better than nothing, I suppose.

I laugh. *You're so cruel.*

Not cruel. I just don't believe in second chances when it comes to people like him.

There's a stretch of silence before I ask, *Are you okay today?*

Much better, thanks to you.

I smile. *Good.*

I pause. *When will we be able to look for Warren?*

Soon, Willow. I promise. I want to get more intel before we make any moves. I have a few things to do today, but I'll be back by dinner.

Okay.

I love you, Willow Woman.

I love you too, Caspy.

Gonna put my wall up now.

I get up to fluff the pillows. *What? You don't trust me to hear what you're thinking about while we're apart?*

No, it's not that at all. He chuckles. **Things just tend to get ugly around here. I don't want to put a damper on your good mood. I sense it, you know. Your happiness.**

I bite a smile, putting my focus on the balcony doors. *I am happy, actually.*

I'm glad to hear it.

I'll see you tonight, then.

You will. I love you, Willow Woman.

I love you too.

CHAPTER 67
WILLOW

WHEN I DON'T HEAR ANYTHING ELSE, OR SMELL chocolate and whiskey, I stand up again and slide my feet into the sandals beneath the chair where the outfit was placed. I open the door and walk down the hallway, taking the curved staircase down until I'm in the foyer.

A delicious aroma floats through the air, and my stomach rumbles as I follow the scent trail and wind up in the kitchen. Juniper stands at the broad island counter, kneading some dough on a cutting board, flour all over her clothes and even on her cheek, and Maeve is pulling something out of one of the ovens. When Juniper notices me, a wide smile sweeps across her face, and she wipes a hand over her forehead.

"Well, good morning! Aren't you a beautiful sight!" she chimes.

"Morning," I return, fighting a smile.

"Mum, look at her. She's so pretty! You did great."

Maeve is already turning to find me. Her loose curls are

pulled up into a thick ponytail, her face free of makeup, yet she's still flawless.

"Look at that. I knew red would look good on you." She winks at me, then taps the counter in front of a stool. "Sit. Have something to eat."

I pull the stool back as Juniper adds more flour to the dough. "What are you making?" I ask as Maeve brings a glass to me filled with green liquid. I take a sip, and it tastes like freshly squeezed grapefruit. I search for the maker of this juice and spot a sliced green fruit on a cutting board behind Juniper. Maeve turns for a cabinet to retrieve a porcelain black bowl.

"Glory Bread," Juniper says, pushing her palms into the dough. "It's *so good* in the morning. Spread some blackberry jam on it, and I swear it's an orgasm in your mouth."

Maeve places a bowl in front of me along with a spoon. She brings a pot toward me, ladling some of the contents into my bowl. The food in the bowl reminds me of oatmeal, with chunks of white and yellow, and it smells mildly sweet.

"It's my famous porridge," Maeve informs me, picking up a container and scooping out some black powder. She sprinkles the powder onto the porridge, as if it's confectioners' sugar. "Now don't knock it before you try it. It's quick to make but takes two hours to set. Literally melts in your mouth. Try it."

I pick up my spoon and take a small bite to test. The flavors burst on my tongue—it's like cream and cinnamon with hints of apple or a fruit that's similar in taste. Pear, maybe? Do they have pears hear? Whatever it is, it's freakin' tasty.

"Mmm. Wow, Maeve, this is *really* good."

I take another bite as Maeve lends me a pleased smile. "I knew you'd like it."

"You'd better enjoy that cause she won't make it again for

another year," Juniper pipes in. "She hardly ever makes it. As a matter of fact, Mum, can you make me bowl? I'm almost done with the bread."

As I continue eating, Juniper collects a pan and dumps the dough into it, then presses it into the pan neatly. She slides the dough into the oven, washes her hands, then carries her bowl of porridge to the counter, sitting next to me.

"You two like cooking?" I ask.

"I don't mind it," Juniper answers.

"Neither do I, but it has to be when I'm in the mood. I used to cook day and night for my triple crew. All they did was eat, especially Killian! My word, he was a bottomless pit." Maeve waves a hand at the sheer reminder.

"I loved cooking too," I tell them. "Me and my brother Warren would cook together every week. We'd make a random dish we found on Pinterest."

"Pinterest?" Maeve's brows bunch together.

"Oh, right. It's an Earth thing. You can find a lot of inspiration on it for recipes, crafts, all that."

Maeve rests her lower back on the counter with a nod. "Do you miss Earth?"

I offer a half-shrug. "Some of the things."

"Like what?" asks Juniper.

"I guess some of the food. The bookstores, especially my best friend Faye's. I miss hanging out with her a lot. Also shopping at Target." I huff a laugh, remembering my last Target run with Caz. That seems like ages ago.

"We have all of that here!" Juniper exclaims. "Well, everything but your friend Faye and this Target you speak of. We have plenty of bookstores, and trust me, the food in Blackwater is incredible. You should try Hatley's. Their pasta is delicious, and they have this hazelnut mousse pie that is to die for. They serve tea all day long, and most nights they have a live band playing."

"Whatever you need, Willow, we can provide it," Maeve implores. "I know this isn't your home, but we're willing to do whatever it takes to make you comfortable and to make you feel at home here."

I work my spoon around in the porridge. "Are you just saying all this so I don't leave Vakeeli?" I ask, smirking.

"Guilty," Juniper laughs over her bowl.

"It's not that we don't want you to leave, but...well, we know about your life on Earth," says Maeve. "We've gotten bits and pieces from Caspian, and Alora may have spoken to me in private about what you told her that first night in her palace. With the thing about your mother..."

I feel a clench in my belly when Maeve mentions my mother. I told Alora that my mother was suicidal. Didn't seem like such a big deal to tell the time. I didn't think anyone would care. "All we want is for you to feel at home here. There is no rush for you to leave. All of us are here to protect you and be there for you, just as we are for Caspian."

"I'm considering it," I confess.

"Really?" Juniper lights up.

"Yeah." I nod, smiling. "I really am. Me and Caz talk about it a lot."

"It's all Caspian wants," Maeve tells me with a gentle smile. "I've never seen him so happy. He's sleeping. He's eating. He's...*alive*. There's even color in his cheeks now." Maeve places a hand on mine, and despite her age, her skin appears satiny smooth, not a blemish in sight. "I don't want you to feel like you're being forced to stay here, though, and I'm certain

Caspian doesn't want that either. At the end of it all, the choice is yours, and we will respect it."

I huff a laugh. "Talk about pressure."

"We just love you," Juniper gushes, wrapping an arm around my shoulder. "I feel like I've found my long-lost sister! It's so refreshing after being surrounded by men all the time!"

I wrap an arm around her, giving her a squeeze.

"Well, speaking of making Caz happy..." I start, and Maeve stands taller while Juniper pulls her arm away but keeps her attention on me. "He's taking Della's loss really hard, and I can tell he's trying not to think about it too much and wants to focus on what's in front of him. Anyway, I was thinking since he will be returning around dinner time, maybe we can set up a nice dinner for him. All of us can be there, maybe some of his close friends. I haven't met any of them, I don't think, but it'd be nice to get to know them."

Juniper and Maeve steal glances at each other, and there's clearly some silent communication going on that I know nothing about.

"What?" I ask, looking between them.

"It's just that Caz doesn't invite many people into Blackwater Manor," Maeve explains. "He likes to keep it to just family and people he fully trusts." I consider that, and a warmth wraps around me when I remember that, not too long ago, I was only a stranger to him. Now look at me, a permanence in his castle.

However," Maeve goes on. "There is a guesthouse just beyond the castle. It's beautiful there, close to the ocean, and there's a large table inside it that seats over twenty people. It's been there since Caspian tore down Magnus' castle to replace it with Blackwater Manor."

"Wait, he tore down his dad's castle?" I ask.

"Oh, yes. It was a whole thing," Juniper says, waving a hand. "He was the new monarch and wanted nothing of Magnus to remain. We celebrated when this place was built, drank ourselves dizzy."

"Yes, I recall you lot drowning yourselves in wine and liquor," Maeve says, shaking her head with a smile. "Anyway, the guesthouse isn't used much, only for meetings or when Rowan wants to sneak some Blackwater whore on castle grounds. Della kept up with it a lot, so I'm sure it's in good shape. Perhaps that could work?"

"It sounds like it could work. Do you think I can see it?" I ask.

Maeve is already walking across the room. "Follow me."

CHAPTER 68
WILLOW

MAEVE LEADS THE WAY OUT OF THE KITCHEN, rounding a corner that takes us to a winding staircase with sharp rails. I recall this staircase leading to Della's chambers, and my heart wrenches at the thought, having once gone up there and seeing Della's side of the castle. She'd patched me up, fed me, was honest with me. She was a good woman who didn't deserve what happened. Fuck Decius for taking her away.

The thought leaves me as Maeve walks behind the staircase to pull a door open. It groans as if it hasn't been used in ages, and we take a flight of stairs down until we're on damp grass.

Maeve trots through the grass, her wide black pantlegs swishing with the breeze. Her curls whip around her face as she struggles to collect them all and tuck them behind her ears. Juniper doesn't have to worry about loose hairs, seeing as hers is in a tight ponytail. She stretches her arms to the sky, indulging in the sunlight, still with flour on her cheek.

"You have a little bit of flour on your face." I point to the area on my face, and she wipes hers.

"Thank you." She rubs her cheek to make sure it's all gone. "I bet Mum would've let me walk around with it all day like an idiot."

I laugh as Maeve wanders down a gently sloping hill. The sound of the ocean intensifies, and birds caw and chirp, flying overhead. The grass is still damp, but that dampness feels good as it drags across my ankles.

Down the hill is a one-story cottage, tall, with black bricks and a wide steel door facing us. The roof is all black as well, with a tiny chimney to the left. Windows line every side of the house, which I'm sure provide a stunning view of the ocean from inside. Trees hover above the back of the guesthouse, creating an ample amount of shade.

Maeve walks toward a bridge with wooden slats and steel railing and platforms. As we follow her along the bridge, I notice the creek below. The water trickles by at a rapid pace, running between smooth black rocks. When we make it across, Maeve goes straight for the door.

"Better not be any bloody squatters in here," Maeve mumbles as she twists the doorknob open. The door creaks, and she pushes it ahead, revealing the interior.

The first thing that captures my attention is the kitchen. Sleek steel counters and a gas stove, double ovens, and a slim fridge. I follow her into the guesthouse and spot that table she spoke of that can seat over twenty people, taking up most of the dining area. The table is coated with dust, and a stack of chairs are on either side of it, black, thick, and sturdy.

To my right, a black leather sofa is pressed against the only solid wall of the cabin, and to the left of the sofa—outside the wide floor-to-ceiling windows—is a wooden deck wrapped in steel with black railings. The deck offers a sideview of the ocean, the black waves rippling beneath the sunny sky. More seating is out there, as well as a built-in firepit.

I turn back to look around, and a folded bed is in the corner next to a door. Noticing the bed, Maeve says, "We can take that out." She then opens the door beside it. "The bathroom."

Juniper flips on a light switch, and the room illuminates with gold lighting. I hadn't noticed before, but there are fairy lights sweeping across the walls, as well as bulbs hanging from thick cords above, giving the guesthouse a comforting glow. I'm certain it looks even better at night.

"Wow," I breathe. "It's perfect."

"You sure? We can always go bigger, book a place in the village," Maeve insists.

"No, no." I shake my head quickly. "This is exactly what we need. Small and cozy. It'll make it more intimate. Special."

"Okay." She smiles, pressing the pads of her fingers together in front of her. "This will make a great surprise for Caspian. So very thoughtful of you. Even before this Mournwrath came along, we were all so wrapped up in ourselves. It will be nice to have everyone together so we can catch up and breathe a bit." Maeve huffs, as if exasperated. "In the meantime, let's work on a menu and the list of guests we want to invite. Once we know who's attending, I'll contact one of my good friends to cater. It's very last minute, but there's nothing she wouldn't do for her monarch. Once that's settled, we can run to the village. Caspian insists that I take you there and let you pick out your own clothes."

"Oh, you really don't have to do that," I assure her.

"I don't mind. Juniper and I can tag along, plus it'll give me a chance to go over my list for house maidens. The sooner we can get one, the better. No one will live up to Della, of course, but it's better to have some extra hands than none at all."

"Well, thank you," I murmur. "I know you have much better things to do than wait around for me to shop."

"Oh, please!" Juniper jumps in. "You think you'll be the only one shopping? No way. I'll show you *all* the best shops. Trust me. By the time we're finished and you have your new wardrobe, Caz won't be able to keep his hands off you. He'll fuck you every way he can."

"Oh my gosh, Juniper." I fight a smile and a blush.

"What? It's fine! We all have sex! It's natural! And mind you, it's a good thing for Caz. I swear he was going to explode one day from all his pent-up frustration. He has to let it out *somewhere.*"

"Jun, cut it out! You're making the poor girl uncomfortable," Maeve scolds, sauntering to the door again.

I follow Maeve out as Juniper goes on about how sex shouldn't be so taboo, and despite the rather naughty turn this conversation has taken, it's still nice to have. Having people to talk to who feel like family. People who understand both me and Caz. Faye would love it here, I bet. I'd love to talk to her right now, tell her how everything is going and to celebrate the fact that Decius is gone. If I could call her, I would, as it would be nice to communicate while away. Hopefully I'll be able to go back soon and catch up. I also have to deal with Lou Ann, and at this rate, I will likely quit because the more time I spend in Vakeeli, the more I realize it's not so bad. I feel more like myself here than anywhere else.

There are many things for me to deal with on Earth, and I'll get to those, but first, I need to put a smile on my mate's face.

CHAPTER 69

CAZ

I HAVE SEVERAL MEN LOAD A TRUCK WITH FOOD, rubies, and guns. After they've finished, we start our venture to Whisper Grove, which is a three-hour drive from Blackwater.

Before we can even enter the territory, I sense something completely off about the place. Rowan has the windows cracked, and I feel a difference in the air as we approach the border. There are no birds cawing, and the air is as stiff as cardboard.

The last time I was in Whisper Grove (when I was stuck in the inn with Willow for the night) there was serenity swarming throughout this territory. You knew you were in Whisper Grove by the way the temperature dropped to a comforting cool and the gentle breeze that drifted by, causing the leaves on the trees to sway. There was peace upon entry—a welcoming energy that was hardly found in any other territory.

I have to wonder if that tranquility and peace was the image Manx wanted to portray. Whisper Grove was always a comforting place, but perhaps he upped the performance when I

369

visited. He increased the energy so that I'd have no suspicion against him.

As a boy, this was my favorite territory because it was so natural, thriving with thick green grass, beautiful bodies of water, and abundant hills with cottages speckled throughout. I'd roll down those hills until I made myself dizzy enough to vomit. It's not like that anymore, and I realize that truth the deeper we get into it.

As Rowan drives on a dirt path that leads downward and overlooks the village, the scenery ahead has become something straight out of a nightmare. The grass is dead, the trees naked and without leaves, their branches reaching to the sky like ancient mythic fingers. The village is dull, lifeless. Several people move across the cobblestone roads, guiding thin, malnourished horses by the reins. The village normally thrives with citizens as they work in markets, or come in and out of shops, but not today. It's a damn near ghost town.

"Where is everyone?" Rowan asks, parking in front of Tribal Hall. I expect this Conan person will be here if he's trying to get things in order.

I step out of the car, and Killian stands next to me, drawing out one of his guns.

"No animosity," I order, focusing on the ivory building. The vines that were once lush as they trailed across the face of the building are now browning and shriveled. The leaves that remain drop to the ground in a sad silence. "Something strange may be going on here, but they probably still have a protection spell over this place. That was here long before Decius took over. No violence unless we're proven wrong."

After my statement, there's a wail in the distance. Killian

raises his gun instantly, Rowan immediately going for his too, as a woman runs out of Tribal Hall.

"Stop running!" Killian shouts, pointing his gun at her.

"Please!" the woman shouts. "Please, m-my son! H-he's not well! I—I need help! *Please!*"

"Lower your weapons," I order as the woman clasps her hands together, dropping to her knees on the ground before us. Her tears stain her chubby, freckled cheeks, and her bottom lip trembles. Killian and Rowan follow my orders, lowering their guns.

"Where's your son?" I ask, taking a step forward.

"Inside." The woman stands, and as she does, a man ambles out of the building with a boy in his arms who can't be any older than seven. The boy is thin, frail, and his skin ashen despite how tan he seems beneath. The closer they move toward us, I can see his lips are cracked and split. Blood lingers between each split. The man holding him is large with almond skin and dark-brown hair. His eyes immediately lock on mine as he stops midway with the boy.

"What's happened to him?" I ask.

"He needs to be hydrated and fed," the man informs me. He speaks with confidence, certainty.

"Kill, Row, go to the truck and get some water," I tell them. They rush off, heading to the truck as several of the other soldiers remain standing next to it.

I move closer, eyeing the large man with the boy. "You must be Conan."

"I am, and I'd shake your hand, Monarch Harlow, but... well." He gestures to the boy in his arms.

"How many more children need to be fed and hydrated?" I ask.

"Oi, Tribal Hall is full of children," he informs me, and though he's mustered a smile, his voice is laced with pain. "I had everyone gather here last night to see what we could all pull together. All the food we grew just...*disappeared*. Right out of our sight, as if it were never real."

Strange. But with Decius and his bloody mind games, it makes sense. He took over and left these people with nothing, and now that he's gone, they *truly* have nothing. Where is The Fucking Council when you need them?

Rowan rushes forward with a large black burlap bag, grunting as he drops it onto the ground. Conan carries the boy to a dry patch of grass, placing him on his back, and the woman lowers to her knees next to the boy.

I dig into the bag, pulling out regular containers of water, nuts, and a few pieces of lakefruit. There's some jerky there as well, but I think the boy needs to work up his strength first before chewing on it.

I drop to one knee as the boy weakly opens an eye. He tenses at the sight of me, clinging to his mother, but she whispers, "It's okay, it's okay."

"I'm not here to harm you." I crack the container of water open. "Here. Drink."

I bring the water to the boys' lips, and he takes a few sips. His eyes flicker to mine, and when I nod, he grips the container, taking it away from me and chugging the remainder, water dribbling down the corners of his mouth. Killian hands me another water, and I open it and hand it to him, letting him guzzle that too.

"You ever had lakefruit?" I ask when one is handed to me.

The boy shakes his head but smiles, revealing dimples. I can't help smiling back as he takes it from me and bites into it.

The juices cover his mouth, and he lets out a small, satisfied moan.

"Thank you," his mother sobs. She touches my arm, and her touch burns through my coat, but I keep steady.

I give her nuts and some of the jerky. "Have some for yourself."

She thanks me again profusely, and I stand, focusing on Conan. "Let's feed your people before we discuss what happened. Babies, children, and breastfeeding mothers first. We brought a little bit of everything, figured you'd need it. Afterward, we'll discuss what's going on and see how we can help."

"Absolutely." Conan bobs his head, gesturing to the entrance. "Right this way."

CHAPTER 70

CAZ

"I REMEMBER THE DAY MANX ARRIVED." CONAN SITS in a wooden chair behind a large wooden desk. The chair creaks every time he adjusts in the seat, and I can't help wondering how long that chair's been around. His hands are steepled together atop the desk, dark circles around his eyes. He looks drained, and I mean that literally. It's as if most of his energy has been taken away from him by Decius, like he was feeding off of these people to stay alive. It clearly wasn't enough. I was what he really needed to be satiated. The thought of it still makes me shudder.

I sit up higher in my chair, finding Conan's eyes again. "What do you remember about it?"

"I remember him being a random visitor," he states, scratching the side of his head. "At first, he kept to himself. He was quiet, didn't really join us for the festivities. He was staying in Whisper Grove Inn for a while. Then suddenly, Nelle died. She was Whisper Grove's doctor. Healed a lot of us. Took care

374

of us. She was never sick, and she drank her youthwater every day. She was healthy, so I thought her death was very strange and not at all expected, but I figured it just happened—that something went wrong, just as it would with anyone else. We had a proper burial for her, put her house up for sale, but the next day, Manx bought the house as-is from Nelle's son. He moved right in without even taking any of Nelle's furniture out. That never sat well with me. I mean, her body wasn't even cold yet, but I understood Nelle's son for wanting to sell it so quickly. He didn't live in Whisper Grove. He was a gunmaker, traveled a lot between Blackwater and Ripple Hills."

I nod, waiting for him to continue.

"After Manx moved in, he opened up a bit more. He came to Trible Hall and introduced himself, then confessed that he'd been running away from bad Mythics and needed a safe place. And you know how we are. We believe in peace here. We don't want anyone feeling unsafe in this world, so when he told me his story, it felt only right that he should stay a while. From then on, we spoke every day, and that's when I learned he could heal people as well, and seeing as we needed another doctor, well...it felt right to give him the position. We'd meet for tea right here in Tribal Hall, or we'd catch a drink or two at the inn." He hesitates a bit, his eyes wandering. "It wasn't until about two weeks after meeting him that my memory started to slip. I couldn't really explain it at first. Simple things would happen, like losing my house key, or not remembering where I placed my shoes. One time I'd even lost my hat, found it outside in a bush." He huffs a laugh. "I told Manx what I was feeling, and he gave me something for my memory. Some kind of elixir. I took it every day as he suggested, and...that's when I felt my sense of being had vanished, or like I wasn't really a *person* anymore, if that makes sense, but more of a vessel, really. *Something* being controlled by *someone* else."

I stare at Conan, trying not to flinch. A vessel...just like Garrett and that snake on earth.

"After that, I agreed to *everything* Manx said," Conan says. "I agreed to step down and let him take over without argument. I agreed to remove myself from Tribal Hall completely, and I kept taking that bloody elixir, because he told me to, even though I felt like it wasn't working. I wasn't able to tell him no. I could only say yes, and it seemed that way for everyone in Whisper Grove eventually. He became our leader, and we relied on him. Trusted him." He pauses, picking up his container of water and gulping some down.

"I will say that at some point, the elixir began to wear off for me," he continues. "I was going to visit Manx to tell him that my memory was becoming fuzzy again, but when I went to his house, I saw someone else inside." Conan's face pales, the dark circles making his eyes appear rounder. "He...he wasn't himself. It's like he'd transformed into this *darker* man—someone I'd never seen before. But he, um...well, he looked like a demon from the tales about Inferno Isle. And he had a man in the cottage with him. The man was in some sort of trance as he stared at the dark man, and dark wisps floated in the air, like he was stealing his energy, or feeding his dark energy to the man. Whatever he was doing, I refused to stand for it, so I banged on the door and demanded him to stop. But that night is the last thing I really remember about Manx...if that was even his real name. It's the last *any* of us really remember about ourselves." Conan scratches at the scruff on his jaw. "I know it all sounds impossible, but it's true. That man...he did something to us. He...*used* us. Harbored the energy of Whisper Grove to keep himself strong. He manipulated the people and the territory, and now that he's gone, we've been sucked dry. We've been left with nothing."

"Believe me," I say. "Nothing about what you've said is impossible. I've seen some mad shit that I *never* would've believed if I hadn't caught it with my own two eyes."

Conan bobs his head and sighs with relief, eyes glistening.

"That person you saw sucking the energy from that man that night wasn't Manx. It was Decius."

Conan frowns at me. "What? No, that's impossible! You mean Decius, from the original Tethered?"

"Yes."

"But...*how*? All the Tethered died. How is that... I'm not understanding. How is that possible? And how do *you* know this?"

"Because he tried taking my life too. My energy."

Conan's jaw drops, eyes rounding. "B-but how did you escape?"

I lift a shoulder. "Got lucky. But this would explain why he could get past the protection barrier of Whisper Grove," I tell him. "He's stronger than any Mythic out there. His energy is very powerful, going back millions of years."

"And I just welcomed him in," Conan breathes.

"Don't be so hard on yourself. Believe it or not, that man practically raised me. Turns out he was only using me."

"Oh." Conan's eyes remain glassy as he looks me all over. "I'm so sorry. No one should ever be treated that way."

I say nothing to that.

"I'm also sorry to have bothered you with this. We felt there was nowhere to turn, really. Vanora has so many guards and hoops to jump through just to get in. We thought to go to

Luxor, seek The Council's help, but it's too far a journey, and I was afraid some of my people would die during their travels. Blackwater seemed like the safest option."

"The Council wouldn't have done a damn thing for you," Killian grumbles behind me. "You were smart coming to us."

"My Gunman is correct." Killian fidgets at my side, grumbling a bit. He hates when I call him my Gunman, though that's what his status is in the Blackwater Clan. He and Rowan are my Gunmen, and they're the only two people in Blackwater with that title. "You can put your mind at ease, Conan. You came to the right man. We will help you," I assure him.

"Conan bobs his head gratefully. "Thank you, Monarch Harlow."

"Call me Caz."

He nods again.

"We've brought plenty of food for you and your people, lots of regular water for the children, and Alora, the queen of Vanora, has agreed to deliver several barrels of youthwater for the adults within the next couple of hours. Your people will survive. As for Decius, he's gone now. You'll never see him again."

"How can you be so sure?"

"I just am. Trust me." I won't get into talking about the Regals. Some people believe in them, but many don't—and for good reason. They practically left Vakeeli to their own devices and went off the grid. I was one of the many who didn't believe in them until we stumbled across Korah. Sure, the stories were interesting to read, but I always had a hunch they were fairy-tales—made up things to give people a reason to meet, pray, and have someone to send their worries to. I don't feel like going into a conversation about whether they still exist or not.

They've kept low profiles for a reason. Best it stays that way before people try to find them.

"Well, that's wonderful. And that puts my mind at ease." Conan sits up taller, looking from me to Killian and then Rowan. "I can't help sensing there's a catch to all of this though."

I press my lips, wanting so badly to pull out a bloom, but these people are practically dying, and I don't think my second-hand smoke will help. Instead, I turn to Killian, who puts his attention on Conan. "Killian? Mind taking the floor?"

"We are more than willing to help your people, but we do request that once your energy is restored, you'll help us," Killian says, taking a step forward from his corner. "As I'm sure you're aware, the ruby caves are in our territory. We have lots of them, and because of a slight hiccup with the monarch of Ripple Hills, we now owe them five million rubies."

Conan gapes. "Oh my."

"There's no way we can have our men mining for that many rubies within a month without some of them dying. We don't want our people suffering because of our errors."

"*My* errors," I mumble. I still don't regret killing Rami though. I'd kill him a thousand more times if it meant saving Willow.

"Once your men are feeling healthier and stronger, we would like to work out a plan to take shifts. Our men mine for a few hours a day and night, and then your men can come and mine as well. With the help of your people, we could get the rubies in no time."

"My men aren't used to mining," Conan says, hesitant.

"Get them used to it." Killian takes another step toward the desk. "Tell them it's this simple favor that will only take a week, or they'll be without food and youthwater for their families for the rest of their lives. Because believe me, the other territories are selfish. You may catch some luck with Alora, but like you said, you'll have to go through hoops to get to her, and by the time you do, it may be too late for your people."

Conan's throat bobs, and he picks up the container of water from his desk again, opening it and taking a large gulp. I notice his hands are shaking. "Very well," he gasps. "I'll see to it that they restore their health and prepare to assist your people in the ruby mines."

"We hate being the kind of people to dangle meat over someone's head," I tell him as wariness sinks into his eyes. "That's not why we came here. We truly did come to help, and that's what we'll do. But in order for all territories to get along and respect one another, we must help each other. We must become allies. Once the mining is done, your people are free, I guarantee it. We'll never ask anything of you again. We'll send food as you need it until your crops grow back in and you start your trades again. Your people are free to come to Blackwater to shop for what they need. This isn't a threat, I guarantee you. It's a bargain. Sometimes these hard decisions must be made for our people to thrive."

"I completely understand," Conan returns, sounding slightly more assured.

"Good." I push to a stand. "Mining will start in exactly seven days. That should be enough time for your men to restore their strength. In the meantime, do let us know if there is anything you need, and we'll take care of it."

"Of course." Conan stands, stretching his arm over the desk and holding out a hand.

"I don't shake."

"Oh."

"Don't take it personally."

Conan nods, snatching his hand away.

"And for the love of Vakeeli, make your lives easier by getting transmitters and bloody cars in this territory!" Rowan says. He can never leave a meeting without saying *something*.

Conan chuckles. "I will work on that as well. In due time."

"Right. Let's go boys." If we leave now, we'll likely make it back by dinner.

When I'm in the car, I feel a cold prickle on the back of my neck. The prickle is familiar and sends goosebumps all over my body. I peer out the window with a sharp gasp, scanning my surroundings but there's no one around buy Whisper Grovians. I search the trees, the hills, but there are so many that it's impossible to tell if someone is watching.

"Alright, Caz?" Rowan asks.

I swallow, facing forward again. That prickle felt just like the iciness from Decius…but that can't be. He's been put away.

No. It's all in my head. *It's all in my head.* No one is coming after me. No one with power of that magnitude. Not anymore. They can't be.

"Yeah," I breathe. "I'm good."

CHAPTER 71
WILLOW

WHEN I FIRST ENTERED BLACKWATER, I ASSUMED IT was a run-down place with poor, violent people. I was wrong to judge this territory so quickly.

Just like Vanora, there are two sides of Blackwater, though they don't really have names, like how Vanora has Iron Class and Gold Class. Here, it all exists under one umbrella, but I can tell the difference between the two sides. I'd like to consider it lower and upper class, just like we have on Earth. We can tell which areas are for the rich and which are for the poor based off the size of the houses and the lay of the land.

In Juniper's car (a very fancy black two-door), we ride past the lower class, where the houses are no more than a story high and about the size of the cabin that once belonged to Caz's mother. The houses range from black to gray, and even brown. The people are dressed casually—pants or skirts and solid-colored shirts. Most of their attire is black or gray.

Juniper drives past one of the markets, where some of the

stands have meat hanging while others sell fruit or gigantic fish. Buyers drop rubies on the counters of the stands after grabbing their food, waving their goodbyes as others in line move forward.

Then there's a shift in the ambiance. The houses grow in size—two to three stories high with a Victorian feel, all assembled in tight-knit neighborhoods. The markets transform to well-built shops, and a large store appears with a sign that reads **Youthwater Kingdom**. Horse carriages provide rides for citizens, and one of the men holding the reins of a spotted white and black horse tips his hat at us as we pass. A school appears, and through the doors and windows, I see children with their heads bowed, likely reading or doing classwork.

Juniper drives up a steep hill, pressing her foot on the gas to increase the speed as Maeve mumbles to herself in the passenger seat. She's reading papers on her clipboard, going over a list of house maidens and their qualities.

"This is where the fun happens," Juniper says over her shoulder, and she makes a right onto a single-laned black street.

Bordering the street on both sides are rippling black waters, and on the other side of those waters are a number of shops. They all stand out beautifully, each one built with unique details. Some have square windows, some have round. Some have gold signs while others are made purely from rubies. Juniper drives beneath a bridge and turns down a dark alleyway, tailing a few other cars until we reach a parking deck. She turns into a space with a sign in front of it that says, **Blackwater Monarch Clan Parking Only**, then kills the engine.

After leaving the car and finding a staircase that leads us out of the parking deck, we cross a bridge, and from the top of it, I can see *everything*. Every single shop, every person walking by, the people riding their horses on the streets beyond the shops, and even teenagers laughing as they rush into stores. I even see Blackwater Castle from here, just the tips of it, looming behind skyscraper trees.

"Okay, now I get why you love Blackwater so much," I say, turning to Juniper and Maeve.

"Once you get to this side of the village, it's a dream!" Juniper replies. "You'll have to try the spice rolls at Petra's while we're here. They're the best thing you'll ever taste, I swear it. Then we can go to Hatley's for lunch."

Maeve stands on the bridge next to me, a clipboard in hand and her nose scrunched. She's been staring at the clipboard ever since we left the castle.

"Let's make this quick, shall we, ladies?" Maeve insists, eyes still on the paper. "There's so much to do, and if we want to keep having more dinners, we need to hire a house maiden immediately. I think I've found one, but he's male. Not sure Caz will like that."

"Why wouldn't he?" I ask as we step onto flat ground.

"Because *you* are now in the castle, dear," Maeve chuckles. "He'd have that man's head if he even cut an eye at you."

"Not if the house maiden likes other men," Juniper quips, her eyes fixing on something to our left. Juniper rushes to a slim silver machine and twists a knob repeatedly until something pops out. When she brings it back, I see that it's two shiny black balls.

"It's a Chew," she says, offering one of them to me. "You just chew it, and the flavor literally lasts forever. There are three flavors. I always hope for blackfruit."

"What are the other two flavors?" I ask, taking one of the offered Chews.

384

"Goldberry and verdeberry."

I pop it into my mouth, and of course, it's verdeberry. I'm instantly reminded of Alexi and Whisper Grove Inn. A sour taste floods my tastebuds. I disregard it, chewing anyway, until the flavors settle.

"I need to interview him," Maeve goes on. "All the others are young girls. They wouldn't know their heads from their asses, and the last thing we have time for is someone who doesn't know what they're doing. Besides, I'm certain a lot of them only signed up so they can be in Caz's face and striving for his attention."

I laugh at that. "Good luck to them on that. It took me days, and I'm his mate."

Maeve can't help smiling. "This man, his name is Makoto. He's much older, has worked for many people in Blackwater. Knows how to cook. Has three children. He seems promising... but he could be lying. I'll have him meet me at Petra's for a quick interview." Maeve lowers the clipboard, her eyes saddening. "It's awful doing this so soon. I feel like an uncompassionate twat. I mean, Della was everything we never knew we needed, and she was a wonderful asset to Caz. She always saw him how I did—like he was her own. She understood him and knew when to give him space. She kept him fed and hydrated because, let me tell you, Willow, he has the tendency to overwork himself and forget to eat. Even when he didn't want to eat, she'd make him. She loved him, and he loved her." Maeve lets out a long sigh, and I'm flooded with emotions again, thinking about the raw ache Caz felt when he lost Della. "Anyway, if this Makoto doesn't work out, I'll have to take on two women who probably won't even be able to do half the work Della could. Because Della was precise, I'll tell you that, and she made a delicious roast with black potatoes. And she always chose the best wine and snacks." Maeve lets out a sigh. "You can't find people like her these days."

"That's very true. Well, how about you call Makoto and tell him to meet you," Juniper says. "Willow and I will shop, and you can meet us at Hatley's when you're done."

"Sure thing, girls." Maeve plants a kiss on both our cheeks, leaving behind red lipstick prints. "Wish me luck."

I smile as she sighs yet again, then watch her saunter away, disappearing across the bridge.

Juniper turns to me with a grin. "Let's go destroy Caz's pockets!"

CHAPTER 72

CAZ

I CAN'T REMEMBER THE LAST TIME I LOOKED FORWARD to going home.

As soon as Rowan pulls into his designated garage, I climb out and walk through the door that leads into the manor. I make my way through the foyer, rounding a corner and finding the kitchen. The kitchen is spotless, and the only breathing things inside are Silvera and Cerberus coiled up on an oversized pillow in the corner.

Cerberus hops up when he spots me and rushes my way. I give him a stroke on the head and behind the ears as Silvera approaches, stretching with exaggeration before wedging her body between my legs.

"Look at you two," I chuckle, rubbing both their heads. "Best of friends now, I see."

Rowan and Killian come in, placing their guns on the counters. "Oh—by the way, Juniper said we have to dress nicely and meet her at the guesthouse," Rowan announces.

"For what?" Killian demands, unstrapping his bulletproof vest.

Rowan shrugs. "Dunno. But she said as soon as we got back to change and come there."

"Jun is always doing something outrageous," Killian gripes.

"Is Willow with her?" I ask.

"She is. So is Mum."

Just as Rowan says that, a door closes outside the kitchen. I march around the corner and look to my left, finding Juniper waltzing through the back door that leads to the lower deck. She's not dressed in her normal attire. She wears a velvety teal dress that dips very low on her chest. Her dark hair has been straightened and rests on her shoulders.

"Where's Willow?" I ask.

"Don't worry, she's fine," Juniper chimes. "She's with Mum in the guesthouse. Why aren't you all changed yet? Come on, be quick! We don't have all night!"

"What exactly is going on in the guesthouse?" I inquire.

"It's a surprise," she states. "And if you want to find out, you must change out of those dirty working clothes and into something easier on the eyes. But also make it a bit relaxing, not too busy. Now hurry!"

She moves forward, pushing Rowan by the arm. "All right, all right." Rowan chuckles while Killian mumbles something under his breath, but he follows their lead anyway.

When they're gone, Juniper's eyes swing to mine.

I need more information than what she's given me. What does she have going on in the guesthouse? And why isn't Willow here with her to tell me? They *never* use the guesthouse. The last time we did was for a meeting with Vanorians—literally years ago.

As if she's read my mind, Juniper says, "Please, Caz. Just let us do something nice and surprise you for once."

I take a step back, studying her eyes. They're bright, hopeful. Clearly no lives are a stake.

I shift on my feet. "Fine."

I don't waste much time getting changed. I find a black button-down shirt and dark jeans, tuck the shirt in, swap boots, and pick up my coat again. When I've returned to the kitchen, Killian is already there, leaning against a wall while swiveling a gun around his forefinger by the trigger guard.

"Is that thing loaded?" I ask.

"Of course, it is," he retorts.

I shake my head. Reckless asshole. "Where's Rowan?"

"Here!" Rowan appears from the foyer dressed much nicer than we are in a gray turtleneck, a dark gray trench coat, and dress shoes. He's even gelled and styled his hair.

"Nice!" Juniper praises.

"You're such a pretty boy," Killian chuckles.

"And the ladies love it." Rowan pops the collar of his coat.

"Right. Juniper? The guesthouse?" I ask, doing my best to cling to patience.

"Yes, yes. Come on." She twirls around, opening the door again and walking across the deck to get down the stairs. The sun has dipped behind the ocean, and the moon is not too far off on the other side of the sky, ready to give a full debut. The sky bursts with purple and orange hues, and a gentle breeze drifts by us, causing some of my hair to fall into my eyes. Juniper leads us down a hill, and I'm surprised to find the guesthouse completely lit up.

There are lights hanging outside the house, wide bulbs that illuminate the area, and a warm glow emits from the windows.

As we get closer, I take notice of the pillar candles perched in the windowsills, the flames dancing joyously. We cross the bridge and make it to the door. Juniper swings it open with a grin, revealing what's inside.

The large table, which is normally vacant, is set with black plates, crystal glasses, and gold cutlery. Candles are lined in the middle, surrounded by centerpieces of Gold Vanorian Blossoms, and more candles are on the counters. Three women are near the kitchen, working with food. They're unfamiliar to me, but not the other people inside.

Simpson and Paulina are here, as well as Veno, my driver, and Jack, Lew, and Hunter, my Blackwater Generals. Veno and Lew have brought their wives, and the quartet mingle in a corner. Jack and Hunter stand near the kitchen with silver beer tins in hand, laughing. Simpson and Paulina are pouring and mixing drinks, their forte thanks to their positions as barmen at Blackwater Tavern.

And then there are the two women next to the window, facing the sunset while chatting. Maeve and Willow.

My gaze locks on Willow, and despite the busyness of the room, she's all I can see. There's a thumping in my chest as I study the curve of her ass in the silk maroon dress she's wearing. My heart beats at a swift, chaotic pace, longing to be close to hers. As if she senses me, and all the mad thumping going on in my body, Willow stops talking midsentence to swing her gaze to mine. Her brown eyes light up, twinkling from the nearby candlelight, and she smiles, revealing two rows of beautiful teeth.

My word, is she a beautiful sight. Her long-sleeved dress cuts into a deep V at the chest, revealing the tops of her voluptuous bosom. Her locs are parted at the top of her head and swim down to her shoulders. She wears a gold crown as well, and I bet a million rubies it was Juniper's idea to put it on her. Willow says something to Maeve before coming my way.

I start to speak, but I'm at a loss for words. I'm not even sure what to say to her. She's so fucking beautiful it hurts. It literally *hurts* to see her—to know she's mine and that I get to have her forever—but in the greatest way.

"Willow, I—" I look her all over, taking her hand in mine. "You look...I mean..."

"Go on. Spit it out," she teases.

I huff a laugh. "You look incredible. Absolutely stunning."

"I know." She taps her temple with two fingers. "I could hear you," she says with a tinker of a laugh.

I can't help smiling wider. "Right."

"This dinner was all her idea, by the way," Juniper says as she passes us.

I focus on Willow's eyes. "Was it really?"

She gives me bashful smile. "I just wanted to cheer you up a bit."

"Well, it worked. Thank you. This is all very thoughtful and beautiful." To fulfill my aching need, I reel her in by the waist and bring her body closer. My heart comes alive again, humming with our energy. The coolness sinks into my chest, familiar and definite. Never a feeling to waver. Our Cold Tether.

I palm the back of her head as she laces her arms over my shoulders and brings her mouth to mine. Her mouth is sweet with wine, and she smells like flowers and sweet spices. I hold her closer, deepening the kiss, wanting to tangle myself in her, to completely rid myself of the ache by taking her right here, *right now*...but then I remember, we're not alone.

I break the kiss, my eyes traveling across the room. All my

cousins are trying *not* to look at us. The other guests are whispering amongst themselves while cutting their eyes at us (it's mostly Veno's and Lew's wives doing the whispering. They've not seen me with a woman before, so I'm sure it's shocking). Maeve looks right at us, though. She's not one to miss a romantic moment...especially when it comes from me.

Heat creeps up from my shirt collar, and I clear my throat before lowering my gaze to Willow's and placing my lips to the shell of her ear. "If they weren't all here, I'd fuck you right on this table," I whisper.

She releases a bubbly laugh. "Don't be naughty."

"We can leave right now, you and me. Run back to the manor and fuck wherever we want. Once everyone starts eating, I bet they won't even notice we're gone."

She laughs again, holding me close and pressing her ear to my chest. She angles her head upward, so I can see her eyes. "We have plenty of time for that afterward."

"Shall we eat?" Juniper calls out. "I'm starving!"

"Absolutely." I turn toward the table. "Let's eat, everyone, and enjoy this night created for us."

After the food is served by the three catering women and we all dig in, I take a look around the table, understanding what Willow meant when she said there are people who care about me.

I see it now. I knew it was here all along, but it was never this apparent. We never really sat down to have dinners, to laugh, to drink and let go. We're all so caught up—so busy with life and trying to survive that we don't get these small moments, nor do we plan them.

But Willow did. She's given this rare gift to us. Her heart is so soft, so kind. She's exactly what we need, and because of her, this will become a night I'll never forget.

CHAPTER 73
WILLOW

THE DINNER IS DELICIOUS, THE DRINKS APLENTY, AND everyone has their guards down for once and are centered in peace.

There's a serenity to this moment, seated amongst Caz's family and friends. I met Veno's wife, Tallulah, who is a beautiful woman and the complete opposite of Veno. Where he's serious and alert, Tallulah is playful and giggly. I've not met Lew before tonight, but when he came in, he couldn't stop staring at me. Not in a disturbing way, but more like he was trying to understand me and how I'd gotten with Caz. Simpson and Paulina did the same, but more in awe. They're very nice, but they have a look to them—one bred from roughness and difficult times. I get the sense that they're two people you should not mess with. Simpson is tall and lean, a light-skinned brown man with a great smile. And Paulina has a very strong build, her skin pale, hair red, and cheeks splattered with freckles. She looks tough, but also carries a feminine grace.

They all have stared, and I bet it's hard for them to understand what Caz and I have. Caz isn't the kind of man who settles down, that much has been clear. He doesn't like people and prefers to be alone. He's their leader, and I'm this woman who literally *fell* out of the sky and is now sitting next to him with my hand in his lap. He holds on to me like I'll float away if he lets me go.

Lew's wife, Nikita, is stunning and in my world would pass as an Asian or Pacific Islander. She'd kept me entertained a bit before Caz's arrival, telling me all about her teenage daughter who was going through a rebellious phase and didn't want to start drinking youthwater yet.

It was interesting to learn that people don't start drinking youthwater in Vakeeli until they're eighteen. Apparently, when a person turns eighteen, a ceremony is placed for them to enter adulthood. They'll drink their first cup of youthwater and celebrate a long, prosperous life.

"She says youthwater is a punishment!" Nikita exclaimed before. "She doesn't understand that it can give her a fruitful life! So many kids would kill to get even a drop of youthwater. But anyway, you and Monarch Harlow, huh? How is that? Is he much nicer than he lets on? No, never mind. Don't answer that. I'm just glad he's finally found someone to be with. I don't want to hex it."

The three women Maeve hired to cater and help with dinner are named Bella, Joelle, and Danica. Bella and Joelle are mother and daughter, Joelle being the mother, and Danica is their assistant.

There is something unique about Danica. Besides one of her eyes being a ghost-gray with a red scar running from the bottom of her brow to the tip of her eyelid, there's something else about her and I can't quite place my finger on it. She's been staring at me since she arrived, which isn't new considering *everyone* has been stealing glances. I'm the new chick around, and I'm sleeping with the monarch of Blackwater, but Danica doesn't know I'm new...I don't think. Regardless, she stares at me with an all-knowing gaze, that one sharp brown eye locking on me every chance it can. Her skin is like porcelain, her hair a soft black collected into one braid that falls down the center of her back. She hasn't said much, while Bella and Joelle were practically gushing to Maeve and Juniper about letting them cater and serve us for the night.

Even now, Danica watches from the kitchen. Her hands are busy, but she cuts her eyes at me sporadically, zoning in, before going back to slicing something with a knife.

A hand drops to my upper thigh and squeezes lightly. I look to my right, into blue eyes. "You okay?" Caz asks.

"Yeah. I'm fine." I place my hand on top of his, giving it a squeeze back. "Did you like the dinner?"

"I did. It was great. How about you? I know it wasn't a cheeseburger, but still good, eh?"

I laugh. "Yeah. It was good. Especially the water beans."

"Told you you'd like them."

Joelle, Bella, and Danica make their way to the table with large trays in hand. On the trays are small plates with slices of yellow cake, berries, and gold cream.

"Have you ever had Gold Cake before?" Nikita asks from across the table as a plate is set in front of me.

"Of course, she hasn't, Nikita," Juniper quips, rolling her eyes. "She hasn't been in our world long."

"I'm only asking." Nikita shrugs, slicing her fork into the

cake. "Whether you have or not, it's so good. In fact, I'll probably ask for seconds."

"It's infused with whiskey," Caz says to me. "Don't eat too much. It'll get you *really* drunk."

"Probably why Nikita here likes it so much," Juniper teases.

"Oh, whatever, Jun! Like you can't say the same. This is, what, your sixth glass of wine?"

Juniper points her fork at Nikita. "Oi, don't call me out like that. I'll stab you with my fork."

Nikita breaks out in laughter, and I notice Tallulah giggling at the conversation. Nikita leans over the table a bit, whispering to Juniper. "What do you say we go to the Silver Swan after this?"

"You think your husband will go for it?" Juniper whispers back.

"I can hear you both," Lew grumbles, and that causes both Juniper and Nikita to break out in laughter again. Yeah, they're pretty drunk.

"We have Yurina keeping an eye on Britt for us, babe. Come on," Nikita whines, clinging to Lew's large, tattooed arm. "Let's go out, have a little fun."

"Not a chance. Yurina is old and falls asleep at the drop of a hat on her porch. I don't trust Britt at home alone for more than two hours. She'll throw a damn bash for all we know."

"You're right." Nikita's head shakes. "That girl, I swear. Caz, can't you, like, instill some kind of monarch law where teenagers *have* to listen to their parents?"

One side of Caz's lips quirk. "I believe that'd be an abuse of power."

"Well, sometimes people need it in order to get in line."

Nikita shrugs, but I don't miss the way Caz fidgets in his chair a bit. "She still hasn't taken the youthwater, you know?"

Caz leans back in his chair, relaxing again. "Just trust her. Let her grow into her own woman. She'll thank you for being patient with her down the line."

Nikita presses her lips, and her eyes soften. "Wow. Are you always this sentimental? Willow, what have you done to our monarch?"

I fight a laugh, and a few others at the table laugh too. I carry my eyes to Caz who has lowered his head a bit, his face turning a bright red. He's so adorable.

CHAPTER 74
WILLOW

AFTER DESSERT, CAZ LEADS ME OUT OF THE guesthouse and toward the beach. We kick out of our shoes, sending them flying across the sand, then I tug the hem of my dress up to walk along the black sand.

The sand sparkles beneath the cool moonlight, glittery silver specks that remind me of a shattered mirror. The ocean's waves gently crash in the distance, and I walk to shore, letting the cool, dark water run over my feet when I reach it. Caz meets at my side, standing so close I can feel the heat of his body. He smells like expensive cologne and bloom. The cologne reminds me of mahogany and smoked wood.

I start to say something, but he tips my chin with his fingers and drops his head, kissing me ever so slowly. The kiss is gentle, applied with minimal pressure, and with the drinks swimming through my veins and the desire I have for him, I sink into the kiss, dropping the hem of my dress to slide my hands over his shoulders.

I curl my fingers into his hair, deepening the kiss, and he releases a guttural groan, picking me up in his arms. He stumbles forward until my back bumps against one of the jagged rocks, and I moan as he shoves the fabric of my dress up to my hips. Our lips tear apart so he can unbutton his pants and lower them just enough to pull his hardening dick out, and when he does, he pushes my panties aside and buries himself into me. I clasp his face in my hands again as our lips collide, pressing and parting, gasps escaping. The rock scrapes my back, but some of the satiny fabric from my dress blocks whatever pain it tries to bring.

"I can't believe I have you," he whispers on the crook of my neck. "Can't believe you're mine. How have I gotten so lucky?"

"It's not luck," I breathe. "It's destiny."

He grins, his beautiful teeth gleaming in the moonlight, and his smile is so infectious I smile too. He finishes in a heated few minutes beneath the burning stars, pulling out with a grunt and coming on my belly. Then, with ease, he whips out a handkerchief from his pocket to wipe the puddle of cum away, then drops my legs so I can stand straight.

Lowering to his knees, he shoves my dress up just enough to put his head beneath it.

"Caz," I giggle as his mouth grazes the front of my thigh. "What are you doing?"

He doesn't answer, at least not with words. Instead, he's pulling my panties down completely, forcing me to step out of them, and when I feel the hotness of his tongue sliding through the lips of my pussy, I gasp. He shoves one of my legs up and rests it over his shoulder to get a deeper taste, his head still beneath the dress, moving carefully.

"Oh...fu—" My breath hitches as he eats me with ferocity,

like this was the meal he's waited for all night—like this is what he's wanted to do to me since he laid eyes on me before dinner —and I throw my head back, staring up at the indigo sky.

This is my life now.

This is happening.

This man is *mine*, and damn, did I hit the fucking jackpot.

It doesn't take me long to finish. With several coaxes of his tongue lapping around my clit, and his grip tightening around my waist so he can bury his hot tongue deeper into my pussy, I'm tipped right over the edge. I cry out his name, my nails digging into the rock next to me.

He doesn't stop right away. He waits until my body has relaxed, licking ever-so-slowly, before pulling his head out.

When he's standing upright, he holds the panties up with a smirk, his lips glistening from my wetness, and says, "Suppose these are mine now." He tucks them into his pocket.

"You're such a..."

"A what?" he asks, cupping one side of my face and planting a kiss on the corner of my lips.

I'm not even sure what I was going to say. He's all man, he's bold, he's loyal, and he's *mine*.

"You should taste yourself," he rasps on my mouth, then he's pressing his lips to mine, spreading them apart with his tongue. I moan, and a heated pulse blossoms between my thighs, as if he weren't just there mere seconds ago.

Love of Vakeeli, I want him all over again.

CHAPTER 75
WILLOW

Caz and I make our way back to the guesthouse where Rowan, Killian, Lew, Hunter, Jack, and Veno are playing a card game at the table.

The table is topped with crystal tumblers halfway filled with amber liquid and a tray of nuts for the men to enjoy.

I fix my gaze on the kitchen, where Bella and Joelle are tidying up, but I don't see Danica with them. The women aren't around either. Juniper, Maeve, Nikita, and Tallulah are gone, as well as Simpson and Paulina.

"Where are the others?" Caz asks.

"Simpson and Paulina had to run back to the tavern. The ladies went to the castle, said they wanted tea," Rowan answers.

"They aren't drinking any bloody tea," Lew grumbles, slapping a card down. This man does a lot of grumbling.

Caz looks at me, smirking. *And you think I'm a grump.*

I can't fight my grin,

"Ready to head to the castle?" he asks.

I nod, smiling, and he takes my hand, leading the way out of the guesthouse. As we approach the castle, I hear footsteps behind us, and Rowan dashes past us in a blur, laughing his ass off as Killian chases after him with a gun in hand.

"What is going on?" I laugh as Rowan clambers up the stairs to get inside. Killian huffs like a bull, rushing past us.

"Who knows," Caz chuckles. "They're always fighting about something."

We enter the castle, and music is playing, something folksy but calming. In the kitchen, Juniper, Maeve, Nikita, and Tallulah are drinking tea and chatting amongst themselves. Danica is in there as well, removing a kettle from the stovetop. Ah. So that's where she ran off to.

"Tea?" Caz gestures to the kitchen.

"Yeah. Let me run to the bathroom first."

He nods, lifting my hand to his lips and kissing my knuckles. "Make sure you come back to me."

I smile as he releases my hand. I make my way down the foyer, past the portrait of the horses with manes of fire and the man riding it into darkness. In this dimly lit section of the room, it's even more mesmerizing than before. The darkness truly does look like a black void a person will never be able to escape.

I find the bathroom, finish up, and wash my hands. As the water pours over my hands, rinsing the soap away, I can't help smiling like a goof at my reflection. I'm too busy thinking about what Caz and I just did on the beach. I've never had an experience like that with anyone, and with him it all comes so...*naturally*. In all honesty, I'm ready for everyone to leave now so we can go to his room and have more fun. I'm not kidding when I say I want him now more than I did before...and before, I wanted him a lot. Something has changed within me. Something internal and soul deep. I can't quite explain it, but Caz and I truly feel like one now.

After I've dried off my hands, I swing the door open and hear the ladies getting louder and chattier in the kitchen. But as I shut the door behind me, someone grabs my arm and tugs me around the corner and into Caz's office.

I feel a drop in my stomach as the person's cold grasp wraps around my wrist, and for a moment I think it's Mournwrath again, coming back for us—here to demolish all the happiness we've aimed to restore—but then I see the brown and gray eye along with the scar on her face. Danica.

She presses my back against one of the shelves and looks me all over, narrowing her eyes. "You're her."

"What the hell are you doing?" I snap, shoving her hand away.

"Willow?" Caz calls from the end of the foyer.

"I know where your brother is," Danica says hurriedly.

My heart drops. *"What?"*

She grabs my hand and rapidly stuffs something into it as Caz calls my name again, then I hear footsteps thundering.

"Find me at this location tomorrow at noon," she says. With that, Danica runs out of the office and toward the front door.

"Oi!" Caz shouts just as Danica rounds the corner. He snatches his gun from inside his coat, but Danica's gone, her footsteps pounding toward the front door. Caz stops at the mouth of the office, glancing at me quickly before running after the woman, and Killian and Rowan are right behind him, guns out and bustling out the front door.

What the hell is going on?

"Willow?" Juniper appears, gripping my shoulders. "What happened? Are you okay?"

"I—I don't know." I swallow hard then open my hand, focusing on the crumpled sheet of paper. I blink at it several times, trying to process what Danica just said. *I know where your brother is.* What does she mean she knows where Warren is? How would she know, and why do I need to meet her to get to my brother? Maeve appears, looking between us, while Nikita and Tallulah stand a few steps back, a mixture of fear and concern on their faces.

"What did that woman want?" Maeve demands, eyeing me.

"I—I'm not sure not sure."

Maeve comes closer to me, taking the paper out of my hand. She unravels it, her brows furrowing as she reads it. "What is this? What are all these numbers?"

Juniper looks with her and says, "They're coordinates." Juniper's eyes then shift to me. All of them are looking at me, awaiting an explanation...but I can't bring myself to explain a damn thing right now.

CHAPTER 76
CAZ

I RUN ACROSS THE FIELD, MY EYES LOCKED ON THE woman ahead of me like a target. She's fast, but that won't stop me. I'm fast too.

She runs toward the forest behind Blackwater Manor, which means she'll be likely to stumble. No one knows that forest more than I do, so I keep running with Killian and Rowan behind me. Cerberus has appeared as well, and he darts past me, his paws pounding into the ground.

He leaps forward, and the woman (who has stripped out of her white button-down shirt to a black tank), looks over her shoulder and dashes to the left. She does it so fast it's outlandish, and Cerberus ends up rolling onto his side. He's back up in a matter of seconds, chasing the woman again, much angrier this time by the way he bares his teeth.

The woman approaches the forest and I raise my gun, pointing it at her back. Suddenly, she stops running, and the tall blades of grass sway past her ankles as she keeps her back to us.

"Turn around!" I shout, my gun still aimed at her. One move and I'm blowing her fucking head off. Then again, I shouldn't be so hasty and should at least capture her first. I need answers. Who the hell is she and why did she go after Willow? I swear if she did something to Willow, I'll kill her. I felt my mate's panic. She was terrified. Is this another one of Decius' traps? Is he still tampering with our lives somehow?

The woman turns slowly, and when her eyes land on mine, it feels like a bolt of lightning has struck me. A shockwave runs through me, but I don't relent. I keep my gun aimed at her as Killian and Rowan stand a few paces behind me, prepared for any surprises.

"Who the hell are you?" I demand.

The woman tilts her head, looking me up and down, and a slow smirk tugs at her lips as the wind whips at the loose tendrils of her dark hair. I wrap my finger tighter around the trigger, ready to shoot her, and I would if any of this made sense. None of it does. I don't know who she is or what territory she's from, but what I just felt—the shockwave—that's new. I've never felt it before, but it's given me a sense of familiarity. Like I know her...or that I should. I shouldn't hurt her, even though I so badly want to. She infiltrated my house, touched my mate. I should fucking *kill* her.

"This was fun. See you tomorrow, Mr. Harlow," the woman finally says, and then she disappears, right into thin air.

"She's a fucking vanisher!" Killian hollers as he and Rowan spin around with their guns in front of them.

I lower my gun. "She's no threat," I mutter, but Killian and Rowan don't lower their guards, not until they see me running past them to get back to Willow.

CHAPTER 77

CAZ

WHEN I BURST INTO THE CASTLE, I MARCH DOWN THE foyer until I've reached my office. Maeve and Juniper are pulling down books from the shelves and carrying them to one of the tables where loose sheets of paperwork are. Nikita and Tallulah are squatting next to Willow as she sits in the chair behind my desk, both of them stroking her arm or back and trying to sooth her.

"Nikita, Tallulah. Find your husbands and get out of here," I command, and they cut their eyes to me before focusing on each other.

"Of course, Monarch Harlow," they reply in unison. They were never supposed to be in here. I've never liked others in my castle, but tonight was different. Everyone was having fun, and I'm certain having tea was Maeve's idea. I can't fault her for wanting to switch up the pace, show off the castle a bit. But this is what happens when we lower our guards too much. Someone is always around, ready to pierce our hearts.

"Please let us know if we can help with anything," Tallulah says to Willow. When they're gone, I lower to a squat next to Willow and collect her hand in mine, but she doesn't look at me. Instead, she remains focused on the top of my desk—not at anything specific, but more like she's in a trance.

"Willow?" I call, squeezing her hand, and her eyes finally drop to mine.

"Caz," she breathes, and her eyes glisten. "I don't understand what's happening. What has she done with my brother?"

"What did she say to you?" I ask.

"She said to find her at the location on the paper. That she knows where Warren is."

I peer over my shoulder as Killian and Rowan stand near the opening of the office, watching Maeve and Juniper pull down several more books.

Releasing Willow's hand, I drop a kiss on her forehead then move across the room to Maeve.

"I am so sorry, Caspian. I thought she could be trusted. The girls wanted tea, and I figured it would be easier to just make it in the kitchen, and that woman who threatened Willow offered to prepare it—"

"It's fine, Maeve. She's safe." I zero in on the book in her hand. "What are you looking for?"

"These coordinates," she answers, and she hands a crumpled sheet of paper to me. I open it.

N 36, 22
L 80, 33

"What is the L for?" I ask. "I've never seen that."

"That's what we're looking for. It's not on the Vakeeli

maps." Maeve props a book open, skimming through the table of contents. When she doesn't find what she's looking for, she passes the book to Rowan, who takes it and puts it back on the shelf. She and Juniper do this for quite some time while I study the coordinates with a frown.

"Found it!" Juniper shouts, pointing a finger on the book.

"'There are four major cardinal directions of Vakeeli—north, south, east, and west, but there is one direction on the map that has not been studied; however, it does exist. This direction is called the Limit,'" Juniper reads aloud. "'The Limit exists beyond the outskirts of Vakeeli, a territory that has not been properly analyzed because of its high levels of toxicity and violence.'" Juniper's throat bobs as her eyes lift to mine. "The Trench."

CHAPTER 78
WILLOW

"We can't go to The Trench. It's too dangerous."

I whip my head up, looking at him. "Caz, we *have* to go."

He stops pacing, looking me in the eye. "Willow, that place is horrid."

"You promised we'd go after him. This woman just told us where he is! We have to save him from that place!"

"This could all be a trap," he counters. "We don't even know how this woman infiltrated us! And I just saw her vanish right before my very eyes when we chased her. She's a vanisher, and I've never trusted them."

Rowan and Killian nod in agreement, arms folded.

"What if this woman is holding him hostage?" I ask.

Caz frowns, holding my gaze for several beats before allowing a sigh to escape him. "Everyone out, please. I need to talk to Willow."

The clan file out of the office one by one. When they're gone and we can no longer hear their footsteps, Caz walks around the desk to stand closer to me.

"Willow, I want to be completely honest with you. The Trench was not designed for survival. It's a toxic place, and I don't want you there. I know you want to save Warren but it's not worth putting your life at stake. We can find an alternative. Seek Danica out again or—"

"Caz, my brother is out there waiting for me to come to him. This woman knows we're related, and you said it yourself, you don't think she's a threat. If I have to go by myself, I will. I'm not kidding."

He holds my eyes, frustration washing over him as he stands tall again. He makes his way toward one of the windows, peering out while shaking his head. "I can send men there in place of us—"

"No. If you do that, there's a chance Danica will change her mind, and I might never see him."

"Willow, you have to work with me here," he snaps, turning toward me again. He moves across the room, his boots thumping on the hardwood. When he stops in front of me, he clasps my face in his hands. "It's not safe, and I swear if something happens to you, I'll burn that Trench to a crisp."

"So do it," I counter, and his eyes stretch, surprised. "If it's a trap, or they lie to us, or we see them hurt my brother, *burn it down.*"

His eyes flicker with something hard to describe. It's not apprehension or worry. It's a cross between pride and astonishment.

"Right. I promised we'd find your brother. Let's go find him."

CHAPTER 79
CAZ

I DON'T WASTE MUCH TIME AFTER THE DECISION IS made. I round my clan up and tell Killian and Rowan to get a fleet together.

"I'll need at least thirty men," I tell them as they stand by the front door of the castle, ready to make necessary calls and moves. "Let them know *no one* is to have their guard down, and to load our best weapons. I want all the gear properly checked so we don't end up with any surprises. I'll meet you all at the Barix."

"Got it." Killian nods, taking off with Rowan.

"Juniper, Maeve." I turn to face the women of my clan, sighing. "Juniper, get Willow dressed accordingly then take her to the armory for weapons. Maeve, I know you have things to do, and you have to see to the new house maiden, so you stay here, keep an eye on castle grounds. If anything happens while I'm not here, you let me know immediately."

"Will do," Maeve returns.

"Come on Willow, I'll help you," Juniper calls, already making her way up the stairs.

Willow shuffles past me, but I catch her hand before she can get far, turning her to face me again. "I have to run to the Barix, but I'll be back."

She nods. "Okay."

"Promise me one thing."

"What?"

"Promise me that when we go, you'll listen to everything I say. I'd prefer you stay here with Maeve, but—"

"Not on my life," she argues rapidly, brows stitching.

"*But,*" I go on, looking deeper into her eyes. "I know you won't. And I respect that, but when we go to The Trench, I want you to respect my wishes as well. I can't protect you if you're reckless. Do you understand?"

Her eyes soften, and she lowers her fingers, clasping my hand. Bringing my knuckles to her lips, she kisses them. Not once, but twice. "I understand."

"Good. Go with Juniper. Get ready. I'll return shortly to pick you up."

I watch her jog up the stairs, and when I can no longer see her, I grit my teeth and step back. I don't want her to go. In all honesty, I'd prefer to run to the Barix, meet my men, then head straight to The Trench to handle it myself, but she'd never forgive me. This is her brother we're talking about. Her twin. I can't do that to her, no matter how scared I am for her safety.

"You can't protect her every second of her life, Caspian." Maeve's voice is nearby, and I look to my right. She's standing near the office, arms folded, shoulder pressed to the wall.

"I know I can't, but I can damn well try."

"She's a lot stronger than you think she is. Once she adapts,

414

I have a feeling no one will mess with her. She has this fire in her that lights up a room. I can't quite explain it, but she's a survivor. Don't doubt her."

Maeve walks away, drifting down the foyer, and I turn for the door, leaving the castle.

CHAPTER 80
WILLOW

I WISH I COULD SAY I'M FEELING CONFIDENT ABOUT my decision to go to The Trench with Caz and his clan, but I'm terrified. All I ever hear are the horrors of The Trench. It's no man's land, and we're strolling right into it.

Caz arrives at the castle to pick me and Juniper up like he said he would. I have to admit, I didn't think he'd return. I could hear him contemplating going there himself and leaving me here.

He pulls up in a large truck with thick armor on the body of it. It reminds me of a military truck, or like the spy trucks you see in movies. It's the size of a miniature bus, with windows tinted pitch black. I bet a hundred bucks they're also bullet proof. The engine of the truck rumbles, the side door wide open as Caz hauls out a black bodysuit and requests that I change into it. Once I do, he offers me a gas mask.

"These are the only things that can protect us from the toxic fumes in The Trench," he informs me. I study the gas mask unlike the type we have on Earth. This mask has a wide, glassy window to reveal the whole face, and near the chin strap are dials for the gas release. The mask goes over your whole head like a motorcycle helmet, no tubes or wires required. You just put the mask on, switch the dial, and you're protected. When we're all set, Caz assists me into the truck, but not without a wary glance.

The inside of the truck is lined with two built-in leather benches on either side. A narrow passageway is in the center, along with dangling leather handles built into the ceiling. In the front, there's a gap that leads to the driver and passenger seat, and that's occupied by Veno. It's very spacious inside.

Now that we're on the road, everyone dressed in their body-suits, gas masks placed on the benches next to them, my decision feels abrupt. Seeing Killian so serious is one thing, but to see Rowan frowning with his jaw locked is another. He's not the one to take things heavily, yet we're all riding into a place unknown. A place that's toxic and so corrupt, Caz has six more military-like vehicles tailing us, as well as a tank.

According to Juniper, it's a twelve-hour drive to the Trench, and since it borders on the dark side of Vanora—a place no one ever ventures because the land is dead and there are no signs of life—we have to cross into Vanora to get through. Caz sent a message to Alora beforehand, so the guards don't stop us. They let us pass right through, bobbing their heads in their white hats.

Vanora, as always, is beautiful, and we take the roads on the outskirts away from the city to not bring attention to ourselves. Still, I see the skyline—Alora's towering palace and the golden tips twinkling in the sun.

We're on the road for hours, and everyone is restless. I try relaxing on the seat, but it's impossible. To know that I'm about to be reunited with my brother makes me anxious. I never thought I'd see the day.

We eat nuts and berries Maeve packed for us, and when the sky shifts from pitch black to hazy gray, I sense a shift in the air.

We're nearing The Trench. I feel it before I even see it. The hairs on my arms raise, goosebumps crawling up my back. There's a friction in the air, and as I rub a gloved hand over my gas mask, it crackles.

"We're fine as long as we're inside the truck," Caz murmurs. "It's when the doors open that we must put our gas masks on."

He peers out a window, and I look with him. Veno drives rapidly along the rocky road, passing charcoal trees with stripped branches and bodies of water so dark, they appear to be made of ink. The dirt on the ground is like ash, as if the land was set on fire and the remains were left. There are no houses, no animals, even the sky is colorless. I can't even say that it's gray, more like a filmy white.

Veno slows the vehicle in front of a small batch of buildings. The buildings were once red brick but are now covered in dark soot. None of them are up to par. Many are missing doors, roofs, and windows. The buildings that are seemingly intact have broken windows or doors hanging off the frames.

I spot people near the buildings, legs drawn to their chests. They peer up as the truck passes, but there is no excitement in their eyes, no happiness or curiosity. There's nothing but...*emptiness*. Their faces are ghostly and sunken in, the clothes hanging off their ill frames. Slowly dying...all of them.

I swallow hard as the truck comes to a complete stop, and Veno says, "As far as I can go, Monarch. There's a bridge ahead, but it's damaged."

"Here is good," Caz says, then he turns to me. "Mask on." He picks it up from the bench behind me and helps me put it on. When mine is secured, he twists the dial, and a hissing noise starts up. Through the window of my mask, I watch as he puts his on as well, twisting a valve to release gas in his too. Numbers appear on the dial he twisted, reading 100%.

"Can you hear me?" he asks. I hear his voice inside my mask. It's staticky, like a radio. There must be speakers built into them.

"Yeah," I answer.

"Good. We should all be able to hear one another." He puts his attention on Killian and Rowan. "We'll go out first. Juniper, you stay here with Willow while we do a surveillance. Keep watch and protect her at all costs."

"Got it." Juniper stands at my side as the truck door slides open with a heavy thunk. The air from outside floats in and is much thicker and heavier, the weight of it clinging to my suit. Caz grunts as he hops out of the truck.

"My legs feel heavier," Rowan says. "That normal?"

"Probably," Caz mutters.

His heard turns, and those icy blue eyes land on me. "Wait here."

The truck door slides closed, and I move closer to the window, peering out as Juniper does the same.

Several of the soldiers who tagged along rush between the buildings with guns aimed forward. In my mask, I hear the words, "Clear. Clear. Clear," until they're near the vehicles again.

We watch Caz, Killian, and Rowan make their way toward the tallest building. Caz pulls out something round from his pocket, reads it, then he looks toward the roof of the tall building. He's reading the paper Danica stuffed in my hand.

The building they face has no windows, only gaping holes spread throughout the length of it. The door is thick and iron like. Several of the other men meet up to Caz, dressed head to toe in armor and gas masks, guns up, red lasers pointing directly at the building.

"Danica!" Caz shouts. His voice fills the inside of my mask. "Where are ya? We came to your location, now come out!"

A thick silence lingers in the air. My heart beats faster as I watch the building with bated breath. There's a thump behind us, and Juniper gasps as the truck door slides open.

A man stands outside the door, pale beneath all the dirt and oil on his skin. He's shirtless, his eyes red-rimmed, a wild grimace on his face.

"Oi! Fuck off!" Juniper shouts, raising a foot and kicking the man in the chest. He goes flying back, but just as quickly as he goes, two more men appear, gripping Juniper by the ankle and ripping her out of the truck. Her gun falls to the ground as she tries snatching it out, and I suck in a sharp breath, running to pick it up.

"Let go of me!" she screams. One of them tries taking off her gas mask, and she screams again, whipping her head left and right to fight them off.

"Let her go!" I shout.

I raise the gun at the men, and they eye me, but they don't react. I suppose they're used to being faced with death. The guns don't scare them. Being shot to death would make a much better fate than suffering here.

I freeze, unable to pull the trigger. I've never shot someone with a gun before, but they're hurting her. She'll die if they get that mask off her head. Just as I wrap a finger around the trigger, both men are blasted in the head. For a split second, I believe I did that. I pulled the trigger and shot both of them... but then Killian and Rowan are on either side of the truck, smoke drifting from the barrels of their large guns. The men's bodies crumple to the ground.

Rowan rushes to assist Juniper after she kicks one of the men's limp arms off of her. "You all right, Jun?" he asks.

"Yeah. I'm fine. Those dirty assholes." She straightens herself up, wiping dirt off her clothes.

"For Vakeeli's sake, Willow. Next time, pull the bloody trigger," Killian grumbles, moving past me to get to his sister.

"I'm sorry," I whisper.

Someone lets out a screeching roar, and when I look to my left, a man is charging my way. I start to raise Juniper's gun at him, but he doesn't make it far. A gunshot goes off, and he falls to the ground with a lifeless thud. I shudder a breath as blood dribbles from a hole in his head, and then Caz steps around the corner, pulling the trigger again and sending a bullet into the dead man's back.

"You can't freeze, Willow," he says, turning to me.

"I'm sorry," I whisper again. I shift my focus to Juniper. "Jun, I'm sorry."

"It's okay," she assures me. "I'm fine. Everything's okay."

But it's not okay. She almost died because I was too scared to shoot people who were *attacking* her. What the hell is wrong with me?

Caz takes my hand and leads me around the truck where the rest of the soldiers are posted.

"Danica! I won't call you again! Come out now!" Caz orders. I notice some people scatter away from a distance, disappearing into the other buildings to escape whatever chaos is going on. I pray no one else attacks us.

A door creaks loudly on the hinges, and I bring my attention to the door of the towering building again. When it has completely opened, a woman appears.

Danica.

She's dressed in all black, no gas mask on her face; however, a large sword is on her back secured by a thick leather band that crosses her chest. Her scarred eye is milky, the scar seeming redder now than before.

"Mr. Harlow, you made it!" She lifts her hands, giving off a slow round of applause.

Caz moves a step ahead of me, raising his gun, and Danica drops her arms, sighing. "Where's Warren?" he demands.

"Inside," she informs him.

"Bring him out."

"I'm afraid I can't do that yet."

"Why not?"

She juts her chin out, eyes landing on me. "I need Willow. Only her."

"Yeah, fucking right," Caz snarls, and he takes another step forward, his finger wrapping around the trigger. "You have ten seconds to bring him out or I'm putting a bullet in your fucking head. I'm done with your games, and from where I'm from, when you cross me once, that's enough for me to end your life."

Danica smirks. "Try."

Agitated, Caz pulls the trigger. As he does, Danica withdraws the sword from her sheath. The sword has a slim silver blade with an angled pointed tip and long handle. To my complete and utter shock, she deters the bullet with the sword and sends it flying toward one of Caz's soldiers instead. The

422

man grunts from the impact and falls, but he's not dead. The bullet is lodged in his chest plate. Several soldiers rush to help him to a stand.

Caz doesn't waver, but I can sense his shock. *Is that a Katana sword?* I hear him asking himself.

Danica tucks the sword back in place without hesitation, raising her hands in the air. "Are we done here?" She takes a step down. "Look, you could have all your men start shooting at me, and I'd ward off every single bullet. And this time, I'd be sure not to aim for the chest. Let's not make this messy. Bring Willow to me so I can take her to Warren."

My heart catches speed, and I move closer to Caz. He tenses at my side and partially lowers his gun. "She only goes in if I go with her."

"Caz, don't be fucking stupid, brother," Killian grouses behind him, but Caz ignores him, focused on Danica.

"All right. Deal. Makes sense you'd want to protect your mate. After all, I'm willing to do the same." Her eyes flicker to mine, and something rocks through me, like a zap to every organ. The feeling is both shocking and intriguing. Still, I frown, eyeing her.

Caz lowers his gun, then shouts for the rest of his men to do the same. They lower their weapons, all but Killian and Rowan.

"Are you sure about this, Caz?" Killian asks, still pointing his gun at Danica.

"I am. Keep watch of the area," he commands, then he's grabbing my hand and leading us toward the building.

CHAPTER 81
WILLOW

"YOU'RE FROM KESSEL," CAZ SAYS AS SOON AS WE'RE inside the building.

"I have Kessel blood in me, yes," Danica responds, standing several steps away from us. "What gave it away?"

"The sword." Caz shifts on his feet, looking all around.

I look with him, smelling something similar to rotten eggs or sulfur. It's dark all over, and soot clings to every wall and surface. There's nothing inside but a couple of broken chairs and tables. Parts of the wall are covered in black residue, concealing the brick, most likely from being burnt. Everything appears to have been set on fire and left here to rot. Was this Decius' doing? Did he try burning this place down when he realized it would be his downfall? I recall the story Hassha told about Decius burning down all the trees in The Trench. Perhaps those flames spread and singed everything.

I hold back a gasp when I spot a rat scurry across the room, twice the size of an Earth rat. Why does she have my brother in this place? And how is she able to breathe without a gas mask?

"There were rumors that the original tribe of Vanorians used the Katana to fight," Caz goes on, his eyes fixed on Danica again. "That was centuries ago, and they aren't made anymore. How do you own one?"

Danica ponders his question a moment, her bold brown eye surveilling him. "It was my mother's," she finally answers. "She belonged to one of the original Vanorian tribes, long before Alora was ever born. Believe it or not, her tribe was blessed by the hands of Hassha, and my mother passed her gifts to me before she died. It's why I can breathe in this filth and not die, and how I vanished before your very eyes last night at your castle."

Caz digests this information, holding Danica's gaze. There are a million questions running through his head. He's confused by this woman just as much as I am.

"Why do you need Willow?" he asks, shifting the subject.

Danica's face changes, an uneasiness stealing her rugged features. "Come this way, I'll show you." She turns away, walking up a curved staircase missing several steps. It doesn't look safe to walk on, but Danica takes the steps with ease. Caz goes after her first, keeping my hand in his as we follow her up. We pass three floors until she ventures down a hallway and pushes a rickety door wide open.

I choke on my next breath when I see a man sitting on a bed in front of a window. The window pours in that filmy white light, and at first, he's nothing but a silhouette. Tall, square shoulders, his head hanging low, focused on the floor. I step closer, taking in the details. His locs are much longer, the roots dark, poofy, and thick. That childhood scar remains on his fore-head when he'd cut himself trying to jump a fence.

I can't believe it. It's my brother, in the flesh.

"Warren!" I scream, pulling my hand out of Caz's and running across the room. I throw my arms around him, holding on tight, hot tears dripping down my cheeks. I wait for him to hold me back, to wrap his arms around me in a tight embrace once he's realized this is me and that it's all real...but he doesn't. He remains stiff, unmoving, and I sense something terribly wrong.

I pull away from him, studying his motionless body. He's breathing just fine, his chest rising and sinking, but his head is still down. He's still staring at the floor, face solemn. I force his chin up to look at me, and he stares right at me—the same brown eyes as mine—but there's nothing inside them. They're empty and cold, and my heart plummets.

"Warren?" I whisper. I drop my hand and his head falls again, eyes gluing to the floor. "What's wrong with him?" I demand, turning to look at Danica.

Danica looks from me to Warren, her eyes now thick with tears. "Warren and I were a source of Decius' power for years. It's how Decius could change forms and blend in while keeping his negative energy at bay." She steps deeper into the room. "I was with Warren the day Decius came for us. We were in Vanora, and I remember feeling this strange pull inside of me, like a magnet being drawn to an iron board. I could sense Warren before we even met—his fear, his panic, and I followed those senses. I left Vanora and made my way to Gilded Forest, and the closer I grew to him, I began to *hear* what he was think-ing. I'd heard his voice many times before, around the time I turned twenty-seven, but my counselor told me it was the guidance of a Regal—that they took on many voices to lead us and help with our decisions. But I didn't believe that because I could have full conversations with this voice. We'd talk about things or confess our deepest secrets." Danica swipes the tip of her nose, bobbing her head toward Warren. "I found him near the ocean. When I saw him, I just *knew* he was my mate and that we were to be together. The moment we locked eyes, we fell in love. But only two weeks later, while we were residing in Vanora, Decius infiltrated. First with our dreams, then in person. We started feeling random bursts of coldness, even when we held each other to keep warm. Eventually, Decius took us both and brought us here to The Trench. He kept threatening how he was going to kill us, but that he couldn't yet—that he needed someone else before he could. He kept saying something about a twin. That he needed both twins together before he could absorb the energy from our Tether."

"What?" I stand up straight. "So, he kept you and Warren locked away in here until he could find *me?*"

"I believe so. We were nothing but his puppets, really. We lost control of our bodies, our minds. I don't remember being able to eat or drink. It's all so dark during the time he had us under his spell. But, only days ago, something changed. That darkness I felt with Decius keeping us hostage lifted, and I suddenly remembered *everything.*"

"Sounds like what he did to the people of Whisper Grove," Caz says, more to himself than to us. His eyes swivel to Danica. "Decius is now gone, trapped in a coffin, and the spell he had over you has lifted. He can't take you or your Cold Tether anymore."

"Are you certain?" she asks.

"More than."

"I could remember everything when I came to. All my skills, my purpose, our Cold Tether...but Warren. He's never really gotten out of whatever it is Decius has done to him," Danica goes on. "I don't think Decius still has a hold on him, but I think his mind remains in a dark place. He won't leave the bed. He won't look at me. He won't speak." Her bottom lip trembles a bit, but she sucks it up and raises her chin. "I didn't know what to do, so I ran to a Mythic in Vanora, who told me he most likely needed a mental recharge. She said he needed to encounter something or someone he remembers before he ever entered Vakeeli."

"That's why you were looking for me," I breathe, and I glance at Warren again. "But I'm here now, and he's still acting weird. He's not looking at me either."

Danica steps forward, digging into her front pocket and pulling out a blue capsule. "The Mythic told me to give you this."

Caz snatches the capsule out of Danica's hand before I can even attempt to take it. "What the hell is it?" he asks, more in a demand.

"She said it will help Willow get into Warren's mind." Danica's brows are furrowed, her lips pinched.

"No. I don't trust you or your Mythic. You won't be giving my mate any of your concoctions." He chucks the pill out the window behind Warren, and Danica's face turns beet red before she reaches behind her and draws out her sword.

"What is wrong with you? Do you know what I had to go through to get that?" she shouts.

Caz already has his gun out, pointed at her, ready for whatever she decides to do next. "I don't care. You're not about to poison my mate."

"It's not poison, you uptight, pompous jackass!" She raises the tip of her sword to Caz's throat, and he points his gun at the center of her forehead.

"Both of you, please stop. Seriously." I step forward, pushing them apart, but they don't back down. Their weapons are still aimed, ready for one wrong move. It's astounding, really, because they're just alike. Defiant. Headstrong. Don't trust easily. It's no wonder they're butting heads. Then again, Caz butts heads with a lot of people.

"Let's compromise," I offer with my hands in the air. "I need to get my brother out of here. We can't do that if you're fighting."

"Yeah, good luck. I've tried getting him up, but he goes right back to the same spot and sits there. He won't leave that bed," Danica says.

"Well, I'll have the soldiers out there rip the bed up and put it in the tank. I don't care," I return. "I just need to get him out of The Trench. Once we're out of here, we'll go to a Mythic Caz and I trust to confirm that capsule is the proper way to get my brother back to his best state of mind, and then we go from there. You can come with us, Danica. It'll be safer for you."

She eases up, lowering the sword, only an inch. Caz does the same, keeping a careful eye on her.

"Fine," she grumbles. "But if this demented fuck tries *anything*, I'll slice his bloody head off."

Caz chuckles. "I wish you luck on that one, vanisher. You're not the only person who loves their weapons."

I ignore their squabbling and lower to a squat, grabbing Warren's hand again. I search his eyes for something—*anything* that will give me sign that he's still in there. Nothing comes. His eyes are vacant, as if no soul exists beyond them. This is not my brother. He was full of life. He was active and outgoing. I have to get him out of this place. "We're going to get you better, Warren. I promise."

"I'll tell my men to come up," Caz announces, pulling out his transmitter. "How the hell did you get into my castle anyway?" He's eyeing Danica, clearly still wary about her.

"I heard through whispers that you were part of a Cold Tether and that your mate was from another world, like my mate. Found out there was a dinner, applied for the position to assist with Bella and Joelle, and showed up. It was quite easy, actually. You should be more careful, Monarch. If I were someone who wanted to kill or poison you, I could have."

He grimaces at her before cutting his eyes to me and offering a hand. "Let's go, Willow, before I blow this woman's head off."

CHAPTER 82
CAZ

THERE IS ONLY ONE MYTHIC I FEEL WE CAN GO TO about Warren, and that's Beatrix. However, after she helped us the last time, I heard she's become very ill.

While I was on Earth, Alora left a message on my transmitter, relieved that we'd made it out, but worried about Beatrix and her health. Apparently, it'd required an abundance of her energy to get us to Earth, and seeing as she was already wounded from the stabbing of those Decius-controlled Whisper Grovians, well, that made it much worse.

Still, we must go. We don't have much time. The Council has granted me another day, fortunately, but my time is ticking. We take the four-hour drive from The Trench to Vanora, riding through the city in the truck, the tank trailing us with Warren as cargo. The rest of my men have gone back to Blackwater.

When Veno parks the truck in front of Beatrix's, the sun is nowhere in sight. It's pitch black, minus the gold glow radiating from her windows. I walk up the steps, Willow trailing behind me, and give the door a rapid knock.

Footsteps thump on the other side, and when it cracks open, I'm surprised to see an unfamiliar woman with round eyes and a hawkish nose. Her skin is dark like a bruised black plum, her thick copper hair pulled into a low ponytail. She tips her chin, keeping the door cracked just enough so I can see her but nothing inside the house.

Right. Another obstacle. Here we go.

"Wha' do ya want?" she inquires with a thick accent. She sounds like she's Vanorian, one of the coastal people. They have their own lives, working in the sun, drowning themselves in coconut water, and surviving off of fish. They hate the city and all its busyness.

"Here to see Beatrix," I tell her.

"Beatrix hasn't mentioned a guest, now go'on away, before I blast ya off."

I sigh. I truly don't have time for this. "Either you let me in, or I kick the door down. Your choice."

The woman narrows her eyes, and they flash a hot silver. "Like tah see ya try, boy."

"Let him in, Kimina!" a voice hollers from inside, one that sounds a lot like Beatrix.

"Best listen to your friend, there, Kimina," I murmur.

Kimina looks me all over before yanking the door completely open. "You come in but touch nothin', ya hear?"

I ignore her, brushing past to get into Beatrix's cottage. Beatrix is sitting on the sofa, wrapped in a blanket. She smiles weakly at me and Willow. "You made it back in one piece, I see," she says with a grin.

"I did." I study her in all her frailness. Her hair is grayer, cheeks hollow. "I heard what you did for me. I'm grateful for it and am now in your debt."

"Yes, well, you can release yourself of that debt. Don't think I'll be alive much longer to request anything."

"Ya about killed my sister, boy," Kimina proclaims, walking around us to get to the table. She picks up a bowl and sits next to Beatrix, spoon feeding her some kind of broth. Beatrix sips slowly, carefully.

"I'm sorry, Beatrix," Willow whispers. "I hate that this has happened to you."

"Ah, well. I've lived for five hundred and sixty years. All our time comes to an end eventually."

"Coulda been longer if ya hadn't been helping these commonas," Kimina grumbles. "Wha' do ya want now, anyway?" She places the bowl and spoon on the coffee table. Some of the broth spills over the lip of the bowl from the impact. "Ya took what's left of her life. She can't help ya no mo.'"

"We didn't come to ask her to use more energy," I assure her, and though the words come out calmly, my fists is clenched so tight I'll probably cause myself to bleed.

"There's one thing we wanted to ask...about my brother." Willow steps forward, taking the lead. "He's still alive, and apparently Decius was using him and his mate to fuel himself. Now that Decius is gone—"

"Gone?" Kimina interrupts. "There's no way that demon is gone! He cannot die! It's been proven!"

I glance at Willow, then focus on Beatrix. "There is something you should know, but I would encourage you to keep it here."

"I'm listening," Beatrix murmurs, eyeing me.

"Korah returned to help us. She's the reason we were able to return to Vakeeli, and she currently has Decius locked away, as well as the dark energy he possessed. Everything he had reign over has washed away."

"I see," Beatrix mumbles, and you'd think I told her I love water or something.

"And why would our Korah help ya? We call on her all da time and she never answer. What makes ya special?" Kimina demands.

I shrug, shaking my head. "I don't know."

Kimina frowns, focusing on the broth before her.

"Anyway, there is one individual in particular who isn't from Vakeeli but has survived Decius. Willow's twin."

Beatrix focuses on Willow.

"Right now, he's in some sort of trance," Willow says. "He won't snap out of it. Won't look at anyone. A Mythic told his mate that he needed a mental recharge or something. She said that I have to take some capsule and get into his mind in order for him to snap out of it."

"That is a possibility." Beatrix mulls over the facts. "But that's the harder way. Taking the capsule could have you both sinking into darkness. There is a much easier option."

"Well? What is it?" Willow asks, desperate.

"Let him sleep."

Willow frowns. "What?"

"Kimina. Grab the slumber elixir from the shelf," Beatrix commands, raising a shaking hand and pointing at the shelf. Kimina rises, moving across the room and taking down an amber jar. This jar is medium sized, about the size of coffee mug. Kimina hands it to Willow with her lips pursed in judgement.

434

"Take your brother somewhere safe, give him about three tablespoons of the slumber elixir, then let him sleep. Fair warning, he will sleep for well over twenty-four hours. Once he wakes the first time, he should gain some recognition, but his mind may still be scrambled, and it is possible he won't be able to form a coherent sentence. If that does happen, it is normal. Just give him another dose of the elixir and let him sleep again. After the second time waking, he should be fine and back to his normal self."

"Are you sure that's all?" I ask.

"Yes. Now, go." Beatrix sighs, leaning back and sinking into her sofa. "Let me rest."

"Beatrix, if there's ever anything we can do to make your life easier..." I trail off, looking the frail woman from head to toe.

"I appreciate the gesture, Monarch Harlow." Beatrix curls into the couch. "If there is, I'll let you know."

Willow lingers, studying Beatrix. I hear her thoughts: **This is our fault. She's dying because of us. This Tether is killing everyone.**

I grip her hand, and she shakes out of it, her glassy brown eyes lifting to mine. She thanks Beatrix for the elixir, and we make our way toward the door. Kimina follows us out, and as we make our way down the stoop, she says, "I fear for ya, Monarch Harlow! Ya name floats through the trees and the clay. Your blood is charged, and people will do anything to have it. Betta watch ya back. Yours *and* hers! She's watchin'. Watchin' ya like a vulture in the sky."

A frown takes over my face, and I whirl around to look at Kimina, but she's already shut the door. "What the hell is that supposed to mean?" I snap.

"Just leave it, Caz. *Please*," Willow pleads, squeezing my

hand. "We have to go." She tugs on my hand, forcing me to move. When we're inside the truck, the bottle of elixir secure in Willow's hand, I peer back at Beatrix's cottage, and can't help sensing there's a warning to what Kimina said. How does she know my blood is charged? And who the hell is watching?

CHAPTER 83
WILLOW

Caz doesn't trust Danica to be inside the castle again. It makes no sense, seeing as she got in once and could easily do it again, but he makes an agreement to let her and Warren sleep in the guesthouse.

Warren remains on the bed we collected from The Trench. I wasn't aware that one side of the guesthouse's wall could lift like a garage door until Rowan pressed a button to do so. They carried the bed Warren was on into the guesthouse in one piece.

I now watch from the corner of the room as Maeve sets up the folded bed, places a sheet on it, and tells Danica it's where she can sleep if she prefers not to lie on the Trench bed. She then waltzes to the kitchen, returning with a spoon. She hands it to Danica, and Danica opens the elixir from Beatrix immediately, pouring the blueish liquid onto the spoon and force feeding it to Warren.

The liquid dribbles down Warren's chin, and Danica wipes it away with her fingers. She presses her hands to my brother's shoulders and lays him back on the bed. Relief fills her eyes and sinks into my veins as we watch Warren finally close his eyes and fall asleep. I move closer, stroking some of his locs away with a smile.

"You don't mind if I stick around until he wakes up, do you?" I ask, side-eyeing Danica.

"No. Just stay in your own space and I'll stay in mine," she mutters.

I take it she has to warm up to me. Well, same here. I need to warm up to her. After Manx, I can't trust a single soul outside of the clan. For all I know, this woman isn't even Warren's mate, but is pretending to be. A bit farfetched? Possibly. But people have lied about things much smaller than mating.

"You also won't mind Juniper popping in, right?" I inquire just as Juniper walks through the front door.

Danica stands up straight, her eyes going up and down the length of Juniper. Juniper has changed from the black bodysuit to jeans and a fitted dark-green T-shirt. Her platform boots thud on the floor as she enters. A belt is around her waist with guns and other weapons strapped into separate sheaths.

"Might as well get used to my face 'cause you'll be seeing a lot of it," Juniper quips before raising a blackfruit to her mouth and chewing.

"What is this?" Danica demands, a deep frown taking over her. "I don't need babysitters!"

"No one said you did," Maeve interjects, raising a hand. "But you infiltrated before and lied about who you were. You're lucky we don't cut you down where you are. After all we've been through, we can't take any chances."

Danica huffs, folding her arms and taking a step back. As

she does, Maeve holds out a hand. "What?" Danica snaps, glaring at it.

"Your Katana. Monarch Harlow says he'd like to keep it inside the castle under his watch until we get more information on you."

Danica scoffs, her frown morphing into pure shock. "Are you serious?"

Maeve's hand remains steady while one of her brows shift upward.

"My Katana is sacred. It is bound by my blood and the blood of my mother. I never let it out of my sight," Danica declares.

"We understand, and we promise to take very good care of it." Maeve gives her a smile that doesn't reach her eyes.

"Look, if you want to stay here, and if you really care about my brother, you'll hand it over," I tell her, standing. "It's your only option. You've met Caz. He'll take your rejection as a reason to kick you out of Blackwater completely."

"Don't make this difficult, dear." Maeve blinks at her, waiting, that hand still firm. Danica looks at each of us, and her eyes may as well be on fire, even her scarred eye. She's livid, but Caz is right to do this. Danica is a vanisher, and she snuck inside once. She could have some ulterior motive that we know nothing about.

With pure reluctance, Danica unstraps her Katana from her body and shoves it into Maeve's hand. "If I find so much as a scratch on—"

"Careful with your threats, dear," Maeve interrupts. "I may seem kind, but I'm much older than you are, and believe me, what I can do is *much more* lethal than what your Katana can."

Danica's mouth clamps shut and she backs away, folding her arms again and facing the window.

"Killian and Rowan will keep an eye out as well, make sure no one leaves the castle grounds." Maeve saunters toward the door as Juniper plops down on the sofa, crossing her legs and biting into the blackfruit. "I will have dinner sent down by our new house maiden in just a bit."

"So, it did work out?" Juniper asks, elated.

"It did, yes! Makoto is a delight. He'll be here soon, actually. He's excited to meet everyone. By the way, Danica, do you prefer sourdough or ivory bread with your soups?"

Danica rolls her eyes, refusing to answer.

"Ivory bread it is." And with that, Maeve is off, leaving the four of us in the guesthouse.

As soon as she's gone, Danica whirls around and glares at me. "Just so we're clear, *as soon* as Warren is awake, we're getting the hell out of here."

I try not to react to her outburst. She's angry right now, and I get that. She's full of emotion and not thinking clearly, so I say, "I haven't seen my brother in two years. We're twins. I highly doubt he'll just up and leave when he sees me."

Her good eye twitches, then she looks around, huffing. She picks up a bag she brought along with her (one that Caz had thoroughly inspected by Juniper) and slings it over her shoulder. "Whatever. Can you two at least get the hell out for ten minutes so I can take a shower?"

"Do you think we were born yesterday?" Juniper laughs. "You can take your clothes into the bathroom with you and change, which, by the way, have no windows. I'm not sure if you've figured it out or not yet, but we literally *don't* trust you."

"When I came here, it was only to save my mate. That's it," Danica declares.

"The fact that you dressed up as a caterer's assistant,

followed us inside the castle and made tea, and then snuck behind our backs to get to Willow was sneaky," Juniper snorts. "Why couldn't you be practical about it and just knock on the fucking door?"

"I considered that, but there were wolves guarding the castle."

I smile at that. "Silvera and Cerberus." Yeah, they'd probably have torn her to shreds.

"Whatever." Danica moves across the room, stopping at the bathroom door. "Like I said, I did it for my mate. Plus, I had to see if Willow was actually his twin. I didn't want to go to Caz until I knew for sure she was Warren's sister. When I saw her, I knew. And I waited for a moment she was alone to speak to her." She enters the bathroom, slamming the door behind her. My eyes slide to Juniper when I hear the shower start up, creating a noise barrier.

"What do you think?" I ask in a low voice.

Juniper shrugs. "I think it is true Warren is her mate, but I still don't trust her. We have no idea what her background was like before bonding with him. There are so many bad people in Vakeeli, Willow. Liars. Thieves. Manipulators. Rapists. Herders, which are people who kidnap children and sell them to molesters. The bloody Rippies." She finishes off her blackfruit, tossing the core into an empty trash bin. "Once Caz gets information on her and it's solid, I'll feel better."

"She's just one woman though," I whisper.

"Yeah, one woman with a Katana sword who can vanish and has Regal power in her blood. We've not seen anything like her before. She's dangerous."

I sigh, sitting on the sofa next to her. "We can't help who we mate with, can we?"

Juniper's head shakes as she wraps an arm around me and focuses on Warren sleeping soundlessly on the bed. "No, we can't. Your brother could be so in love with her without knowing a thing about her past. All he could know is what she presented to him when she met him."

"That's true."

"It's no different than when we took you in, if you think about it. None of us really trusted you, but you grew on us. And if this Danica person isn't a piece of shit, we'll know that. Until then, don't stress about it much. She'll be okay. At least we didn't make her pitch a tent on the beach." She laughs, and I laugh with her.

"Caz would literally do something like that just to piss her off."

"He definitely would. The asshole."

We laugh again, leaning back and staring out the window. My hope is that we can trust Danica in the end. She seems passionate about Warren, and protective, just like Caz is about me. What would she even gain by lying to us about being his mate? Nothing, really. Decius is gone (for now, at least) and no one can get to him because they'll have to go through Korah, one of the strongest beings of Vakeeli. Then again, the only reason I am thinking all this is because the last thing *any* of us needs is a betrayal. After Manx, I'm not sure I can handle any more.

CHAPTER 84

CAZ

THERE'S A KNOCK AT MY OFFICE DOOR JUST AS I SPARK a bloom. Killian walks in with a sheet of paper in hand and closes the door behind him.

"Got the information on Danica," he announces, sitting on the opposite side of the desk.

"Go on, then." I release a cloud of smoke. "Read it."

Killian clears his throat. "Danica Harmon. One hundred and thirty-four years old and orphaned at the age of fifteen. It says here that her mother was slaughtered in her own home by burglars. Apparently, the mother had been drugged so she couldn't use her powers, and then killed."

"If she was killed so suddenly, how would Danica have received her energy?"

"I'm not sure. Perhaps it's something that happens by ritual or is simply connected by bloodline. I don't know."

"Right." I flicker off some of the ash onto the ashtray. "Continue."

443

"She was sent to live in an orphanage in a cathedral in Vanora called Pupils of Sky, stayed there for three years before running away. From here, the details on her get a little slim, up until she turns one hundred and two. At that age, she'd murdered a man named Tuttle Lament and stole something from him when she fled."

Tuttle Lament? Why does that name sound familiar? "What did she steal?"

"That Katana she's carrying."

I frown. "So she lied. The katana never belonged to her."

Killian places the paper on the table. "I don't know, but I tell you what, Caz. I don't trust her. We've been through enough shit with your and Willow's Tether alone. We don't need another to come in and drown us more."

"I know, brother, I know. But what can I do? I can't kick them out right away. It's Willow's brother we're talking about. She'd never stand for it. She'd go right along with them if I removed them from castle grounds."

Killian is quiet a moment, mulling it over as I take another pull from my bloom.

"I need more intel on this woman," I mutter. "Who is the Mythic she sought in Vanora that gave her the capsule? Who did she hang out with? Where was she working? Who was she involved with? What happened to her bloody eye? Who the hell is Tuttle Lament? That paper does not give me enough, and if I have to kill her, it'll kill Warren. There has to be something that proves she can be trusted."

"I'll keep digging." He gestures to my transmitter on the desk. "Have The Council contacted you yet?"

My eyes flash to his. "No and I'm finding it a bit suspicious.

They were in such a hurry to get us to Inferno Isle and now they aren't responding to any of our messages."

"Yeah. They're too quiet for my liking. Means they're planning something."

"Or waiting things out. After that run-in with the Regals, I have even more questions about this quest The Council want me to take to awake Selah. They claim it will limit violence in Vakeeli, but Hassha and Korah seem to think otherwise and have purposely closed themselves off to the world *because* of such violence. If that were the case, wouldn't they be waking Selah themselves to restore the peace? Hassha and Korah seem to be completely against this plan The Council has, though they won't admit it to me."

"It's literal suicide, that's why." Killian rumbles.

"All of them are lying. I know it."

"And we're stuck in the middle of it." Killian pushes out of his chair with an exasperated sigh. "In the morning, I'll be off to the Vanorian coast like you asked. Find out more about this Kimina woman and the threat she made."

"Thanks, Kill."

"Always, brother."

"Oi," I call before he can leave the office. He stops to look back at me. "Have Rowan check in with Willow and Jun. Tell them to take shifts if they have to."

"Got it." Killian thumps down the foyer, and when his steps disappear, I pick up the sheet of paper with Danica's information, rest an elbow on the desk, and rub my forehead as I read it again.

I frown a bit and stab out my bloom when I spot something familiar—a detail Killian forgot to read off next to Tuttle Lament. No wonder his name was so familiar.

"Shit," I hiss. I push out of my chair, grab my gun, and flee the office.

CHAPTER 85
WILLOW

DANICA WALKS OUT OF THE BATHROOM WITH DAMP, bone-straight hair, avoiding our eyes as she moves across the guesthouse and drops her bag in a corner. She then sits on the bed next to Warren and strokes his forehead with the pad of her thumb while studying his face.

I glance at Juniper who seems to be bored with all of this as she leans forward on the sofa, her chin propped in her hand. Danica begins to hum, collecting some of Warren's locs and moving them away from his neck.

"He's cute when he sleeps," she laughs, and I think she's talking more to herself than to us. She stares at him a little while longer, then pulls away, pointing her gaze in our direction. "I'd like to go to the beach," she states.

"Sure." Juniper stands. "Let's go."

Danica stands with a grimace. "Whatever."

"I'll come with you two." I follow them out the door, but not without a glance back at my brother. He should be okay for a bit.

I'm surprised Danica finds her way to the beach without our help. There are several footpaths, and only one leads to the beach from the guesthouse. The others drift off to the forest or castle grounds.

When my feet touch the cool sand, I'm filled with a sense of calm. It washes over me as I stare ahead at the ocean. The full moon is large and pale white, the light of it reflecting off the dark rippling waters.

Danica trudges forward until she's close to shore, then she sits and brings her legs to her chest. She stares at the ocean a while, her chin on her knees. And then, to my surprise, her forehead falls, and she breaks down in a sob.

"Oh." Another shockwave hits me—the same one I felt when I first saw Danica. Everything in me wants to comfort her, be there for her. "She's crying, Juniper," I say as if that'll help the matter.

"I see." Juniper's eyes are wide with surprise. "Perhaps we have been a bit mean to her."

"We were just taking things seriously, that's all. But, regardless, she's human." I sigh, shifting on my feet. "I'm gonna go talk to her."

I leave Juniper, who marches toward a nearby boulder to sit on. When I near Danica, she looks at me through the corner of her eyes and swipes at her face.

"I don't need your sentiment," she grumbles. "I just wanted a moment alone."

"There's nothing wrong with crying," I return with a soft voice.

She wipes under her eye with the pad of her forefinger, and I take in a deep breath before releasing it, claiming the spot next to her. I feel her suspicious glare on me as she sniffles.

"How long have you been with your mate?" she asks, and I meet her eyes. Her gray eye is murky, the brown one burning with curiosity.

"I think about three weeks now...maybe?" I shrug. "Feels like it's been longer."

"Only three weeks?" she balks. "How? I mean, you two seem to have known each other for much longer."

I smile. "It does seem like it. But no, we literally *just* met. So much has happened since we met, though. I think all of it has sort of pushed us together."

"I understand that. It was the same with Warren. I only knew him a few weeks before..." She clenches a fist. "Before Decius came for us."

I study the profile of her face, how her mouth pouts, the dimple in her chin. Right now, she looks like a little girl. A sad, lonely, lost little girl.

I allow a few seconds of silence to pass before asking, "What were your nightmares like?"

She lifts her head, peering up at the star-splattered sky. "They were...dark. Cruel. Sometimes I'd be in total darkness but could feel myself running, like something was chasing me. I'd run forever, never finding a destination. But those weren't as bad as Warren's."

"What were his like?"

"Oh, his were awful. He'd wake up in cold sweats, panicking. He'd tell me it felt like something was choking him while he slept or trying to strangle him. He described this...monster with red crescent eyes. It haunted him. Sometimes threatened him. He always had dreams that he was someone else...or at least he felt like he was. I did a lot of reading on what it was, sought a few Mythics before Decius came for us. I believe he felt like someone else because he *was* someone else then. Decius was showing him how he'd died in his previous life."

"Yeah." I lower my gaze. "I had similar visions before we took him down. I could never see my face, though. I would be running in a dress." I squeeze my eyes closed, trying to remember. "I could feel the fear of those people in our former lives, as if it were my own, right up until he takes them. It was always the same dream. Blood soaking my dress, hands that weren't mine. A voice telling me not to run to my mate."

"It's dreadful." Danica sniffs. "I keep asking myself why this is happening to me? Apparently, it's not up to anyone who carries the Cold Tethered babies. A woman winds up pregnant and eventually discovers her baby is special when they mate. But isn't it terrible that when they birth us and watch us grow, they all disappear? They're all either scared off by someone, murdered, or end up killing themselves."

"Yeah." I pause, thinking about my own parents. It never felt like my father to walk away from us. He spent so much time with us as children, even more so when our mother died. When he never came home that one day, it was devastating. We thought he'd gone missing, but the truth is he no longer wanted to be around us. Warren told me the story all the time about how he tracked our father down, found him mowing the lawn of some house he bought in Charleston. Our father couldn't even look at him. He yelled at Warren, told him to leave and never come back. He found Warren's number and tried apologizing over the phone, but it was never the same. I attempted calling him several times afterward to hear his voice—to see if he still loved us—but the conversations were always brief. I stopped calling eventually...and so did he.

"Before Decius came for you, what was Warren like?" I ask after another wave of silence. "I mean, was he still goofy and adventurous?"

"Oh, he was." She grins, and I hate admitting it, but I know that grin. It's the grin of a fool in love. "He was so romantic too. Once he got used to Vanora, he'd run to the city and bring me food to eat in bed or flowers. He helped me wash my hair. He did my laundry, even though I insisted on using the maid in our duplex. And his jokes—love of Vakeeli, they were so silly! But he was so full of wonder, you know? He wanted to see everything, do everything. He loved swimming, loved going out to dance. We drank *a lot*," she emphasizes. "But we always had fun. We were one, you know? And I felt at ease with him. For the first time in my life, I could be vulnerable around a man. Only he could do that to me. It's incredible how this Tether has the power to change so much about us."

"This Cold Tether thing is insane, right?" I laugh.

"It is!" Danica's head shakes, and slowly her smile slips away. "He worried about you a lot, though."

I study her eyes and see nothing but truth. "I worried about him a lot too."

"He hated that he couldn't go back—that we couldn't find a way so he could tell you he was alive. He knew you'd think he abandoned you." She clears her throat. "He told me all about your father...your childhood."

I can't look at Danica anymore. I stare at the ocean instead, despite my blurry vision.

"Anyway, that's probably something you two should talk

about when he comes to," she goes on. "It's hard seeing him like that."

"I know. He's so...*empty*."

"The complete opposite of himself." She drops her legs to cross them. "I worry he'll never recover. I mean, Mythic elixirs and energy is powerful, but it doesn't restore everything. I'm worried he'll forget what it was like when we met."

"That can't be possible," I murmur, placing my hand on top of hers. "You're his mate. He has to remember."

She looks down at my hand, her face softening. "Thank you for that."

I pull my hand back, sitting straight again. "Do you mind if I ask you a question?"

"About my eye?" she asks, smirking.

I fight a smile. "You guessed it."

"You know, I thought Warren would find my eye hideous. That he'd have a hard time looking at me." She bites a smile. "He told me my eye was beautiful. That it suited the woman I am. That he wouldn't change it."

I smile at that.

"I used to be a bit of a rebel. Still am, actually," she chuckles. "But before I met Warren, I fought...*a lot*. And I stole from the rich. I protected orphaned kids—kids who were just like me, living in this violent world with no parents or guidance. When my mother was murdered, I was sent to a cathedral to live as an orphan. It was such a boring place. And they wanted all girls to grow up to be submissive virgins. We were required to cover our faces with veils in public, couldn't eat certain foods like fruits or treats like cake and candy. I eventually ran away, and that's when a man named Ossan found me. He caught me stealing from one of the markets, plucked me right off the street, and asked how I was going to pay for it. I started panick-ing, of course. The last thing I wanted was to be sent to a dungeon, so he made a deal with me. He had me start selling fruit from his stand instead. And later, I learned Ossan was part of the original Vanorian tribe. He wasn't a warrior, but he was a counselor and had helped warriors sharpen their abilities. He told me he knew who my mum was and the power I possessed. He knew what I'd gone through, and what had happened to my mum, and he told me I had to right this wrong. I'm not sure why he cared so much, but he did, especially when it came to women and children. He taught me how to infiltrate, how to disguise myself. But even while doing everything he needed me to do and growing stronger from his training, there was one thing I wanted from it."

"What was that?" I ask.

"I wanted to kill the man who murdered my mum."

"And let me guess. This man is Tuttle Lament, lead coach of what was previously known as Buckley's fight club." Caz's voice catches me completely off guard, and I whip my head to find him. He's walking along the beach in his boots, dressed head to toe in black. He approaches us, and Danica hops to her feet with a frown.

"How do you know that?" she demands.

"I gathered information. You're Tuttle's daughter, aren't you?"

She grimaces, looking away.

"That's all right. I already know you are. And I take it you lost your eye because you went out of your way to murder the man who slaughtered your mother. Your own father did it, correct? And he did it because you sought him as a teenager, wanting so desperately to know who he was. But that was a mistake, you see, because your father had no clue you existed up until that point, and he wanted to keep it that way. He had a status to uphold. Tell me, am I hot or cold?"

I put my attention on Danica who is vibrating with rage. Her whole face is beet red. "I didn't ask you to dig up that sort of information on me," she snaps.

"As monarch and as a man who doesn't trust you, it's my job."

"So, what? You think I'm a horrible person because I killed my own father? Tell me you wouldn't have done the same!" she challenges, stepping closer to him. "I've heard the stories about you, Caspian Harlow. I heard how your father took you to those caves to fight, how he punished you for losing, how he dunked your head in a tub of water and nearly made you drown because you were so weak and pathetic!"

Caz tries not to react, but I notice the ticking of his jaw and the way one of his fists clenches at his side. Despite the visible anger on the outside, I feel the clench in his chest too, the lurch of his heart. He's equally as hurt by her remarks as she is by his.

"But you grew out of that, didn't you? You proved to him you weren't weak or pathetic because you're still here now while he rots in his grave."

Danica is in his face now, and I notice three people behind Caz—Rowan, Juniper, and Killian. They're watching the altercation, keeping a safe distance in case things blow out of proportion.

"You think you know me, but you don't," Danica seethes. "And sure, you may not trust me because I infiltrated your precious life and found my way into your castle, but I did it because I felt I had no choice! I had to be sure that you were with Willow. I needed to be certain before I told her a damn thing. I couldn't get this wrong when it came to Warren because I've gotten it wrong once before with someone I love, and it cost her life—my mother's life! I've lived in confusion and denial, *riddled* with anger because *I* fucked up! It's *my* fault she's dead! So yes, I took my Katana and sliced my father's head off with it. Yes, I did that, and I'd do it again if I had to because he was a piece of shit who ruined my life and took *everything* from me. Don't you see it? You and I, Monarch Harlow, aren't so different. We do what must be done to survive, so don't stand there looking down on me with that disgusting judgement in your eyes when your past is filled with vengeful actions too."

They stare at one another, Danica breathing rapidly through her nostrils, chest heaving, and Caz staring into her eyes, unflinching. With a huff, Danica backs away and takes a look at everyone before throwing her hands in the air.

"I know you don't care for my presence, or trust anything I'll do next, but I guarantee you, if I wanted to hurt you, I'd have done it already. All I want is my mate to wake up, and I'll be out of your hair. You'll never hear from me again."

"Well, if you know this, why don't you go for now and return when he's better?" Caz questions.

Danica scoffs. "Never. He's half of me, just as she's half of you. She completes you. You know how all of this works. We literally *ache* when we're apart."

Caz shifts on his feet, his eyes swinging to mine briefly. There's a snap in his chest that transcends to mine, like the snap of a rubber band.

"I'm going to bed. Do I need a babysitter for that too?" she asks, but she's already moving, trudging through the thick sand

and making her way toward the path that leads to the guesthouse.

When she's gone, I look into Caz's eyes. "Why did you do that?"

"Do what?" he asks.

"You intentionally upset her, Caz!"

"Of course, it was intentional! Now I know everything about her. It was necessary."

I step away, shaking my head. "That wasn't right."

He bridges the gap between us, closing a hand around my elbow. "It had to be done."

He's right, but still. She was finally opening up to me. All that did was close her like a clam again. "Are you staying in the guesthouse?" he asks.

"After that shitshow, no." It'll be too awkward with Danica.

"Will you return to the castle with me then?"

I press my lips. "Fine." I take his hand, and he leads the way toward the castle as Juniper, Rowan, and Killian take the path to the guesthouse.

CHAPTER 86
WILLOW

WHEN WE'RE INSIDE, TUCKED AWAY IN HIS BEDROOM, Caz plops down on the edge of the bed and releases a deep sigh.

"You triggered her," I say sitting next to him.

"I triggered *her*?" he counters. "She spouted off about my father trying to drown me in a bucket! I'm the one who's triggered."

"Caz." I grab his chin, forcing him to look at me. "I think it's time to admit that she's not a threat. I know you don't want to believe it, but I do. I really think Danica means well, despite how intense she is. She was forced to be that way. And now that I've heard her side of it, it makes sense that she snuck into the castle. Like she said, she had to be sure it was actually me. How else was she going to know if not seeing it firsthand?"

"I don't care, Willow," he grumbles. "My trust has been abused and is now peppered in bruises."

"Do you not trust her because she reminds you of yourself?"

"What?" he scoffs. "I am *nothing* like that woman."

I release a dry laugh. "You're a lot like her, Caz. I think we all can see it."

"I'm not a thief or a liar or a manipulator."

"Maybe not, but you've done bad things, just like she has. Just like we all have."

He sighs, rubbing the center of his forehead. "Can't believe you're comparing me to this woman. She carries a Katana, for Vakeeli's sake. I use guns."

"What does that have to do with anything?" I laugh.

The left corner of his mouth twitches. "Guns are better."

"Oh, come on. You can't deny that Katana is cool. The way she swings it like that, so effortlessly. She literally blocked your bullet without so much as a blink."

Caz chuckles, softening. "That was pretty interesting." Then he frowns again. "But no. I still suggest we keep our guards up. I won't feel better about her until your brother's memory is restored and he can tell us more of what he knows about her."

"Fine." I strip out of my clothes. "But if I'm right, you owe me."

His eyes travel down the length of my body as I climb onto the bed in just a bra and panties. "Owe you what, exactly?"

"Favors."

He pulls his shirt over his head, then kicks off his boots. "Tell me about these favors," he rumbles, climbing onto the bed with me and wedging his body between my legs. His dick rubs between my thighs, and I can't help smiling as I circle my legs around his waist.

"All sorts." I kiss his lips, a charge sweeping through me.

"You know I'll do anything."

"Oh, speaking of. I was wondering if you could teach me how to shoot."

He tips his head back, more serious now. "Yeah, you froze in The Trench."

"I know." I swallow hard. "I told you I'm no good with guns." He's quiet a beat, so I continue. "If there's ever a time when I need to protect myself and you're not around, I want to be able to use a gun properly. I want to be confident when I use it. I don't ever want to freeze again." I draw in a breath. "I almost got Juniper killed."

He studies my eyes a bit longer, his shining from the moonlight. "Killing someone isn't easy. And your first kill will fuck with you mentally, so I understand why you froze."

I nod. "How do you all just...do it? Kill people without thinking about it?"

"Oh, we think about it. Why do you think we all smoke and drink so much?" He cracks a boyish smile.

I huff a laugh. "I'm serious, Caz. Does it not bother you?"

His face hardens as his eyes shift a bit. "Every day, Willow. There was a point in my life when I told myself I'd never hurt anyone, let alone kill them. But that time was before my mother was tortured and murdered." He sighs. "It's not easy to live with, but it's the hand we were dealt. All we're doing is using our cards and playing them correctly."

"Yeah. I get it."

He sighs, carrying his gaze to mine again. "How about we practice in the morning?"

I bob my head. "That sounds good."

He presses his lips to mine before collapsing onto his back next to me. "It's really not that hard though. You're just aiming and shooting."

"I don't think I have very good aim," I counter.

Caz considers this, propping himself up on his elbow and

looking me all over. "Seeing as you're from Earth, you're probably right. I saw how you drove your car. Bloody horrible! How hard is it to stay on the road? We'd better start practicing right away."

"Shut up!" I laugh, and he chuckles deep and sweet, making his way on top of me again and claiming my lips.

CHAPTER 87

CAZ

W<small>ILLOW AND</small> I <small>SPEND THIRTY OR SO MINUTES</small> together in my bedroom, taking a moment to breathe. We don't have sex, though I'd be willing. We lie in each other's arms, our thoughts crossing until they become unbearable.

When she finds herself restless, she asks, "Can we go back to the guesthouse?"

"If that's what you want."

She climbs off the bed and makes her way to the closet. She takes down comfortable black pants and a T-shirt with the words *Blackwater Bitch* on it.

"Let me guess." I gesture to the shirt. "Juniper picked that out."

Willow laughs, nodding. "Definitely. It's nice knowing there are graphic shirts around. My wardrobe at home is, like, 99% graphic tees and biker shorts." She takes my hand after I've put my clothes back on and leads the way out the door.

We pad down the stairs and past the kitchen, walking out

the back door. When we're at the guesthouse, I give the door a knock, and Rowan answers. His eyes are tired, but there's a cup of tea in his hand.

"Caz, brother. Thought you'd be sleeping," Rowan says, letting us in.

"Not tonight."

I shift my gaze to Juniper who is slumped over the counter, hardly awake.

"Where's Killian?" I ask.

"He took off for Vanora, said he was getting a head start." Juniper yawns.

"Oh. Well, why don't you two go and get some rest? I'll cover the rest of the night," I offer.

"You sure?" asks Rowan.

"Positive."

"Don't have to tell me twice." Juniper is the first one out. "See you in the morning."

Rowan trails behind her, capping my shoulder. "Stay vigilant, brother."

When they're gone, Willow makes herself comfortable on the sofa but focuses on the bed Warren lies on. He's not alone. Danica is there as well, spooning him from behind. She snores loudly, and Willow's eyes get bigger as she switches her gaze to me.

Loud, I hear her think, and I smile as she taps the spot next to her. I withdraw my gun, setting it on the table then sitting next to Willow.

"I'm curious about something," I whisper.

"What?" she asks, resting her head on my shoulder.

"When Warren comes to, and he remembers everything…do you think he'll want to stay here, or go back to Earth?"

Willow is quiet a moment, and the guesthouse goes still, minus the crickets chirping and frogs croaking outdoors. "I'm not sure."

"Do you want to go back?" I ask softly, and she picks her head up.

"I want to be wherever you are."

"So, let's settle this right now." I straighten on the couch, and she gives me all her attention. "Would you rather go back to Earth and return to the life you once had, or will you stay in Vakeeli with me? And I want an honest answer, Willow. No beating around the bush. I want to know what you want."

She considers my question, holding my eyes a split second before lowering her gaze. "I think...there are things I need to settle on Earth before staying here."

"Like what?"

"My job with Lou Ann. I'd have to tell her that I quit."

"Okay. That's an easy fix."

"But there's Faye. I love her, and she's my best friend. I'd want to keep seeing her, or at least visiting her."

"I'll try to find a way for you to be able to do that."

She nods, dropping her chin again. I lift it with my fingers, forcing her eyes on mine. "Tell me what's really on your mind."

"It's just that Vakeeli brings out the worst in people. It's clear this is a violent, dangerous place. What if I want kids one day?"

That causes me to pause. Children? I hadn't thought about it before, but if we are to be together, that eventually would happen, right? I throw up my mind's wall, hoping she doesn't hear how terrified that idea makes me.

"I'd protect you...and our child, if that time ever comes," I say.

"I know...but sometimes the thought of it scares me. I just...I can't help feeling like I belong here somehow." She huffs a laugh. "I'm beating around the bush."

I chuckle. "You are."

"I'm just saying, I want to be with you, but I'm scared. You've worked so hard for everything you have in Blackwater. I'd hate to be the reason it all gets ruined."

"But none of it matters if I don't have you." I collect her hands in mine. "I don't care about these material things, Willow. I don't care about the castle, or being monarch, the fucking rubies or any of it. None of it will ever be enough to fill the void I have when I'm without you."

Her eyes glisten as she holds my gaze.

"I want you, no matter where we are or what we do," I continue. "I can work something out so that you and any children in the future are never harmed. I'll beg the Regals if I must, ask them to protect you all from dangers. I'll drop to my knees before them and give them all of me if it means you're safe and happy. I'm willing to do whatever it takes to protect you, Willow. Yes, I know Vakeeli is a wicked place, but I won't let the ugliness of it infect your golden heart. My child, whoever they may be, will never face the horrors I did. They will never be threatened. *Never*. Not while I live and breathe."

A tear slips down her cheek. "You promise?"

"I promise you this now and forever, Willow Woman. Oi, look at me." I press my fingers to her chin. "Now and forever. Do you understand?"

"I do." She closes her arms around me, hugging me tight, and I sigh, leaning back and letting her rest against my body. I hold the side of her head, planting a kiss on her forehead. "I love you. I only ever want you to be happy."

"I love you too. And I want the same for you," she mumbles into my chest. "I'll stay. I'll be here with you."

"You sure?"

"I am." She yawns. "But promise you'll find me a way to visit Faye—something that isn't a one-way chant."

"I promise you."

She sighs, and it doesn't take long for her to fall asleep. The side of her face nestles into my body, her breaths soft as they spill on my skin. I hold her close as I replay the conversation over again in my head.

She has every right to be afraid. Hell, I'm afraid at the mere mention of children. I suppose I should tell her that I never planned on having them. I didn't want any of my own, and to continue the Blackwater monarch lineage, I'd have adopted a child and taught them everything. They wouldn't be mine, but they'd be a good leader thanks to me, and that would be enough.

There's something frightening about bringing my own child into this world, though. A person derived from my loins. I never wanted it because I know how dark my heart is, but with Willow, so much has changed.

What will she do when she realizes I'm not fit enough to be a father, and that, despite us being mates, I'm not worthy of such an intimate title?

I look down at her with an aching chest. I want to make her so happy. I want to be the man who gives her *everything*. But how can I be the man who gives it all to her, while also being the one who could cause her demise?

CHAPTER 88
WILLOW

A DEAFENING SCREAM FILLS THE AIR, AND MY EYES pop open. The guesthouse has turned to absolute chaos as Caz shoots off the sofa and flies across the room while Danica shouts at Warren.

"Warren! Please, stop! It's just me!" she shouts with her hands in front of her like she's taming a wild animal. And perhaps she is. Because standing on the other side of the bed, holding a knife, is my brother. He's fully alert, eyes wide, as he swings them from Danica to Caz while slashing the knife in the air.

"Easy," Caz warns, one of his hands up too.

"Back up!" Warren barks. He breathes rapidly as I stagger to a stand. "Who is this man, Danica?"

Danica's eyes shimmer from the sunlight. "You remember me?"

"Of course, I remember you." The sun has made its appearance, just a blip over the horizon.

"That's Caz," Danica urges. "It's okay. He's been helping us."

"Warren?" I step around Caz, focused on my brother. Caz notices how close I am to Warren and the knife and shifts in front of me. Warren finds my voice, and when he does, his eyes grow rounder, his brown irises glinting in the light. He lowers the knife, mouth ajar.

"This a dream," he breathes. "No, a trick. It's a trick. It's a trick."

"No." I move forward. "It's not. It's *me*, Warren. It's Willow. I'm here."

The knife that was in his hand clatters to the floor, and he rushes my way, instantly crashing into me. It's so fast, so sudden, that Caz has to take a quick step back while we embrace.

"Oh my God. Willow! It's really you?" Warren gasps over my shoulder. He leans back, grabbing my face, looking me deep in the eyes. "Still beautiful and ugly at the same time."

I burst out in a sob-laugh, then reel him in again to hold on tight. "You had us all worried."

He releases me and focuses on Danica. "What the hell happened? One minute we were together in bed, the next we're...*here*."

"You don't remember all the stuff with your nightmares? Or what I told you about the Cold Tether?" Danica asks.

Warren's face warps. "No."

"Do you remember how you got here?" Caz asks, and Warren takes a step back to look at Caz.

"Not really. I'm sorry—Willow, who is this man?"

"This is Caz," I tell him, wrapping an arm around Caz's waist. "He's my mate."

Warren studies my arm around Caz, looking between us. "Your *mate?*"

"Yes," Caz replies sharply.

Warren looks Caz in the eyes before taking another step back and sizing him up. A slight frown takes over him as he looks between us, then he shakes his head, rubbing a palm over the top of it. "I'm so confused right now."

"You are, and there's a lot to explain, but don't worry about that right now." I throw my arms around him, hugging him again. "I never thought I'd see you again, Warren."

"I know, sis. Same."

Danica clears her throat, and I pull away as Warren faces her. I look at Danica's face, the longing she has, then at Warren, whose eyes narrow a bit before he walks toward her.

For a split second, I'm worried for her. He's not looking at her like she's his long-lost mate. He's not looking at her with hearts and stars in his eyes or anything of the sort. He just *stares* at her, clueless—like he doesn't know what to do with her.

She drags herself across the room, taking his hands and clasping them. "Tell me you still feel this?" she whispers. "Us."

Warren drops his eyes to her hands. "I feel...something."

"Do you remember all the time we spent together? Or how we fell in love? How we met, even?"

Warren looks all around the room, digesting the question. Then he drops his eyes on hers again. "I...I can't say that I do, Danica. I remember your name, but...that's it."

Her eyes well with tears, and before I know it, she's shoving his hand away, marching past him, and running out of the guesthouse.

"Wait—Danica!" I start to run after her, but Caz catches my hand.

"Give her a moment," he advises.

"I—I don't understand why she's upset. What did I say?" Warren wonders, his eyes tear-filled too.

"Do you feel her sadness?" I ask.

"I—I do, yes. I want to comfort her. I should go after her... but she's so sad. Feels like her heart is breaking."

I look at Caz, and he returns a look, one to match my worry.

"Perhaps your memory will come back in time," Caz offers.

Warren drops down on the edge of the bed, his face falling into his hands. "She's saying she hates her life. She wants to die. I can hear her."

"Go to her, Warren. Please," I plead.

"How am I supposed to find her?"

"You will," Caz responds. "You're Tethered. You'll find her."

CHAPTER 89
WILLOW

I CAN'T BRING MYSELF TO EAT. AND THOUGH MAKOTO, the new housemaid with soft black hair, almond eyes, tan skin, and a rather cute button nose, is a wonderful man with incredible culinary skill, my stomach doesn't want any of the food he's prepared.

My brother is awake again. He's alive and breathing, and he remembers me. That's great. However, he can't remember the love he shares with his mate. That is a problem.

On the way back to the castle, all I could think about was Danica. The hurt was all over her. What would happen if I somehow forgot Caz, or if he'd forgotten me? I can't imagine that pain, knowing the one person you're bound to has no recollection of the intimacy you shared or your time together. I get the sense Warren doesn't even know about Decius, or how he lost part of his memory with Danica in the first place.

"It'll come back," Caz murmured as he opened the back door

for me. "Beatrix warned us about this. He just woke up. Give it some time."

Now, Caz is eating toast (because he doesn't quite trust Makoto yet, go figure) while Makoto talks about the restaurants he's worked at and reminds us all how it's a pleasure to serve us.

"I just can't thank you enough," Makoto goes on, sautéing meat in a pan. "I promise, I will never let you down, Monarch Harlow. It is my honor to serve you, and it will be my duty to keep you fed, hydrated, and to make sure all your home affairs are in order. I even gave the wolves some lamb. They loved it."

"Easy on the excitement there, Makoto," Rowan says. He's seated at the table while I'm at the island counter on a stool. Caz is at the head of the table, Killian in the chair next to him, Rowan opposite of Killian. Maeve is next to Killian, doing a cross between sipping tea and smoking a bloom, and Juniper is perched on a stool beside me at the counter. She seems stressed.

"Sir?" Makoto calls, grinning.

"You'll soon find out it's not all gold blooms and rainbows around the castle," Rowan goes on. "Shit gets crazy around here. You'll probably want to quit."

"I doubt that. I served for the Blackwater fleet during the 1926 battle against Ripple Hills." Makoto dumps the sautéed meat onto a dish.

"The 1926 Fleet?" Caz asks, and that's gotten his attention. He takes his eyes off the papers, looking to Maeve. "Maeve, you didn't tell me he was a soldier."

Maeve shrugs. "Didn't think it mattered."

"Of course, it matters. Any man who fought for Blackwater

should be highly respected. Those battles weren't easy, were they, Makoto?"

"Not at all. I actually still have nightmares about them, believe it or not."

"Yet you continue to smile," I say, and Makoto winks at me.

Caz winds up next to me, offering a hand to Makoto. "I'm sure you're aware I hate being touched, but if you're on board to work for me and you're a veteran soldier, I must shake your hand as monarch of Blackwater."

"Is that custom?" I ask Juniper.

"Yep," she whispers.

Makoto places a dish down and wipes his hands on his apron before grabbing Caz's and giving it a shake. "A pleasure, Monarch Harlow. I will not fail you."

"You'd better not," Caz says with a faint smirk.

Makoto chuckles, returning to his cooking. Caz starts to say something to me, but something behind me catches his eyes. I look with him, and across the room is Warren and Danica. They're standing hand in hand, shifting about nervously. Danica's eyes are puffy and red, but she looks somewhat better.

"Come," Caz calls, gesturing to the table. "Sit. Grab a bite to eat."

Warren and Danica trek across the room, taking seats at the end of the table.

Makoto gets straight to work, putting food on plates and carrying them to the table. "An honor," Makoto says, bowing at them before returning to the kitchen.

I climb off the stool to get to Warren, giving his shoulders a squeeze. "Everything okay?"

"Think so," he murmurs. He stares down at the food Makoto has served them with a slight frown before shifting his gaze to Danica. Danica is already staring at Warren, a mixture of concern and hopelessness stealing her features.

She immediately reaches for the knife next to Warren's plate and places it next to her, out of his reach. I can't help frowning at the action, but I don't say anything as they begin eating.

Everything's fine. Just takes time.

Heat brushes my side, and Caz collects my chin in his fingers, fixing his eyes on mine. "Let's go to target practice."

CHAPTER 90
WILLOW

THIS IS THE THIRD DAY OF SUNSHINE IN BLACKWATER. Caz believes it's an omen from the Regals. In his mind, they're watching over us. They can see and hear things we can't and have a much deeper connection to Vakeeli than we do...but he still doesn't trust them.

With the sun in the sky, us making the trek toward Blackwater forest with guns, the forest doesn't seem so daunting now. In fact, the leaves on the trees are emerald in the sunlight, the trunks and branches sharp black. A coolness drifts in the air, but it's a pleasant cool, one that mingles with the warmth. Tufts of clouds linger in the sky, bringing a possibility of rain, but I've learned Blackwater is a lot like the beaches of Florida. The rain is sporadic because we're so close to the ocean, and when it does shower, it's brief.

The sounds of panting rise beside me, and I carry my eyes down to my wolf Silvera who trots next to me. Cerberus is on

Caz's side. They're protectors of Blackwater Manor and the castle grounds. A badass concept, I won't lie.

When we meet the forest, Caz pushes a thick brush of trees aside to let me by, and we keep walking, going well past my portal, stepping over clusters of bushes and mangled branches until a thicket appears.

Caz takes the machete out of the sheath attached to his waist, the sunlight glinting off of it as he raises it and slices through the thicket.

"Haven't been here in ages," he sighs.

"Where are we, exactly?" I ask.

His lips quirk on one side. "You'll see."

He chops some more until an opening appears then tucks the machete away. He presses an arm against one side of the bush to keep it propped open.

"Go on. Step through," he insists.

I put a foot through, guiding my body through the hole. I immediately notice the difference in the grass. It's much denser and plusher, and the scent of lilac floats past my nose, as well as honeysuckle. When I make it through, I drink in my surroundings, completely in awe.

We've reached a field, the blades of grass ankle-deep and black flowers peppered throughout. The flowers glisten with a fresh coat of dew, tall, thick trees wrapped in thriving green vines leaning inward as if protecting this particular space. Each tree slopes toward the next, the tips of their branches touching. At a glance, it would seem these trees are whispering to one other. I squat, taking a closer look at the flowers with their golden centers and petals that are a soft, rich black. At the far end of the field are three wooden pedestals, which I find out of place.

Caz meets up to me as Silvera and Cerberus sniff around. "We call this place the Monarch Terrain," he says, looking upward.

I look with him, allowing the sunlight to bathe my skin with its gold warmth. "Why is it called that?" I ask.

"It was created as a place for all monarchs to practice, whether it be with swords, knives, or guns. See how the trees curve?"

"Yeah."

"A Mythic made it so that the trees keep everything inside it. Whether a bullet goes astray or a dagger ends up flying too far across the field, it won't escape this area. Originally there were people living in this forest. Lots of commoners, and the previous monarchs didn't want anyone getting hurt during their practice, so this place was created. I like to think of it as a bubble of sorts. I actually heard someone accidentally got shot in the ass before the barrier was created."

"You did not!" I bust out laughing.

"I swear it!" he laughs. "Anyway, those posts," he says, pointing to the wooden pedestals. "They help us practice. Watch this."

Caz jogs away, stopping at a tree next to the posts. This tree is not like the others. It looks to be more of a black pole with the design of tree bark. He presses a button on the pole, and the pole whirs to life. It splits into three sections, revealing spin dials. The dials wind with aging creaks, and the pedestals next to them rise in the air. They fly toward the center of the field, floating midair as Caz makes his way back to me.

One of the pedestals shoots something out. I can't make out what it is. A boomerang? A disc? Whatever it is, it comes flying down, whirling around the terrain rapidly until Caz whips out his gun, cocks it, and shoots it down.

I walk with him, and he picks up the object. It's a wooden bird with a bullet smackdab in the center.

"This," Caz says, raising it in the air, "is the best target practice you'll ever get. You learn to shoot down one of these with a weapon, and you're good as gold."

I look up again at the floating pedestals. They shoot out another bird, but Caz doesn't shoot it this time. Instead, he gestures to me. "Right. Go on. Let me see what you've got."

"Oh my God," I gasp. "I'm nervous. What if I miss?"

He smiles graciously. "Then you try again."

His eyes fall to the gun attached to my hip. "Retrieve your gun." I do, and he takes a step toward me. "Don't be afraid of it."

"Hard not to be. They're so dangerous."

"Wrong. It's the person who has it that makes it dangerous. If your intentions are good, there's nothing dangerous about it. You're only using it to protect yourself."

"I'm not really a gun-positive person," I say, half-joking.

"I get it." His cerulean eyes shift up to the top of one of the trees. "Your world is not like this. On Earth, I bet it's frowned upon to love guns so much."

"Meh. Guns are a hot topic on Earth. Lots of debates about them."

"Well, this is Vakeeli. And like you said, you want to be able to protect yourself. If push comes to shove, I want you to protect yourself too. So, we'll start with guns, and then we'll move on to knives and daggers. How's that sound?"

"Sure. Sounds good."

"Right." Caz steps behind me, and I'm not prepared for him

to wrap his arms around me. His warm fingers slide down my forearms until his palm is resting on the back of my hand. I feel a shiver ride through me, that same feeling I had when we first kissed, and I bite a smile as he whispers on the shell of my ear, "Let me teach you."

"'Kay," I breathe, holding the gun with both hands.

"Raise your gun and aim," he whispers again, breath warm. Goosebumps crawl up my spine, the heat of his body flush against my back. "Focus on the target," he murmurs, and I do my best to focus on the wooden bird which is impossible seeing as he feels so good against me...

Focus, Willow.

He chuckles, and I'm certain that thought slipped out.

The bird floats everywhere, not as fast as the first bird, but still pretty quick. It bobs back and forth over the pedestals, nearly hitting the trees. I align my gun with the angle of the bird.

"When you lock on your target, pull the trigger," Caz says, and I press my finger to the trigger, sending a bullet flying toward the bird. The gunshot echoes along with a hollow *thunk*, and the wooden object flails to the ground.

"Holy shit!" I gasp when Caz pulls away. "I shot it!"

"I knew you could do it!" I jump into his arms, and he holds me tight with a deep laugh. "You see? You're a natural."

The whirring of the pole becomes faster, and this time *two* birds come flying out of the pedestals.

"I'll try by myself this time," I tell him, and Caz grins, gesturing to the open field with a slight bow.

"Be my guest."

I miss my second bird, and it takes me three tries before I finally shoot it down. Caz whips out a dagger, throwing it into the air at the other bird. The bird sails across the field and pins to a tree trunk.

"Show off!" I yell, and he throws his hands in the air, a guilt-less gesture.

"Hundreds of years of practice, babe!"

We spend an hour on the field, wooden birds springing out of the pedestals, a gentle breeze going, and the honeysuckle scent stronger. The daggers are the hardest part, and he informs me that it's really about force and the use of my wrists.

I only knock down one bird with a dagger, but I'm determined. Hopefully with a few more weeks of practice, I'll be just as good as he is—as all of his clan are, really.

There's a serenity to this—being outdoors in a picturesque field and practicing with my mate. Moments like these, I realize, are irreplaceable. We're bonding, allowing our Tether to go much deeper than we imagined. I could *never* get this on Earth. I'm starting to think everything I need is all here. I wonder what Warren thinks about this new life...well, from what he can remember. Does he like it here? Does he want to stay forever? Would he want to go back to Earth?

I throw a dagger ahead of me as one of the five wooden birds floats nearby. Sometimes they thrust high, sometimes they bobble low. I barely hit the bird, but it does fall, my dagger going with it.

Then I feel a sense of unease wash over me. There's a tightness in my stomach, almost a cramp, and my heart races, the hairs on my arms rising. Silvera and Cerberus are on their feet in seconds growling and baring their teeth and I look over my shoulder at Caz, who rapidly whips out his gun and points it directly at the opening of the thicket.

"Who's there?" he barks, brows furrowing as he moves

closer toward it. My heart continues its race as I remain stuck in place. Fuck. Here I go freezing again.

There's rustling near the thicket, and Caz presses the gun hammer down, his finger wrapping tighter around the trigger.

Who is it? I ask him.

Don't know.

"It's just me." A person appears, climbing through the opening. Her hair is pulled back in a thick braid, and loose tendrils hang around her face. Her eyes are still puffy, and the gray eye seems sadder than the good eye, but her face is clear, a little brighter. She's also changed clothes, dressed in all brown, with boots to match.

Danica forces a smile, looking from Caz to me, and I relax a little, breathing a sigh of relief. God, this place makes me so on edge. That could have been anyone coming to hurt us.

Caz drops his arm with a frown. "Why are you sneaking up on us?" he snaps.

"I'm not sneaking up on you. I was *looking* for you."

"Well, you found us. Now what do you want?"

Danica takes a thorough look around, moving closer. "I was hoping to ask for a favor."

"Of what kind?" Caz moves my way. He does that a lot, no matter the person. Stands close to me, just to avoid any surprise attacks.

"It's about Warren. He's hanging out with Rowan right now, but I'm a little worried." She wrings her fingers together. "You, um...saw me this morning. How I ran off. He found me through our bond, and he tells me he can still hear my thoughts, still feel how I feel. But...something is different now. Besides the fact that he can't remember anything we've experienced together or falling in love with me, his thoughts are...well, they're *disturbing*."

"Disturbing how?" I ask.

"Earlier, I heard him thinking about killing himself. But it's a different voice, one that sounds like his but more sinister. Truthfully, I don't think it belongs to him at all."

"Whose do you think it is?" Caz inquires.

"I know you said Decius has been put away, and that Korah has him locked up, but that doesn't mean all his energy has fully disappeared, does it? I think...I think this voice that's in Warren's head is telling him to kill or harm himself so that his half of the Cold Tether can be dispensed. And I know this is a stretch, but what if Decius is *still* controlling him somehow? He *was* stuck in that trance before, and sure, the elixir woke him up and brought him back to reality, but it didn't erase everything. And I hate saying it, but Warren is the weakest of us all. He'd be the easiest to take down. Decius' energy is still working through him, regardless that he's been put away by a Regal. It won't be until he's dead that we're all truly safe."

I glance at Caz, my chest growing tighter by the second. "Would that be possible? For Decius to still have energy around?"

"Honestly, anything is possible these days. But even so, what do you want us to do about it?" Caz asks, frowning at Danica. "There is no Mythic strong enough to penetrate a hold like that. Even the Regals said they can't fully kill him, they can only weaken him. And the only Regal who can remains in a slumber."

"Please," Danica pleads. "T-there has to be something." She steps closer, gesturing to me. "Willow, he's your brother, and you know I'm telling the truth. These thoughts are dangerous, and they're not like him. I've heard him three times this morning thinking about killing himself."

So that's what that was at the table—why he was frowning, and she put the knife out of his reach. The idea of Warren using that knife to hurt himself sends my mind spiraling. I find it hard to swallow, to digest. The Warren I know would *never* do such a thing.

"You're right. It's not like him," I agree.

"Is there anyone we can talk to who can restore Warren's mind? Get Decius completely out of him?" she requests.

Caz lowers his head with an irritated sigh. "Look, Danica, I already know what you're hinting at, but it's not possible and frankly, I don't want to do it.."

"Why not?" she counters rapidly.

"Because for one, I don't trust the Regals. And two, they are not easy to find. We have no clue where Korah is, and as for Hassha, I highly doubt she'll allow us on her island twice."

"You mean in Kessel?" Danica asks. "No, she wouldn't. My mother told me stories about her journeys to Kessel. The warriors would kill you before you even make it to shore. But I have their blood. Perhaps she'll allow us."

Caz says nothing, only stares at her.

I grab his hand. "There has to be a way we can get in touch with them, Caz."

"There must," Danica insists. "I know I come from nothing, but if you help me, I'll owe you tenfold. I will forever be in your debt. I—I work hard and fight harder, and I can hold my own in any situation I'm put in." Danica raises her head, though her mouth is quivering. *"Please."*

Her tears fall, slowly skating down her cheeks.

Caz sighs. "Love of Vakeeli, I don't do well with tears."

"Caz. We have to do something," I murmur.

"I know. I know." Another sigh escapes him, and he tucks his gun into his holster, eyeing Danica. "Fine. I'll do my best to send a message to Hassha, but I can't promise it'll get to her."

Danica swipes at her face, nodding eagerly. "Yes—okay, yes. I understand. Anything is better than nothing at all."

"I'll express that it's urgent, and if that doesn't work, I'll ask around, see if any Mythics can assist us with Warren or ward off those dark thoughts, even if it's temporarily."

"Okay. That could work." Danica closes the gap to offer a hand to Caz. "Thank you. I promise you, I'm forever in your debt. Anything you need me to do, it shall be done."

Caz glances at her hand before locking on her eyes. To my surprise, he takes it, his jaw clenching. The pain spreads all over him, and I feel a hint of that sensation in me, but he shakes while nodding at her.

With that, Danica turns away and jogs across the terrain and through the thicket.

"I can't help feeling like that was a mutual understanding just now," I tell him.

Caz is quiet for a while. "Perhaps it was." He glances at me. "Do you get odd sensations when they're around? Like little shocks?"

"I do. You feel that too? I couldn't figure it out before."

"I think it's in our blood," he murmurs. "The Cold Tether has an effect on all of us. It's a bond that unites us, whether we know each other or not. What I gather from her is similar to how I felt when I met you. I knew you weren't a threat and that she wasn't one either."

I wrap an arm around him, and he closes me in his. "Are you saying you believe her? That you trust her?" I ask.

"I never said all that."

"Caspian Harlow? Trusting a stranger? That would be *very* new."

"Pipe down, Willow Woman."

I laugh into his chest, but the laughter is short lived as someone shouts his name.

"Caz!" Rowan calls, bursting through the thicket. Caz pulls away, looking in his direction. "Finally got contact from The Council!" he pants. "Better come now. They say it's urgent."

Caz's eyes fall to mine, a sense of dread sinking into us both. Regardless, he wastes no time taking my hand and leading the way out of Monarch Terrain and to the castle.

CHAPTER 91

CAZ

"I DON'T LIKE THIS." KILLIAN'S VOICE ECHOES IN THE darkness, and I feel the heat of his body as he stands nearby. I told him to hurry back to Blackwater Manor as soon as we got word from The Council.

Shadow's Peak is notorious for its sharp, jagged rocks, bumpy trails, and ominous caves. For the most part, only teenagers venture this way, sparking bonfires and getting drunk off wine and whatever else they can get their hands on. Even Killian, Rowan, and I used to come near Shadow's Peak, proving how brave we were to get near it. We never ventured *into* it though. Hardly anyone does. Shadow's Peak is no place to party. There are things that lurk in the night here, and I'm not talking bears or wolves. No, there have been stories about literal *monsters* who drift in and out of this place, just like Rukane Forest. It's the most annoying thing having all our forests practically haunted in Blackwater. Fortunately, many people are smart enough to stay away, minus the rebellious few. Shadow's

Peak isn't barricaded like Rukane, but it still holds a mystery I can't explain.

Many of the tales mentioned how the monsters were made by vengeful Mythics. These monsters were human at one point, who fed on animals and eventually began to feed on humans, devouring them limb from limb like wicked carnivores. When I took over Blackwater, I made it my mission to send fleets into Shadow's Peak to make sure there were no lurking monsters and that my people could enter this area safely if need be. They never found any monsters, but I get the sense some are still out there…somewhere.

"Why would they have us meet here?" Killian snaps, waving his torch in the air. "Why not at the castle or the fucking tavern?" He narrows his eyes, craning his neck to see ahead.

"Because they don't want to be seen," I answer.

"It's creeping me out," Rowan mumbles, holding out his torch and peering around. His eyes dart around the darkness. "Where the hell are they anyway? The sooner we get out of here, the better. The last thing any of us needs to be going up against is one of those blood-sucking monsters."

"Those stories are fake," Killian grumbles, but that doesn't stop his eyes surfing the area.

A crackle sounds in the distance, followed by a loud snap, and Rowan whirls around with the gun he loaded with Luxor Ash bullets. He points it in the direction the noise came from, his breaths quickening. My gun is already in hand, chin tipping, eyes narrowed. It's hard to see past the light of the torches. There's nothing but darkness, and with the roar of the distant ocean, we can only hear so much.

"There." Killian points, and three figures appear. They float over the jagged tops of the mountains, their lengthy silver cloaks billowing with the wind. They follow the light of our torches, mouths turned down. It's The Council, also known as Callista, Arie, and that shithead Vassilis.

They land several feet away from us, their silver eyes shifting among the three of us.

"I was hoping I wouldn't have to see your face until *after* your journey to Selah," Callista announces, taking a minor step forward.

"Oh, don't be that way, Callista. I'm certain my face is much better to look at than that asshole brother of yours." My eyes snap to Vassilis, and an immediate growl erupts from his body. Rowan can't help stifling a laugh. "Let's get this over with. Why did you have us meet here?"

"We had to be sure you weren't followed and that you're not being watched. This is a gray area and is hardly ever surveilled by the Regals." Callista's silver eyes drag from the top of my head down to my feet. They flash a heated silver, then cool again. She's reading me.

"Watched by whom?" I ask.

The silver of her eyes seems to darken, muting in color. "The Regals."

"And why would the Regals be watching me?" I ask, clinging to obliviousness.

"Oh, kill it with your bloody arrogance!" Vassilis snaps, taking a giant leap forward. "We heard through the winds that you were with Hassha in Kessel and that Korah is the reason Decius has been defeated. You think we're imbeciles? That we wouldn't find out? You forget we are aware of many things!"

"I assumed you would figure it out, but I don't see how any of that matters or what it has to do with me," I respond calmly, and I can tell the calmness in my voice is really getting under Vassilis' skin by the way he grimaces.

"It matters much more than you think, Monarch Harlow," Ares responds.

"What my brothers are trying to say is this changes everything we had planned for your trip to Selah," Callista says. "With the Regals once again making their presence known, we can't be sure about their intentions, nor can we ask them, seeing as they are above us...in a sense." Her face tightens, nostrils flaring, as if she hates the idea of *anyone* being above her. How terrible that is for her ego.

"Why didn't you just have one of the Regals go and wake Selah in the first place?" I study all three of them. "They're sisters, after all. Well, according to the history. And they're powerful. Who's to say they can't get the job done?"

"The Regals have their reasons to not like us, just as we have our reasons for not liking them. You think they aren't aware that it is *your* blood that can bring Selah back? You don't think it's quite simple for them to travel to an island they created to wake their sister?" Callista inquires, eyes narrowing. "They're well aware, and yet their sister remains in a slumber on a fiery, man slaughtering island."

"Well, that's clearly for a reason, isn't it?"

"Whatever their reasons may be, we have other plans. We still have a goal to obtain, and we *will* meet that goal, but only after we figure out what Hassha's and Korah's true intent is. Until then, the boat ride to Inferno Isle will be postponed."

Some of the tension melts from my body, seeping into the ground. This was what I wanted, but I figured it would never happen. Now it is. Thank the Regals.

As if reading my mind, Vassilis says with snark, "Don't be so comforted by this, Harlow. You *will* make that journey to Inferno Isle, whether it's now or within a few weeks."

"Well, until then, I'll enjoy the time I do have not seeing your ugly face, Vassilis."

Vassilis' eyes flash, and he lunges toward me, but Ares presses a hand to his chest, forcing his brother back. Killian's and Rowan's hands shift just a little, twitching for their guns.

"Those rubies are still due," Arie reminds me, a flat palm on his brother chest.

"I'm aware, and we're working on it," I state.

"And the boy of Rami's," Callista adds. "He will still need guidance and training."

"I'll be getting to him as well."

"I suggest you spend your time wisely, Monarch Harlow," Callista says. "Armistice Night will be here soon." Ah, yes. A night where everyone gets shitfaced drunk, dances, and fucks like rabbits.

"You especially better enjoy the time you have left with your mate. There's no guarantee she'll survive long in Vakeeli if Selah doesn't rise." Another sneer takes over Vassilis' face, and I'm going to break his fucking neck in half. I'm going to murder this ignorant wannabe Regal, I swear it. I will crush every bone in his body and gouge his eyes out with my own fingers.

It takes me a moment to realize my hand is tight around his throat, his pulse beating beneath my palm. I only come to the realization when I feel the searing heat of touch and the weight of Rowan's and Killian's hands on my shoulders, trying to reel me back. I bring the barrel of my gun under Vassilis' chin, and he gulps beneath my palm, his eyes darting to his brother and sister, who are both floating nearby, their eyes a blinding silver.

"Did I not tell you that if you threatened my mate again, I'd pop those silvery eyes out of your fucking head?" I don't recognize my own voice, but I've heard it before, this primal side I hate revealing but will if it means setting any record straight.

"Monarch Harlow, stand down immediately," Callista commands.

But I don't move. I swear on all Vakeeli I'll kill this fucker right here, right now, and still sleep like a baby tonight.

Vassilis grips my hand, struggling for breath while looking into my eyes. That silver is gone, as if it's drained and he's nothing but a meaningless bag of bones, flesh, and organs. There's power in my hands, a power I've never felt before. It's hot and tempting, begging me to crush his windpipe with one more squeeze.

"I said stand down!" Callista shouts, this time with more bass in her tone.

I glare into Vassilis' eyes, narrowing mine, and his flash with something I'm *very* familiar with. Fear.

Then it hits me. I realize that I *can* kill him. I'm not like the commoners. It was stated with their words that *my* blood is charged—that I have enough power in it to wake one of the most powerful beings of Vakeeli. They can't kill me either, or they won't get what they need.

A smirk tugs at my lips, and I finally release him. He wraps a hand around his throat, drawing in rapid breaths as he falls to his knees before me. When he peers up, he raises a brow, but that fear is still rooted deep in his eyes.

"I should kill you!" he snarls.

I cock a brow. "Try it."

Arie rushes to his brother, helping him up. They both float into the air, Arie shoving Vassilis on the back to get him farther away from me.

"We'll be in touch," Callista grumbles, and The Council takes off, disappearing in the night.

"WHAT. THE HELL. WAS THAT?" Rowan shouts. "Caz, *what*? You just choked out a Council! You've got some balls on you, man!"

"He did warn him the last time," Killian tosses in, shrugging.

"Oi, that was literally insane! Did you see how scared Vassilis was?" Rowan laughs. "Bloody hell. Wait 'til I tell Mum about this!"

I can't help my smile as we walk away from the cliff to find the SUV parked on the path near the trees. I lift the hand that held him, and if I'm not mistaken, my palm is red—an abnormal red that appears to glow. It fades rapidly and I draw in an even breath.

I'm still pissed about Vassilis' threat, but I have to admit, it feels good knowing one of the members of The Council is afraid of me. Power is...well, *powerful*. And I'll use every ounce of it if it means protecting Willow.

CHAPTER 92
WILLOW

I EAT BREAKFAST WITH CAZ ON THE UPPER TERRACE of the castle. The terrace is as wide as my apartment, swathed in vines and embellished with Vanorian blossoms. Caz informed me the blossoms were Della's idea. They still thrive, almost like a reminder that she'll forever live on in our hearts.

The terrace is two floors up from his chambers and overlooks the garden. There is another kitchen on this floor that I didn't know was there, as well as an attic crammed with chairs, tables, and dusty boxes. In its own wing is another armory that isn't as large as the lower-level armory, but still pretty spacious. More weapons on castle grounds. Can never be too careful, I suppose.

Makoto makes use of the garden, watering plants and picking fruit. I spot him as I sip my tea in a chair at one of the terrace tables. His lean frame weaves through the tiny paths to get where he needs to be. He's made himself acquainted with the castle and has truly been on top of everything. He's washed everyone's clothes, allowed them to air dry outdoors, and then ironed and folded them, and he never confuses them. He delivers baskets of fresh laundry to each of us every day. Around noon, he ventures to everyone's rooms, knocking politely and making sure we've been fed or hydrated. Breakfast, lunch, and dinner are served to us on time, along with snacks for us to grab when we pass the main kitchen. He also makes this delicious fruit-infused water that I can't get enough of. I'd watched once as he prepped the fruit, slicing delicately with a knife as he told Juniper and me stories about his kids (who are adults now), and even his time during battles against Ripple Hills. For a man who has been through so much, he's amazing. A part of me wants to not trust him. After all, nobody is perfect. But there is something about Makoto. He seems like the kind of person who wants to just live his life after so much hardship. Plus, I'm sure if Caz finds anything out that betrays his status, he'll have his head, so there's that. I have no doubt Caz has been doing some digging of his own.

"I have to run off," Caz says after wiping his mouth with a napkin. "Would love to stay, but I have to get to Vanora. Killian says he's found a lead on a Kessel connection. Thinks someone there may have information."

"Okay." I stand with him and start to clean my area.

"Leave it!" Makoto's voice shoots up to us. I peer over the thick railing, and he's standing in the center of the garden with a basket of vegetables tucked beneath his arm. "Don't mean to interrupt, but I can clean it, Lady Monarch! Stop doing my job!"

I can't help laughing. "Fine, Makoto! I won't do your job!"

Caz chuckles, offering me a hand. I take it, and he leads the way inside again, taking two staircases down until we've reached the kitchen. Makoto has made it inside with the basket. He sets it on the counter and gives us a wide smile.

"Is there anything I can get you?" he asks.

"Nothing right now, Makoto. Thanks," Caz says.

Makoto nods, removing various vegetables from the basket.

"I'll see you in a bit." Caz plants a kiss on my cheek. "Juniper is around if you need her."

"'Kay." He gives me one more kiss—on the lips this time—before leaving the kitchen.

"Young love," Makoto chuckles, carrying some of the vegetables to the sink. "So beautiful."

"Are you married?" I ask when he turns in my direction again.

"Was. We split apart. Turns out she favors fighting people in caves more than spending alone time with me."

"Oh." I'm not sure what to say to that so I don't respond at all.

"A good thing, though. No wife, and all my children away creating their own lives gives me time to live my life." His eyes wander, as if reminiscing about something. But just as quickly, he perks back up and asks, "Would you like something to drink, Lady Monarch? Are you thirsty?"

"No, that's okay, Makoto. I'm fine."

When he turns for the vegetables again, I leave the kitchen to find the deck. Outside, the air is humid and thick, the clouds hanging low. No sunshine today, I presume.

I turn my head left, spotting someone sitting in the middle of the field. His legs are crossed as he focuses on the view of the ocean, his brows bunched together, as if deep in thought. Warren.

Not too far away from him near a line of trees is Danica. She has her Katana in hand and whips it in the air with precision. Caz gave it back to her this morning. A truce, I presume. Danica's eyes shift to Warren every so often before returning to her sword training, her back and arms stiff, lips pinched tight.

I walk inside again and ask Makoto, "Actually, I do need something. You wouldn't happen to know what a peanut butter and jelly sandwich is, would you?"

CHAPTER 93
WILLOW

WITH A STEEL CUP OF MILK IN ONE HAND AND A Vakeeli version of a peanut butter and jelly sandwich in the other, I leave the castle and walk toward Warren.

As I approach, his head turns a fraction to find me, and a whisper of a smile claims his lips. I take the spot beside him on the grass, and his eyes fall to the sandwich and cup of milk.

"Didn't eat breakfast?" he asks.

"I did, actually. But I gather you didn't."

He shrugs. "Not really hungry."

"Do you remember peanut butter and jelly sandwiches?"

Warren huffs a laugh. "How could I forget? We practically survived on them every summer, especially when Dad started working more."

I avoid the topic of our father for now. It's a sore spot, and I want to cheer my brother up, not bring his mood down. "Mine were always better," I say, bumping his shoulder.

"Yeah, okay. You wish." He cracks a half-smile. "You always

put too much jelly and not enough peanut butter. Made it so sloppy."

"Those are the best kind!" I laugh, offering him the sandwich. "Try this one. It's not our usual, but maybe you'll like it. Makoto said it's pecan cream and blackfruit jam. It's the closest thing we could find." I extend my arm, holding it closer to him. He's so much skinnier than he was the last time I saw him. Even through the gray T-shirt that hangs off his body like a cloth, I can see the ridges of his spine.

Warren takes the roll from me, studying it carefully. The eggplant colored blackfruit jam spills over the edges, and the tan pecan cream merges with it. He takes a big bite, then moans with a sigh.

"It's really good," he says.

"Yeah? Break me off a piece." I take the piece he offers, popping it into my mouth. "Wow. It *is* good! I didn't think pecan cream would be."

"Just like home, really," he chuckles. He takes another bite and turns his gaze ahead. As he chews, the smile slowly fades away and his eyes sadden.

"What's really been on your mind, Warren?" I ask, though I have an idea. Death, death, and *more* death. Danica has been keeping a watchful eye, but I want to hear it from him personally.

He's quiet so long I think he's either ignoring me or didn't hear me.

"I never told you the whole truth about Momma and Dad," he finally says.

I try not to frown. "What truth?"

He lowers the roll to his lap, glancing at Danica who is already watching us but keeping her distance. He swings his eyes to mine again, mashing his lips together. When his head drops, I worry he won't tell me anything at all, so I place my hand on top of his.

"Warren?" I call.

He looks down at our hands as two tears skid down his cheeks. "That time I visited Dad," he starts, swiping at the tears. "It was because I had this dream of Momma. It was so… vivid. I remember every detail. She was in the bathtub. She'd slit her wrists, and as she bled, she looked at me and told me to find Dad."

My throat closes in on itself. Momma died in the clinic. She'd swapped pills with another patient, built a concoction over a period of time, and died from overdose. I wait for him to continue.

"I went looking for him, and it's true he sent me off and wanted nothing to do with me, but not before telling me why. I demanded to know, told him I wasn't leaving until I knew why he abandoned us." He sucks in a breath. "We were never their children, Willow. Momma was never pregnant with us. She fostered us first, then adopted us."

"*What?*" I choke on a breath, staring at him incredulously.

"She found us after a late shift. He said she found us in a basket next to her car. Dad says Momma brought us home, took care of us. She reported that she'd found us to the police, and social services stepped in, but she told them she wanted to keep us. I guess because she couldn't have kids of her own."

"You're lying," I mutter. "Tell me you're lying." He has to be. There's no way he's telling the truth. All my life, I ached for her. I still do. And even though I didn't see the resemblance I had to them, I figured it was just a coincidence—that I'd grow into my face and look just like Momma. She was beautiful, with sable skin and bright brown eyes. Her hair was always nice and neat, never a hair out of place...at least not at first. How could she have just *found* us?

Warren rubs his jaw as if it hurts. "Dad said as soon as Momma took us in, she changed. And when we turned two, she started having nightmares about someone coming for us. It drove her to hysteria, you remember? And when she died, those nightmares shifted to Dad, apparently. He said he tried enduring them, but he couldn't because they were so vivid. He swears there was a voice in his head, telling him to kill us. He said..." Warren's voice cracks. "He said one night, he remembered raising a pillow above my face to suffocate me, but he snapped out of it."

My heart sinks. I drop my gaze, trying to remember all the moments spent with Dad. He'd changed toward the end of the time he was with us, yes. He'd lost job after job, and we continuously downsized until we were in a one-bedroom apartment on a shotty side of Charlotte. Now that I think about it, I do remember him mumbling to himself a lot. Staying awake all night. He carried this bottle of pills with him all the time and told me once they helped him stay alert. "B-but how?" is all I can muster.

"I don't know. But that day I found him, he described the thing that was tormenting him in his sleep. He said it was shaped like a woman, and that she was always red. She had hair of fire, and her eyes were like hot coals. He said she took over his dreams every time he fell asleep, and he couldn't take it anymore, so he left. He walked away. He told me the dreams immediately stopped when he left us. He never had them again. He thinks...he thinks we're possessed by something evil."

"Do you think it was Decius?" I whisper, jerking my head up to find his eyes. "You think he was tormenting them?"

"I don't know. I'm not sure what all Decius is capable of."

"He couldn't have reached their minds, could he?" I shake my head, pondering it. "He's not strong enough for that—not to tap in with people on Earth. *Good* people, at that."

Warren nods, but still looks unsure. "I'm sorry I never told you the truth."

"It's okay." I take his hand, squeezing it lightly. "Warren, it's okay."

"I have the same nightmares as he does, even now."

"What?" I gasp.

"About the woman with hair of fire. They're stronger now that I'm in this world."

I swallow hard, unsure what to say.

"She hurts me in my dreams. Tries to strangle me. Her hands are always on fire. It's clear she wants me dead. Between her and Decius' evil thoughts lingering, I feel like I'm losing my mind, Willow." He huffs a laugh, but there is no humor to his tone.

"I know, I know." I collect him into my arms. "It's okay. We'll get you better, I promise."

"But what if I don't get better?"

"You will. You have to. For Danica. For *me*."

He shudders a breath, and I hear footsteps shuffling in the grass behind us. Danica approaches, looking between us.

"Everything okay?" she asks.

"Yeah, we're good. Just having a heart to heart." I smile up at her, but she doesn't return the smile.

Danica cuts her eyes to Warren. "You closed me out,

Warren. You promised you wouldn't close me out while you're like this. Open minds only, remember?"

"I'm sorry," he responds, pulling away from me. "I just wanted to talk to my sister alone."

Danica's lips press, her eyes bouncing between us. "Okay, well, I'm going back to the guesthouse." She lingers a moment, as if waiting for Warren to come with her. When he doesn't, she shakes her head and turns away, tucking her Katana into her sheath.

Warren watches his mate go, then says, "What if that Hassha woman doesn't take me in? Danica says there's a possibility she won't because I'm a man."

"If she can't take you in, hopefully she can at least heal you, clear your mind. Rid you of those nightmares. Maybe she knows what the nightmares mean."

Warren says nothing, but he does inhale before exhaling. "I don't think we were born on Earth. I think someone brought us from here and placed us in that parking lot. They were trying to get rid of us, or save us...maybe? I don't know."

"Yeah," I murmur. "After hearing all that, I think so too." But who would do that? The only people who can are the Regals. Korah found her way to Earth, but she ventured there long before we were ever born. Did she return when we were born and swindle us to Earth? If she did, I would assume she did it to protect us from Decius. Perhaps our previous selves died, we were reborn, and she moved us. But that would be a vicious cycle, wouldn't it? Constantly going back, knowing we're going to die, only to bring us to Earth when we're reborn?

None of this makes any sense, and now that I know all this about our parents and what they suffered on Earth, I need to find answers.

CHAPTER 94
WILLOW

RUBY FALLS IS A SERENE PART OF BLACKWATER THAT many visit during the spring and summer, according to Caz. It's also where Hassha has agreed to meet us.

It wasn't easy finding a way to deliver a message to Kessel. Kessel's High Guard (aka Milandra) keeps a transmitter in her bungalow for emergency purposes only, in case any women who ventures from Kessel to the mainland needs their assistance. Caz had to travel to Vanora, and it turns out his lead belonged to a Mythic brothel. According to Juniper, Mythic brothels are a place where Mythic women make anyone's fantasies come true visually...while also performing sexual favors. I wasn't fully comfortable knowing Caz went to a brothel of all places, but I understood. Plus, I know him. The last thing he would have wanted was to be touched, and I trust him. He found one Mythic woman who claimed to have encountered a Kessel woman once. She said she had the transmitter information. It took Caz paying the Mythic prostitute a ton of rubies just to retrieve that information. Fortunately, the woman wasn't lying because Milandra responded to his transmitter request the same day.

Caz sent his men out with orders to keep everyone away from Ruby Falls for the day so we can meet Hassha privately.

Just off the shore, I find myself comforted as we step out of the SUV. Caz removes himself from the driver seat while Danica and Warren climb out of the back. We stand on black sand that squishes beneath my feet, but ahead, past smooth rocks swathed in moss, is an incredible view of a waterfall.

The water cascades down protruding rocks tinged red, pooling into an oblong gorge. We climb over smooth stones and boulders to reach the gravel on the other side, closest to the waterfall. The scent of mud fills my nostrils, the gravel beneath my feet sparkling in the light. When I'm closer, I realize exactly where that glint of red on the rocks is coming from. These aren't simple rocks that make up the waterfall. They're interwoven with rubies. The rubies twinkle beneath the gray sky and adorn the rocks on either side of the falling water. From where I stand, a cave is behind the waterfall's belly.

"Does the name of this location make sense now?" Caz smirks as he stands next to me.

"It does," I breathe. "Wow. It's so beautiful here."

"To be here, it must be reserved. We collect a list of visitors, seeing as some would come to mine the place and collect rubies. We don't allow that here. We like the rubies at the falls to stay in place. It keeps the area sacred. Mining here is against Blackwater Law."

I nod. "I see. That's good. It makes it all the more special to be around it."

Warren and Danica meet up to us, facing the water too.

They're hand in hand, though Danica is hanging on much tighter to him than he is to her. She informed me this morning that she caught him standing on the guardrail of the guest-house, like he was about to jump off. I look at my brother now, and though he looks the same to me, I can't imagine the thoughts running through his head.

"Come," Caz says. "I'll show you the cave."

Caz leads the way across the gravel to a set of built-in stairs in the rock wall. The gurgling of the waterfall grows louder, the water crashing into what appears to be a bottomless black gorge.

With the final step up, we're inside the cave. The roar of the water is louder, but soothing. The cave leaks inside, water trickling from the ceiling. Some drips onto my cheek, and I wipe it away with a smile, taking in the view of rubies glinting marvelously inside the cave. I look through one of the gaps on either side of the waterfall, and ahead is plush green land that travels to the beach. It would make a great place to spread a towel, bring a picnic basket, and enjoy the day.

"We can do that today," Caz murmurs in my ear. He's standing behind me, the heat of his body pressed to mine. He circles his arms around the upper half of my body, and I melt in his arms.

"Blackwater is beautiful. I didn't realize there was so much more to it," I admit.

"Oh, there's lots to be discovered," he says on the shell of my ear. His warm breath sends a spiral of heat through me, creating a puddle between my legs. "We can discover it together."

My eyes shift to Danica and Warren. Warren is facing the

waterfall, zoned out, while Danica claims the space next to him, her sword in hand.

"How long must we wait?" Danica asks, wiping the sword with a handkerchief.

"There's no wait at all." A voice rises behind us, and Caz pulls himself away from me to spin around. In the depths of the cave, I spot lustrous blue eyes. They move closer, along with soft, damp footsteps, until Hassha appears. She stands several paces away, dressed in a sleeveless tan top and matching skirt. Her crown is rooted to her head, her white hair braided into singles down her back. She smiles at me and Caz, then her eyes shift to Danica and Warren, who are staring at her in complete shock. Danica plants the tip of her sword in the ground, dropping to one knee and bowing her head.

"My Regal, Hassha. I am so grateful to be in your presence," Danica says. "I never thought this day would come."

"Rise," Hassha commands, and Danica immediately stands upright again, but not without staring at Hassha with glistening eyes.

"All the Cold Tethered children in one area. I've not been a witness to this for centuries." The glow of her eyes fades, and two women step up behind her—Milandra and another built woman with blonde hair. Warriors who are all business and no smiles, unlike their leader.

"Hassha, thank you so much for doing this." I move closer, wanting badly to take her hands and hold them, but I know better not to. Milandra is already looking at us like she seeks a challenge.

"Come." Hassha holds her arms out to me, and I hesitate before stepping into them. She holds me close, hugging tight, and her warriors tense, gripping the handles of their spears tighter. "Such wonderful energy." Pulling away, Hassha clasps my face in her hands and presses her forehead to mine. She closes her eyes to breathe a moment, eyeballs moving behind her lids, then she opens them again.

"I've seen what has happened since you returned to Blackwater. Decius is gone. That is good." Her gaze shifts to Warren and Danica. "Come," she insists, waving her hands for them to approach.

They make their way toward her, Warren a lot more wary than Danica. When they're close enough, Hassha takes Warren's hand and wraps hers around it. Her eyes shut again, those eyeballs swiveling behind the lids, until she hitches a breath and her eyes pop open, glowing fiercely now. She releases Warren's hand and takes a minor step back.

"I felt the dark energy seeping out of him from a distance, but it's much worse than I thought," Hassha states.

"How do you mean?" Danica asks rapidly.

"Though you can't remember, I saw exactly how Decius used your energies to get by. Warren's is much stronger than yours, Danica, so he used him twice as much. I believe he was using Warren to tap into Earth as well, hence the nightmares Willow previously had, as well as the snake attack and the attack from our prisoner. Warren was his only link to Earth."

Garrett. I put up my mind's wall because I know Caz is going to flip if he even hears me thinking about Garrett's well-being. I don't know why I care. I shouldn't at all, and he deserves to rot, but I'm too damn empathetic sometimes. I still don't think he deserves to die. Tortured? Sure. But death? No. Still, Caz is tense next to me, and the back of his hand brushes mine, a mutual understanding.

"So, what are you saying? That there's nothing we can do?" Danica inquires.

"No, no. There are things we can do. The only issue is that it'll require a lot of time. I suggest you two come to Kessel, remain in Wellness Bay until we can piece his mind back together and rid him of any lingering energy from Decius. We do that, and his memories with you should be restored and his heart will be clear. I would also like to run other tests, just to make sure"

"Why is it that I know who Danica is, but I can't remember anything I did with her?" Warren asks. "It's strange because I feel like I've developed some form of amnesia about our bond, yet I trust her and still care about her very much."

"His wicked ties can't taint virtue," Hassha returns with a smile. "The good will always triumph. Once we're done, it will all come back. Trust me." She points her eyes to Milandra. "Milandra, Lilith, take them to the portal so we can clear him immediately."

"Yes, your grace." Milandra and Lilith step back, gesturing toward the darkness of the cave. Warren and Danica stare at each other, hesitant, before following their lead.

"Wait—Warren." I rush after him, and when he turns a fraction, I wrap my arms around him and press my ear to his chest. "Get better, you hear me? I can't lose you again."

Warren nods when I look up. "I will."

Thank you, Willow." Danica's voice is soft as she touches my hand. I nod, watching her take Warren's. They follow Milandra and Lilith, disappearing into the darkness. I notice a flicker of blue light, almost like a camera flashing, and then the cave is dark again.

My brother is in Kessel. He'll get better, and when he does, we'll find out exactly what happened in our past. If our parents on Earth never birthed us...who did?

CHAPTER 95

CAZ

"HASSHA, DO YOU THINK I CAN HAVE A WORD?" I ask when Milandra and Lilith have disappeared with the other Cold Tethered couple.

"I was going to ask the same thing." Hassha stands taller, crossing her fingers together and resting them in front of her. "What's on your mind?"

"I feel there's something I should mention to you about The Council." I glance at Willow, who nods her head. She's the only reason I'm bringing this up. She believes the Regals can help us because the last thing she wants is this burden over our heads or me taking a trip to Inferno Isle. Juniper took it upon herself to show Willow images of that wretched place in textbooks while I was meeting The Council last night, and now Willow is losing her damn mind over it.

"Go on." Hassha's eyes lock with mine.

"They've told me they're aware the Regals are making

appearances again. They sense you and Korah have come out of hiding and that it will deter their plans."

"Their plans to do what, exactly?"

"They've mentioned that my blood is charged and that it's powerful enough to wake Selah. Apparently, she's resting somewhere on Inferno Isle."

Hassha doesn't react with the body, but her eyes tell it all. There's a slight flinch at the mention of Selah, but she blinks it away.

"Something tells me you already knew this," I add.

"Of course, I knew. Why wouldn't I know where my own sister is?"

"So, if you knew, why haven't you gone to wake her yourself?"

"It has not been in my plans. I've been preoccupied with Kessel." She drops her hands, closing the gap between us. "I'd advise you *not* to take the journey to Inferno Isle, Caspian. It's a death sentence and impossible for any man to survive. I should know. I helped design it."

"So, if you designed it, surely you can clear it and set your sister free."

Hassha blinks but doesn't answer my statement. Instead, she says, "Don't listen to The Council. Remain in Blackwater, where it's safer."

"Why shouldn't I go? Waking Selah will restore everything. Violence will end, everyone can be healed, and the world can be renewed. This is what The Council has told me."

"The Council is *lying* to you." There's a difference in her tone. It's sharper, huskier. Still, her body is relaxed, neutral. She knows how to play her cards, hold them against her chest. I'd expect nothing less from a woman who's been alive for hundreds of thousands of years.

"How do you know?" I ask.

"They're a group of bored liars. Everyone knows this." She waves a dismissive hand.

Frustrated, I take a step forward. She's lying through her teeth, I know it. "Hassha, why won't you go after your sister? Why won't you wake her?"

She holds my stare. "It's much more complicated than that, Caspian, and I don't have the time to explain it to you right now. If The Council is awaiting our next move, they'll be waiting a very long time. We'll keep our heads down, and I'll find a way to inform Korah of this news about them. As long as they're unaware of what we're doing and think there'll be consequences to their actions, they won't send you. This, I know for a fact. Why do you think they haven't responded to you? They know not to cross us."

"They said you *knew* my blood was charged," I add quickly. "That it's enough to wake her. Why was that never mentioned to me in Kessel? And if Decius has been stored away, as well as most of his energy, how is Selah *not* awake yet? All the stories say Decius is the one who defeated her—who put her to rest. Shouldn't she be able to free herself from whatever slumber she's under if Decius is weaker now? Surely, she can break out of it. She's one of the most powerful beings in all Vakeeli. Hell, she created us *and* him. Even if she can't wake somehow, The Council is *very* adamant about getting this done, while you and Korah couldn't seem to care less. Where is your loyalty to her?"

"Don't you dare question my loyalty!" Hassha roars, and though I don't flinch, Willow gasps and backs away.

Hassha glares at me, her eyes lit in silvery flames. Her

nostrils flare as she breathes raggedly through them. Of course, it doesn't take those eyes long to cool and for her calm demeanor to be restored.

Silence thickens the cave as she draws in a deep breath, then exhales through her mouth.

I sigh. "I'm just saying that it feels like there's much more to this than *any* of you are letting on and I don't want to be stuck in the middle of it," I murmur.

"Oh, Caspian. There is *so much* more. It is far beyond anything you will ever understand. Selah is my sister, yes, but she is *not* who you or The Council think she is. The less you know, the better. Trust me."

"What is that supposed to mean?"

Hassha's lips part. She studies me for a very long time, not blinking, breathing softly. It seems she's about to say something until she clamps her mouth shut, places a hand on my shoulder, and says, "Don't let your curiosity of Selah ruin everything you've built."

"I can't help feeling like a bloody puppet," I grumble as she backs away. That causes her to freeze.

"You are *far* from a puppet. Do you not realize just how powerful you are?" She scoffs. "Honestly, your energy could tear down this entire cave and all of Blackwater if you wanted it to! You felt it last night, didn't you? That power in your hands? It's within you. If you truly learn how to use your gifts, just as your mother did, there is *nothing* you can't do. But if you wake Selah, that energy will be gone, do you understand? It will be stripped away from you until you're left to be nothing but ash."

I feel a clench in my chest and glance at Willow, who is staring at Hassha, confused and slightly afraid.

"I must go, Caspian. Enjoy your life. *Live* it. Take pride in your Cold Tether and in all you do." Her eyes shift to Willow, a complacent smile taking place. "We'll take care of Warren and Danica and alert you when they're ready to come back."

"Hassha, I seriously think we should consider—"

Hassha turns her back to me and vanishes into thin air.

"Fuck!" I hiss, planting a hand on my hip. Willow moves closer to me. "There's something going on here, Willow. I feel it in my bones. They're all hiding something, and if we don't figure it out, The Council is going to use us until they get what they want, while Hassha and Korah idly stand by, twiddling their fucking thumbs and living their untouchable lives."

Willow releases a breath. "Maybe they won't," she offers. "There's a reason The Council put a hold on that trip for now. They're afraid of what the Regals will do now that they're revealing themselves to commoners again."

"We're not just commoners though, don't you see? We're descendants of the Tethered, and whatever goes on with us also affects them. There is something much deeper at play here and not knowing is frustrating the hell out of me." I swallow hard. "I need to do more studying. Talk to more people. Perhaps Alora will have a clearer idea of the history between all the Regals. I just...I can't stand by with bated breath, waiting for The bloody Council to pop up again and whisk me off to my death. If push comes to shove, they will do it."

"Then we'll talk to Alora. But listen to me, Caz." She collects my face in her hands, forcing my eyes on hers. "Right now, we don't need to worry about it, okay? Let The Council's fear of the Regals be our peace for now. If anything changes, we'll know, and I have a feeling they'll warn us. Hassha will sense it. I'm sure she'd tell us first."

I shake my head. "You have too much faith in these Regals.

You forget they stood by while all those Tethered couples from the past were murdered by Decius. They did *nothing*, Willow. *Nothing*. The only reason they helped us this time is because we found them and they were forced to face us. What makes you think they won't let the same happen to us?"

Willow purses her lips, hesitating. "I—I don't know. I just...I don't think Hassha would do that. I know it sounds crazy, but I trust her. And Korah saved us, remember? She saved us from Decius and his tricks and returned to Vakeeli after so many years when she didn't have to. I really think they want a change for the better, and whatever their reasons are for not waking Selah is probably because it won't benefit us...or them. They know much more than we do. For all we know, Selah is no Regal at all. The history could be wrong. Trust me, I grew up in a world where the history is completely wrong. Turns out the people we thought were heroes, were never really heroes. Maybe the same applies here." She holds my hand, kissing my knuckles. "Let it be, Caz. Sure, you can study and seek answers, but don't allow this to stop us from living. Our lives will always be in danger because of things we can't control. Let's at least enjoy the parts of it we can. We have each other. We're happy. I want more happiness with you."

Damn.

Her words are soothing, like ice to a hot, swollen knot. Some of the tension fades away as I reel her into my arms, but as I peer over her shoulder, past the waterfall and toward the pastures that lead to the ocean, that worry still sits in my gut like a block of steel.

Whether Willow realizes it or not, we're in the crossfire of the Regals and The Council. They're much more powerful than we are, and one rash decision from them can tarnish our lives.

Of course I want to be happy with her. I want that forever, but how can I be with such threats lingering?

How do we know Hassha and Korah won't just kill *me* to deter The Council's plans? How can I be certain The Council won't return, despite their fears?

There are too many what ifs, too many doubts...but regardless, my mate is right. I'm still monarch, and I'm still in control of what I have before me. There is a power within me that I need to develop. I am the son of a hybrid Mythic and a cold tethered child. It starts with me and if weapons form against us, I'll make sure I'm ready.

So, I let it be...for now.

CHAPTER 96

MIDNIGHT IN KESSEL

INSIDE THE VISITOR'S HUT, HASSHA STANDS OVER ONE
of the Cold Tethered children with her heart beating slowly. Her
eyes hold a subtle blue glow as she studies the man with hair
like a lion's mane and dry, brown skin. She's scanned him
several times, had him treated to remove the dark energy within
his soul, but none of it is working.

Now, it's late, and she's made her presence unknown,
cloaked in a shield of invisibility. While she watches them in
their slumber, they can't see or hear her, though they probably
could sense her presence if they were awake, feel as if someone
were watching. But they aren't, and she's made sure of it with
the sleeping spell she's put them under.

Warren's partner, Danica, rests next to him, one arm draped
over his waist, her face buried into his body. She has Kessel
blood in her that's pure and strong. *A lovely couple*, Hassha

516

thinks, and as badly as she wants to smile, she can't help sensing something is so very wrong with them. Or perhaps it's just him. It's not just that the energy of Decius remains in Warren's soul, but something much heavier is thriving in his mind—something that feels equally as powerful as she is...and terrifyingly familiar.

The only option is to get into his head, dive deeper, and see what's really keeping his virtuous soul at bay.

Something crackles outside the hut and Hassha peers back. Through the window she spots a glow of lavender. The hairs rise on her bronze arms, like static is in the air, and a familiar warmth sinks into her chest, settling around her rib cage. She's only ever felt this with one person of Vakeeli—this comfort that can't be denied. This warmth brings a trust that is rooted so deeply inside her, it's impenetrable.

A smile graces her lips as the heat of a body arrives next to hers. This person's energy is potent and charged, fed off land, water, and Vakeeli air. She smells of ocean, grass, and golden blooms. She smells of *love*.

"Korah." Hassha utters the name in a gentle voice, her heart beating a notch faster. She doesn't move her head, too afraid of how she'll react when seeing her sister again after so many centuries. They've spoken only through thoughts and messages for so long. In the cozy confines of this hut, she'll cry if she looks too soon.

"What is it? Afraid I'm even more beautiful than the last time you saw me?" Korah's laughter is infectious and Hassha finally turns her head to digest an eye-full of her sister.

There is no denying that Korah is beautiful. In fact, Korah has always been the prettiest one of all. The candlelight bounces off her dark skin and reflects off her purple eyes as if they're a mirror. Her hair is collected into one large ponytail, bushy and beautifully unkempt, giving off that edge only she can bring. She dons her signature colors—green, brown, and beige. Hassha's vision blurs and all the colors as well as the silver of her sister's irises merge into one.

"Aw, sister." Korah turns fully to face her, drawing her in for a hug. She's missed her just as much, and her heart comes alive as they hold each other chest to chest. "I've missed you," Hassha whispers.

"I've missed you too." Korah leans back, gripping the tops of Hassha's shoulders. She can't help noticing her sister is wearing armor, which is odd considering it's so late at night and she's in protected land. She should be dressed comfortably, for peace, not like this.

"What's troubling you?" Korah asks.

"Oh, many things, sister." Hassha takes a minor step back, inhaling before exhaling.

"Not my nieces, eh? They're okay?"

"Yes, they're fine. They're quite rebellious, but so full of life." Hassha pauses. "They'd love to see you."

"Perhaps another time, when things are a bit clearer." Korah takes a step away too. She loves the twins, but she can't see them. She saw them once, through sequences Hassha sent her mentally, and longed to hold them. To be there. But she felt such guilt for leaving. How could she return when she'd abandoned Hassha while she was pregnant with the girls? She searches for that answer in Hassha's eyes, but as always, Hassha reveals nothing. Either Hassha doesn't see it the way she does, or she's pretending that it doesn't bother her.

"Tell me what's on your mind," Korah encourages.

"It's him." Hassha gestures to Warren. "He's a product of the Tether. A cold tethered baby."

"Is he?"

"Yes. He's one of the twins. *Willow's* twin."

Korah swallows. "Ah. I see."

"I agreed to bring him here in hopes that I could rid him of the dark energy inside him, but I've tried everything, Korah. I've exhausted all my methods. Decius still lingers inside him, and I feel he won't let go unless we kill him. But in order to kill him, we'll have to..." Hassha trails off, staring vacantly.

"Well, we can't do that." Korah folds her arms, lowers her gaze. "How do you feel about Willow and Caspian? Have you seen them recently?"

"I have seen them, yes." Hassha nods. "They contacted me about Warren and his mate." Hassha surveys Korah. "Have you heard what I've heard recently?"

"About The Council trying to send that boy to Inferno Isle? Of course, I've heard. Who do you think it was that gave them warning not to send the sad sap off?"

"Yes. I told Caspian to let it go as well, but he knows I'm hiding something. He's lost trust in me, which is the last thing I wanted. Are you not worried?"

"We made that place impossible to survive," Korah says, though that doesn't answer the question. "He and anyone with him will die if they ever set foot on that island."

"What did you say to The Council?" asks Hassha.

"I told them to cease their plans or I would slice of their heads and plant them on a stake." Korah raises her chin, smirking. "They know better than to test me."

Hassha's head shakes slowly, her gaze turning the other way. "We cannot be so confident, sister. This new generation of The

Council is bold. And strong. Something tells me Selah has been speaking to them somehow. Though she's at rest, it doesn't mean she can't still speak. If a mind is dark enough or suffering...she can get there."

Annoyance wraps around Korah. "That is true."

"Willow and Caspian, they're not like the previous Cold Tethered children," Hassha continues. "Their bond is one of the most powerful bonds I've ever encountered in my life. I can feel their energy, even now. I know you felt it too when they came to see you."

"Yes, I felt it. Still do." Korah's head hangs, her focus on Warren now.

"I believe someone else is speaking to Warren in his dreams. I just hope it's not who we think it is." Hassha's belly clenches as she focuses on Warren again. It's been so long since she's felt what she does right now. *Fear.*

Korah takes Hassha's hand and gives it a squeeze. "Shall we go in together?"

She peers up at Korah. "Yes. That would be good."

"Very well."

Hassha closes her eyes and Korah does the same, and as they clasp each other's hand, Hassha uses her other to touch Warren's forehead. The pull is instant, as if his body has been awaiting her touch. She sucks in a sharp breath as Warren shifts in his sleep with a slight moan, and before she knows it, she's inside, seeing what he sees. Breathing his air. Drowning in his stress.

She looks down at the fractured black ground beneath her feet, the gaps filled with fiery orange lava, then up, at the razor-sharp mountains gushing with even more of it.

The land is empty, no trees, grass, or signs of life, however when she looks up, the sky is full of creatures—dark creatures with massive wings, visible ribs, and slimy gray skin. They fly in a circle, hovering above something in the distance. Hassha looks left, and Korah is with her, radiating with soft purple light.

When Hassha moves, Korah does too. They walk until they approach a crater in the ground, a crater so deep it seems a bomb has dropped on it to open it up. But there are no bombs here. Only energy. *Bad, bad* energy.

Hassha hitches a breath when she spots the gold coffin planted at the bottom of the crater, however it's not as she and Korah left it. The coffin is wide open and the body that's supposed to be inside it is gone.

A screeching noise fills the air, and Hassha peers up as the dark-winged creatures come flying toward them, but instead of hitting or landing on them, they swoop right past, blocking their line of sight. They zip by in large whooshes and flaps...and then they're gone.

The land is still.

The air is thick and suffocating.

A figure wrapped in fire appears from a distance. It walks toward them, closer, *closer*, and Hassha's heart beats like a caged bird when the figure stops, the flames die, and it transforms into a woman. The woman is completely naked, with skin as white as snow and a thin frame. She grins as Korah grips Hassha's hand tighter, but just as quickly as the woman appears, she vanishes.

Hassha and Korah spin around, searching for her. When they turn again, an invisible force drops them to their knees, and a searing hot hand lands on both their shoulders, burning their skin.

Before them is the woman in fire, a sly grin covering half of her face, and her eyes lit into bold red flames. Her red hair floats in the air and she uses her flamed fingers to tip their chins, so their eyes are only on hers.

They can't move from her grasp.

Can't resist.

Can't *run*.

Here, she has full control and based off her wicked smirk, she knows it.

"Hello, sisters," she says.

Hassha gasps, and the fire and lava drifts away. Their surroundings melt, returning them to the presence of the hut.

Hassha pulls her hand away from Warren's head, staring at him in utter disbelief as her back slams into the nearest wall. She turns her eyes to Korah whose eyes are cloudy and damp. Then Hassha hisses when she feels a broiling heat on her shoulder.

Korah rushes toward her sister, helping her take off the gold chest plate, and when Hassha's removes her shirt, she finds an imprint of a hand. It has claimed her skin, branded her. It's a warning that's as clear as ever.

"Selah's back," a deep voice says, and the Regal sisters hitch a breath when they look up to find Warren now standing. But this isn't the kind, timid kid from hours ago. His eyes are fiery red, just like Selah's...and he now has talons so dark and sharp, they could slice through steel. A crackling noise fills the air, like the sound of bones crunching and breaking, and greasy black wings rip through his shirt and sprout from his back—wings twice as large as his body. "Regal Selah is back. And she's going to *kill you all*."

MORE CAZ + WILLOW

If you've made it this far, I'm going to assume you enjoyed the wild ride of *Wicked Ties*! Thank you so much for reading! If you're like me and couldn't get enough of Caz and Willow together, I have good news! There's a deleted scene with Willow and Caz spending some much needed time together at Ruby Falls. It's sweet, hot, romantic, and I love it! If you want that bonus chapter, please scan the QR code below withy your phone or type this link in your web browser: https://bit.ly/rubyfallschapter

Lethal Souls, the final book of the Tether Trilogy releases on August 13th, 2024 and can be preordered now! Just typed this link to preorder yours: https://mybook.to/lethalsouls or search for the title on Amazon!

Brace yourself for the Regal sisters and their intense history, Caz and his newly discovered power, (what the hell is going on with Warren?), and of course more romance between **Callow**... See what I did there? ;)

For updates, teasers, and more fun exclusives:
Follow Me on Instagram @reallyshanora
Follow Me on TikTok: @theshanorawilliams
Twitter: @shanorawilliams

Visit www.shanorawilliams.com for more info, details, or to shop for signed books and merchandise.

MORE BOOKS BY SHANORA

WARD DUET
THE MAN I CAN'T HAVE
THE MAN I NEED

CANE SERIES
WANTING MR. CANE (#1)
BREAKING MR. CANE (#2)
LOVING MR. CANE (#3)
BEING MRS. CANE (#4)
TEMPTING CLAY (4.5)

NORA HEAT COLLECTION
CARESS
CRAVE
DIRTY LITTLE SECRET
MY PROFESSOR

<u>STANDALONES</u>
<u>BAD FOR ME</u>
<u>COACH ME</u>
<u>TEMPORARY BOYFRIEND</u>
<u>MY FIANCE'S BROTHER</u>
<u>DOOMSDAY LOVE</u>
<u>DEAR MR BLACK</u>
<u>FOREVER MR. BLACK</u>
<u>UNTIL THE LAST BREATH</u>

SERIES
<u>FIRENINE SERIES</u>
<u>THE ACE CROW DUET</u>
<u>VENOM TRILOGY</u>

<u>THRILLERS:</u>
<u>The Perfect Ruin</u>
<u>The Wife Before</u>
<u>The Other Mistress</u>

Most of these titles are available in Kindle Unlimited.
Visit <u>www.shanorawilliams.com</u> for more information.

Made in the USA
Middletown, DE
30 August 2024

60015549R00298